The Surleighwick Effect

THE SURLEIGHWICK EFFECT

by

Charles H. Cutting

ZOILUS PRESS

First published in Great Britain
by Zoilus Press, 1993
45, Tower Hamlets Road, London E17 4RQ

ISBN 0 9522028 0 8

Printed in Great Britain by Antony Rowe Ltd.,
Chippenham, Wiltshire, SN14 6QA

British Library Cataloguing-in-Publication Data

A catalogue record for this book is available from the British
Library

ZOILUS PRESS
45, Tower Hamlets Road, London, E17 4RQ

to Ellis Sharp

non ita certandi cupidus, quam propter amorem
quod te imitari aveo

Note

CONTENTS

CHAPTER ONE

THE DEATH OF PROFESSOR HOUGHTON AND WHAT HAPPENED TO HIS BOOKS

'At Christie's New York sale of early scientific books, a first edition of William Harvey's Latin treatise on the circulation of the blood (*De motu cordis*, Frankfurt, 1628) was sold for 250,000 dollars (275,000 dollars with buyer's premium)'— Saleroom Notes, *The Times*, 24 June 1985.

'Nemo peius iudicat de ignorantia quam ignorans' (Petrarch, *De sui ipsius et multorum aliorum ignorantia*)

The death of any professor, particularly one who was also the head of a department, is invariably the occasion of great public sorrow and private joy. The death of Professor James Houghton, Professor and head of the department of English at the University of Surleighwick, was sudden and surprising, and the sorrow and the joy were on that account all the greater. The cerebral haemorrhage had struck without warning, and Professor Houghton died— of shock as was later said—in the very act of reading a letter from the Vice-Chancellor increasing his department's funds on the grounds of its excellence in research. The bluff, brusque but genial, cheroot-smoking wiseacre was no more, and although they did not yet know it, none of his rejoicing colleagues was to be unaffected by the suddenness of his passing.

Professor Houghton's widow had expressed a wish that his ashes should be scattered on the grass outside his favourite hostelry, the Three Blind Mice, adjacent to the Surleighwick campus. On the day after his cremation, a group of friends, colleagues and senior administrators joined her in one of the private bars. To a man and to a woman, the members of the Surleighwick

English department were there to witness the event, to drink deep to the memory of their departed leader, and to speculate with guarded optimism about the possibility of a replacement. As a token of respect, classes had been cancelled on this last Thursday of the autumn term, so the staff members of the Surleighwick English department could liquor themselves up with beer and brandies and pernod and champagne, without needing to think about the afternoon. The department's three resident alcoholics and Senior Lecturers, Doctors Beaver, Festering and Sword, had been at their whisky bottles since early in the morning, and did not need the excuse of Professor Houghton's death to become even drunker as the day progressed.

"He's bound to be replaced of course," said Mr Jack Napes, the diminutive Cornishman and authority on the works of Shakespeare, who was perhaps the most earnest and naive member of the department. "After all, we *are* the biggest and most important department in the university."

Although all members of the Surleighwick English department agreed with these sentiments, there were nonetheless frowns of disapproval at this rash and presumptuous remark, which seemed to be tempting the fates. But further discussion was cut off by Professor Eustace Toady, the fat Dean of the Surleighwick Arts faculty and Professor of Industrial Archaeology, who banged on the table several times with his pewter beer mug, slopping its contents on to the battered wooden table. For Professor Eustace Toady, like many of the regular Surleighwick drinkers, kept his own well worn, much discoloured vessel, hanging on a hook for his exclusive use.

"Gentlemen, gentlemen, ladies and gentlemen, Mr Vice-Chancellor Sir, Mr Registrar Sir, colleagues, friends"—Professor Toady endeavoured to make himself heard above the chattering throng, who were now beginning to enjoy themselves as the alcohol worked its soothing charms on minds and bodies wearied by the stresses of the term, and emotionally drained by the dramatic events of the last few days. Silence fell at last.

"Mr Vice-Chancellor, Sir, Mr Registrar Sir, Mrs Houghton, colleagues, friends—this is a very sad day for all of us at Surleighwick. We are gathered here today to pay tribute to one of the most outstanding scholars that Surleighwick has ever produced. Jim Houghton's death is a tragedy for scholarship and a tragedy for all of us in the Arts faculty. It is a tragedy too for his department. We must hope first of all that one of his colleagues will come forward to complete his major edition of the minor poems of Kirke White, on which as you know he had spent the last thirty years of his life, which will be *the* edition when it appears and for which he had already gained in anticipation an international reputation."

Little Jack Napes, ever anxious to make a good impression, raised an eager hand, but slowly and uncertainly lowered it as the Dean continued to speak. The Dean placed his hands on his paunch, and tried to make the tips of his fingers touch each other. There were few things in academic life that Professor Toady enjoyed more than the sound of his own voice pronouncing platitudes before an audience of his colleagues.

"Yes"—he continued, "it is a tragic loss to scholarship, and it is a tragedy for the department. You all know what Jim did for the department in his fifteen years as its head. No one did more than he to put the Surleighwick English department on the map. He made it what it is today, one of the few departments in the country with a star for the excellence of its research." (For this was December 1990, when memories of the award of 'Grade 5 stars' for international research excellence were still fresh in everybody's mind. These had been allotted the previous year in a random and arbitrary fashion by the Universities Funding Council, chiefly as a result of departments' own inflated claims about their productivity. But only a few departments had them, and most were classified either 'above average', 'average' or 'below average'.

"Yes, it's not too much to say that the star was largely Jim Houghton's doing."

A tear emerged from the bifocal spectacles of the fat Dean of Arts, rolled down his chubby cheek and fell into his fifth pint of beer.

"Yes, he got you your star," continued Professor Toady, with a note of grievance in his voice. (His own department was only 'average', and yet, if you actually counted pages, his department had produced more per head than the English department, which was most unfair.) He tilted his tankard, and drained a good half pint of ale in one gulp, and continued.

"But we don't just miss Jim as a scholar—we miss him as a *person*. As Dean of the faculty of Arts"—and here Professor Toady puffed out his stomach and swelled like a frog, tugging at his waistcoat, "I know as well as anyone that Jim ran a pretty tight ship." He savoured the phrase. "Yes, English was a pretty tight ship. A very ship-shape department indeed. Good at the paper-work." He paused, and looked into his tankard, and lost the train of his thought. "Where was I?"

"Pretty tight ship," whispered little Jack Napes, helpfully, ever an eager-beaver.

"Ah yes. Ship. Well, now Jim's launched on another voyage. The Last Journey, as E.M. Forster calls it, if I remember aright."

Jack Napes was about to correct the Dean, but thought better of it.

"Yes, the Last Journey," said the fat Dean, thoughtfully, for he was a religious man, and went to church every Sunday. "The undiscovered country from whose bourn no traveller returns— Milton, what?—" he laughed. "I may be only a professor of archaeology, but I flatter myself that I do read English literature now and again. Well, Jim's on his last journey. I ask you all to raise your glasses and drink the health—I mean, to the memory, of Professor Jim Houghton, colleague, teacher and above all *friend*."

Professor Toady drained the last of his beer, ordered himself another pint, and looked round with satisfaction. He was pleased with his speech, which he considered to be an appropriate tribute to his old drinking crony. When the understatements had been written up in more laudatory language, it would serve as the basis for his obituary notice of Professor Houghton in the *Independent*. Then, with suitable digressions, it would appear, with a picture of Professor Houghton and a title, *A Great Loss*, in the university's fortnightly *Factfile* of news and information. Expanded yet again, Professor Toady's tribute would appear in the university's annual *Review*, under the title 'Years of Achievement: In Memorium to the Memory of Professor James Houghton, scholar, teacher friend....' Yes, thought Professor Toady to himself with great satisfaction, with a little legerdemain and juggling with titles, he could claim three publications as a result of Houghton's death. And with the increasing emphasis being placed on publication nowadays, three publications would come in quite handy, especially as he hadn't written an article for ten years. It was an ill wind....

Mrs Houghton wiped away a tear and passed the little metal urn containing the ashes of her husband to Professor Toady. Then, led by the Vice-Chancellor, Mr Henry Tinker, MBE, B.Soc.Sc., (Hon MA, Surleighwick), who was assisted on to his crutches by his shapely Principal Personal Assistant, Miss Sarah Carstairs, the assembled throng left the warmth and went outside into the raw air. At the side of the Three Blind Mice, Professor Toady removed the lid of the urn, and shook a few handfuls of ash over the spot where Professor Houghton had so often walked. The ceremony over, the Vice-Chancellor hobbled away to his chauffeur-driven Silver Shadow (Surleighwick bought its Vice-Chancellor a new Rolls every year as a perquisite of his high and responsible office). The Registrar too left in his university Daimler. The rest of the party hurried back inside to the warmth of the bar. Silently congratulating himself on the excellence of his speech, Professor

Toady looked around at the various members of the Surleighwick English department. The three alcoholic Doctors Beaver, Festering and Sword were now completely plastered and laughing uproariously. Slumped in a chair all by himself was the departmental grouch, the scowling, frowsty figure of the unfortunately named Mr Ivan Hoe ('Taffy' to his friends, 'Rowena' to the students), declining as ever all contact with his colleagues. Propping up the bar were two of the department's feminists, Mrs Pauline Quick, Senior Lecturer in Charlotte Brontë, a trim, lean, outgoing woman, in her late thirties, with lined face and greying hair, and her inseparable companion, the glamorous and attractive Dr Antonia Crumpet, an expert on Emily Dickinson. There too in his motorised wheelchair was Professor Bodgering, the second professor of English and Director of the Centre for Marlowe and Elizabethan Studies, his head lolling back against the headrest of his wheelchair, his tongue protruding from between his stained yellow teeth, wheezing heavily as usual—for he was dying of a fatal lung disease. Oblivious to his surroundings Professor Bodgering was slurping vodka and lime from a plastic straw, ministered to by his personal research assistant, a faded young woman of thirty-two years old, Jennifer Olive Lavinia Prendergast, ('Jolly' for short). The fidgety and diminutive Jack Napes broke in on Professor Toady's reverie.

"Who is going to take over the department, Mr Dean? We'll get a replacement, won't we? Our publication record is so good, you know. We got a star for international excellence."

"Ah yes, that reminds me." Professor Toady banged his tankard on the table, and called for silence again.

"Jack Napes here has just asked about the future of the department. I have discussed the matter with the Vice-Chancellor, and we have agreed that in view of the department's excellent research reputation we ought to move quickly to attract a distinguished scholar to fill the chair. A search committee has been set up, and I am reasonably hopeful that within three or four years we will have succeeded in finding the right man—or woman of course—to take over. Certainly by the beginning of the next decade...In the meantime, Professor Bodgering, as second professor of English, will take over as acting head of the department."

There was a sudden shocked silence. Professor Bodgering! The most notoriously incompetent member of the English department, a chronic invalid and an inveterate absentee who after ten years at Surleighwick was still a stranger to almost all his colleagues! Surely Professor Toady couldn't be serious?

But Professor Bodgering was grinning feebly, a wizened and mummified figure, as Professor Toady made the announcement. So it must be true!

Apart from Professor Toady, probably the only person in the room who was not appalled by this announcement was the diminutive Mr Napes, but then, as a Cornishman of Breton extraction, he had little sense of English practicality. Even the departmental drunks were shocked as the news penetrated their fuddled brains.

Mrs Quick made her way speedily to Professor Toady.

"Professor Toady, is that a wise decision? Professor Bodgering is a sick man. Ought we to place this extra burden on him?"

"Sick? Nonsense my dear. He's not on the sick list. I have every confidence in him."

"But he's a dying man," whispered Mrs Quick urgently. "You only have to look at him to see that. Believe me, he's just not up to the job of running the department."

"Well, I'm sure the department will rally round for the good of the cause and help him out. Anyway, he's a man of vast experience. Look at the way in which he built up the department at Skelmerdale." (Before appointment at Surleighwick, Professor Bodgering had held a chair in the department of English at Skelmerdale. There, Professor Bodgering had gained a certain reputation for glibness and for specious charm.)

"But that was years ago," protested Mrs Quick insistently. "He's changed since then, believe me."

"It's no use arguing, Mrs Quick," said the Dean coldly. "The matter is settled. Bodgering is the next senior man, and so, under our rules and traditions at Surleighwick, he must take over the department."

Professor Toady prepared to take his leave. He found Mrs Houghton standing by Professor Bodgering's wheelchair.

"So kind of you to do the tribute to Jim," said Mrs Houghton. "And it was good of you to come too, Percy," she said to Professor Bodgering, who nodded his head very slowly, and fought for breath.

"It was the least I could do," answered Professor Toady. "If ever there's anything else I can do to help?"

"Well, there is one thing, if it's not too much trouble...?"

Professor Bodgering gazed up at Mrs Houghton with lacklustre eyes. She wasn't his type.

"I was wondering if you and Percy would advise me about Jim's books? He's got rather a lot, and I'm anxious to clear them out as quickly as possible. Some of them may be of interest to someone, and I'd value the advice of his friends."

"Of course," replied Professor Toady, easily. "Percy and I will be only too glad to help. And why don't I get the university librarian to come along as well? I'll have a chat with him and ring you when I know when he'll be free."

Professor Toady and Mrs Houghton left, and shortly afterwards Professor Bodgering's research assistant helped push his wheelchair down the steps of the Three Blind Mice bar.

Mrs Quick looked bitterly after his departing figure.

"My god," she said with feeling to Dr Crumpet. "It's not that I mind so much this university being run by men, but I do object to it being run by geriatric incompetents. 'He's the next senior man'"—she mimicked Professor Toady's pompous and complacent tones. "I tell you, Antonia, Bodgering is going to be a complete disaster as head. He's gaga, he's deaf, he's terminally ill—we all know that his lung disease is incurable—he's a complete incompetent administratively. You know he lost all the marks to the Marlowe papers last year, and had to make them up off the cuff at the examiners' meeting? Moreover, I'm pretty sure that he's suffering from senile dementia. He's sixty-four, you know. I ask you! When did you last have an intelligent conversation about literature with him?"

"I've never actually spoken to him at all," answered Dr Crumpet. "Our paths have never crossed."

"Oh no, I forgot, you've only been here for five years, haven't you? You've hardly had time to meet him yet. Well, I can tell you Antonia, this is a catastrophe for the department." Her eyes narrowed. "I wonder if it's a plot," she said thoughtfully. "That awful Toady always resented the fact that English got a star whereas his department was only average. Maybe he thinks that Bodgering will drag us all down—and he will, too. After all, what has Bodgering ever written, apart from that fifty-page guide to *Tamburlaine* in the 'Skelmerdale Notes' series? And that was twenty-five years ago. Since then, what? Half a dozen worthless essays at the most?"

"Then how come he got his chair if he'd published so little?"

Mrs Quick laughed cynically.

"Well, he was a man, he was over fifty-five and he had written *one* thing that was all his own from cover to cover. So he fitted the Surleighwick professorial profile. Anyway they never advertised the job. He was appointed on the old-boy network."

The gathering broke up. The three drunks remained carousing in the bar. Mrs Quick and Dr Crumpet returned to their rooms to mark essays. Little Jack Napes went home to write an elaborate and flowery letter of condolence to Mrs Houghton. Ivan Hoe returned to his house to nag his wife. Professor Toady, sleepy from six pints of 'Surleighwick Special', the rich dark local real ale, waddled off to do battle about funding on behalf of the faculty of Arts with the clear-headed Deans of Medicine, Science, Engineering and Law, all of whom had dined frugally in secret conclave on bread and cheese and water, resolving to take Toady to the cleaners. Which they proceeded to do.

*****

When an academic dies, it is usual for many of his books to be disposed of. Some, of course, his family will wish to keep for reasons of sentiment, but reasons of space will dictate the disposal of the rest, since most serious academics, particularly in the humanities, attract books to themselves like iron filings to a magnet. And many of these books will be of no use to any of his family after his death. Such were Mrs Houghton's sentiments in the days that followed, as she mounted a small step ladder and ran her eyes along the books in her husband's study—who for instance would want thirty-five books of 'fifties and 'sixties criticism on the works of Kirke White? Or the vast pile of dissertations on Lake poetry left over from the days when Professor Houghton used to edit *Romantic Studies Weekly Bulletin*? Or the text editions that had survived from his undergraduate days, heavily annotated with ink underlinings and pencilled annotations such as "How true!" or "This line is v. beautiful." Or the vast pile of battered paperbacks now falling apart, their yellowed pages weary on the eye and almost unreadable? Still, who knows, there might be something of interest to someone there, and someone might, she fondly believed, like to have a memento of her husband's scholarship and learning—perhaps she could present all the members of the department with half a dozen books of their choice.

The sensible thing for academics with books to do is to make a will, perhaps inviting friends and colleagues to choose fifty books each. Then, in years to come, their colleagues might be reminded of them as they tugged a dusty volume off the shelves. "Ah yes, this was Jim Houghton's copy. Such a tragedy that his major edition of Kirke White's minor poetry never appeared. He'd been working on it for thirty years but died before he could complete it. His notes were given to his department for them to make use of, and of coure that was the end of the matter. It's still a desideratum of scholarship you know." But, like many academics, Professor Houghton had a strong ego, and simply could not bear to think of the days when for him no more the blazing hearth would burn, and he would not be around any more to needle all his staff. So from year to year he put off making a will, and thus abandoned his books to the fates and to a wife who did not know what to do with them. And, although he did not even know it himself, Professor Houghton had owned some interesting and valuable books.

Mrs Houghton had done what wives usually and under-standably do in these circumstances. She had consulted her husband's colleagues and friends, and Professors Toady and Bodgering had agreed to call round with the Surleighwick University librarian to look over the collection. Poor Mrs Houghton was not to know that she could not have chosen three worse counsellors.

Professor Bodgering had scarcely read a book for thirty years, since his first appointment as Assistant Lecturer at the University of Righton in 1952. For since his tenure was confirmed, he had gradually narrowed his teaching down to just five works of English Literature—*Wuthering Heights*, *Pride and Prejudice*, *Tamburlaine*, Marvell's *To his Coy Mistress* and Beckett's *Waiting for Godot*. For the two first works, he relied on his memory of reading them as an undergraduate, and truth to tell, he knew them principally through the 1939 film of *Wuthering Heights*—(as a spotty adolescent he had fallen in love with the screen image of Merle Oberon as Cathy)—and the 1940 film of *Pride and Prejudice* starring Greer Garson and Laurence Olivier. For *Tamburlaine*, the subject of his own scholarly disquisition (as he liked to think of his Skelmerdale Notes pamphlet), he relied on a pirated videotape stolen from the ante-room of a Haitian prostitute in New York whose favours he had unsuccessfully attempted to purchase for a thousand dollars. (But that is another story.) This was his most prized possession. *Waiting for Godot* he knew chiefly from a student production at the University of Righton. He had been been made to learn *To his Coy Mistress* at the age of fourteen, as a precocious schoolboy. And, attracted as he was even in those days to its arguments in favour of seduction, he had never forgotten the poem. And those five works were the foundation of Professor Bodgering's career! This range of authors, Emily Brontë, Jane Austen, Marvell, Marlowe and Beckett had gained him the reputation, at the University of Righton, of being a man of phenomenal range. This reputation had followed him to the University of Skelmerdale, that wonderful new university in the northwest of England whose English department had been one of *the* success stories of the 1960s, and which boasted incessantly that it had gained an international reputation under Professor Bodgering's leadership—particularly for its unconventional syllabus and for the fantastic quality of its undergraduate teaching. At Skelmerdale, Professor Bodgering had been quite the nonpareil! But the fact was that he was not interested in books, and knew nothing about them. When he himself died, the problem of disposing of his library would not arise, consisting as it did of no more than thirty-seven books wedged unread between a pair of broken bookends, and containing little more than Dr Moffat's translation of the New Testament, the Reader's Digest condensed version of the works of Karl Marx, a disbound copy of the Penguin translation of the works of Aeschylus that he had filched from the back of a rag-and-bone cart in Righton, and three old numbers of *La Vie Parisienne*. A more unsuitable person to advise on the disposal of Professor

Houghton's books could hardly have been found in the whole University of Surleighwick.

Except perhaps for Professor Toady. It wasn't that Professor Toady didn't know anything about books. He did—in his own subject. He had himself once even written a coffee table book about eighteenth-century mills copiously illustrated with colour-plates of spinning-jennies found on digs; and he owned a few hundred books personally. But he was not interested in books outside his own subject. Moreover, as was natural at Surleighwick, since entering upon a career as a professional committee man, one of the sound men in whose hands the future of Surleighwick lay, he had simply abandoned any interest in books, learning and scholarship. His reading was now confined to the *Sunday Times* and university official papers. Professor Toady might have been able to give some not utterly worthless advice on a collection of industrial archaeology books—but Professor Houghton did not have any books on industrial archaeology. Nevertheless, ignorance of books was not likely to deter Professor Toady from laying down his opinion with a great air of plausible confidence and authority. And Professor Toady had of course suggested that the university librarian Dr Pratt should be asked along too.

Dr Peter Pratt, the librarian of the University of Surleighwick, was a very modern librarian, so he was not interested in books either. The library of the University of Surleighwick had in fact been one of the better university libraries in the country. From the 'thirties to the 'seventies, it had been well-funded, and in the happy days, long since vanished, when Surleighwick had appointed scholars and men of humane learning to its chairs, some of them had built up the library by judicious and well-timed purchases. Since its foundation in 1882 the University of Surleighwick had not only acquired most of the important books that were published in the United Kingdom, and sometimes abroad, but had also built up a respectable collection of books printed before 1882, including a surprisingly large collection of early books from the seventeenth century and before. Often a curious book could be found only in London or Oxford or Cambridge or Surleighwick. But since the late 'sixties, no university in the kingdom had a more unerring record of appointing unsuitable people to senior posts than Surleighwick, and by the mid-'seventies it unfailingly appointed those who had done no research to its research chairs, and those who were inarticulate and inaudible to its important teaching departments. True to form, it appointed as its librarian a man indifferent and even hostile to books. As a student, Dr Peter Pratt had firmly believed in the once influential doctrine proclaimed by Marshall McLuhan in *The Gutenberg Galaxy*, that the age of the book was over, and that the new age of electronic culture, the new orality, was here to stay. Dr Pratt envisaged a time, not far off now, when all the books in the world would have been optically scanned and stored on a central computer. The scholar who wished to read a book would then simply sit at a terminal, dial the computer, and the book and page he wished to read would appear on a screen before him. Hence libraries would cease to be repositories of books, and would instead become buildings housing vast banks of terminals. His own doctoral thesis in library science had been devoted to this very theme; and since appointment at Surleighwick, Dr Pratt had endeavoured so far as possible to remove books into store, and replace them by computer terminals. Dr Peter Pratt, truth to tell, regarded his visit to Mrs Houghton as an unutterable bore. The last thing he wanted in the Surleighwick library was Professor Houghton's tedious tomes! Confound that wretched Toady for dragging him in to this—but he thought it as well to keep in with Toady, one of the Surleighwick power brokers, whose support he might need at any time.

At the appointed hour, Professor Toady drove Professor Bodgering and Dr Pratt to the old Victorian house up the hill from the Surleighwick campus where Professor Houghton had lived.

"It's so good of you to come," Mrs Houghton greeted her guests.

"Not at all, anything we can do to help," answered Professor Toady, clambering out of the driving seat of his Land Rover, from which he and Dr Pratt proceeded to lift the backward-facing and wheel-chair-bound figure of Professor Bodgering, who peered soulfully from the open rear of the Land Rover with his red nose and beady brown eyes, looking for all the world like a bewildered horse in the back of a horse box. Professor Bodgering was well muffled against the cold, wearing an old tweed overcoat and a checkered muffler around his withered neck. He breathed noisily and loudly as Dr Pratt and Professor Toady wheeled him into the house.

Mrs Houghton showed her three visitors into her husband's study, and excused herself for a moment whilst she went off to make her guests some tea.

"Please do look around," she invited them. "Jim's books are all here in this room. I'm anxious that they should go into good hands or be otherwise properly disposed of."

Professor Bodgering slumped almost unconscious in his wheelchair, and gaped at the perhaps fifteen hundred books that lined the room on three sides, in shelves running from floor to ceiling. They were carefully arranged by size, with oversize books at the bottom of the shelves, and smaller volumes at the top. The fourth side of the room was a picture window that overlooked the green lawns and stark shrubs of an elegant garden, for Mrs Houghton was a keen gardener. It was a long time since Professor Bodgering had seen so many books. He had not dreamed it possible for any Professor of English to own so many.

Professor Toady and Dr Pratt went up to the shelves and riffled through the pages of a few volumes in a desultory fashion.

"I'm sure all this is a bit of a bore for you, Peter," remarked Professor Toady complacently. "But one likes to do what one can for a colleague's widow. Of course all he'll have is the usual old Eng. Lit. stuff—of no great interest to you, I suppose? The library no doubt has copies already."

"Looks rather like it," replied Dr Pratt without enthusiasm, casting his eyes along the rows of texts and volumes of criticism. Pretty standard stuff, most of this, I'd say. We're certain to have it all." He stifled a yawn. Heavens, these books were boring. Of course English wasn't his subject, but why anyone should think that the library would be interested in volumes of Lake poets or Kirke White criticism he simply didn't know.

Mrs Houghton returned with a tea trolley containing plates of sandwiches and fancy cakes, and poured four steaming cups of tea into delicate china cups.

Professor Bodgering held his tea cup with frail and trembling hand, spilling tea into his saucer and licking it from there like a cat.

"Well, what am I to do with Jim's books?" she asked after a while. "I don't suppose there's anything very special. But perhaps the library would like a couple of hundred of them as a memento of Jim?...And perhaps his colleagues too would like to choose three or four apiece. What do you think, Percy?"

"Ah yes," muttered Professor Bodgering, who had not really heard the question, and was now dopey with sleep in the warmth of Mrs Houghton's centrally heated house, perspiring in the overcoat which he had refused to remove on entering.

"That's very kind, Mrs Houghton," replied Dr Pratt briskly. "So far as I can tell the library has all these books anyway, but perhaps I might just choose a couple say for the library, and if we haven't got them I'll be glad to put them in the library with a little sticker saying that they were from the library of your husband."

Mrs Houghton seemed somewhat disconcerted at this lack of interest.

"What about you, Percy? Is there anything you want for the Centre—or for your own collection, of course?"

"No, I've stopped collecting books, haven't got house room for them any more," replied Professor Bodgering ungraciously, spilling tea down his overcoat. "And of course the Centre is really only interested in Renaissance plays—we don't do Lake poets there you know." He drew his lips back over his gums, revealing his stained and yellow teeth in the ghastly simulation of a smile, and wheezed with laughter at the thought. Just fancy, he, Professor Bodgering, had outlived old Jim Houghton. He hadn't expected to do so, and now he was offering advice on Houghton's books!

"That reminds me," interposed Mrs Houghton. "Jim did have one or two Renaissance books." She went to a corner of the room, and climbed two steps of a short stepladder, and handed down a vellum quarto. She climbed down and placed it open at the title page on Professor Bodgering's knee. "It's a Latin book, I think, from the year 1628."

Professor Bodgering looked down, and there, mouthing the words slowly with his lips, slowly and painfully, with great effort, he made out the words on the title page: *Exercitatio anatomica De Motu Cordis et sanguinis in animalibus, Gulielmi Harvei Angli, Medici Regii et Professoris Anatomiae in Collegio Medicorum Londinensi.* Below this was a picture of an angel with wings, who supported in his left hand an upside down shield bearing the number 4 and the letter W. Then came the words 'Francofurti. Sumptibus Guilielmi Fitzeri. Anno MDCXXVIII.'

Professor Bodgering looked at the book with complete lack of interest. He opened the book once in the middle, and saw that it was a plain text.

"No, it's not the kind of thing the Centre would want," he said at last. "We're not interested in anything later than 1593. We specialise in Marlowe at the Centre, and that's the date of his death, you know—and in any case, we're not interested in anything but plays, and then only plays in English." He handed the book back with indifference.

"May I see it, Mrs Houghton?" enquired Professor Toady tactfully. He strolled over to the picture window where the light was better, and spent a moment or two flicking through the pages. Then he prepared to indulge his favourite avocation—pontificating authoritatively.

"Well, I can tell you one thing," he started confidently. "This is not a Latin book, Mrs Houghton. You see, the Romans died out before the invention of printing—a good few hundred years before, in fact." He laughed. "And as this book is clearly not a printing of a classical author, it follows that it can't be in Latin."

Dr Pratt nodded in agreement with Professor Toady's impeccable reasoning.

"No, Mrs Houghton," Professor Toady continued. "As a matter of fact this book is in Romanian. It's quite understandable that you should have thought it was in Latin," he went on smugly. "The two languages are rather similar. Romanian descends from Latin, you know."

Professor Bodgering glowered with resentment from his wheelchair. Trust Professor Toady to be showing off his knowledge of languages again! Soon after arriving in Surleighwick, Professor Bodgering had learned that five years previously Professor Toady had been invited to read a paper in France, and this, at Surleighwick, had served to mark him out as a scholar of international reputation and a linguist to boot! Whereas Professor Bodgering's knowledge of languages went no further than that smattering of half-forgotten demotic German that had served for mouthing his frustrated sexual longings to the Hamburg prostitutes, when he had taught for a couple of years in that ruined city after the war.

"Yes, my Romanian is a little rusty," Professor Toady rejoiced to state. "But one can tell from the very title page straight away. It's by a man called Demotu Cordis—look, the printer made a mistake and split the name in two. And Demotu is a Romanian name. Nothing is more characteristic of Romanian than the *u* ending—Marshall Antonescu, President Ceausescu, Radu Lupu, Dinu Lipatti, the list is endless."

"Malibu," nodded Professor Bodgering sagely, determined not to be outdone.

"Quite," said Professor Toady crossly. "And just look at all the words ending in *u* inside the book." His finger flicked through the pages and pointed out more or less at random words like *hiatu, ictu, manu, circuitu, visu, sensu, impetu, impulsu, connexu, inflexu,* and so on. "Take it from me, Mrs Houghton, this is Romanian. And it's not printed in 1628 either. See the M at the beginning and the VIII at the end in the date here? That means it was printed in the 1800s. Now, I don't know what you think, Peter, but I should say that a Romanian book printed in 1885, which is what this date really reads—see the CXX is the Roman way of writing 80—you add up the two *X*'s and subtract from the *C*, which is a hundred, and this gives you 80, and the *D* of course is 5, hence 1885—a Romanian novel in fact, printed in 1885, though perhaps a trifle curious, isn't really going to be of much interest to anyone. Percy, you're a professor of literature. What was the Romanian novel doing in 1885?" Professor Toady laughed in a condescending way.

Professor Bodgering seethed with black bile, sullen in his wheelchair. How he hated his colleagues when they tried to expose his ignorance. Sometimes he wished he had never come to Surleighwick! At Skelmerdale, he had been regarded as *the* authority on everything, and no one had ever dared to ask him such impertinent questions.

"Quite so," he muttered, and broke out into a fit of coughing. His hollow cheeks gradually became purple, and he called frantically for oxygen. Mrs Houghton turned on the cylinder of oxygen which was strapped to Professor Bodgering's chair, and clamped the mask to his face. At the onrush of the pure gas, Professor Bodgering's normal muddy colouring slowly returned.

"So it's a novel, is it?" remarked Mrs Houghton at last.

Professor Toady flicked through the book again. He pretended that he could read the odd sentence or two. "Yes, it's an allegorical novel about the adventures of an angel," he said in a very final tone, taking his cue from the engraving of an angel on the title page. "Don't you agree, Peter?"

Dr Pratt, not being a scholar, felt no qualms about admitting his ignorance of Romanian. Nonetheless he flicked through the book again in a cursory fashion before replying.

"Well, certainly the library has no great interest in Romanian literature," he said thoughtfully. "Still, it's a nicely printed book if you like that kind of thing."

"Well do please take it for the library," said Mrs Houghton. "Jim also had a German edition of *Das Kapital*—I think it was the first—with Lenin's signature on the title page.

Professor Toady laughed. "Didn't know Jim was a Marxist," he joked. "But no, I fear that's of no great interest. Books with Lenin's signature in them are very common." (Well, they must be, mustn't they, if Jim Houghton had one in his library?) "And all that Marxist stuff is madly out of fashion nowadays you know."

"Still, I thought that as an association copy?" persisted Mrs Houghton.

"A kind gesture, Mrs Houghton," said Dr Pratt. "The book is valueless of course, but why don't we take it too for the library as one of the mementos of your husband. And now I fear I must be going."

The three experts thanked Mrs Houghton for their tea, advised her to accept not less than £600 from the sale of Professor Houghton's books, loaded Professor Bodgering into the back of the Land Rover, and drove back to the Surleighwick campus conscious of a good day's work done.

Mrs Houghton watched them go, a little disappointed that her late husband's books had not attracted more interest—but then in the immediate aftermath of his death it was hard for her to be objective about them; and after all, she was not a knowledgeable academic like Professors Toady and Bodgering.

CHAPTER TWO

THE PRATT FACTOR

'It will be worth while for the patrons of public libraries, even in appointments to small offices, to have an eye on bookish men for filling them.... The usual testimonies to qualification—steadiness, sobriety, civility, intelligence etc.—may all be up to the mark that will constitute a first-rate book-keeper in the mercantile sense of the term, while they are united in a very dreary and hopeless keeper of books.' John Hill Burton, *The Book-Hunter* (London, 1863)

William Harvey's treatise on the circulation of the blood is one of the rarest of all scientific works, and copies are virtually never found on the market nowadays, although some fifty-seven copies are known to exist. The rarity of a book is not absolute. A book may exist in only one copy, but if no-one wants it its rarity will not be recognised. Whereas a book extant in ten copies which two thousand people would like to own will always be a rare book. Nearly all of the extant copies of Harvey's *De motu cordis* are in institutional libraries and are unlikely to come on the market. Rather more than two thousand people would love to own a copy. Medical men have traditionally been great bookmen, and have often been attracted to collect key works in the history of medicine. The copy of the *De motu cordis* sold at Sotheby's on Tuesday 6 November 1979 at the famous sale of the Honeyman collection fetched £92,000 (£102,900 with buyer's premium). That was the first time the work had been auctioned in London since before the Second World War. The prestige of medicine and science in modern society has led to a surge in the prices of important scientific works since the 1930s onwards. The *De motu cordis* is a seminal work. Hence, apart from the Gutenberg Bible, no Latin printed book commands higher prices on the rare occasions when it is for sale.

How did Professor Houghton, who was neither a polymath nor a man of wide interests (even by the admittedly mediocre standards of Surleighwick), come to have such a book on his shelves? And why did he not know what it was? Professor Houghton had inherited the volume from his aunt, who in 1952 had left him £500 and a trunkful of books, most of them of little enough interest, apart from the Harvey volume and the volume of Marx with the incredibly rare signature of Lenin. She had acquired these books at the death of her husband, Horatio Croaker, who was twenty years older than she was. The books had come down to *him* from his grandfather and great-grandfather. One fine morning in June 1819, on the fourth anniversary of the battle of Waterloo, old Ebenezer Croaker, who had once thought of studying medicine and retained a dilettante interest in the subject, had seen the volume in the corner of a dusty bookshop in Chancery Lane in London, and had paid out three golden sovereigns to make it his own. The book had made its way to London when old Sir Frank Kynaston, last of the line of that fine old family, the Warwickshire Kynastons, had died, and his effects were sold by his executors. A hundred years earlier, in 1717, the young Sir Thomas Kynaston had bought Harvey's book in Padua on his Grand Tour of Europe. It had come to Padua in 1645, when Signor Francesco Pallavicino, one of the more lively members of the medical faculty of the famous university of Padua, had brought the work home from Vienna, where in 1640, not long after its first printing, he had purchased it. In London in 1819, Ebenezer Croaker had read the work with interest; but his interest in medicine was not shared by his son. The son kept his father's books out of *pietas*, and 'father's', later 'grandfather's' and then 'great-grandfather's books' had remained undisturbed on the shelves of the Croaker household as the decades went by. When old Mrs Croaker, Professor Houghton's aunt, sold her London house to move to a cottage in the country, she had packed up a trunkful of books. And, being proud that her nephew was now a 'college professor' she had left the books to him in her will. Professor Houghton had been duly grateful for the £500, had looked at the trunk of books without interest, and with hardly a second glance had melded them into his own collection. As a university teacher of English the youthful James Houghton was not so foolish as to think that the book was a Romanian novel. He thought it was in Italian, and misled by the engraving of the angel on the title page, a religious text at that. From 1952 to the day of his death, he never opened the book again.

Such was now the book that Peter Pratt tossed carelessly into an armchair in his room, on the second floor of the Surleighwick University library, on his return from Mrs Houghton's house.

"Make me a cup of tea, will you Sarah-Jane? I need it!"

What a bore the afternoon had been, he thought to himself. As he had suspected, Jim Houghton's books had been the usual boring collection of unreadable academic texts and dull editions of minor English poets and prose writers. Confound that wretched Toady for getting him in to this! It was not as if he had ever been close to old Jim Houghton at all.

His secretary, the dark-haired, pretty Miss Sarah-Jane Moore entered the room carrying a large, white, bone-china cup of piping hot Earl Grey.

"Thanks, Sarah-Jane," he replied appreciatively. "As I thought, there was nothing of interest to us in Houghton's books. Still, I suppose one has to go through the motions."

"Do you have any more correspondence this afternoon?" enquired Sarah-Jane, standing near his desk.

"No thanks." Dr Pratt looked at his watch. "Look, it's half past four now. I shan't need you again this afternoon. You can buzz off if you want. I shall be OK here by myself. I think I'll do a couple of hours on my paper on bibliometric ergonomics, and then call it a day."

He gave her a quick smile.

"Thank you Dr Pratt—goodnight then."

"Goodnight."

Sarah-Jane Moore returned to her own office, ran a comb through her chestnut curls in front of the mirror on the wall, collected her car keys, donned her warm grey overcoat against the damp chill of a Surleighwick winter's evening, switched out the light, and left the building, glad for once of a chance to beat the rush hour and return to her flat to soothe away the stresses of the day in a hot bubble-bath. One had to admit that there were worse people to work for than Dr Pratt...tiresome and irascible though he could sometimes be.

Left to himself, Dr Pratt finished his tea, and then with a sigh went to his desk, pulled out a folder from the bottom righthand drawer of his office desk, and with a satisfied grunt settled down to revise his paper for the *Journal of Library Science*. Dr Pratt had been the Surleighwick University librarian for three years now. He was young for the post, in fact only just turned thirty-five. Normally, appointing committees at Surleighwick were extremely reluctant ever to appoint anyone younger than fifty-five to any senior post, fearful of what rash and heedless youth might do. But when three years ago a new librarian had had to be appointed, the appointments committee had been emboldened to break with tradition. The powers that be at Surleighwick were vaguely conscious that their university was in decline. It had become a trifle stale, a trifle conventional perhaps. It was perhaps time to act in an utterly uncharacteristic way and make an imaginative, *different* appointment.

The Vice-Chancellor in particular had been impressed by Dr Pratt's vision of the library of the future where books had been replaced by terminals. That sounded to Henry Tinker, MBE, B.Soc

Sc., Hon MA (Surleighwick), like dynamic new thinking. Perhaps Surleighwick could lead the way, he thought to himself, and be the first university library in the country with no actual books of its own. What a saving that would be in library staff! Pratt might be a young man, but the Vice-Chancellor liked him. Someone with modern interests, who'd be very good with modern technology. And after all, Surleighwick was mainly a technological university. Whereas previous Surleighwick librarians had been interested in old-fashioned fuddy-duddy subjects. Why, the last librarian but two had actually written a monograph on libraries in Ancient Greece! And that wasn't the way to get Surleighwick known at all.

Dr Pratt had not disappointed his masters and was now making quite a name for himself with his theory of bibliometrical ergonomics. He was slowly groping towards a theory that was later to become quite well-known in the British university library system. This was, that the value of a book could be quantified by its frequency of use. Dr Pratt started from the belief that the basic 'unit of use' of a book was when one undergraduate borrowed one book for one week. That represented one 'Pratt' as the unit was later to be called. When a post-graduate research student borrowed a book, one could assume that the book was read at a higher level—hence the same book borrowed for a week by a postgraduate researcher counted as two Pratts. A member of the academic teaching staff borrowing a book for a week counted for three and a half Pratts. Later, Dr Pratt realised that these measurements were not precise enough, and he refined his basic unit, for sake of convenience, to a hundred pages. Thus a Pratt became a hundred pages per undergraduate per week. Hence an undergraduate who borrowed a 500 page book for ten weeks bestowed fifty Pratts of use upon the book. Unknown to anyone, Dr Pratt, who knew about computers, had programmed the library's computer to record the number of pages of each book checked out on loan, and the status of the borrower. (This was in fact a very simple operation.) He had already compiled some absolutely fascinating information about the Prattage of books in different subjects. For example, he had proved quite conclusively that students of English literature operated at a higher Prattage than medical biochemists! Nor was this all. His programme had enabled him to identify some books in the library that were hardly used at all. His computer print-out showed, for example, that since the University of Surleighwick had axed its Italian and Russian departments two years ago, the Prattage of books in Italian and Russian had been dramatically reduced. Now bibliometric ergonomics was, when all was said and done, the science of the efficient use of books!

One drowsy summer day, when Dr Pratt was dozing on the sofa of his home in the Hilly Beeches suburbs of Surleighwick, whilst his wife was tending the flowers in the garden and his two young daughters were playing good humouredly in their playroom, a revelation had come upon him with a blinding flash. Bibliometric ergonomics was a measure of the efficiency of libraries. But the low Prattage of Italian and Russian books reduced the *average* Prattage of the Surleighwick books. Hence, by getting rid of such books into store one would increase the Prattage, and hence the efficiency of use of the library!

So, excitedly, Dr Pratt had put this idea informally to Professor Bodgering, at the end of a meeting of the library committee, and Bodgering, who resented any book that he had not himself read, had seen the point at once, and wholeheartedly endorsed it. (It was most uncharacteristic of Professor Bodgering to serve on university committees—but Mrs Quick, one day, had maliciously pulled his leg, and told him that members of the library committee did the interviewing of the female counter assistants. Professor Bodgering, whose office overlooked the library steps, lusted impotently after the pretty girls he saw skipping blithely up and down them. Mistakenly, believing them to be counter assistants not students, he had accepted nomination to the library committee.) In

due course the library committee had adopted Dr Pratt's idea, glad
to clear out of the way books in languages that no one at Surleighwick was now studying or was likely to read. Dr Pratt was confident of increasing the efficiency of his library by a factor of three
or four.

Dr Pratt was now refining his theory still further. It had
occurred to him that a book that was borrowed fifteen times for
one week was actually being more intensively used than a book
which was borrowed once for fifteen weeks. (This was true.
Professor Bodgering, for instance, needing a book a fifth of an inch
thick to support an uneven chair in his kitchen, had sent his
secretary to the library to borrow his own little Skelmerdale Notes
pamphlet on *Tamburlaine*, which met the case exactly.) So Dr Pratt
had now built a 'frequency of use factor' into his calculations. And
so his statistics multiplied. It was easy to find the ratio between the
total number of books in the library and the total number of
academic staff; or the total number of research students; or the total
number of undergraduates. And these could be compared with the
figures for other university libraries in this country and abroad.
These figures could be broken down between the humanities and
the social sciences and the sciences. Moreover, the figures were in
constant flux. They altered year by year as fortunate younger
members of the academic staff succeeded in their unending quest
to escape from Surleighwick. Dr Pratt's flow charts and graphs
multiplied.

Then there was the problem of books that were merely
consulted in the library but not borrowed. To cope with this Dr
Pratt had devised a lengthy form which was wrapped round the
front boards of certain books in the Surleighwick library. This
invited users of the books to identify their status with a tick in the
appropriate column, and to say whether they were consulting the
books for research, teaching or other purposes; how much of it they
had read; how long they had spent reading it; whether they had

used the book before, and so on. Every five weeks these forms were collected and replaced by fresh ones. The information on the old ones was then fed into Dr Pratt's computer simulation of the ergonomic efficiency of the books under his control.

Dr Pratt had now at his command many fascinating statistics, which his computers could print out at high speed, or represent in a shimmering array of changing coloured circles on VDUs. The Surleighwick Vice-Chancellor had been fascinated by these, and had pounded his crutches on the table with great excitement when he saw them.

"Well done, Pratt. This is splendid stuff. Keep up the good work."

For Mr Henry Tinker, the Surleighwick Vice-Chancellor, was sure that this modern, innovative, *exciting* project would assist the long campaign he had been waging in Whitehall to get his MBE upgraded to OBE—his greatest, indeed obsessive, ambition.

Since Dr Pratt had arrived at Surleighwick the amount of money spent on the library had greatly increased, much against the national trend. New computers and expensive software had been purchased, installed and regularly updated. Programmers, inputters, and technical staff had been engaged. The secretarial staff had been expanded. The number of books purchased for the library had declined year by year, and was now only half what it had been at the time of Dr Pratt's appointment. The average ergonomic efficiency of each book in the library had therefore been much increased.

A year ago, Dr Pratt had been authorised to increase the ergonomic efficiency of the library even further by removing to store books in other subjects too which Surleighwick no longer taught. A large hole had been dug on waste ground to the north of the Surleighwick campus, and an air-conditioned concrete bunker constructed. Its walls had been lined with steel. In the vast underground concrete hanger thus created, steel shelves had been crammed in, to which library staff alone had access. On to these shelves had been placed, first, all the books in Italian and Russian that had been removed from the Surleighwick library and stored in packing cases in a furniture warehouse. As modern languages collapsed at Surleighwick, books in Spanish and German had followed them. Then the principle of disposal had been extended. A start had been made on books which had not been borrowed for more than twenty-five years (which could be ascertained from the date stamp of the loan slip). These books were dragging down the overall ergonomic efficiency of the Surleighwick library, and as they were removed, the remaining 'working collection' of the Surleighwick library became more and more efficient on Dr Pratt's charts. He was now wrestling with the difficult problem of eliminating these books from his computer model, and had arrived at the concept of 'virtual inefficiency'. These books were 'virtually inefficient', because they were no longer used at Surleighwick. Therefore, they could be 'virtually ignored' from the point of view of his computer model.

Although of course, on rare and irritating occasions, a persistent enquirer could still consult these books. Such pests had to fill in a lengthy form in triplicate, pay a fee of two pounds towards the inconvenience caused, and hand it to one of the counter staff. Once a fortnight, a reluctant assistant would drive an electric trolley to the bunker, and would spend an hour extracting the twenty or so books that had been requested since the last fortnightly visit. On the Wednesday afternoon of the week following such retrieval, the books were available for consultation for a two hour period in the rare book room of the Surleighwick library.

These loans made Dr Pratt's calculations untidy, and he was often tempted to zap the books from the computerised catalogue, which he could do with three keystrokes. But so far he had hesitated to do so.

Now he sat in his office pondering the problem of adapting his computer calculations of ergonomic efficiency to periodicals.

At eight in the evening, for he had been so carried away by his thoughts that time had flown, Dr Pratt put down his file with a sigh, switched off his VDU, put on his coat, and went off home. Williamn Harvey's treatise on the circulation of the blood lay unheeded and forgotten in his armchair.

*****

A fortnight later, on the 8 January 1991, when the Christmas and New Year's festivities were fully behind him, and the Surleighwick campus was bathed in the cold cheerless light of the endless midwinter, Dr Pratt stood in his warm office on the second floor of the library, gazing pensively at the muddy grass, in front of the library courtyard, still bespattered with last October's fallen leaves. He saw the infinitely depressing, jarring mixture of modern concrete, dispiriting functional redbrick buildings of the 1950s, and dirty Gothic pinnacles of the Victorian buildings that constituted the Surleighwick campus.

Miss Moore entered the room, neat as ever in her white blouse, simple grey skirt, black stockings and comfortable slip-on shoes.

"Here, take this." She proferred Dr Pratt the first of his morning cups of tea, served in the usual large white porcelain cup, with two digestive biscuits in the saucer.

"Thanks Sarah-Jane. How I hate Januaries at Surleighwick. They're so depressing." And indeed that extensive conurbation of rusting factories and derelict canals was not seen to best advantage in the early months of the year, when damp chill winds swept in from the west, and the sun was scarcely seen.

Dr Pratt looked without interest at the wire in-tray of letters that his secretary had opened and removed from their envelopes, and which she now brought for his attention. She had already been through the correspondence and attached the relevant files, and, where necesssary, had provided background information in the form of neat, succinct memos.

"Anything of interest in the post today?"

She shrugged her shoulders and gave a quizzical smile.

He sighed. "Silly question, I supppose."

"Oh, there is one thing." She gestured towards the two volumes of Harvey and Marx that were still in the armchair in the far corner of the room, where Dr Pratt had left them in the week before Christmas. "I wondered about those books there. Are they for cataloguing?"

Dr Pratt suddenly remembered the books, about which he had thought not at all until that moment, and on the instant, at the thought of a book, he snapped out of his mild mid-winter blues and was once more instantly decisive.

"No, not for cataloguing." The ergonomic efficiency of those books was obviously zero. Who at Surleighwick would read a Romanian novel or Marx in German? The very idea was laughable. "I took them off Mrs Houghton's hands to do her a favour. We don't want them in the library, though. It's only a boring volume of Marx and a Romanian novel. I suggest the Marx for the salvage bag and the other one for Odds and Ends."

Recently Dr Pratt had persuaded the library committee that certain books in the library were unnecessary and ought to be disposed of—for example, copies of out-of-date textbooks in electrical and mechanical engineering which dated from the 1920s and were of no conceivable interest to anyone. The committee had endorsed this very reasonable suggestion. Then there was a small number of books in Oriental languages—which Surleighwick had never taught. These books, the result of chance donations and bequests, had never found a borrower in sixty years, and their cataloguing had always had to be farmed out to the School of Oriental and African studies at the University of London—it not being worthwhile for Surleighwick to employ a cataloguer with the requisite expertise. Again, to dispose of such books seemed eminently sensible, and would free valuable shelf space. Such books would never find a reader at Surleighwick. Then again, Surleighwick had a large collection of books on theology, but a lot of it was, as the committee agreed, complete and utter rubbish. Who nowadays was interested in the bad-tempered polemic waged by various sects of methodists and presbyterians against each other in the 1850s? Certainly such texts were not needed in more than one edition. Let the library by all means keep the first and perhaps the last edition—the ones in between could be regarded as superfluous.

The committee then turned to the question of disposal. There were two possibilities. The books could be sold; or else disposed of to a salvage merchant for pulp. Professor Zigmund, of the department of Applied Economics, argued strongly that all the books should be sold for pulp. The great advantage of this was, as he pointed out at tedious length, that the income from books sold for pulp was predictable. They fetched 50p per hundredweight. Hence it was possible, by weighing the books, to know exactly what they would fetch. Thus forward planning about what to do with the money could proceed on a confident basis. But there were some pretty smart professors on the Surleighwick Univerity library committee. One of them was Professor Middleton, the emaciated, bearded, bright-eyed professor of philosophy. Professor Middleton suddenly had an idea, a flash of pure inspiration worthy of the highest traditions of creative professorial thinking at Surleighwick. Could not some of these books be sold instead? That way, the books might fetch more than they would as salvage, and, as an added bonus, the books might find a readership that Surleighwick could not provide. Thus, the university would at one and the same time gain money and advance its duty to promote knowledge. Professor Zigmund guffawed! Trust a philosopher to come up with crazy, impractical ideas! Any economist knew that certainty of price was the conclusive factor in any sale. Professor Middleton disagreed. He argued that there was no essential difference between selling a book and sending it for salvage. A book sold for salvage always had the *potential* to be read, just as a book sent for sale had the *potential* to be pulped. Professor Middleton rather lost his colleagues at this point, with his philosophical musings. But that was not the point. What mattered at the end of the day was how much cash in hand a transaction produced. After a three and a half hour debate, by five votes to four, Professor Bodgering abstaining on the grounds that he was asleep, a compromise was adopted: the books would be sold for salvage, except for those that, in the opinion of the library staff, would fetch more by being sold.

In the last year, five and a half tons of dross had been cleared from the Surleighwick shelves and sold for salvage, and the very useful sum of £55 had accrued to library funds. The value of the shelf-space freed was of course considerably greater than that, so the committee prided themselves on a very sharp move. A further 5000 redundant books, carefully selected by the junior counter assistants for their bright bindings or illustrations, had been saved from salvage and sold in job lots for a total of £800 to Odds and Ends books in Hay-on-Wye. It was to this shop that Dr Pratt had been referring when he consigned the Harvey volume to Odds and Ends.

Miss Moore obediently picked up the Marx and the Harvey from the Librarian's armchair, and returned to her room to carry out his instructions.

*****

Miss Sarah-Jane Moore was not only a personable and attractive young woman: she was also clever and intelligent. So much so that the more perceptive and thoughtful members of the male academic staff at Surleighwick wondered what she was doing working for the distinctly uncompetitive—in fact downright parsimonious—salary offered to her grade by the niggardly University of Surleighwick.

The answer was quite simple. Miss Moore had come to Surleighwick because her boyfriend was a student there. That romance had however finished six months previously, and she was now unattached. But, having settled herself into a flat at Surleighwick, she did not wish to leave the city just yet. She carried the two books back to her office, closing the communicating door of Dr Pratt's office behind her. She poured her own tea into a mug embellished with a William Morris floral design. (Dr Pratt was very status conscious, and just as his office and carpet were bigger than Sarah-Jane's, so too she knew that he would be made uneasy if his secretary sipped her tea from porcelain as nice as his own.) And she was willing to humour him in this matter of the utmost triviality—for she had not been a secretary for more than ten days before the correspondence which passed across her desk brought it home to her how important trivialities were at Surleighwick.

She sat at her desk, and examined first of all the volume of Marx. That did not particularly interest her, and so with a shrug of her shoulders she tossed it onto the trolley on the far side of her room marked 'for salvage'. The other book however caught her attention. For a start its vellum binding felt so smooth. She ran her hand over the spine and front boards. Their smooth whiteness had an almost sensual feel. She turned to the spine, which was lettered in black ink with the words 'De Motu Cordis'. She looked at the lower boards. She pressed the cool vellum flat against her left cheek, and inhaled the distinctive, slightly musty, but nevertheless not unpleasant, odours that the book exhaled. She inhaled this with the same pleasure which the fragrance of certain cigar tobaccos sometimes gave her, though she did not smoke herself. Then Sarah-Jane gently opened the book. She admired the elegant device of the angel on the front. She admired the paper, still white and pristine after so many centuries. The well-inked letters stood out clearly to her eye, as the print flowed on in its crisp and clearly defined columns page after page.

She turned again to the title page. Miss Sarah-Jane Moore had never been to university, but she had studied Latin for three years at school. She instantly recognised the work as a medical treatise 'On the motion of the heart' by William Harvey, Englishman and London professor, published at Frankfurt in 1628. The name of Harvey was familiar to her from her sixth-form course in the history of general science. She did not know the market value of the work, but she realised that she held in her hands a handsome and noble book, a book that would grace anyone's collection. And to think that it had been printed in 1628, over three hundred and fifty years ago! It seemed almost unimaginable that books could have been so well printed then. She checked the date again, but there was no doubt about it. Sarah-Jane strolled over to the far wall of her office where Dr Pratt kept a library copy of the compact *Dictionary of National Biography* (in two volumes complete with magnifying glass). And this confirmed the date. It seemed a pity that such a book should go to Odds and Ends. She returned to her desk and called up the entries for William Harvey from the computerised catalogue. Surleighwick had no copy of the 1628 edition, though its medical library had some nineteenth-century editions and translations.

Sarah-Jane thought for while. Dr Pratt had said it was a Romanian novel, and that it was to be sold to Odds and Ends. One thing was instantly clear to her. It would be folly to call her findings to the attention of Dr Pratt. She had been at Surleighwick long enough to know of the blind irrational rages into which so many of the senior administrators and professors would descend, the very second that their authority or status or position was compromised or threatened, or their knowledge impugned. She remembered how at a meeting of the library committee (whose minutes she took) Professor Bodgering had actually cried and gnawed the rubber of his wheel-chair wheels when he learned that he had not been invited to a farewell party for one of the female counter assistants. She remembered too how white with anger Dr Pratt had been when Dr Hanwell, a historian of science, had once suggested that the ultimate value of a book was not dependent on how often it was borrowed. Most of all she remembered how a junior counter assistant on the humanities floor had dared to suggest to Dr Pratt that he should not be pulping the library's duplicate copy of the *Poems* of Currer, Ellis, and Acton Bell. Dr Pratt had exploded with fury, and dismissed the girl on the spot for insubordination and insolence. Dr Pratt had exclaimed anyone who knew anything knew that the minor poetry of unknown Victorians was worth absolutely nothing. Why, the Bell brothers had simply paid to have the work printed out of their own pockets! And everyone knew how dreadful poems published on vanity presses were!

Sarah-Jane was an honest young woman. So: to Odds and Ends the book must go. But first Sarah-Jane took out her pad and jotted down a few details in a neat hand. The idea came into her mind that when the book had reached Odds and Ends, she might take a trip to Hay to see if she could not buy the book herself. She placed the book on the Odds and Ends trolley, drank her mug of tea, and turned to her other duties.

Two days later, Howard Cantelow, the rather careworn, shabbily-dressed proprietor of Odds and Ends arrived in his ancient van, on his fortnightly visit to purchase the unwanted books from Surleighwick. It was a profitable business for him, and all his colleagues in the trade envied his fortune in having such an arrangement with the university. Mr Cantelow was usually able to recoup his investment in a reasonable period of time by the sale of just a portion of the Surleighwick books. Then, the rest was clear profit. Gradually, he had stopped looking very much for books elsewhere, and let Surleighwick supply him with letters, poems, plays, the belles-lettres of the eighteenth and nineteenth centuries, theology, and other general books. After the first few visits, one hundred pounds a trolley had been established as the going rate. Mr Cantelow handed over £800. Eight trolleys were loaded from the back of the library on to his van. The *De motu cordis* started on its journey to Hay-on-Wye.

And what of the priceless copy of *Das Kapital* once owned by Lenin? That was now lost to the world, recycled into a cardboard yoghurt carton.

CHAPTER THREE

THE BASKERVILLE FELLOW IN THE HISTORY OF SCIENCE

'There can be good men even under a bad emperor.' (Tacitus)

'A wise man knows an ignorant one, because he has been
ignorant himself; but the ignorant cannot recognise the wise,
because he has never been wise.' (Persian saying)

In 1967, Mr Surleighwick P. Baskerville, the great American
chemical magnate and philanthropist, had tried in vain to give a
hundred million dollars to the University of Surleighwick, from
which his Christian name had been derived. Mr Surleighwick P.
Baskerville's mother had, as Miss Harriet Peachtree, been one of
the first female students of chemistry at the University of Surleighwick in 1908. There she had met and married Mr Hiram P.
Baskerville III, a charming, relaxed, and very clever student visiting Surleighwick from the USA to work for his doctorate in
chemistry (for ages long ago, in the long-distant days of 1908 the
chemistry department at Surleighwick had been one of the leaders
in the field).

In 1911 Hiram P. Baskerville III had returned with his bride
to the United States, and during the great expansion of the chemical
industry that resulted from the First World War he had, through
his uncommon intellectual, financial and chemical acumen, laid
the foundations of one of the great American fortunes. Mrs Baskerville had no relations in England. She never returned to Surleighwick; and so, over the years, the happy times she had spent there
became, in nostalgic recollection, still more golden and mellow.
The reality of latter-day Surleighwick never broke in to destroy her

illusions. Her marriage was an extremely happy one, though there was but one child of the union, Surleighwick P. Baskerville, born in 1913. As she grew into serene old age, Mrs Baskerville often spoke to her son in fond remembrance of her halcyon days at Surleighwick, that old, grey, industrial English city. In 1946, with the Baskerville fortunes diversified, invested and multiplied a further ten-fold through judicious investment in the booming industrial economy of World War II, Mr Hiram P. Baskerville III died, leaving his widow and son as multi-millionaires on a grand scale. In 1963, Mrs Baskerville was dying of a rare blood disease, but her final days were made easier through her happy memories of unclouded youth at Surleighwick. She left all her millions to her son, and, as she lay dying, suggested to him that he should approach the University of Surleighwick with a view to endowing the university with a foundation in her memory.

Mr Surleighwick P. Baskerville was a keen amateur of history. Both his father and mother had been chemists. What better way of commemorating both his parents, and of perpetuating the Baskerville name, (for he had never married), than by endowing a putative Harriet Baskerville Institute for the History of Science at the University of Surleighwick, England? By 1965, his plans were made.

Mr Baskerville envisaged a purpose-built building on the extensive and roomy Surleighwick campus, with a Director of international standing, a staff of ten full-time researchers paid at professorial rates, a teaching staff of twenty, limitless funds to build up its library, a librarian, abundant secretarial assistance, facilities for conferences, a publications fund, generous travel and accommodation grants. No expense would be spared to attract academic talent, and to make Surleighwick *the* leading place in the world for the History of Science. In general terms, Surleighwick P. Baskerville wrote to the University of Surleighwick propounding his idea.

That was when his difficulties started. The first reaction at the University of Surleighwick was to laugh at his name. Fancy anyone being called Surleighwick! Who ever had heard of such a thing! So after desultory discussion a reply was sent to the effect that Surleighwick was not very interested in that kind of research. Mr Surleighwick P. Baskerville persisted, and revealed a little more of his plans, and the generous scale of his funding.

The matter was remitted to faculty Boards for consideration. The Science faculty, ardently supported by the Medical faculty, was bitterly, not to say fanatically, opposed, on the grounds that the history of science was the history of superseded science. And who wanted to know that? Such out-of-date knowledge ought positively *not* to be taught! To do so would in fact corrupt youth, not educate them. It was analogous to teaching herb-medicine or the works of Galen and Paracelsus to medical students, as one uncharacteristically erudite medical professor said, to the mysti- fied stares of the anatomists and physiologists and specialists in rheumatoid arthritis. (Galen? Paracelsus? Who on earth were they? Were they African witch-doctors perhaps?)

The Arts faculty, with the historians in the van, were just as bitterly opposed.

Then too that smart young lecturer in archaeology, Mr Eus- tace Toady, in the third year of his appointment at Surleighwick, garlanded with the fire-new academic honours of his Oxford MA, had made a particularly brilliant and witty speech at the faculty Board, leaning back in his chair and sticking his thumbs into his waistcoat pocket.

"The History of Science, Mr Dean Sir, is, Sir, I submit, Sir, neither History, nor, Sir, certainly, is it Science."

This terse, clever, wittily antithetical intervention had quite carried the day at the faculty Board. But throughout the whole University of Surleighwick, the thought of an infusion of inde- pendently funded academics in an unknown discipline was anathema. Anyway, who needed the money when government funds with no strings attached were flooding in?

So the University of Surleighwick wrote a curt note to Mr Surleighwick P. Baskerville explaining that the History of Science was not a discipline with which it wished to be associated. Baffled, but writing it off to English eccentricity, Mr Surleighwick P. Baskerville offered his monies to the University of Surleighwick, Arkansas, as the next best thing. His offer was promptly accepted, and, when he died in 1972, the University of Surleighwick, Arkansas, received the sum of two hundred million dollars 'to endow an Institute for the History of Science or otherwise at its absolute discretion', as the trust deed stated. The Harriet Baskerville Institute at the University of Surleighwick, Arkansas, is now *the* place in the whole world for the study of the History of Science.

By that time Mr Eustace Toady's clever little witticisms had put him on the road to academic success at Surleighwick, England, and he was now a Senior Lecturer with as many as three five-page articles and two two-page reviews to his credit. But Mr Surleighwick P. Baskerville, out of respect for his mother's wishes, had not forgotten Surleighwick, England, entirely. He left a million dollars in his will to fund one post in the History of Science, with the proviso that should the bequest be rejected, the money was to be used instead for a series of adverts calling attention to the university's stupidity in turning down untrammelled funds of some two hundred million dollars. Chastened, the University of Surleighwick had accepted the money with a bad grace. It still did not believe in the History of Science, but it feared ridicule and bad publicity even more.

*****

In 1990 Dr Charles Hanwell had been Harriet Baskerville Fellow in the History of Science at the University of Surleighwick,

England, for seventeen years. He had been appointed in October 1973, shortly after his twenty-second birthday. The University of Surleighwick, having accepted the Baskerville bequest in as surly and ungracious mood as was possible, was determined that no distinguished scholar would be appointed to the post. Not that anyone at Surleighwick would have been able to recognise scholarly distinction in the History of Science anyway. So they had appointed as young a man as possible, partly on the grounds that although the endowment of the post could not be applied to other purposes, any portion that was not spent would aid the Surleighwick cash flow. The post had been advertised only once—in the *Times Literary Supplement*. That way, it was hoped that no one with scientific interests would see the advertisement. The powers that be at Surleighwick were narrow minded and prejudiced; they therefore made the mistake of judging others by their own limited capacities, and had not the wit to see that a historian of science who read the *Times Literary Supplement* might be a man of deep and broad interests—the very qualities that Surleighwick had wished to avoid.

The advertisement had produced three replies—a pleasingly small number. One of the candidates was thirty-four years old, and had written a well-received book on the history of scientific method. This was sufficient to turn against him the four Surleighwick professors on the interviewing board who had not written books. The second candidate, Dr Clare Tunbridge, was a young woman twenty-nine years old with ten good papers to her name on the development of magnetism and electricity. Dr Tunbridge was working towards a major book on the subject. Hating her intellect and competence more than they lusted after her beauty, the board declined to appoint her. Dr Tunbridge's seminal book on *Magnetism and the Mind of Man* was published three years later to outstanding and universal acclaim, and she went off to a research post at the Institute for Advanced Studies, Princeton. That left Dr Charles Hanwell.

"He's only twenty-two, Isn't that rather too young?" asked the Dean of Science doubtfully.

"But at least he hasn't written as much as the other candidates," replied the Dean of Arts, coming to Dr Hanwell's support. "I'm very much against the view that one can judge a man's scholarship by his publications."

"He seems well dressed and polite, apart from his bright socks. I'm for him myself," put in the Senior Lecturer in Law. (It was traditional at Surleighwick for all appointing committees to include at least three people who knew nothing about the subject of the post.)

"After all, his doctoral thesis is on the history of botany from Clusius to Darwin—and Darwin is a big name," remarked the Vice-Chancellor.

Darwin, at least, was a name that most of the committee recognised.

"He's the cheapest candidate on the wage-for-age scale," added the Registrar helpfully. "And we won't have to pay him an increment till he's twenty-five."

A very definite plus! Dr Hanwell got the job.

Yet the appointing committee, in spite of their best efforts, had made a mistake from their point of view, for Dr Hanwell, although he had no publications at the time of his appointment, turned out to be a publishing scholar. His Ph.D. yielded five articles, and then, in his early years at Surleighwick, he set out to immerse himself in his subject.

When asked at his interview about his knowledge of foreign languages, Dr Hanwell, a modest man, had turned the question aside in a deprecating way. That was fortunate for him. If he had admitted the truth, namely that his father had been an International Civil Servant working for UNESCO in Geneva, and that he himself had a good working knowledge of French, Spanish, Italian and German, with a smattering of Dutch and Portuguese, a little Czech and Polish, and six years Latin and Greek at a variety of good schools, he would never have got the job, for linguists were regarded with extreme suspicion as somehow not 'playing the game' at Surleighwick, particularly in the mainstream humanities departments. Most people at Surleighwick, in fact, did not believe that foreign languages *really* existed. Almost by definition, knowledge could not be said to exist unless it was in English! To refer to material in any other languages, unless you were doing your degree in them, was low, underhand, and caddish, and not at all in accordance with the traditions of Surleighwick. That certainly was the view held no less firmly by Professor Bodgering than by Professor Toady or the late Professor Houghton.

Dr Hanwell was interested in his subject, and he had the background to make a go of it. His first degree was in biology from Manchester. Then, finding that the history of science was his real interest, he had studied for three years at Sussex, and completed his thesis on time. Arriving at Surleighwick at what was recognised twenty years later as the very moment when the university began its precipitate decline, he set to work with a will to turn himself into a scholar. He sharpened up his Greek by reading Theophrastus. Clusius, Matthiolus, Linnaeus, Pliny the Elder and Columella strengthened his Latin. He read through Rapin's Latin poem on gardening, *Hortorum libri cultura hortensis*, Vanier's *Praedium rusticum* and Zanchius' *De horto sapientiae*. He enjoyed these fascinating albeit obscure poems, and started to look out for other Latin (and French, Italian and German) poems on gardening. He even looked at English poems such as Granger's *The Sugar-Cane*, in four books, about the West Indian plantations. Dr Hanwell started to publish notes and articles on poetical books about horticulture in the botanical and even literary journals. He started to catalogue the flora (and fauna) of this poetry. The search for botanical poems caused him to stumble across the vast literature of poetical science from the sixteenth to the eighteenth centuries. He read Cardinal de Polignac's *Anti-Lucretius*, with its long excursuses in majestic hexameters on Boyle's law. He read Carlo Noceti's *Poesie Scientifiche* (Florence, 1755) and started to make notes about poems on rainbows. This led him to Zarrius' monumental verse metaphrase of and commentary on Diego Sarriana's Latin translation of the influential twelfth-century writings on optics of Ali Ibn Ali al Rajal, the famous Arab scientist. By the late-1970s a major work on scientific learned poetry was in the making—an area that conventional historians of science had ignored because it was poetry, and students of literature because it was science (and in foreign languages at that).

The study of scientific poetry extended Dr Hanwell's interests in the History of Science. From reading sixteenth-century Latin poems about pulleys, he progessed to a general knowledge of mechanics from Philoponus to Walter Burley. From mechanics he was led to the study of motion from Aristotle's *De physico auditu* to Nicholas Oresme's treatise *On the Kinematics of Circular Motion*, and thence on to Galileo and beyond. The study of motion led him into astronomy, from Ptolemy to Copernicus, from Copernicus to Newton. Then his interests widened to include the field equations of J.C. Maxwell and the birth of modern physics. Thence he proceeded on the one hand to a study of the history of electricity from the earliest Latin writings on Lichtenberg figures in the eighteenth-century scientific journals, and on the other hand to a general knowledge of the quantum theory, from Bohr and Heisenberg and Dirac, to Fermi and beyond. From the study of Newton Dr Hanwell was led into higher mathematics, to Euler, the court mathematician to Catherine the Great, to Boole, to Hilbert. Dr Hanwell was the first person in the University of Surleighwick to be interested in the fractal geometry of Mandelbrot. All the while he kept up his early interests in botany, biology and zoology, and

throughout the seventies and early eighties followed with amusement the passionate controversies about cladistics and phenetics
waged in *Systematic Zoology*. By the mid-1980s, with a firm
command of two ancient and four modern European languages,
with a rough and ready smattering of four other tongues, with an
extensive knowledge of the history, philosophy, and sociology of
science, and with a vast body of reading in original sources behind
him, Dr Hanwell was one of the best read and most intellectually
alert members of the University of Surleighwick. He was, as was
only natural, also one of the least regarded.

Naturally, Dr Hanwell was not popular at Surleighwick.

When he was first appointed way back in 1973, The faculties
of Science, Medicine and Arts in that order declined to admit him
to their faculties. Hence his position was labelled 'extra-faculty' ,
and in effect he formed an independent research institute all by
himself. In his early days at Surleighwick, Dr Hanwell had offered
to teach courses for various departments, but found that:

1) The department of botany was not interested in courses
either on Theophrastus or on the early history of the potato in
Europe.

2) The Greek department disclaimed any interest in Theophrastus and Philoponus or in Greek science.

3) The Latin department had never heard of Clusius, Matthiolus, Zanchius, Vanier, Rapin's poem on gardening or any of the
other poets, and did not consider them suitable for their students
to know. (This was before Surleighwick decided to close its Greek
and Latin departments as an economy measure in 1983.)

4) The physics department considered that physics from
Aristotle to Galileo, and also the early history of electricity, was
irrelevant to its students.

5) The medical faculty had not the slightest interest in Galen,
in Bombast von Hohenheim, or in the school of Paracelsian medicine. Their students were too busy learning to be doctors to have

much time for anything else but going down sewers and holding wild parties.

6) The chemistry department was not interested in the early development of alchemy into chemistry. Dr Hanwell's offer of some general background lectures was declined.

7) The archaeology department, guided by the unerring hand of Mr Eustace Toady, who in 1970 was quite the coming man, was not interested in the early history of archaeology. (From Politians's *Panepistemon* Dr Hanwell had been led to Politian's *Epistolae*, and thence to a consideration of that antiquarianism in the Italian Renaissance exemplified in them, a topic on which he published three papers.)

8) The French department refused to have anything to do with courses on the scientific background to the French Revolution.

9) The Italian department was not interested in *Poesie scientifiche*.

10) The German department had never head of Bombast von Hohenheim, and was utterly uninterested in courses, or even one general lecture, on his cultural importance. In any case, their students were too busy reading *The Tin Drum*.

11) The Spanish department declined a course of lectures on Raymond Lull as a scientist, and on Arabic science in Spain in the twelfth and thirteenth centuries.

12) The mathematics department had no real interest in Euler.

13) The department of zoology regarded Gesner's *Historia animalium* as hopelessly out of date.

14) The department of anatomy saw no point in studying Vesalius.

15) The English department did not consider lectures on scientific poetry to be appropriate for their critical methodology.

("Confounded fellow is offering lectures on the sugar cane," grumbled Professor Houghton, misunderstanding Dr Hanwell's phone call. (Professor Houghton had never heard of *The Sugar*

Cane.) "Dammit, this is the *English* department, not the department of agriculture.")

16) The department of veterinary studies had no interest in horse-doctor books from Pelagonius to the eighteenth century.

17) The sociology department disclaimed any interest in the sociology of science.

18) The department of economic history did not favour a course exploring the connexions between scientific development and ecomomic progress.

19) The history department was bitterly opposed to its students being exposed to the history of science, which they considered not to be a part of history at all. To a man and to a woman, the Surleighwick historians eschewed ideas, theories, the intellect, for the tedious gathering of population statistics and details of pots and pans bequeathed in wills.

20) The bitterest and most hostile reaction came in 1982 from the Centre for Marlowe and Elizabethan Studies. Professor Bodgering had greeted the offer of a lecture on the magical background of *Dr Faustus* with genuine fury. He went incandescent with anger when he opened Dr Hanwell's memo, his whole body trembled, his heart raced, he fell back in his chair and he had to call for his oxygen mask. How *dare* anyone at Surleighwick presume to think of lecturing on Marlowe, an author who was his, Professor Bodgering's personal intellectual property? he reflected. "Marlowe is *my* author, and no one else at Surleighwick must be allowed to misinterpret him."

Moreover, Professor Bodgering cowered at the mention of the words magic. He tried to pretend that magic was not important in the Renaissance, and certainly formed no part of the background to *Dr Faustus*. Professor Bodgering chose to believe that Faustus was not really indulging in magic, but was suffering from paranoid delusions. He was thinking of writing an article about this—it would be his *fifth* journal article in thirty years—but he preferred, as always, to let the ideas mature in his mind first for several decades (which was why his own articles were so stimulating!—or so he believed). No-one at Surleighwick deplored the vulgar rush to publication more strongly than Professor Bodgering. Besides, everyone knew that renaissance magic was all mumbo-jumbo and didn't work.

Except that Professor Bodgering believed in magic himself! He firmly believed that the Haitian prostitute whom he had insulted in New York had put a hex on him! Somewhere in Harlem, he was convinced, she was sticking pins into a waxen image of himself, and this was the cause of his lung disease—which had certainly got much worse of late. (In 1977 Professor Bodgering moved from one walking stick to two, in 1978 from two sticks to a frame, in 1980 from a frame to the motorised trike to which his withered and shrunken body was now confined.)

Here Professor Bodgering was unjust. Pins were being stuck into his waxen image not by the Haitian prostitute, but by his colleagues Mrs Quick and Dr Antonia Crumpet.

Dr Hanwell found in fact only two departments at Surleighwick who were interested in his courses.

1) The metallurgy department, which welcomed his lectures on Agricola's *De re metallica* with open arms. (The Surleighwick department of metallurgy, by some strange chance, was one of the few civilised and respectable departments in the university.)

2) The theology department, which accepted both a suggestion for lectures comparing the accounts of creation in Genesis and Clarambald of Arras, and the offer of special subjects on creation theory and the history of cosmology.

So Dr Hanwell went his own way. Every two years or so the occasional bright and inquisitive student of theology found her way (it was usually a her) to his room, obscurely hidden away in the very basement of Surleighwick's Gothic central building, there to sit in his comfortable room, lit only by thick panes of glass set into one side of the ceiling, and furnished with many bookcases and battered armchairs. Such rare inquirers would listen, interested but sometimes slightly bemused, whilst Dr Hanwell lit a Don Diego cigar, a luxury which he allowed himself once or twice a day, and paced up and down in a relaxed but authoritative fashion. Then, casually dressed in corduroy trousers and checkered shirt, clasping his cigar in one hand and twirling his silver-framed granny glasses in the other, Dr Hanwell would pace up and down the faded red carpet, discoursing on Bridget of Brnö and Gerhoh (the Great) von Reichersberg, on Oderic of Oppenheim and Englebert of Admont, on the mysticism of Raymond Lull, on geology and belief in the nineteenth century, on the *mumia* and the *vis medicatrix naturae* of Bombast von Hohenheim, until the light faded, and Dr Hanwell would bring his class to a halt, and offer his student a cup of tea in a large brown mug from an old pewter teapot. The few students who came into contact with Dr Hanwell found his lectures among the most interesting and informative of their Surleighwick career.

Dr Hanwell found when he arrived that the Surleighwick library was well equipped for the study of the history of science. Why he never knew, but it subscribed to *Annals of Science* and *Ambix*, to the *British Journal of the History of Science* and to *Medical History*, to the *Journal of Small Animal Practice* and to *Tijdschrift voor Geschiedenis Wetenschappenlijk*. It possessed facsimiles of the complete works of Raymond Lull and of Agrippa von Nettesheim, and of the encyclopaedias of Vincent of Beauvais in the Douai, 1624 edition. It had the original Latin writings of Lichtenberg. It even possessed a Clarambald of Arras. And anything not in the library, Dr Hanwell could buy from the funds attached to his Baskerville Fellowship, over which he gained more and more control the longer he was at Surleighwick.

So gradually, in his late thirties, with his 948 page magnum opus on scientific poetry now in the press, with several dozen publications to his name, Dr Hanwell accepted his obscure fate at Surleighwick with reasonable contentment. As much as anyone not possessed of great wealth could, he lived a life that was free of stress and allowed him the leisure to cultivate his interests. True, Surleighwick had not been the best university in the world at the time of his appointment, and throughout his years there it had fallen into a catastrophic decline. But Dr Hanwell gradually recovered from his early disappointment at not being allowed to teach, and settled into a comfortable routine as early middle-age approached. The occasional female students from the department of theology provided an agreeable and not too demanding contact with students, enough to maintain his interest in teaching without suffering the overwhelming pressure of marking and examining that was the fate of many luckless contemporaries. His general lectures in metallurgy and contact with that department kept him in touch with modern science—for many Surleighwick metallurgists had been trained as physicists. To these Dr Hanwell would chat, as he joined them most mornings for coffee in their departmental coffee lounge, tucked away in a remote corner of an inner courtyard, but only fifty yards from Dr Hanwell's office.

Dr Hanwell had started to collect books as an undergraduate, and as a postgraduate had acquired some interesting books in his field. On arriving at Surleighwick he proceeded to add to his collections, scouring the not very interesting bookshops in Surleighwick and its environs, and making excursions into the towns and villages around. From time to time he would unexpectedly come across some central works for his discipline, and these he would buy if he could afford to—the works of Lagrange on mathematics, of Monulcka on mathematics and physical science, of Delambre on astonomy. He owned copies of the magisterial works of Kopp on chemistry, of Poggendorff on Physics, of Sachs on botany, of Zittel and Geikie on geology, of Klein on mathematics, and of Burtt's *Metaphysical Foundations of Modern Physical*

Science. One glorious day he had found for £5 in a Surleighwick junkshop all five volumes of Anneliese Maier's monumental *Studien zur Naturphilosophie der Spätscholastik* (Rome, 1949-58). The Surleighwick copy of this work was still waiting for its first reader other than Dr Hanwell, and now he would not need to borrow it any more. In a Cotswold village one autumnal day he stumbled across copies of Hélène Metzger's *Newton, Stahl, Boerhave et la doctrine chimique* (Paris, 1930) and of Karl Holtzmann's fascinating work on the calorific theory of heat, *Über die Wärme und Elasticität der Gase und Dämpfe* (Mannheim, 1845).

Yes, anyone who knew the University of Surleighwick found it easy to see why Dr Hanwell would not fit in there! To Professor Bodgering and his numerous ilk, he appeared a terrifying and threatening figure, profoundly demoralising and subversive, with a breadth of reading that was deeply suspicious and a knowledge of languages that seemed almost praeternatural. Professor Bodgering, after the one occasion when he had talked by mistake to Dr Hanwell, wondered if Hanwell had not sold his soul to the devil, like Dr Faustus. Such a man was to be shunned, and kept at arm's length.

*****

The spring term had started at Surleighwick, and at four o'clock on the first Tuesday of term, the 15th January 1991, Dr Hanwell had just finished his weekly tutorial on the creation theory of Matilda the Hermit of Debrecen, that intriguing example of Germano-Hungarian contact in the thirteenth century, whose views on creation were unconventional and unexpected to say the least! The recent completion of the six-volume Hungarian Academy of Sciences edition of her total *oeuvre* was welcome news to Dr Hanwell. His class consisted of a single student, Ruth Henderson, a third-year theologian with tousled fair hair, a lively expression on her face, and an attractive impish grin. She sat in her dark red woollen dress and black tights, glad of the warmth of the three-bar electric fire on that dark and cheerless day. The light had almost faded, and Dr Hanwell had switched on both the fluorescent lighting of his room, and the lamp on his desk. The class over, he indulged himself by removing one of the favourite Don Diego cigars from its tube, lit it and puffed away with satisfaction, whilst waiting for the kettle to boil. The subtle aroma of that most wonderful of all cigars filled his room, cosy now in the mingled natural and artificial light. Dr Hanwell was fortunate that in his room was a small sink and supply of water. Originally his room had been the annexe to a lab. He had conjured this long-disused and unwanted room out of the Estates Office when he had arrived at Surleighwick all those years ago. Now he was glad that the science and arts faculties had both refused to give him a room. Truth to tell, the Estates Office had forgotten all about this little bunker, below ground level, hidden away in the manifold rambling outbuildings of the main Surleighwick administration and chemistry building, and accessible only from the outside by a separate stairway leading to a door that was otherwise unmarked except for the words 'Radiation Hazard' (a legacy of its previous use).

Ruth Henderson stood up and wandered over to the large oak bookcase that lined one side of the room.

"Do you mind if I look at some of your books?" she asked.

"No, of course not. Do browse away," replied Dr Hanwell, pouring out the tea and putting a few biscuits on to a plate.

Ruth browsed among the books on botany, and then turned to an eclectic selection of books of various sizes and bindings, jumbled together in no particular order—books on chaos theory, popular books on quanta and reality, a few science fiction novels including a signed first edition of Iain M. Banks' *Consider Phlebas*, some Westerns, a biography of Lavoisier, some German books on Paracelsus, some books on computer programming, some works on the history of mathematics, a large thick floppy tome *The Psychotronic Encyclopaedia of Film*, half-a-dozen books on jazz, a book on *Snooker: the Cruel Game*. Next to them came Granger's *The Sugar Cane* in a nice eighteenth-century binding, an odd volume of Duheme's *Systeme du monde*, a novel about Galileo, *The Star-Gazer*, by Zsolt von Harsanyi, then a mass of books on magnetism dating from the nineteenth-century. Then came another shelf of books on modern politics and green issues, and a few joke books.

"What a strange collection of books you have," she remarked.

"Well, they're all related to my interests in one way or another you know."

"What about the *Psychotronic Encyclopaedia of Film*?"

He laughed. "Yes, even that. It's all about mad scientists you know. Most horror and shocker films simply pick up old and distorted ideas from the history of science. After all, take the Frankenstein movies—you've seen them on TV I'm sure. How is the corpse animated? By pulsating an electric charge through it. And how is that charge produced? By a Van der Graaf generator which emits its sparks from a huge dome whilst the wheel that generates the charge turns. We see here a filmic adaptation of the old ideas of Galvani of course. And the whole idea of the man created not by God but by man himself goes back at least as far as the homunculus or Golem (you've perhaps seen *The Golem* on TV?), of Aureolus Philippus Theophrastus Bombast von Hohenheim, better known as Paracelsus. His ideas were often discussed in the sixteenth and seventeenth centuries you know, and received a new lease of life in the nineteenth-century, first with Mary Shelley's *Frankenstein*, which I expect you know, and then later on with the rise of the Theosophists."

Dr Hanwell handed Ruth her tea and biscuits, which she sipped and nibbled, not fully understanding, but interested none the less, as he passed from one topic to another.

From Frankenstein's monster the talk passed to Vampires, from Vampires to Zombies, from Zombies (by a natural progression of thought) to the Surleighwick professors, from Surleighwick professors to mad professors, from mad professors to *The Nutty Professor*, from Jerry Lewis to Alaskan Polar Bear cocktails and the filmic theory of comedy, from Polar Bears to Gesner's *Historia animalium* with its wonderful wood-engravings, from wood-engravings and film-theory to Pabst's *Paracelsus*, one of the rare films of the Nazi period that could still be shown without apology or careful setting in context; from *Paracelsus* to books used in movies, and their authenticity or otherwise. Dr Hanwell had observed disapprovingly that the grimoires in horror movies were generally printed in a type far too modern for the period in which they were supposedly set.

He pulled down from his shelves a couple of battered sixteenth-century vellum quartos of Pacius' commentary on Aristotle's writings about the soul to show her the kind of thing he meant.

"Where did you get these?" asked Ruth, fascinated, for she had never seen books so old before.

"From Hay-on-Wye, the 'Town of Books'," he replied.

"Oh, I've heard of that, but never been there. I should love to see it."

"Well, I go there once a month, he replied. "In fact I'm driving down tomorrow. You can come with me if you like."

Ruth thought for a moment. She had a lecture on nineteenth-century moral theology tomorrow from Professor Bohring—but as he was a Middle-European with a guttural accent and a cleft palate, his lectures were usually rather hard to follow. Hay-on-Wye with Dr Hanwell seemd a more attractive option.

"OK, why not? " she replied. "Thanks, I should like to. I've got a lecture, but I can easily cut it."

"All right, I'll pick you up at say—9.15 at—where?"

"I live in Second Hall on the edge of campus—the other side of the pond." (At Surleighwick the student residences had been most imaginatively entitled First Hall, Second Hall, Third Hall, Fourth Hall and Fifth Hall, after the order in which they were built).

"Second Hall it is then."

Ruth took her leave, and Dr Hanwell poured himself a glass of Jack Daniels to accompany the last four inches of his Don Diego cigar, before returning to his flat to cook himself a lasagne and to catch up on the latest bitter (but hilarious to one who was not personally involved) controversies about cladism.

CHAPTER FOUR

THE BEGINNING OF TERM AT SURLEIGHWICK

'Great grief is indeed dry-eyed'(Seneca, *Phaedra*)

'Even in the remotest corner there will be none of you on whom the dogs will not piss.' (Paracelsus, Preface to *Paragranum*)

All through the Christmas vacation large numbers of the late Professor Houghton's colleagues had been hugging themselves with barely suppressed joy.

The Vice-Chancellor was glad that Houghton was dead, because Professor Houghton had ventured to disagree with him slightly at Senate three times out of the last forty-five meetings. Moreover, letters and memos from Professor Houghton had always been addressed to 'Henry Tinker, Esq., MBE, B. Soc. Sc.' Professor Houghton had *invariably* omitted the 'Hon. MA (Surleighwick)'! And Vice-Chancellor Tinker knew full well that this omission had been intended as a deliberate insult!

"Good riddance to bad rubbish," he had thought to himself with pleasure, as he had hobbled from the Three Blind Mice into his Silver Shadow, and retired to his office to sleep on the soft-leather couch of the dressing-room of the private suite that he had insisted be attached to the Vice-Chancellor's office before he would come to Surleighwick. (He knew that Surleighwick had been *desperate* to appoint him, as he was now the 184th candidate whom they had approached.)

Professor Eustace Toady too was particularly pleased at Houghton's death, and could hardly contain his joy. At dinner on the evening of his memorial speech at the Three Blind Mice he opened two bottles of champagne to drink with his wife and daughters.

In the first place, as Dean of the Arts faculty, he would play a leading role in the search for a successor—and this would feed his vanity and self-importance. With any luck, he would be able to stretch the process out for three or four years. For months and years to come, he would sit in the faculty of Arts coffee room, whilst the likes of Jack Napes would sycophantically approach and ask if there was any news on the headship front. At which Professor Toady would shake his head in feigned sorrow. He would miss submission deadlines, linger for months in approaching external assessors, set up a subcommittee chaired by himself and reporting to himself as Dean to review 'the future of the English department', and initiate a protracted debate about what kind of a person they wanted to fill the chair—that would really set the English department tearing themselves to pieces, he thought with pleasure as he sipped his champagne in great good humour. Then, at a higher level in the university, he could argue against any new appointment on grounds of expense! In three or four years time, with any luck, the gloss would have worn off the English department, Professor Toady thought grimly—for he would never forgive them for getting a 'star' when his own department had been dubbed 'average'! But the whole faculty was tired of hearing nonentities like Napes and Ivan Hoe boasting about their department's star, which had quite gone to their heads. It had been a masterstroke to rush the Vice-Chancellor into appointing Professor Bodgering as acting head of the department. That way, Professor Toady would be able to say there was no rush to fill the chair, because it had a professorial acting head—yet Bodgering was such a hopeless, stupid, boorish incompetent that even the other Arts professors at Surleighwick noticed it! Bodgering would soon run the department into the ground, without a doubt.

Yet now that the department had no permanent head, Profes-

sor Toady as Dean of Arts could really put the boot in! Already,
he had had Professor Houghton's room cleared, and the large
carpet of which he had always been so envious was now on the
floor of his, the Dean's office! He had too appropriated Professor
Houghton's stand-alone computer system for his own use as
Professor of Industrial Archaeology—and this now stood, an impressive and unused status symbol, in the centre of his own desk!
He had had the lock on Professor Houghton's office changed
before his body was even cold, and now none of the English
department could get in with any of their keys! Now he could have
a lot of fun by dangling the enticing prospect of an extra room in
front of three or four professorial cronies. That would certainly get
him bought one or two drinks at the bar! With Bodgering in charge,
he would find it easy to cut the English department's funds, and
switch the money to Archaeology! He would be able to inflict a
swingeing increase in their student-staff ratio! He would terminate
their temporary posts! He could cut their book-grant! All through
the Christmas vacation, his family found Professor Toady in an
unusually beneficent mood, as he gloated over the prospects of
reducing the English department to 'average'!

Then, Professor Bodgering was also pleased by Jim
Houghton's death. As a dying man himself, he was always pleased
to outlive a colleague. Moreover, as acting head of the department,
his own status and power would be increased, and he would pick
up a head of department's allowance of £1,500 a year, which would
pay at least a portion of his drinks bill. He could delegate all the
boring administration, such as exams, admissions, the question of
the department's future (about which he didn't care since if he
didn't die, he was due to retire in two years anyway). He could get
his hands on the department's hospitality and other funds, and use
them acording to his whim! He could block the promotion prospects of his junior colleagues! He could make post-graduates do
all his teaching, instead of just four-fifths of it as at present. And

he'd always fancied Professor Houghton's secretary, Josie. Now at last he would be able to get close enough to her to make a pass! So, though less ecstatically than Professor Toady, Professor Bodgering savoured the news of Houghton's death, as he sat slumped in his wheelchair throughout the Christmas festivities, in a hazy blur of burgundy, vodka, tranquillizers, and oxygen from his cylinders, gazing vacantly out of his bedroom window towards the Ratford river, just visible from the second floor of his country cottage, conveniently located in the market town of Ratford, a mere forty-five miles from Surleighwick. From Ratford, one day a week, he made the slow and painful journey to Surleighwick, driven by Jolly in her old Marina.

Others too of the English staff were happy at the news. Mrs Quick was glad that Professor Houghton had died, because he had several times called her 'my dear'. She regarded him as a sexist who deserved to die. Perhaps now a woman could be appointed to the post—maybe she would apply herself. Her little volume on the *The Women of 'Shirley'* had been called 'an interesting venture' and 'competent and workwomanlike' by its two reviewers. And at 107 pages it was certainly longer than Bodgering's Skelmerdale Notes volume, which had got him his chair; but then, he had been a man. Life was so unfair.

Dr Antonia Crumpet was also not a mourner for Professor Houghton's passing. He had once made a joke about her research on Emily Dickinson, implying that it was not the most important subject in the world, and she could not forgive him for that.

Dr Beaver, Senior Lecturer in English, was glad that Professor Houghton was dead, because Houghton had recently enquired how Dr Beaver's research was coming on. Dr Beaver, who drank heavily and never published, knew when he was being got at. He went straight home after the Three Blind Mice gathering had broken up, opened a bottle of whisky, and drank damnation to the soul of Professor Houghton, before collapsing into a stupor with great satisfaction.

Dr Festering, Senior Lecturer in English, was glad that Professor Houghton was dead, because Houghton had recently enquired how Dr Festering's research was coming on. Dr Festering, who drank heavily and never published, knew when he was being got at. He went straight home after the Three Blind Mice gathering had broken up, opened a bottle of whisky, and drank damnation to the soul of Professor Houghton, before collapsing into a stupor with great satisfaction.

Dr Sword, Senior Lecturer in English, was glad that Professor Houghton was dead, because Houghton had recently enquired how Dr Sword's research was coming on. Dr Sword, who drank heavily and never published, knew when he was being got at. He went straight home after the Three Blind Mice gathering had broken up, opened a bottle of whisky, and drank damnation to the soul of Professor Houghton before collapsing into a stupor with great satisfaction.

Little Jack Napes, though he had not disliked Houghton with the same intensity as most of his colleagues, nonetheless enjoyed the speculation and gossip about who would take over the department. This enjoyment and curiosity and speculation was naturally shared in all other English departments in the UK as soon as the news broke. Jack Napes had started to spread the tidings of Professor Houghton's death by phone, telex, and e-mail to friends and contacts in every other university in the UK within thirty seconds of being informed of its occurrence, which was within five minutes of the event itself. And already, those members of the profession who were truly desperate for a move (but only those) were trying to nerve themselves for the appalling prospect of having to apply to Surleighwick to escape their own institutions.

The other Arts professors at Surleighwick were pleased that Professor Houghton was dead, because like Professor Toady, they saw a chance to do down the English department. Moreover, Houghton's tedious, re-iterated, boasting about his star had caused them great offence. Serve him right! Pride goes before a fall! "Jim always was too bumptious for my liking, and between you and me, Arthur old man, I had my doubts about his work on Kirke White." Good riddance. Already four other professors had written to the Dean requesting his room for their own departmental needs....

Dr Blodgett, Reader in Victorian Literature, was glad that Professor Houghton had got his come-uppance, because he, Dr Blodgett, had published more than Houghton had—yet Houghton had refused to support him for a personal chair!

Josie, Professor Houghton's secretary, was glad that he was dead, because he had been sarcastic when she made mistakes in his typing, and kept her in her office till 5.15 pm every day. She had always envied her colleagues who worked for more indulgent professors, and could get off early.

So no-one at Surleighwick shed a tear at Professor Houghton's passing, except the woman who cleaned his room, to whom he had once given a box of chocolates.

*****

At four o'clock, on Tuesday 15 January, as Ruth and Dr Hanwell were just starting to drink their tea and gossip about Paracelsus and Zombies and Jerry Lewis and Matilda the Hermit of Debrecen, the Surleighwick English department assembled in a square, unattractive room, lit by harsh fluorescent lights, for their first departmental meeting under their new leader. Their pleasure at Professor Houghton's death was still upmost in their minds, though already several of them had been disturbed by the rumours which Professor Toady had enjoyed circulating to the effect that the university's finances would not allow a replacement, and that the chair might be disestablished.

"But they can't do that," whined Jack Napes. "We're the biggest and most important department in the university, and we did get a 'star' for our international excellence."

"Oh yes they can," said the more realistic and cynical Mrs Quick. "They've closed many whole language departments, after all. Look what happened to Latin and Greek." (Five members of these two departments had been forced into early retirement; whereupon three others had speedily got posts elsewhere, and the last remaining lecturer, Mr Pondering, had been redeployed as Assistant Audit Clerk in the Envelope Section of the university Stationery department, where his slow but meticulous pedantry made him a valued and useful 'second checker' of the stocks of Surleighwick envelopes.)

"Yes, but they weren't as big as us."

"Look, Jack," said Mrs Quick impatiently, "shut up. You know nothing about it. There's a lot of people at Surleighwick who don't like us."

"But we got a star."

"You idiot!" responded Mrs Quick who did not believe in mincing her words. "Can't you see that that's *why* they don't like us? And how good do you think Bodgering will be at protecting our interests?"

And indeed, things were already starting to go wrong for the Surleighwick English department. On the first occasion when Professor Bodgering found himself alone in the room with Josie, the secretary after whom he had long lusted, he had raised a withered paw with difficulty from his wheelchair and had pinched her bottom.

"Josie, you're beautiful," he had gasped.

Josie had promptly punched him on the nose, invalid or no invalid, picked up her hand-bag, left the room, and resigned forthwith to take up a more agreeable job, with better pay and conditions and a nicer atmosphere, at the British Steel Corporation.

Gleefully, Professor Toady had frozen her post. He promised that the Secretarial Review Committee (of which he was Chairman) would consider the matter sympathetically at its next meeting. He pencilled in the following July as a possible date for that and declined to act before then.

Professor Bodgering however still had his long-suffering research assistant and amanuensis Jolly, and she had produced the agenda for the first English staff meeting of term.

The meeting opened with two minutes' silence in memory of the death of Professor Houghton. The whole department rose. Even Professor Bodgering was made to stand upright, gripped by his shoulder pads on one side by Jolly and on the other by the surly but burly Ivan Hoe, whose name was the cause of so much merriment to members of other departments. Between these two, Professor Bodgering hung with legs dangling, like a marionette. The University of Surleighwick was very big on two minutes' silences for dead professors, maybe to savour and prolong and relish the fact that the dear departed was no longer there to put in his oar. Later, two minutes' silence would be held for Professor Houghton at the Board of the Faculty, at the Senate, at the Council, at the Court of Governors, and at the next meeting of each of the fourteen committees on which Professor Houghton had served.

Then the minutes were agreed, subject to Mr Ivan Hoe observing that he had been present at the last meeting, but that his presence had not been recorded. Dr Blodgett pointed out that his name had been spelt wrongly, with only one *t*. Dr Crumpet observed that her initials had been wrongly entered as A.D.C. Crumpet instead of A.A.C. Crumpet (she was Antonia Annette Catherine Crumpet). When these important points had been put right, Dr Beaver observed that *concensus* had been wrongly spelt as *consensus*. The point was corrected. Finally, when the minutes had been fully editorialised, the meeting moved on.

Professor Bodgering, speaking with difficulty, sniffing from time to time from his oxygen mask, then explained that owing to the stress and confusion of Professor Houghton's death, on none of the matters on which it had been agreed that the 'Head of dept. to report to the next meeting' had progress been made. (In fact Professor Bodgering had attended to very little of the correspondence which had accumulated in his in-tray since the end of the vacation, and which, since his secretary had left him, was now piling up unopened in his office. Hence the deadlines for application for money for part-time teaching and for new equipment and for the updating of computer terminals had already passed, with no bids from English. The department did not yet know this, however.)

The next item was the future development of the department for the next five years, particularly its research plans, and its need to make some financial economies to meet the university's financial targets. This information was needed in response to various governmental and university questionnaires, and was to be used chiefly to determine the department's level of funding.

"Well, from the past, which Jim did so much to make illustrious, we come to the future," observed Professor Bodgering, vaguely. "Yes, the future. We got a star, you know. We're well regarded. One of the best departments in the country, in the world I mean of course. International reputation for our research—that's what a star means." This was the longest speech that any of Professor Bodgering's colleagues had ever heard him make. Professor Bodgering paused, exhausted by the effort of six sequential sentences.

Little Jack Napes nodded vigorously.

"May I say how much I agree with that?"

Mrs Quick entered the discussion.

"Still, even so Mr Chairperson, we have to think of the future."

There was general agreement with that. The whole Surleighwick English department could agree that the future had to be thought of.

A rambling, unstructured, inane discussion followed. Professor Bodgering gradually fell into a light sleep. His head lolled back on his chair, as he lay back semi-comatose, breathing heavily, his mouth open and his tongue hanging out. Ms Helen Elton, the lecturer on modern fiction, consulted her knitting pattern, and clicked away at the bottom of the table, occasionally intervening to say, "I absolutely agree."

Dr Spark, the Milton lecturer, ticked off items from a book catalogue and then sensibly started to mark a small pile of student essays.

Dr Showman, visiting on an exchange scheme from the United States, carefully checked references to the footnotes in his latest set of proofs.

Dr Antonia Crumpet listened carefully to the proceedings, alert for any instances of sexist language.

"What are we saying, Mr Chairperson?" asked Mrs Quick, who had been sitting at the far end of the room, and had not observed Professor Bodgering's comatose state. "I don't understand."

"He's asleep, he hasn't been listening," said Dr Festering, taking a silver flask from the pocket of his brown tweed jacket, and tilting a generous slug of the amber liquid down his throat.

Mrs Quick looked concerned, rose from her seat, and came up to the recumbent figure of Professor Bodgering.

"Is he ill?" she asked with apparent anxiety, but also with the wild hope that the pins which she had been sticking into his waxen image were working to good efffect.

"No, don't worry, he's always like this," replied Jolly.

She jabbed him in the ribs with her left elbow.

With a start Professor Bodgering awoke, and looked around him.

"Well," he gasped. "I think this has been a very useful discussion. I think it's clear, though, that we can't decide anything here today. We need more consideration of the issues involved. I suggest we defer them to our next meeting on Tuesday next. I have to go now."

Without a further word he signalled to Jolly to push him out of the room, and the assembled members of the English department were left gazing at the symbolically empty place at the head of the table.

Dr Showman gathered up his proofs and left. Ms Elton gathered up her knitting and left. Doctors Beaver and Sword lurched out of the room to seek the solace of the whisky in their rooms. (Unlike Dr Festering, they were not quite at the hip-flask stage.)

Mrs Quick looked round defiantly.

"Look, we can't just abandon the meeting now," she said with feeling. "There are some decisions which need taking. Like examinations, like drawing up the sabbatical term roster. Like the arrangements for Open Day."

At Jack Napes' suggestion, Mrs Quick moved into the chair, and the rest of the business was despatched with a modicum of efficiency. Dr Crumpet acted as scribe now that Jolly had left.

At the end of the meeting Mrs Quick and Dr Crumpet retired to the former's room to discuss the writing up of the minutes. In her pleasant modern room, lined with works on nineteenth-century fiction and feminist literary theory, facing north over the Surleighwick waste land, Mrs Quick poured two generous tumblers of Manzanilla sherry for herself and Dr Crumpet.

"That man is a disaster—a complete and utter disaster. God help the department if he is left to run it. He's a sick man. They should make him go on permanent sick leave. He's just not up to the job."

"I'll drink to that," replied Dr Crumpet with feeling.

"Like I said last term, it may be a plot," continued the shrewd Mrs Quick. "I wouldn't put it past that Toady to try to do us down by putting an incompetent in charge. I think I'll go and see him in the morning."

"Or maybe we ought to stick some more pins in him," suggested Dr Crumpet with a laugh.

On a recent visit to the United States, Mrs Quick had acquired a popular book called *Do down your Enemies!* at New York's JFK airport, and, intrigued by the title, and thinking that such a book would certainly be useful in academia, had bought it for ten dollars. The volume had turned out to be a popular, though not very well-written guide to low-level black magic, and, one evening the previous October, in a giggly and frivolous mood, as she and Dr Crumpet relaxed after Mrs Quick's autumn party for her under-graduates, the two ladies had in fun decided to have a go at one of the spells in *Do down your Enemies!* Following its instructions, they had found some plasticine in Mrs Quick's children's playbox. (Mrs Quick was separated from her husband; her children were at boarding school.) This they had fashioned into crude figures representing Professors Houghton and Bodgering. They had wrapped them in cloth, placed a matchstick representing a cheroot in 'Professor Houghton's' mouth, and a piece of red plastic in the other model to serve as Professor Bodgering's bulbous and mottled nose. Then, refilling their glassses with fruity and full-bodied Moroccan wine, with much laughter and shushing, for they were both by then pretty drunk, Mrs Quick had read out the little incantatory charm.

"Stick the pin in
See it go in
Do it with a grin
Stick it in his skin
Pin go in
And die die die!

Jeteh hantz dure!"

Almost out of control with laughter, they had then each stuck a hat pin into each of the models, before setting about clearing up, finally consigning the two figures to Mrs Quick's kitchen drawer.

"After all," said Mrs Quick, thoughtfully, as she and Dr Crumpet sat in Mrs Quick's room at the end of that first frightful meeting chaired by Professor Bodgering, "We did it as a joke, but 'poor old Jim'"—she mimicked Professor Toady's tones—"*is* dead. Maybe it works after all?"

They both burst out laughing. At least 'poor old Jim' was no longer with them, and that was one cheering piece of news to alleviate the endless gloom and dullness of the the Surleighwick Spring term!

Mrs Quick refilled their glasses with Manzanilla sherry.

"Yes, good riddance!" interposed Dr Crumpet. "It's enough to make you believe that there's a divine plan in the universe. The only thing is that 'Psycho' is going to be even more of a bore than Houghton."

(Mrs Quick and Dr Crumpet had privately dubbed Professor Bodgering 'Psycho', by metonymy, from what they saw as his amazing resemblance to the mummified Mrs Bates in the Hitchcock film. Mishearing and misunderstanding, the Surleighwick students called him 'the Sickko', thinking this to be a callous allusion to his ill-health.)

"Well, I'm going to do something about it," remarked Mrs Quick. "One way or another, 'Psycho' has got to go. I'll go and see the Dean in the morning. If that doesn't get me anywhere— well, we've got nothing to lose by skewering the old plasticine again!"

They collapsed into hysterical laughter, and settled down to polish off the remaining half-bottle of Manzanilla, and to turn to more lady-like subjects of gossip.

*****

At ten o'clock the next morning, Mrs Quick was closeted with Professor Toady in the Dean's office, pouring out her tale of woe about Professor Bodgering's incompetence.

"So you see, Dean, you've got to do something about it. Professor Bodgering is a sick man. He's in no fit state to run the department. I hope you'll take action to see that he's replaced as acting head. He ought to be sent on sick leave, really."

Professor Toady clutched his stomach, and peered at Mrs Quick over his bifocal spectacles from the other side of his desk.

"As I see it Mrs Quick, you seem to be making two points. First, that Professor Bodgering is ill; secondly, you don't like the way he chaired your departmental meeting yesterday. Now, as to the first point, it would be improper for me to comment on that. Medical matters are confidential, you know. All I can say is that Professor Bodgering is not ill. If he were, he would be on sick leave."

"But you know he's ill," she protested. "You only have to look at him to see that. Look at the oxygen mask he carries around with him wherever he goes. He's a dying man."

"No, Mrs Quick," replied the Dean gravely, in the dignified, judicious tones he liked to cultivate. "I do not know that. I repeat: Professor Bodgering has not asked to go on sick leave. So far as I am concerned he is fit and active, and there's nothing more to be said about the matter."

"But he only comes in to the department once a week."

"You're simply confirming my point that he's a regular attender, and not ill."

"But he's only in for three hours a week!" she objected.

"My dear Mrs Quick! You're surely not suggesting that just because a professor is not in, he's not working, I hope. Really! I've no doubt that in this day and age he can keep in touch with his department perfectly well by the telephone. And his research can no doubt be done in any decent library. Doubtless his absences are occasioned by his next book. No, I really can't discuss that point any more. Now"—pursing his lips—"as to his conduct of the meeting. I don't think I can involve myself as Dean with that. I see that as a purely internal departmental matter. And aren't you being just a little precipitate? You are complaining after just one meeting. Let us accept for a moment that the meeting was badly chaired. We all have our off days. And heads and acting heads of departments are under a good deal of strain now, with all these questionnaires and performance indicators you know. But there's another point. Tell me, what was the first thing you did at your meeting yesterday?"

Mrs Quick thought back.

"We had the minutes of the last meeting."

"But even before that?"

"We stood for two minutes' silence in memory of Jim Houghton."

"Exactly! Poor old Jim! 'There's a great sprite gone,' as Shelley put it so well." The Dean sighed. "Such a tragic loss, such an irreplaceable personality. He'd done so much for the department.....And his death so sudden. I was quite cut up about it myself. Absolutely devastated in fact. As Dean, I had come to rely on his wise words of advice in so many different situations. His memory will live on in all our hearts. Now, don't you think it possible that Professor Bodgering was still affected by the death of his professorial colleague? And after all, you are a large department you know. You'll all have to rally round the flag, work for the good of the cause, all pull together with a little give and take. Try to help Professor Bodgering in his hour of need. He needs your support, your *loyal* support, Mrs Quick." He gave a little smile. "So why don't you give him another chance?"

Mrs Quick rose to leave. "Thank you for seeing me, Dean.

But my opinion has not changed. Professor Bodgering is sick, and not capable of running the department."

Professor Toady ushered Mrs Quick to the door. As he closed it behind her, his grave, solemn features were replaced by a broad smile. As he had anticipated, Bodgering, as a chronic invalid, was a hopeless head of department. But this was even better than he had expected! He danced a little jig around the room, like Hitler after the fall of France in June 1940. Already, Bodgering had missed some important deadlines in bidding for funds. And the less money for English, the more for everyone else, especially Archaeology. Now to screw the English department up a bit more! He telephoned the Stationery store, and asked that as a mark of respect to Professor Houghton, all the supplies of English department stationery, which bore his name at the masthead, should be destroyed. Then he fired off an independent memo to Stationery asking that all Arts faculty departmental requisitions for stationery should be remitted to him first, on the grounds that a committee of the Arts faculty was reviewing departmental secretarial and office practices. Then he sent off a memo to all heads of departments asking them to nominate a representative to such a committee. Then he fixed in his diary the date of the first meeting of that commmittee for July 18th next, in six months' time. With any luck, the English department would run out of stationery in three or four weeks—then they would find themselves completely fouled up, and unable to get any more for months!

Feeling very pleased indeed with himself, Professor Toady thrust his hands into his pockets, and strolled up and down the carpet he had removed from Professor Houghton's office on the day of the latter's cremation. He crossed to his bookshelf, and picked up a battered copy of *The Screwtape Letters*, looking for the hints on the infliction of minor torments that he had underlined, until the university clock struck 11 am, and it was time for the most enjoyable part of Professor Toady's day—reposing his fat form in the corner of the faculty coffee room, enjoying being sucked up to, and dispensing snippets of university gossip to favoured cronies.

*****

'Woman of outer darkness, fiend of death,
From what inhuman cave, what dark abyss,
Hast thou invisible that spell o'erheard?'
(Walter Savage Landor, *The Meeting of the Weird Sisters*)

At the end of the first week of term, two days after Mrs Quick's meeting with the Dean, Mrs Quick and the glamorous Dr Crumpet had dined well *à deux* at Mrs Quick's country cottage, a dozen miles to the south-west of the outer suburbs of Surleighwick. Over generous slugs of gin and tonic, they had together prepared the vegetarian goulash in the spacious, well-lit, modernised kitchen of Mrs Quick's cottage.

Two empty bottles of excellent Chianti—for Mrs Quick was a good judge of wine—testified to the success of the evening. Now both women could relax, as they sat over their apples and oranges and cheese, sipping cointreau, and discussing Mrs Quick's visit to the Dean.

"My worst fears were confirmed," said Mrs Quick. "Toady is useless—he's a pompous old bore, and we're not going to get anything out of him. Maybe it was hoping too much to think that this university would ever take action against a professor. The more I think about it, the more convinced I am that it's all a plot. Toady wants to do us down."

"But why should he want to do that?"

"For two reasons. First, he resents that we got a star and his department was only average. Second, all the departments in the faculty hate us—they always have done."

"But why?" asked Dr Crumpet, who had only been at Surleighwick for a comparatively short time, and knew little of all the faculty squabbles.

"Basically, because they think English is a soft option, and that no particular skill is needed to read a novel or a poem, or to enjoy a play. And at the same time, because we're so much more successful than they are in getting students—and better students at that. Do you know that French only got fourteen applications for their fifty-five places last year? French is only asking for two E's at A level now, whereas you still need three D's to do English at Surleighwick," said Mrs Quick proudly. "And we got 185 applications for our seventy places. Naturally, they hate us. They think they're better than we are, because some of them do languages and we gave up Anglo-Saxon and Middle English and even Chaucer seven years ago. Anyway, they all think they know something about our subject. You heard that fool Toady quoting 'Milton' in his ghastly memorial speech."

They both laughed.

"Come on, let's go and make the doll."

Giggling, and clutching one another, Mrs Quick and Dr Crumpet lurched into the kitchen. There Mrs Quick poured them both a generous half tumbler of brandy, and then went to the drawer in which, hidden under a pile of tea-cloths, were the two plasticine images of Professors Houghton and Bodgering, still skewered with hat pins from the date of Mrs Quick's party last October.

"Why don't you do one for Professor Toady as well?" asked Dr Crumpet, collapsing hysterically and putting her hand to her mouth.

"Great, what a good idea!" said Mrs Quick enthusiastically.

Screaming and laughing, the two women rolled plasticine into a huge ball, to represent Professor Toady's fat stomach. They added on short little legs, and a large head. Two fragments of perspex represented his bifocals.

Carrying their tumblers of brandy they went into the comfortably furnished lounge at the front of the cottage, where the light of a standard lamp cast a subdued glow, and an open log-fire flickered cheerfully and comfortably.

They drank their brandies and looked at the two skewered dolls, and the fat one they had just made, as yet unskewered.

"Well, it worked for Professor Houghton!" remarked Mrs Quick maliciously.

The two ladies sniggered hysterically.

"You know what I ought to do?" Smilingly she removed the pins from the doll representing Professor Houghton. "I think we ought to cremate the 'Houghton' doll. After all, if I understand the theory, this kind of stuff works by assuming a correspondence between the object and the person. And Houghton got burned up didn't he!" With a wicked drunken grin Mrs Quick tossed the doll into the flames, and tossed a little brandy on to it. There was a sudden flare of the fire. Both women drank their brandies with great satisfaction as the image of their last head of department was consumed by fire. For there was nothing mealy-mouthed about Surleighwick feuds and hatreds, which lasted even unto death and beyond. No quarter was given or expected.

"Oh, Pauline, you are wicked!" said Antonia Crumpet, rocking with paroxysms of laughter as the plasticine baked in the coals, and throwing her arms around Mrs Quick's shoulders. They settled comfortably against each other, and Mrs Quick stroked Dr Antonia's hair away from her forehead and gave her a gentle kiss.

"It's been a long day, but things will be better now. You'll see. Just leave it to Pauline. Come, let's say the spell."

They removed the pins from the image of Bodgering, and first Mrs Quick sang in a low voice:

"Stick the pin in
See it go in
Do it with a grin
Stick it in his skin

Pin go in
And die die die!
Jeteh hantz dure!
Die Percy die!"

Closing her eyes in a little prayer, Mrs Quick drove the first pin into the model of Bodgering at the chest.

Then Antonia Crumpet, in her lighter, clearer tones, a gentle smile playing around her lovely lips, sang:

"Stick the pin in
See it go in
Do it with a grin
Stick it in his skin
Pin go in
And die die die!
Jeteh hantz dure!"

And with a pretty smile she hissed "Die, Bodgering, die" as she drove the pin through his neck.

Forty miles away, tossing restlessly and sleeplessly in his cot at Ratford, Professor Bodgering felt stabbing pains in his chest and throat.

Mrs Quick looked on with approval.

"Now for Toady,
Stick the pin in
See it go in
Do it with a grin
Stick it in his skin
Pin go in
And die die die!
Jeteh hantz dure!
Die, Toady, die!"

Mrs Quick drove the pin viciously and with heartfelt longing into the fat paunch of 'Professor Toady'.

Then the sweeter almost angelic, tones of Dr Crumpet (for

her voice was most delightfully melodious, and she sang in the university choir):

"Stick the pin in
See it go in
Do it with a grin
Stick it in his skin
Pin go in
And die die die!
Jeteh hantz dure!
Die, Toady, die!"

Maliciously, she drove the pin into the heart of 'Professor Toady'.

Far away in his modern four-bedroomed detached house, Professor Toady awoke with heartburn and indigestion, and grumpily waited for his wife to bring him an Alka-Seltzer.

I wonder what 'Jeteh hantz dure' means?" asked Dr Antonia dreamily, as she leaned her head against Mrs Quick's shoulder, and looked at the two skewered dolls in the flickering light.

"Oh, I don't know. I expect its nonsense like 'abracadabra'," said Mrs Quick, carelessly.

Neither of the two women knew Dr Hanwell. He would have recognised it instantly as being the anagram of a well-known eighteenth-century Haitian curse, in a corrupt form of the Creole French spoken on that island. And he would have given them a little lecture on sympathetic magic through the ages, on charms and incantations in European learned poetry, on the folklore of the Melanesians, and on the curses of the Siberian shamans, and magical African queens and their powers. Dr Hanwell would have told them about seventeenth-century metallurgical treatises discussing the metal from which pins were to be made, and of eighteenth-century discussions in Italian of the best type of wax to use. He would have lectured them on the witchcraft statutes, and told them when the last women were burnt alive in England,

France, Spain, Italy, and Germany for doing what Mrs Quick and Dr Crumpet had just done. He would have observed where the horror films got the details wrong. He would have told them of Obeah men and Shango dancers and hexes, of herbs that should be sprinkled on the dolls to gain a greater potency, of the best astrological times for making curses, and of the market value of seventeenth-century grimoires. But whether any of it worked or not, Dr Hanwell did not know, for he had never applied the theory he had learned.

Back in Mrs Quick's cottage, lulled by the wine and brandy, by the meal and by the warmth, Dr Crumpet slowly fell into a restful slumber in Mrs Quick's arms. Mrs Quick remained where she was, cradling Dr Crumpet against her breast, then she too leaned her head against the sofa, and fell into a dreamless sleep.

CHAPTER FIVE

A TRIP TO HAY-ON-WYE

'A grey town sits up aloft on the bank of the clear, flowing river, / As it has sat since the days when the Roman was first in the land. / A town, with a high ruined castle, and walls mantled over with ivy, / With church towers square and strong and narrow irregular streets.'
(Sir Lewis Morris, *The Physicians of Myddfai*)

'I picked the book up on a stall. Oh, it's amazing what good books there are on stalls.'
(Queen Charlotte)

At 9.11 am on the morning of Wednesday 16 January 1991, Dr Hanwell drove his elderly, but still reliable, red TVR into the forecourt of Second Hall, one of a pair of gloomy concrete student residences on the northern edge of the Surleighwick campus. As he emerged from the car in his cords and black leather jacket, Ruth recognised him from behind the plate glass windows of the foyer. She hurriedly pulled a black beret over her hair, and came out to meet him, well-protected against the damp and chill of the overcast January day by black woollen stockings and a grey flannel skirt, by a warm silk blouse and cardigan, surmounted by a bright red donkey jacket.

"Hullo there, it's cold today isn't it. I say, what a super car! I've always wanted a ride in one of these."

Dr Hanwell ushered her into the low bucket seat, and they began the three-hour journey to Hay-on-Wye. For the first half-hour or so they did not speak much, as Dr Hanwell slowly and cautiously made his way through the heavy and unpredictable

Surleighwick traffic, bouncing over the pot-holes of the broken roads, slipping through the unending, drab, cheerless streets of the Surleighwick suburbs, past petrol stations and advertising hoardings, through rusting wastelands of derelict factories—for Surleighwick had been hard hit by the Thatcherite recessions of the early and late 'eighties, as its metal-bashing industries succumbed to high-interest rates and bleak despair. At last they climbed a steep hill to the west of Surleighwick, the traffic thinned, and the dank fields of an English winter, still startlingly green, emerged from the mists. Dr Hanwell pulled past a couple of overloaded lorries and started to relax as the countryside sped by, warmly cocooned with Ruth in the heated compartment of the TVR.

"So how often have you been to Hay-on-Wye?" enquired Ruth, looking curiously at the black and white houses that they passed intermittently.

"Oh, I've lost count," he answered. "I suppose sixty to seventy times in the last ten years. I like to get down there every six weeks or so, because the stock turns over very quickly. Anyway, there are so many books there that it would take a fortnight or so to do the place properly, so even if you went every week you could always find something new."

"And you say you got those old seventeenth-century books there?"

"Yes."

"What's your oldest book?"

"Well, for quite a long time now it's been a copy of Alexander of Aphrodisias' commentary on Aristotle's *Meteorologica*, printed at Bologna in 1502."

Ruth put her hand to her mouth and giggled.

"You're making it up, aren't you?" she asked. "Surely no one can be called Alexander of Afro-disias! I thought an Afro-disiac"— for this is how Ruth thought it was spelt—"was a kind of love-potion. Anyway, the term Afro-disiac can't be that old. It means from Africa, doesn't it, like in Afro-Caribbean or Afro-Asian hair?"

Dr Hanwell smiled, cutting neatly past another lorry, and zooming ahead on another clear piece of road. But after a few years teaching at Surleighwick, he had become accustomed to the false etymologies of students, and had ceased to be surprised at the things they did not know. It was usually safest to assume that they knew very little.

"No, that's a different word," he explained carefully.

"Afro with an *f* does indeed derive from Africa, but Aphrodisias, with a *ph*, derives from Aphrodite, the Greek goddess of love. The city of Aphrodisias, which takes its name from Aphrodite, was in the Peloponnesus and has nothing to do with Afro I'm afraid. The word aphrodisiac derives from Aphrodisias, the city famed for its knowledge of the arts of love."

Dr Hanwell went on to talk of aphrodisiacs in classical antiquity, of medieval scientific poems detailing the aphrodisiac properties of fish, of how early botanists such as Clusius and Matthiolus in the sixteenth century had recorded the belief in the aphrodisiac powers of the potato, of beliefs about rhinoceros horn in the seventeenth century. From there he digressed to talk of love-potions and charms, of amulets and incantations, of the properties of herbs and the therapeutic powers of potable gold, of Albert the Great's *Book of Secrets*, of the great storehouse of magical learning that was Martino Antonio Delrio's *Magicarum disquisitionum libri sex* (Lyons, 1606). From Martino Antonio Delrio he passed on to the films of his presumed descendant Dolores del Rio and her appearance in *Flying down to Rio* (1933), from Rio to magic in Brazil, from Brazil to Amerindians in the sixteenth century, from the Amerindians to the Incas, from the Incas to Aztec astrological beliefs, from stars to film stars, from film stars to Jerry Lewis again, from Jerry Lewis to his classic parody *Cinderfella* (1961), from *Cinderfella* to the legend of Cinderella, from Cinderella to the Ugly Sisters, from the Ugly Sisters to Goneril and Regan, from *King Lear* to Merlin, from Merlin to bardic prophecies, from prophecies to charms again, from charms to potions, from potions to *Romeo and Juliet*, from *Romeo and Juliet* to Queen Mab, from Queen Mab to fairies, from fairies to fairy-cakes, from fairy cakes to Pontefract cakes, from Pontefract cakes to liquorish, from liquorish to the medieval theory of humours, and then back back to aphrodisiacs and Alexander of Aphrodisias. "Who I assure you does exist," he said with a smile. "He was a philosophical commentator of the third century A.D., though I fear he's not read very much today."

Ruth smiled to herself. She could well imagine that Alexander of Aphrodisias did not attract many readers now, if indeed he had ever done so.... But she enjoyed Dr Hanwell's digressions, and enjoyed picking up snippets of curious learning. She would enjoy telling her chums back in Hall about the aphrodisiac properties of the potato—particularly since potatoes were served every day of term, year in year out at Second Hall. Maybe, when you thought what went on there, such as the high-jinks in the corridor last night, it was true that potatoes were an aphrodisiac after all.

"So your copy was printed in 1502? Golly! I didn't know that printing went back as long ago as that!"

So Dr Hanwell told her about the early printers, Gutenberg and Fust, about Sweynheym and Pannartz, and Aldus and Paulus Manutius, about the Stephanus family and the Elseviers, about the Juntas and the Cat Printer. From the Cat Printer he digressed to an Italian sixteenth-century treatise on cats that he had been reading, from Cats to Black Cats, from Black Cats to Black Magic, from Black Magic to witches' familiars, from witches' familiars to the history of pets in Western Europe from Ancient Greece to the late Renaissance.

They were now approaching Tenbury Wells from the north, after an hour and a half's drive.

Dr Hanwell drove into the car-park on the edge of the little town.

"Coffee time," he announced. "I need my daily dose of caffeine. I usually pause here to stretch my legs on the way to Hay."

They walked past the strange, ruined, rusting pagoda that bordered the path from the car park into town—a melancholy relic of Edwardian days, surrounded by high nettles and straggling shrubs. Dr Hanwell led the way to a little coffee shop near the marketplace, and ordered coffee and scones for Ruth and himself.

"And what books do you collect, Ruth?" he enquired.

"I'm not sure that I'd call myself a collector," she replied. "I buy second-hand books on my subject if they're cheap enough."

"You'll find lots of theology in Hay," he promised her.

"Then again, I collect books on pre-Raphaelite painting, and on Sibelius, my favourite composer. I buy interesting cookery-books, because I like cooking and trying out new recipes. I'm interested in the early history of needlework. I like reading works of nineteenth-century travel. I read books on the history of France. I'm also interested in books about Amazons, and cultic figures like Snake Goddesses, because they seem to be role-models for women that don't exist today."

Dr Hanwell warmed to a kindred spirit, and told her that once at Hay he had bought Robert Briffault's mighty work *The Mothers*, with its wonderful excursuses on matriarchies in the South Sea Islands, on the ladies of the Troubador poets, and its chapters on just such topics as vatic goddesses and Amazons.

"That sounds like my kind of book," said Ruth thoughtfully. "I've never heard of it, though."

"Well, it's in three volumes," Dr Hanwell explained. "Not many people read it nowadays, even in universities. Its range is too wide."

They returned to the car. Ruth took off her donkey jacket, and snuggled down into her seat as the car headed westward into the pale sunshine, a warm draft of comfortable air whooshing out of the heater, the dreamy music of the complete choral version of Franck's *Psyché* coming from the cassette player. Up the hill from Tenbury Wells, past the now deserted buildings of St Michael's musical college, and soon they were heading west through the serene and still unspoilt Herefordshire countryside. Soon they were driving round the ring road at Leominster, home, as Dr Hanwell observed, of that mysterious German exiled monk Waldemar of Leominster, about whom nothing was known, but whose Latin treatise on mineralogy, written at Leominster Priory, remained in manuscript in the British Library, and had, unaccountably in view of its importance, not yet been edited.

"So how come you know so much about magic and charms and witchcraft?" asked Ruth, comfortable and relaxed after her coffee and scones, and feeling that she could talk familiarly to her teacher. "Are you a wizard?"

Dr Hanwell gave her a little lecture on the etymology of the word wizard, and the historical reasons why there were male wizards and warlocks, but only female witches. Then he smiled at her.

"But no, I'm not a wizard. The reason I know about it is quite simple. Have you ever heard of a book by Lynn Thorndike called *A History of Magic and Experimental Science*? It's in eight volumes, and is one of the monuments of twentieth-century scholarship. It was reading that as a postgrad. that got me into it—it's simply that science and magic are pretty well inextricably connected in early times."

West of Leominster the traffic thinned out considerably. At a steady fifty-five miles an hour, they drove through the lonely country lanes, the landscape punctuated by gaunt steeples piercing the sky, and green fields bleak with leafless trees. Groups of cattle, six or seven at a time, turned lacklustre brown eyes towards them as they passed. They were through Weobley and Dilwyn, and cut across the main north-south Shrewsbury-Hereford road, to the lonely outposts of Monkland, watery in the weak sunlight. It was twelve-fifteen, and five miles short of Hay-on-Wye Dr Hanwell pulled off the road for lunch at the Wayside Inn, a pleasant pub overlooking the placid river Wye.

The bar was almost empty. The comforting warmth of a real fire greeted them in the lounge. Dr Hanwell ordered a half of bitter for himself, cider for Ruth, and scampi and chips for them both. They moved to a table overlooking the river.

"This is fun," laughed Ruth. "I'm glad I played truant from Professor Bohring's lecture today. Don't suppose I'd have missed much though. Nineteenth-century moral theology is a bit of a bore, anyway."

"I've never met him," answered Dr Hanwell easily. "But from what I've seen of the Surleighwick professors, most of them *are* five star solid copper-bottomed bores."

"You don't have any professors in your department, do you?" asked Ruth.

"No, I've been very fortunate," he answered. "There's just me, so I don't have to worry about the funny little habits of professors. You've never been to Hay, have you? Let me tell you something about the place."

"I first went there in 1973," he continued, "shortly after being appointed at Surleighwick. It's one of the most remarkable places in the country for books that I know of. You never know what you're going to find there. There are about fifteen different book-shops there, scattered all over the town. So it's deservedly called 'The Town of Books'. I believe it started with Richard Booth in the 1960s. When I first went there he had the Old Cinema, and the Castle and its outbuildings. Then he expanded and opened shops all over the place—in the centre of town, in the old workhouse, and so on. He operates on the theory that for every book, no matter how bad, there's a buyer somewhere." (Though the fifty copies on

Mr Booth's shelves of Professor Bodgering's Skelmerdale Notes on *Tamburlaine*, priced at 15p each, not one copy of which had been sold in fifteen years, were bidding fair to disprove his theory.) "Later though I believe he sold the cinema to another dealer. Anyway, he put Hay on the map, and declared its Independence from the UK in the mid-seventies. Gradually more and more people started to visit, and this attracted other book dealers into the area. It's remote, but as Booth once pointed out somewhere, nearly ten million people live within easy driving distance of the place. Like us—we've taken it pretty steadily, and we're just ten minutes drive away. I always find it very relaxing to come here."

Dr Hanwell looked out of the picture windows at the tranquil meadows and river below.

"It's good to shake the dust of Surleighwick off one's feet from time to time, isn't it? And what is so interesting and exciting is that one never knows what one is going to find here. Some of the dealers buy stock in vast quantities, and turn it over pretty quickly. In my own field I've bought some pretty scarce items. But then you see, you can't expect bookdealers to know about every book. In lots of cases, they just price them generically."

"How do you mean, generically?" asked Ruth, curious.

"Well, what I mean is, they compare a book to stock that is similar to what has been through their hands before. There is so to speak a 'going rate' for books. Suppose one has say a three-decker Victorian novel—a novel in three volumes, that is. Well, unless it is by someone famous like George Eliot or Dickens, they'll tend to price it at say £100-£150 , whatever it is. Or take 16th and 17th century Latin prose treatises, like the ones I showed you yesterday—the volumes of Pacius' commentary on the soul. Well, that kind of book has a market value of say £150, and if a bookseller gets a Latin prose treatise or something like that, that's what he'll usually tend to charge for it. Now, some books are of more interest than others, according to the customer. I myself would not be very

interested in a work of seventeenth-century Latin theology say—
whereas a seventeenth-century Latin commentary on Aristotle's
Physics might interest me a good deal more. But then again, it
would depend on the author. Magirus on the *Physics* would interest
me a good deal more than Burgersdijk on the *Physics*. But that
opinion is based on internal knowledge of the subject. Now, to a
bookseller, they're all pretty much of a muchness. And of course,
there might be other collectors who would pay more for theology
than for Aristotelianism. Essentially, what it boils down to is this:
a book is worth what someone is prepared to pay for it. Hence, the
pricing can only be very rough and ready, within very wide
boundaries. Ah! here's our food."

"So you can pick up bargains at Hay?" asked Ruth as she ate
her scampi.

"Sometimes. Perhaps less so now that there are so many book
dealers in Hay. They tend to wander round each other's shops you
know, looking for items for which they already have customers.
But no one can know the value of all books. For example, I was
reading a couple of weeks ago that early books on golf—some of
them—can fetch many thousands of pounds. But which ones?
Well, I've forgotten—I'd have to look it up. If I saw a book on
early golf priced at say £500 I wouldn't know if that was cheap or
not. But a collector of golf books would—and a dealer in golf
books certainly would. But supppose you're not a dealer in golf
books. You might price it generically as "early Victorian printing"
and get it all wrong."

They ate their meal, and then it was time to drive the last five
miles to Hay-on-Wye, over the strange toll bridge, and through the
lane, past Bredwardine, the reputed birthplace, as Dr Hanwell
reminded Ruth, of Bishop Bradwardine, author of a strange *Liber
de proportionibus*, a fourteenth-century treatise on acceleration
which was groping towards the concept of the exponential curve.
Then they coasted down hill, came to a sudden sign *Powys*, and

they were in Hay-on-Wye, in the principality of Wales, where the post office sold stamps with a dragon on them. Up they drove through the long main road through the town, past houses and pubs and cafes of pleasant grey stone, past the gaunt towering ruins of the castle visible on the left, and then into the giant carpark.

They left the car.

"I think the best thing is for us to start off at the Cinema," said Dr Hanwell, "and then it would probably be best for us to split up. We both no doubt have different books we'll want to look at. We'll get you a map of Hay showing where all the shops are at the Cinema, and then I suggest we arrange to meet for tea at 4 pm or thereabouts in one of the teashops. Will that suit you?"

"Fine!" answered Ruth, jamming her beret back on her head, as they entered the grounds of the Cinema.

"See, here's where we are; there's the carpark; the centre of town is down there; and all the bookshops are indicated on this street plan," said Dr Hanwell, handing Ruth her guide to the Hay bookshops. "Look, there's Cook Book, the new cookery bookshop that has just opened. I usually start at the Cinema, and then go to Richard Booth's Limited, and then browse around some of the more specialised bookshops. So I'll see you at 4 pm in this tea shop here?" He pointed out a tea shop near the clock tower in the centre of Hay.

"OK," said Ruth. "I think I'll start here too, as we're here already, and then I'll go to Cook Book."

Ruth entered the cinema, and was immediately lost in the vast number of shelves with which it was lined upstairs and down. She made her way to the theology section, and was soon absorbed in the search for books that might be useful for her course. After an hour or so she had selected three books and then she started to browse among the novels, eventually selecting a copy of Disraeli's *Lothair* for 45p. She looked at her watch. Heavens! It was now two o'clock, and there was no sign of Dr Hanwell. Ruth paid for her books, and stood in the forecourt of the Cinema bookshop, breathing in the clear, bracing Welsh air. To the west, the Brecon Beacons could be seen. It started to rain a bit. She shivered, and drew her donkey jacket around her, consulted her plan, and headed for Cook Book, further down the town. There she was at once engrossed by the hundreds of volumes of cookery books, both new and old. Eventually, she purchased a couple of books of Greek and Tunisian recipes, and then walked through the town of Hay, drinking in its strangely peaceful atmosphere, which reminded her of her childhood. The streets were almost deserted on this cold, damp, unseasonable January day, far out of the tourist season. There were shops with unmodernised fronts, sweet shops with gobstoppers in tall glass jars such as she had not seen for a long time, old fashioned stationers, ironmongers with spades and wheelbarrows and hoes and hosepipes spilling out on to the pavement, corsetieres with garments in the window whose like she had never seen before, which made her giggle. On impulse, as a gust of wind swept with scurries of rain down the street, she darted inside Universal Books, and there her eye was caught by the New Age section, a mélange of modern reprints and original editions of works by Edgar Cayce on prophecies and earthquakes, works on Atlantis, books about gnomes and elves. There was a shelf or two devoted to works on UFOs and ley lines, to ghosts and the abominable snowman. Her eyes passed quickly over a shelf devoted entirely to Scotland's most famous tourist attraction: *Loch Ness Monster*, *The Elusive Monster*, *The Loch Ness Story*, *The Loch Ness Mystery Solved*. The last one sounded quite interesting, and she was about to take it down when she suddenly saw there was a section of books about films. The time sped quickly by.

Ruth looked at her watch. It was 4 pm, time to meet Dr Hanwell for tea. She consulted her map, and as chance would have it, they arrived at the door of the tea shop together. Soon they were seated at a dark wooden table in the warm and cheerful tea shop, with an open fire glowing in its stone hearth, fortifying themselves after their labours with large cups of strong tea, piles of hot buttered toast, and a plate of gateaux and cream buns. Ruth, who did not have to watch her weight, ate heartily.

Dr Hanwell looked at her books.

"What did you buy?" he asked. "May I see?"

Ruth passed over her little pile of books. She had bought one book on Pelagianism, a history of the Tractarian movement, and a nineteenth-century copy of Paley's *Evidences*. There were the two cookery books, there was *Lothair*, there was Jung's *Flying Saucers: A Modern Myth of Things Seen in the Skies*, and, from the same shop, a copy of Mircea Eliade on *Shamanism*, a book on *Minoan Snake Goddesses*, which looked rather curious, depicting on its frontispiece a bare-breasted female deity intertwined with snakes, finally a curious book from the 1820s for which she had hesitated before paying £5, called *Les Chançons des Sortilèges*— which amongst its songs had some in English. Then finally, with a little smile, she said "And this is for you to thank you for taking me here today."

And Ruth passed Dr Hanwell a little book in French, *Les films de Jerry Lewis*, in the Cinéma d'aujourd'hui series.

"Oh Ruth." Dr Hanwell flushed with genuine pleasure. "How kind. Just the kind of book I like."

He flicked it open at random and read out aloud in his faultless and idiomatic French accent:

"'Julius, professeur d'université ridiculisé par ses élèves et par ses chefs, est amoureux d'une de ses plus séduisantes élèves. Pour la conquérir, il expérimente sur lui-même un élixir miraculeux qui lui permet de se transformer pour un temps en un chanteur de charme irrésistible au physique de Don Juan.'

Well, what a place for the book to fall open at! It's a résumé of the plot of *The Nutty Professor*, or *Docteur Jerry et Mister Love*, as the French call it. Look, and it's illustrated too! Ruth, thank you so much. The French are very keen on Jerry Lewis, you know. And there's hardly any critical writing about Jerry Lewis in English. I shall treasure it."

Ruth poured out more tea for them both, and then said.

"What about you? What did you get?"

Dr Hanwell began to unpack the two plastic bags that he had with him, emblazoned on their sides with 'Hay-on-Wye, Town of Books'.

"Well, I had quite a good day, really. I've got my usual mixture of old and new." And one by one he handed over his purchases for her to look at. First, a copy of Evans-Wentz's *Tibetan Book of the Dead*, with the notes of Jung; then *Researches on Magnetism, Chemistry and Electricity* (Edinburgh, 1856) by Baron von Reichenbach, the inventor of pitchblend; then a zany book on *The Sciences in Hungary in the Eighteenth Century*; then an Italian biography of Kepler; then half a dozen odd paperback novels, and some little books of poetry, then finally a couple of old books. First he passed over to Ruth a treatise by Meibomius entitled *Tractatus de usu flagrorum in re medica et venerea* (1645), a slim vellum octavo for which he had paid £50.

"What a lovely little book!" said Ruth, looking at the neat clear type, and taking the volume in her hands. "What's it about?"

"It's quite a curious work, really," answered Dr Hanwell. "It's a treatise on the therapeutic value of flagellation. I've never read it, but I'll be interested to do so."

"I didn't know they had that kind of book in the seventeenth century," said Ruth with an impish smile.

"Oh, don't worry. It's a perfectly scholarly teatment of the subject, you know!" answered Dr Hanwell, ever so slightly on the defensive. "It's a work of anthropology, really. Look, it starts off by discussing what happened in the ancient world."

Then he passed over the larger vellum quarto, with an engraving of an angel at the front.

Ruth carefully opened the book, and saw the words *Exercitatio anatomica De Motu Cordis* at the top of the title page.

"What about this one?" she enquired.

"That's quite an interesting work, actually," Dr Hanwell replied. "It's an early edition of William Harvey's famous work on the circulation of the blood. History of medicine isn't really my line, but it looks interesting, and I can't say that I've seen one before."

"So if history of medicine isn't your line, how come you've just bought a book on the medical uses of flagellation? That sounds like a naughty book to me."

"Tut, tut, my dear Miss Henderson," he replied with a smile as he buttered some more toast. "I bought it because I am interested in Meibomius, that's why, and not for any ulterior motive! Anyway, you may rest assured that any indelicacies will be veiled in the decent obscurity of a learned language, as Gibbon puts it. Meibomius wrote other Latin works, you know. I first came to him from reading his treatise on optics. That's such an impressive work it made me happy to read all his other works."

Ruth examined the price tag inside the Harvey volume.

"Golly! You didn't really pay £480 for it, did you? That's an awful lot of money for a book."

"Well" he answered, "they knocked £30 off, so it cost me £450. It *is* a lot of money I know. But fortunately they took Visa, and I put it on that, and then I'll pay it off at £50 or so a month. I suspect that £400 or so is probably about the going rate for a Harvey. Maybe I paid a bit over the odds. But I'm unlikely to see one again. With this kind of book, if you see it and want it, it's usually better to snap it up when you can, otherwise you might regret it. Most of these kind of books seem cheap five years later, you know."

Dusk was now falling, and in the half-light, Ruth and Dr Hanwell walked back through the deserted streets of Hay. The town was still and tranquil all around them. The TVR stood lonely in the vast car-park, overlooked by the unchanging Welsh hills. They loaded their books into the boot of the car. Dr Hanwell started the engine, put a recording of Rachmaninov's second symphony into the cassette player, and drove east for Tenbury Wells, on the first stage of the journey back to Surleighwick, carrying back to that city the self-same copy of Harvey's *De motu cordis* which had left it just four days previously.

Yes! It was the very copy that had belonged to the late Professor Houghton.

Odds and Ends books had paid £800 for eight trolleys of unwanted ex-Surleighwick University library items. When Mr Cantelow, the proprietor of Odds and Ends had unpacked his sacks immediately on return, he had noticed the Harvey. But old books were not the kind of thing he dealt in. Recognising it as a Latin book, he had offered it to his next door neighbour, the Antique World bookshop, for £100, thus recouping a portion of his stake at Surleighwick. Antique World had quickly identified it as a Latin book, but not a classical author. Hence, two hours later, Antique World had passed it on to Old Leather Bindings for £200 and was content with a quick profit of £100. Old Leather Bindings was not really interested in books save as objects. This shop specialised in fine and handsome bindings, and in elegant sets of books which it sold to those who wanted a little instant culture on their shelves. The Harvey was a handsome book, though in vellum not leather. Old Leather Bindings had added on £280 as a holding price till they could be bothered to investigate the matter further. In the two days that it had been on the shelves, four people had looked at it for ten seconds each. Then Dr Hanwell had looked at it for ten minutes or so before deciding to lash out. Old Leather Bindings had been content with £250 speedy profit after knocking off £30 discount, and the book was sold.

In companionable silence, Dr Hanwell and Ruth left the lights of Tenbury Wells and drove north again. Twenty-five miles before they approached the outer suburbs of Surleighwick, Dr Hanwell looked at the dashboard clock, which showed that it was now five to seven.

"I need to rest my eyes," he said. "And you're not going to get back in time for dinner at Second Hall. Let's stop here and have a steak."

He turned the car off the road, into The Bell, a brightly lit timbered roadhouse set back from the road and bedecked in coloured lights. "This is a pretty decent place. They do a good fillet here."

"Okey-dokey," murmured Ruth, drowsily.

They left their books in the boot of the car, and were soon sitting in a warm and cosy booth, sipping a very decent claret, and waiting whilst their fillets were grilled at the kitchen at the other end of the room.

"You'll have to drink most of this," remarked Dr Hanwell. "But I guess a glass or two with food won't put me over the limit."

Dr Hanwell rubbed his forehead and eyes.

"Well, that was a pretty good day, I think. I rarely go to Hay without coming back with a couple of seventeenth-century treatises and a few odds and ends and novels."

"It's been fun, hasn't it?" said Ruth.

"And what's the programme for tomorrow?"

Ruth pulled a face.

"Another boring lecture from Professor Bohring," she replied—"on theological symbolics, whatever they are."

Dr Hanwell told her.

"Tell me, Ruth," he said, as they waited for their fillet. "What made you come to the University of Surleighwick?"

"I thought my A levels were going to be poor," she explained. "So I only applied to universities I hadn't heard of."

"Ah, that explains it. And what's it like living in Second Hall?"

"A bit of a wild madhouse" she said with a smile. "I lived there in my first year, moved out in the second, and moved back in the third. It's noisy, but the Surleighwick flats and bedsits are so grotty, I thought I'd rather live near campus and have some chums to keep me company. It's a bit noisy, and the food's stodgy and overcooked, but there it is."

Their steaks arrived at last, with chips and onion rings, and a fresh green side salad with French dressing.

Dr Hanwell carefully rationed himself to two glasses of wine, and topped up Ruth's glass.

"Yummy yummy yummy, this beats Hall food any day," she said appreciatively. "And what about you, what's your programme like tomorrow?"

"Tomorrow's my day off. I'll probably read Meibomius, or maybe even Harvey. It generally takes me two or three days to get through my Hay books after each visit. And then maybe I'll write a little note on Meibomius, or follow up some of his footnotes."

"Is the Meibomius valuable?" she asked lazily.

"I don't know. As I said, a book is worth what people are prepared to pay for it. One could of course look up *Book Auction Records*."

"What's that?"

"It's a record of the prices paid for books at auction, chiefly Sotheby's and Christie's auctions. But of course, that's not an infallible guide. Say two multi-millionaires both want a book badly and don't care what they pay? The book will fetch a lot at auction. One of them will get it. Next time it comes up, there's only one person wants it, say. It may well go ten times cheaper. It all depends on the market and the market alters. For Meibomius, there's probably not much demand, as most people haven't heard of him, and most people can't read Latin now."

The meal over, they took their coffee to the lounge, where Dr Hanwell bought Ruth a crème de menthe, whilst he extracted a Don Diego from its tube, and felt relaxed and at peace with the world, as they lingered over coffee and chattered inconsequentially, both feeling pleasantly tired from the rather wearisome business of trekking around bookshops and reaching books up and down off shelves.

It was now a quarter to ten. They returned to the car. Lulled by four glasses of claret and a crème de menthe, by the soothing bubbling of the exhaust, by the warm air and the dreamy music of Rachmaninov, Ruth snuggled back into her seat and quickly fell asleep, her head resting against Dr Hanwell's leather jacket. At 10.20 he drove into the court of Second Hall, and there the mingled sounds of horseplay, shrieks, ghetto-blasters and the distant drumming of a disco woke her up.

"Thanks. That was a really great day. And thanks too for treating me to lunch and dinner. That was nice of you." She scrambled out of the car, collected her books from the boot, blew Dr Hanwell a friendly kiss, and vanished into the seething foyer of Second Hall.

Dr Hanwell revved up, backed out of the car park, and went back home to read his books.

CHAPTER SIX

A LETTER FROM ARKANSAS

'And all was Ignorance, and all was Night' (Thomas Gray, *Hymn to Ignorance*)

The week following Dr Hanwell and Ruth's visit to Hay-on-Wye, a few minutes after his arrival for work at 11.15 am, the Vice-Chancellor of the University of Surleighwick sat at his massive desk in his opulent office, drinking his morning coffee, and reading a letter that aroused his interest as few letters he had received that session had done.

```
Baskerville Institute for the History of Science
University of Surleighwick
Surleighwick
Arkansas
Ak 875056


28 January 1991

Dear Mr Vice-Chancellor Tinker Mbe,

We want to buy a copy of the 1628 edition of Harvey's
Circulation of the Blood. Do you have one to sell
us? We'll pay up to a million dollars for one in
nice condition. Xerox of title page enclosed.

Cordially yours,


(Embury T. Jenkins
Director)
```

A million dollars! What could the University of Surleighwick not do with that sum! The Vice-Chancellor's eyes lit up. That would go some way to buying the executive helicopter he had long maintained that the Vice-Chancellor of Surleighwick ought to have to avoid the Surleighwick trafic, on the 600 yard drive from his house to the campus. Yet one thing he did not understand—had there been a mistake? The appended photocopy did not seem to match the letter. The letter spoke of the *Circulation of the Blood.* Yet the xerox showed—he pulled himself with difficulty on to his crutches, and muttered the words audibly in great perplexity:

"X-er-sit-tatt-yo ana-tom-ica—blast it, what does it all mean?" he exclaimed aloud, in perplexity and irritation, as his five secretaries and three personal assistants crowded anxiously around him.

Fred the porter from the Post Room overheard him as he came in to pick up some outgoing letters.

"Anatomical exercise—and I think you'll find the *c* is hard in Latin, Vice-Chancellor." And Fred was gone.

Latin!

"Miss Carstairs,"—he spoke decisively to his Principal Personal Assistant. "Get the professor of Latin on the phone at once."

"I'm sorry, Vice-Chancellor, I can't do that", replied the cool and competent Miss Carstairs.

"What do you mean—*can't*," (irascibly). Not many people at Surleighwick dared to contradict the Vice-Chancellor of Surleighwick to his face.

"We got rid of him in '86, as a result of the cuts," she answered, unfazed.

The Vice-Chancellor searched his memory. Had they? The professor of Latin had made so little impression on him, he didn't even know what the fellow looked like. And then, through the mists of time, he dimly remembered. Wasn't that the professor who had got into the student newspaper when he had slipped on the ice one winter's day, and lain, half-frozen and unnoticed in the snow, for several hours? The Vice-Chancellor of Surleighwick rarely smiled, but that episode had made him laugh. Ah yes, Professor Brewster! That mousy, little, nervous, whey-faced man, who had sat cowering in a chair at their last meeting, when the Vice-Chancellor had told him he was being sacked. ('Thank you so much, Vice-Chancellor,' Professor Brewster had whispered, and had tiptoed out of the room never to be heard of again.)

"Hmpph. Well, get me the acting head of the department then."

"The department no longer exists, Vice-Chancellor. It closed totally in 1988."

The Vice-Chancellor grunted, and settled down to some serious thought.

He looked at the letter and its enclosure again, and ordered several copies to be made of both. The photocopy that had reached him from the Baskerville Institute must surely be from a book, he reasoned, perhaps of the title page of a book. After a while, he dictated a number of memos, determined to divulge as little as possible of his motives and interests in the matter. For at Surleighwick knowledge was power. Surleighwick operated on the 'don't need to know principle.' Only information that no-one needed to know was ever divulged publicly—such as the fact that the chemistry building was now being used as the backdrop for a series of dog-food commercials. Whereas any information that people actually did need to know, such as the latest government circular outlining the prospects for Surleighwick for the next ten years, was confined to as small a circle as possible. Even Dean Toady had not been told how far this would affect the Arts faculty.

As Vice-Chancellor of Surleighwick, Henry Tinker, MBE, B.Soc. Sc., Hon. MA (Surleighwick) trusted no-one and loved no-one; certainly not his professors. And in his heart of hearts, he knew that no-one loved him, not even the Surleighwick professors.

It was his absolute rule, therefore, to divulge as little information about anything to anyone.

To the librarian then, he wrote a laconic memo, enclosing just the photocopy of what he assumed was the title page:

'Do we have one of these? Please inform me soonest.'

Then he looked again at the covering letter. What was all that about 1628? He couldn't see any such date on the title page, if it was a title page.

Then an idea came to him.

To the head of the maths department he wrote, with another photocopy.

'Comments on the mathematical and numerical aspects of the enclosed to be forwarded to me forthwith.'

What had Fred the porter said? Something about exercise?

To the head of the Gymnastics department Vice-Chancellor Tinker wrote:

'Comments please on this Exercise.'

Then he looked at the xerox again. No department of Latin, eh? What faculty did that use to be in? Arts, wasn't it?

Right, now to make that fat Toady do some work! For as the Arts faculty at Surleighwick had always been the least regarded, so also had its Deans—who in truth did not present the faculty in its best light. The nervous, low-profile Professor Brewster, then the incomprehensible Professor Middleton, now the complacent Toady. All that Toady had going for him was his obsequiousness and deference, thought the Vice-Chancellor. Apart from that, he was a pompous ass!

To Professor Toady he wrote:

'I should like to read this book. Please find me a copy.'

That would get that fat Toady scurrying about, he thought to himself with satisfaction! Toady would certainly sweat himself into a lather trying to please his Vice-Chancellor. Moreover, Toady would be terrified if he couldn't come up with the goods!

What was that date again? 1628.

"When was 1628, Miss Carstairs?"

"I don't follow you, Vice-Chancellor."

"When was 1628? It's a perfectly simple question. Like, when was it? In the Dark Ages? the Middle Ages? the Reformation?"

"Ah, you mean what historical period did it fall in, Vice-Chancellor?"

"That's what I just said, didn't I. When was it?"

"I should say late Renaissance, Vice-Chancellor."

"And who professes the late Renaissance?"

"I should say Professor Bodgering, Vice-Chancellor. The Centre for Marlowe and Elizabethan Studies has the Renaissance in its remit."

To Professor Bodgering, he wrote simply:

'Please comment on this.'

Then, finally, because he did not trust any of his professors, he sent a copy by special messenger to Mr Arthur Singleton, a fellow Mason, the discreet and reliable proprietor of Creeps Detective Agency, who was paid a handsome retainer to make himself immediately available to the Vice-Chancellor whenever Mr Tinker wished to check up on what his professors were up to, or to find out what was really happening in his university.

Dear Arthur, (he wrote) I should be obliged if you would let me have a short report on this book (copy of title page enclosed) as a matter of urgency. Look forward to seeing you at the Lodge meeting next week,

Yours as always,

Horace Tinker, MBE, B.Soc.Sc., Hon. MA (Surleighwick)

Vice-Chancellor

University of Surleighwick

*****

This latter missive was despatched by the hand of the Vice-Chancellor's third Personal Assistant, who was allowed, as a special favour, in view of the urgency of the matter, to ride in the Vice-Chancellorian Rolls, driven by Mr Tinker's under-chauffeur! Mr Arthur Singleton scrawled a short note of acknowledgement, 'Dear Henry, Leave it to me, AS.' He then passed it straight on to Mr Hill, his consultant on handwriting and forgeries. Mr Hill recognised the photocopy as being in a foreign language, and consulted his neighbour, a retired schoolmaster, who translated the title page as meaning roughly: 'Anatomical Exercise on the Motion of the Heart and Blood in Animals, by William Harvey, Royal Physician and Professor in the London College of Doctors'.[Printed at Frankfurt, 1628].' Mr Hill gave his neighbour two bottles of decent claret for his pains (for he believed in paying well for information). He then spent an hour or two in the Surleighwick Reference Library, typed out the translation of the title page, summarised the *Dictionary of National Biography* article on William Harvey, checked the Index to the *Times*, added a note to the effect that the work was exceedingly rare and valuable, and had sold for £102,000 at the Honeyman Sale in 1979, and sent his report to Mr Singleton. Mr Singleton paid him £250 (for he believed in being generous to his consultants), and later that same afternoon forwarded the reply to the Surleighwick Vice-Chancellor by special messenger, with his compliments and a bill for £5000 for professional services rendered, inclusive of £2500 supplement for the urgency factor, but exclusive of a £1000 'search fee' and £1000 expenses. The report was on the Vice-Chancellor's desk at 3.40 pm that same day, before anyone else at Surleighwick had taken action. Vice- Chancellor Tinker regarded this as money well spent.

At 3.45 pm, that same day, the Vice-Chancellor smiled, as his personal hospitality hostess, the seductive and alluring Miss Cheryl Bimbaud, brought him his afternoon tea in a Meissen tea service on a silver tray engraved with the university coat of arms. Vice-Chancellor Tinker smiled benignly at her, delighted to have stolen a march on so many of his professors, and the librarian too, at one go. He drank his tea and summoned his chauffeur, speculating to himself what his professors would have made of his memos, and knowing by experience that he could rely on the accuracy of Singleton's information, and on his discretion.

*****

That same afternoon the Vice-Chancellor's memo was delivered to its addressees in the distinctive and sumptuous 10" by 8" envelope which Henry Tinker used for all his correspondence. It was made of specially moulded hand-made rag paper, embossed front and back with the university crest, and adorned in Italic printing with the words: from the Vice-Chancellor of the University of Surleighwick, Henry Tinker, Esq., MBE, B.Soc.Sc., Hon. MA (Surleighwick). Its contents caused suspicion and consternation.

"What's he up to now?" thought the professor of mathematics, Professor Anstruther, early the next morning, scratching his bald head in bewilderment. One thing he knew: it must be a trap. He photo-copied the enclosure, and called an instant brainstorming session of his department, without however telling them the reasons for his request.

"We have an urgent problem, gentlemen (and lady!)," he said as his department sat round the long oblong polished tables in an unattractive seminar room surrounded by blackboards. "What are the mathematical implications of the document you have in front of you? Our departmental grant may depend on the answer. To work!"

The assembled mathematicians set to work on the photocopied title page before them, trying to turn the letters into numbers in various ways, first taking a as 1, b as 2, c as 3 and so on. Then they looked at the figures, and manipulated them in different ways. Soon the blackboards were covered with equations, and the calculators were churning out their print-outs.

Professor Anstruther left them to it. Three hours later, he looked at what his department had produced. The answers ranged from the number of stars in the milky way to the sign of the Beast and a new way of calculating large primes.

The youngest and most junior member of the department, Dr Margaret Hascombe, D.Sc., the temporary Assistant Tutorial Assistant, had written simply.

"I may be naive, but aren't the letters at the bottom 1628 in Roman numerals?"

Professor Anstruther pondered. Were they? And if so, could the answer be that simple? It was such a long time since his schooldays. Then a brilliant idea came into his mind. Where had he seen Roman numerals before? Of course! He hurried to his video-recorder, on a table in a corner of his office, and to a pile of video tapes, and fiddled with the controls. Professor Anstruther was a golfing fan; he had on tape every golf match shown on TV since 1978. Moreover, his own mathematical interests were in calculating the trajectories of golf balls as a function of variable factors such as the wind, the force with which and angle at which the ball was hit etc.... He had it! There at the end of the tape was a notice: Copyright BBC MCMLXXVIII. 6 years later it had changed to MCMLXXXIV! He *was* on the right track after all! Forty minutes later, he had worked out from scratch the system of Roman numerals, apart from *D*.

That night he posed a question to his twelve-year-old daughter.

"What is D in Roman numerals?"

"500, silly daddy." she replied. "Do I get 10p for knowing that?"

He had the answer! Thoughtfully he gave his daughter 50p.

What was the Vice-Chancellor up to? Best to make him reveal more of his hand. Next morning, back in his office, after an hour and a half of drafting and careful thought, Professor Anstruther despatched the following non-committal reply.

'The date at the bottom reads 1628 in Roman numerals.'

That was true, guarded, did not preclude the possibility of the document having further significance, and put the ball right back into the Vice-Chancellor's court. Let him reveal a bit more of the purposes of his inquiry! Reasonably satisfied, Professor Anstruther lit his pipe, put 'In Conference' on his door, told his secretary to bar all calls, poured himself a glass of Talisker malt whisky, and proceeded to watch a re-run of the last Open at Troon.

*****

The Professor of Gymnastics was equally suspicious of the Vice- Chancellor Tinker's memo. 'What's he getting at now?' he thought to himself. 'Best play this one with a straight bat.'. After a little thought he wrote, on the same principle of being factual, non-committal, and saying as little as possible until he knew more of what was going on.

```
Dear Vice-Chancellor,
Thank you for your memo and enclosure. I can confirm
that this Exercise is not done in my department.
Yours sincerely,
J P Crummit
Professor of Gymnastics
```

*****

Sitting in his room, Professor Toady started when he read the memo, the morning after the Vice-Chancellor had despatched it.

That was surely a photocopy of the title page of the Romanian novel by Demotu Cordis which Mrs Houghton had shown him at the house of the late and unlamented Jim. Yes, he remembered the name. But why should the Vice-Chancellor be interested in Romanian novels? He was up to something. Strange—it was not like the VC to be interested in a book....

Greatly daring, he reached for his telephone and tried to speak to the Vice-Chancellor.

He got as far as the Principal Personal Assistant's secretary's secretary, a young woman of twenty-two who had worked for only three weeks in the Vice-Chancellor's secretariat at Surleighwick, but already knew that the Dean of Arts could be safely scorned.

"No, I'm sorry. The VC's PPA can't possibly speak to you for at least ten days. She's terribly busy you know. What's it about, anyway?" she asked idly, painting her nails.

"Well, the VC's asked me to get him a book and I was just wondering—" "Look here, Professor Toady," she said, not unkindly, as she applied the nail brush to her left finger nail, and spoke into the amplifier of her latest hands-free telephone. "If the VC's asked you to get him a book then if I were you I'd get it, no questions asked. One of the things the VC hates most is ditherers. Goodbye." She put down the phone.

"Yes, of course, I must apologize for troubling you, it's just that I thought....." But the fat Dean of Arts was speaking into a dead instrument.

The Vice-Chancellor's memo to the librarian was as usual opened by Sarah-Jane Moore. She too recognised it as a title page of the book that Dr Pratt had told her to add to the pile for sale to Odds and Ends books. However, she also was mindful of the usual Surleighwick rule: never tell anyone about anything that they do not need to know—and never commit yourself. So she merely attached a short covering memo of her own to the VC's missive, stating that the book did not appear to be in the Surleighwick catalogue.

The librarian felt a twinge of unease when he saw the VC's memo. Yes, who could forget the angel and that odd Romanian name, Demotu Cordis? What was going on? Thank goodness Sarah-Jane had apparently just put the book on the disposal trolley, otherwise she would have pointed out that he had disposed of the book only a few days previously. So he could control the situation a little, and if necessary follow the usual Surleighwick practice when caught out in any misdemeanour: deny it, then lie, then deny it again, then complain of misrepresentation, then delay, delay, delay and hope that in time the affair would be forgotten. Still, the memo had to be answered.

Again, after a pause, with perfect truth, he wrote:

'Vice-Chancellor from Librarian. I can confirm that this book is not listed in our catalogue." That was a nice touch. It didn't say whether the book was in the library—which of course it wasn't—merely that it wasn't in the catalogue, which was true. So far he was covered.

Just then his intercom made him jump.

"Professor Toady on line one for you," came Sarah-Jane's voice.

He lifted the phone and she put him through.

"Ah hello Peter. Eustace Toady here," came the fat Dean's complacent and insincere tones down the line. "I can't find Demotu Cordis in your catalogue."

Peter Pratt gave a nervous start.

"Sorry, I'm not with you."

"You remember, old man, Demotu Cordis, that Romanian novelist that Mrs Houghton gave you a copy of from the library of dear old Jim—poor old Jim, such a tragic loss, such an irreparable loss to the university. How we miss him! I thought I'd like to read

Demotu Cordis in tribute to his memory, but I can't find it in your catalogue."

"Well, cataloguing takes a little time," replied Peter Pratt, guardedly.

"But Peter old man, when we gave you that £2,000,000 for new computer software, you promised us no book would take more than 3 days to catalogue," pressed the Dean.

"Oh surely not"—

"Minute 126/84 of the Library Committee," interposed Professor Toady smugly, for he had put his secretary to some trouble to look the matter up. He felt tremendous satisfaction at having put the librarian at a disadvantage.

"In theory, Eustace old fellow, yes—but pressure of work, staff sickness—you know how many people are always down with 'flu in January."

"Very well then—anyway, when can I have a sight of the book?"

"Don't know where it is at the moment, Eustace old fellow," lied Dr Pratt, not liking to say he had disposed of the book. "I expect it's being accessioned—and then of course Romanian books are on special reserve—takes a few days to get them, you know."

"I want to borrow that book, old man—and soon, if you don't mind," said Professor Toady, with an undertone of menace.

"That may not be possible just yet a while. Special reserve books—which is what this will be of course, as a treasured bequest from a valued colleague, have to be read in the library."

Professor Toady was now suspicious.

"Peter old man, I must say I'm just a trifle disappointed in you. I've always supported you in the past, both on library committee, and as Dean in the higher levels of the university. Now, I want the Demotu Cordis book—just to have beside me for its inspirational qualities, as one of dear old Jim's books—poor old

Jim, what a tragedy—when I write his obituary for the university *Review*."

"Well," said Dr Pratt, "all right. I'll see what I can do."

"That's better. I shall expect to see it in the catalogue within the week."

Professor Toady rang off, delighted to have been able to establish his ascendancy for once.

Sarah-Jane Moore, who had been listening to every word, silently replaced her extension, and wondered how Dr Pratt would get out of the mess into which he had blundered. Thoughtfully, she decided to advance her proposed trip to Hay-on-Wye, and arranged with Dr Pratt to take a day's leave the following Wednesday.

The memo sent by the Vice-Chancellor to Professor Bodgering remained unopened for a couple of days. With Professor Bodgering in control of the English departmeet, its administration was just not getting done, and correspondence was piling up unanswered. But the prominent, flashy, envelope was spotted by Mrs Quick, when she raided Professor Bodgering's room in his absence to pinch his departmental stationery, stocks of which were now almost exhausted. Seeing the envelope on top of a huge mound of unopened correspondence, and intrigued by the words 'From the Vice-Chancellor of the University of Surleighwick,' she slipped the missive between the covers of a file and abstracted it without compunction. Inspired by the fact that she had taken the chair at the last meeting of the English department, and luxuriating in the thought that if the university wanted another token woman it was just possible that she might get Houghton's chair when it was advertised, Mrs Quick had come to regard herself as already the *de facto* head of the department. Later that evening, in her country cottage, when the marking of her essays was complete, she steamed open the envelope, photocopied the VC's letter and title page of the *De motu cordis* on her own photocopier, and carefully sealed the memo, ready to replace it on Bodgering's desk in the morning.

Mrs Quick was intrigued, because once, at one of Professor Houghton's boring parties, she had slipped into his study to get away from the noise and inane chatter, and had looked at some of his books. And the *De motu cordis* had stuck in her memory, partly because of its vellum binding, partly for being one of the very few books on Houghton's shelves not in English. But why should the Vice-Chancellor be interested in it? She sniggered. If *he* was interested in a book, it would be the first time for thirty years.

But knowledge was power, and driven by her curiosity, there and then she poured herself a glass of whisky and sat down to telephone Mrs Houghton to sound her out on the book.

Mrs Houghton answered the phone.

"Oh, hello Margaret. It's Pauline Quick here. I was wondering how things were after your sad loss—we miss your husband terribly, you know, especially me—the department just *isn't* the same without him. I would have rung before, but I thought you'd prefer to be left alone with your grief for a while. 'Grief for a while is wild, and so was mine'," she quoted.

"Well, I'm not too bad, all things considered, thank you, Pauline," replied Mrs Houghton. "It's good of you to enquire."

"I was wondering if there was anything I can do to help? Perhaps you'd like some help in sorting out Jim's books, for instance?"

"How very kind. But as a matter of fact, Percy Bodgering and Eustace Toady and the librarian have already been round. I shall probably sell most of them."

"I was just thinking how much I'd *love* to have one of Jim's books as a memento of a fine scholar," said Mrs Quick unblushingly. "It would mean *so* much to me. I once saw a super book at your house during a party—a nice old vellum book, in Italian I think it was. *De motu cordis*,or something like that, I seem to remember," she went on, looking at her photocopy. "I'd gladly buy that one off you for whatever you think is a fair price—say £20?"

"Oh that one's gone," said Mrs Houghton. "You mean the Romanian novel? At least that's what Eustace Toady said it was. It was a nice book, wasn't it. So I gave it to the library in memory of Jim."

"Well, thanks. See you around sometime," said Mrs Quick, thoughtfully, putting down the phone.

She was puzzled. Why was the Vice-Chancellor interested in this *book*, indeed *any* book. He was well-known for his complete and utter unbookishness. And surely it wasn't Romanian. It was Italian for sure. Trust that fool Toady to have made a mistake....She poured herself another half-tumbler of her favourite malt, Maid of the Mountains, chosen for its title and its subtle, feminine texture, and started furiously to think.

Mrs Quick rose bright and early the next morning. At 9.05 am she entered the library, and for twenty minutes she input every word of the title page into the title and author search sections of the computer. She drew a blank. Back in the Arts faculty, she replaced the original memo from the Vice-Chancellor on Professor Bodgering's desk. He was due to make his weekly visit to the department later that morning. Then she too phoned the librarian.

"Dr Pratt? It's Pauline Quick here, English department. Can I have a look please at that *De motu cordis* book which Mrs Houghton gave you for the library—from her husband's books? It doesn't seem to be in the catalogue."

"Er, it's not catalogued yet," answered Dr Pratt, by now distinctly nervous. Perhaps he had better try and get the book back from Odds and Ends. "It's being accessioned—and then it goes to reserve. It will be some time before it's available I'm afraid."

"So when can I see the book? It's just that I'm thinking of writing a little tribute for the *Romantic Studies Weekly Bulletin* that poor old Jim—we're all devasted by his death by the way, such a tragedy—used to edit. I want to do a piece on 'The Scholar and his Books—the Making of a Mind'."

"Er—that may not be possible for some time. Sorry, must go now—got a meeting."

Mrs Quick was now deeply suspicious. What was going on? All morning she puzzled over the mystery. Why should the VC be interested in a *book*. Clearly, not because of any interest in the contents of the book. One only had to make such a suggestion to see how risible it was. Mrs Quick went to the coffee lounge for a cup of coffee, took it back to her room, and paced up and down her threadbare carpet. And then the idea how to find out what the VC was up to popped into consciousness.

It was 11.30am. Vice-Chancellor Tinker had just arrived in his room for the day's work when Mrs Quick rang his office and was, as usual, answered by the Principal Personal Assistant's secretary's secretary. In a deep voice, and mimicking a horsey upper-class accent she said.

"This is the Countess of Bloxborough speaking. Connect me to Vice-Chancellor Tinker *at once*." she commanded.

The Vice-Chancellor was beside himself with excitement at being rung up by a Countess.

Galvanised into sudden energy, he spoke into the voice-box in his most emollient and oleaginous tones.

"Countess, your ladyship, such an honour, your ladyship."

"Look here Tinker," barked Mrs Quick. "Bunny Mellingham—the Marquis of Mellingham you know—has just told me of your interest in the *Exercitatio anatomica de motu cordis*. I understand you want a copy. I have one in my library at Bloxborough Hall, and may be able to help you. Now, why do you want it?"

"Your ladyship! Such an honour to speak to you. May we meet for tea, coffee—dinner perhaps—to discuss the matter? I have been longing to make your acquaintance. We have for some time had it in mind to honour your ladyship with an Honorary Degree."

"Dammit man, don't beat about the bush. What are you offering for the book?"

"Er, we could go to £100,000," said the Vice-Chancellor, thinking quickly. That would still leave about £500,000 towards his helicopter.

So that was it! The book was valuable.

"I'll think about it," Mrs Quick answered abruptly. "I'll be in touch, Tinker. You've been helpful. Goodbye. I'll certainly speak to the Prime Minister about your MBE when I see him next weekend at Chequers," she added wickedly—for the VC's cravings for honours were well known all through the University of Surleighwick.

"But it's an OBE I want, I've got an MBE already," wailed the Vice-Chancellor.

But Mrs Quick had already rung off.

£100,000! what could she not do with that. Together with her alimony, it would enable her to fulfil the dearest wish of virtually all the Surleighwick academics, to leave Surleighwick and do something else!

Then a further thought came to her. If that crook Tinker was willing to pay £100,000 for a copy of the work, then it must certainly be worth a lot more than that.

Mrs Houghton had said that Eustace Toady thought it was Romanian. But when she had flicked through the book at Jim's party, she herself had thought it was Italian. But what was this book? Who at Surleighwick could resolve the matter categorically?

*****

Meanwhile, Professor Eustace Toady, seated snugly deep in

the cushions of his favourite armchair in the SCR, was trying to pump the cronies and placemen who had crowded round him, taking it in turns to offer to buy him a cup of coffee and chocolate biscuit.

"I've been thinking about the novels of that great Romanian writer, Demotu Cordis," he said cautiously.

Little Jack Napes felt a thrill surge through his heart. What a learned man Professor Toady was! How proud it made one to be at Surleighwick! There couldn't be many universities in the UK where the coffee time conversation was on such a high level. Yet some of his colleagues affected to despise the place!

"Ah, yes, Demotu Cordis—a most interesting writer," remarked Professor Cecil Stevenson, the Professor of French, a hunched, gnome-like, red-faced little man.

"And what would you say is his most important work?" probed Professor Toady.

"Ah—that's a tricky one," parried the Professor of French. "One could say that they're all interesting."

"Ever come across his novel about angels? Quite a handsome book, I seem to remember," remarked Professor Toady, casually.

"Not for some time," replied Professor Stevenson, more confidently now. "I read it when I was twenty-three, but that was way back in '51." He flushed with unaccustomed pride at having scored a learned point in the presence of the Dean's attentive circle. He sometimes suspected that behind his back other people in the faculty regarded him as an ignoramus. That would show them!

"Well, if you do see a copy, let me know, will you?" asked the Dean casually. "Especially the 1885 edition with an angel on the title page."

"With pleasure, Mr Dean," smirked Professor Stevenson. "Anything I can do to help, Mr Dean."

"I can tell you where you might find a copy, Mr Dean," put in little Jack Napes, eager to make a contribution. "That's just the kind of book you'd find at Hay-on-Wye, the Town of Books. I've been there twice in the last eighteen months, and they have a lot of foreign language books there. I bought a lovely book about angels in Italian there myself. And I remember seeing some Romanian books there too in the Limited shop."

The fat Dean grunted. Hay-on-Wye. Mmm. It was just possible that for once in his life that fool Napes had said something sensible. He said not a word, but drained his coffee and held out his cup for the eager Napes to take it to the counter for a refill.

"And remember—I take three sugars, and I'll have another chocolate biscuit whilst you're at it."

Yes! Maybe he ought to take a trip to Hay to see if they had a copy there. He was sure the Vice-Chancellor would be grateful. It was a pity, though, that Demotu Cordis didn't seem to be in any of the reference guides to world literature that he had checked. Maybe he was a minor writer....And anyway, it hadn't been easy to find many books that dealt with nineteenth-century Romanian literature. The only ones the library had were all in the bunker. And that left only books such as Cassell's *Cyclopaedia of World Literature* (strange that such a misprint on the title-page should have escaped notice!), and the *Encyclopaedia Britannica*. And neither of them had said a word about Cordis.

"Tell me, Dean," enquired Professor Stevenson, greatly daring, "why this interest in the Romanian novel?"

Professor Toady thought quickly, and then lied:

"This is strictly between ourselves, Cecil, old man. This is 'Deans' Eyes Only' information, so keep it under your hat. But the fact is that we are likely to get some of the funds which the UFC is putting into the 'minority languages' initiative. I gather that the Romanian government is behind the project. They're rather keen for us to support Romanian, so, as I like to enter into the intellectual life of all Arts departments here so far as lies within yours truly's humble powers," he laughed with mock self-deprecation, "I thought I'd brush up my Romanian, which is I fear a little rusty by now."

Returning with the Dean's coffee, little Jack Napes overheard every word open-mouthed.

At 12 noon, the Dean returned from his coffee break,

He poured himself a glass of pre-prandial whisky, and thought for a while. He supposed he had got the date right, but one never knew. Best to check it out again. Then, on the blackboard in his room, he wrote in white chalk.

DEMOTU CORDIS: MDCXXVIII = ?

Yes, that was 1885 alright, he felt almost certain. He pondered what he had written, and drank the rest of his whisky. Then he wandered off to the Three Blind Mice there to tuck into a game pie and drink a few pints of Special with his buddies from the central administration, until three o'clock struck and it was time for him to get his secretary to drive him home before the Surleighwick rush hour traffic built up.

*****

That same day Professor Bodgering arrived for his brief weekly visit to the department. He sat gasping for breath in his wheelchair whilst Jolly went desultorily through the pile of letters on his desk. The Vice-Chancellor's note caught her eye, and she passed it over. Dimly, Professor Bodgering felt that the picture of an angel on the title page was familiar. Yes—he tried to concentrate through the fog of wine and vodka that fuddled his brain. Wasn't that the book that that dead Jim used to have? He laughed a wheezy laugh. Yes, that Romanian, Demotu Cordis, that was the man. But what did it mean. *What* had the VC said? "Comments please?" He thought for a moment, and then gasped out his reply for Jolly to type.

```
My dear Vice-Chancellor,
How kind of you to send me that splendid facsimile.
This is something, which, had I chanced to own it
earlier, I should always have treasured. I shall
treasure it even more as coming from your hands,
I am, my dear Vice-Chancellor, ever yours,
Percy Bodgering
Director,
Centre for Marlowe and Elizabethan Studies,
Professor of English Literature
Acting Head of the Department of English
```

There! That was an answer to be quite proud of, he thought to himself. Who said studying English Lit. didn't make you a good letter writer? What a charmer he was! No wonder he had always been such a success with the ladies!

His thoughts were interrupted by a knock at his door. Little Jack Napes had been waiting for Professor Bodgering's arrival, to waylay him.

Napes stood by Professor Bodgering's wheelchair, and whispered urgently into his ear.

"I suppppose you know that famous Romanian novelist Demotu Cordis?"

Professor Bodgering started. Demotu Cordis again—he must be quite a fashionable writer. Trust that bumptious, cocky, uppity Jim Houghton to have been up with the latest literary fashions, he thought to himelf bitterly. Then he cheered up, and smiled. But Jim was dead! The only book he'd be reading now was the 'book where all his sins were writ, and that's himself', as Marlowe had put it in *Dr Faustus*.

"Well, I have some news you ought to know, professore," said Jack Napes excitedly (for he burst into snippets of Italian when over-excited). "Il Professore Toadyo, he tell me two days ago of his interest in Demotu Cordis. It seems that there will be funds available, many many funds for universities that study Romanian. It's part of the UFC initiative to encourage minority languages."

Jack Napes now poured into Bodgering's ear the story which he had already spread in confidence throughout the faculty, namely that funds from the Romanian government were about to be poured into Surleighwick via the UFC to encourage Romanian studies. It was very plausible, thought Professor Bodgering. After all, twelve years previously Surleighwick had conferred (in absentia) an Honorary Doctorate of Laws on President Ceausescu when he had visited England in 1978 on his State Visit, together with both an Honorary Doctorate in Science and an Honorary Chair in Chemistry on his so charming and learned wife, Mrs Ceausescu. And now at last the university was getting the hoped for kickback!

"Yes," continued little Jack Napes excitedly. "The Dean said it's confidential of course, so not many people know about it yet. But we do literature here don't we, Professor Bodgering. In fact we are *the* literature department in the faculty. We got a star, and none of the others did. And we make our students read Penguins like *Madame Bovary* and *War and Peace*. We'd be well placed to claim some of this money. And there are lots of Romanian books at Hay-on-Wye. I saw them there on my last visit. What we ought to do is go down to Hay and buy them. That would strengthen our case for this new money."

Professor Bodgering grinned feebly.

"Well done Jack, go ahead and organise it will you?"

"Oh Professor Bodgering! Thank you! I thought what we ought to do is have a departmental trip for staff and students. Then we could really comb the town thoroughly."

"See to it will you, Jack?"

And then exhausted by this discussion, Professor Bodgering called Jolly to drive him home.

*****

After despatching his reply to the Vice-Chancellor, Dr Pratt had sent down the photocopy to the competent assistant who really ran the accessions section of the Surleighwick University Library, and had said:

'As a matter of interest: if we had this book, how would you catalogue it?'

And she had correctly identified it as a work in Latin, by William Harvey, entitled *Exercitatio anatomica de motu cordis*, printed in Frankfurt in 1628. Dr Pratt was staggered. So the work was not a nineteenth-century Romanian novel, as that crass Dean Toady had said, but a seventeenth-century medical work by an Englishman! Instantly he rang up Odds and Ends books, explained that owing to an unfortunate mistake a vellum quarto had been placed in the last lot of books sold to the shop, and offered to buy it back. The proprietor of Odds and Ends explained that it had been sold on, but undertook to try to repurchase it, which comforted Dr Pratt somewhat. Then, back in the library, to cover his tracks and lay a false trail, Dr Pratt started to create false entries in the computer catalogue for the *De motu cordis* volume. First he tapped in the author and subject and classmark entries, as supplied from the accessions department, and added the note: Unavailable: Special Reserve Collection: In Binding: for loan to Shanghai Exhibition. Note: readers wishing to consult this volume should now type in their library card number." He programmed it so that this information would show up on his own terminal.

Then he created another false entry for an author called Demotu Cordis, author of *Exercitatio anatomica*, a novel about an angel printed in 1885, with an identical Note. That should enable him to keep tabs on those who were after the book whilst he thought what to do next in the event that Odds and Ends could not get the book back. Satisfied for the moment, he returned to his desk to read *The Journal of Library Science*

*****

Mrs Quick had applied her ingenious and inventive brain to the problem of finding out more about the fate of the *De Motu Cordis* book, and at last she had formulated a plan of suitably Surleighwick-like deviousness. She knew Sarah-Jane Moore slightly, and always smiled at her when their paths crossed on the muddy Surleighwick campus. So she rang her up and said:

"Sarah-Jane? Its Pauline Quick here, English department. It seems so long since our paths have crossed. Look, I'm having some of my students round for drinks in my room after classes tomorrow, and I thought it would be so nice if you would come and join us. We don't see as much of you as we would like. Do say you'll come—there'll be some nice young men there, and I think you'll find it enjoyable."

Sarah-Jane was a little surprised to be invited thus by Mrs Quick—but it was a nice gesture, and she accepted readily enough. It was in any case the evening before the day she had decided to take a trip to Hay-on-Wye, so she did not have to worry about work the next day.

Pleased with herself, Mrs Quick called on Dr Crumpet to tell her about the party. She had not as yet told even Dr Crumpet of her discoveries about the *De motu cordis*.

However, there was nothing unusual in Mrs Quick holding a drinks party for her students in her room. She did this two or three times a term, as well as having a larger termly party at her cottage. Ten minutes' consultation between Dr Crumpet and herself sufficed to draw up a list of fifteen or so names of students to be speedily invited for drinks, and soon Mrs Quick was delivering little notelets to the English department student pigeon-holes, reinforced by pressing verbal invitations to selected students whom she saw in classes and corridors during the day. In one respect, though, Mrs Quick had not been entirely honest with Sarah-Jane. She had no intention of inviting any nice young men for her to meet! None of the young men in the English department were in the least worthy of Sarah-Jane! Such at any rate was Mrs Quick's opinion. Moreover, it was Mrs Quick's invariable aim in her small parties that the male students should always be outnumbered two or three to one by women—and she liked to invite the cleverest and prettiest girls in company with the stupidest and most booby-like young men she could find. That way, the young men would appear at an obvious disadvantage, and Mrs Quick's sense of the superior abilities of the female gender at literary studies be reinforced.

When Sarah-Jane arrived in Mrs Quick's room, at 5.50 pm the next day, the party was in full swing, and the room was crowded with ten young women and three young men.

"Hullo my dear, come in. Let me get you a drink. I bet you've had a tiring day. I've often said that you library staff work far harder than we academics. Here, try some of this, I think you'll find it very drinkable." And she handed Sarah-Jane a large tumbler of full-bodied Californian wine.

"Thanks very much, Mrs Quick."

"Oh, *please*, I'm Pauline. I don't really like my surname. It's my husband's you know, and that's all he left me when he abandoned me." She affected to dab at her eyes with a handkerchief.

"I'd change back to my maiden name, but it's too much trouble professionally. Writing articles, you know. If I started writing as Pauline Haysborough, no-one would know who I was.

Now let me introduce you to one or two people. I don't think you've met my colleague Antonia Crumpet? Paddy, will you make yourself useful by handing those crisps around? Thanks so much." She flashed an insincere smile, and took Sarah-Jane's arm, and steered her towards Dr Crumpet, who was chatting to her first-year tutees, Charlotte and Emma and Elizabeth and Simon. Mrs Quick and Dr Crumpet were delighted with Simon, whom they had nicknamed Simple, because in the first week of term, when asked by Mrs Quick if he had read Eliot's *Middlemarch*, he had replied that he had only done *The Waste Land* at school.

Mrs Quick kept the flow of wine circulating generously, and moved from group to group chatting merrily.

"Yes, it was such a tragedy about poor old Professor Houghton," she answered in response to a query from Charlotte. "What a bolt from the blue. I don't know how the department will manage without him. But doesn't literature teach us that in the midst of life we are in death? 'And with a little pin, bores through his castle wall, and farewell King'. Do you know where that comes from Simon? I'm sure Charlotte does. Anyway, one thing I *do* know. Professor Houghton wouldn't have wanted us to *grieve* for him. He would have wanted the department to carry on *exactly* as before. So let's all cheer up and have some more wine. Paddy, will you top up everone's glass please?"

When Sarah-Jane had drunk her third tumbler of Californian wine, and some of the students had taken their leave, Mrs Quick topped up Sarah-Jane's glass, manoeuvered her into a quiet corner of the room and started on a tête à tête conversation with her.

"And how do you like working for Dr Pratt, Sarah-Jane?" she enquired.

"Oh, it's not too bad, though he can be a bit tedious and irascible at times."

"Oh, don't I know it! That sounds just like my husband who deserted me. I'm afraid that is just typical male behaviour, my dear. They just lack the tact and emotional empathy of us women. As a matter of fact, I was speaking to Dr Pratt only the other day. You know that we lost our head of department last term? Such a tragedy. Poor dear Professor Houghton died of a cerebral haemorrhage you know. You may have seen Professor Toady's obituary notice in the last *Factfile*. Anyway, I gather that Mrs Houghton left one or two of his books to the library, One of them was a rather nice book called *De motu cordis* or something like that. I was just wondering when it would be catalogued so I could have a look at it again. I saw it at his house once, you see."

Sarah-Jane's tongue had been loosened by the wine, and by Mrs Quick's sympathique personality.

"Oh Pauline—I say, if I tell you something, you won't tell anyone else will you? But it's something that's been bothering me a bit, and I'd like to confide in someone. And I feel I can trust you."

"Of course you can trust me, Sarah-Jane. And of course I won't tell. I'm the very soul of discretion, I assure you. What is it?"

"Well—but this is *strictly* confidential. The fact is that Dr Pratt sold the book to a bookshop, Odds and Ends, in Hay-on-Wye! I think he thought that no-one at Surleighwick was ever likely to read the book, and he couldn't be bothered with it. But for heaven's sake keep this to yourself. He'd kill me if he knew that I knew what he'd done and had told anyone."

"Your secret is safe with me, Sarah-Jane. Trust me. Would I get a nice, helpful young woman like you into trouble with Dr Pratt? Don't worry about it."

"It's just that quite a lot of people seem to be after the book. The VC's been enquiring about it, and so has Professor Toady. Though why, I don't know."

"What is the book about exactly?" enquired Mrs Quick innocently.

"It's a copy of William Harvey's treatise on the circulation of the blood. That's what *De motu cordis* really means—literally 'on the motion of the heart' as I'm sure you know."

Mrs Quick nodded sagely.

"And is it valuable?" she probed, anxious to find out all that Sarah-Jane knew.

"I don't know. It's a first edition, but I haven't checked out its value," replied Sarah-Jane.

Mrs Quick was satisfied that she had learned all she could from Sarah-Jane, and she was very pleased with her cunning. Now she could relax.

"Let me give you some more wine, Sarah-Jane," she said smoothly. "I've brought in a little picnic basket for supper. You will stay to help Antonia and me eat it up, won't you? Just the three of us? Good."

Simon and Paddy stacked up the glasses, and then the last remaining students took their leave.

"Thank you so much for being such helpful waiters tonight, Simon and Paddy," said Mrs Quick. "It was sweet of you. Now remember, Emma and Charlotte," she said teasingly, "you're *positively not* to tell Simon where 'And with a little pin bores through his castle wall' comes from. I shall expect him to have found out all by himself before the next tutorial."

The students departed, and Sarah-Jane and Dr Crumpet flopped down into Mrs Quick's two small armchairs, for they were both merry and loquacious after four or five large glasses of wine apiece. Mrs Quick handed round some chicken legs, scotch eggs, tomatoes, and salad on cardboard plates. Sitting at her desk, sipping a glass of Perrier water, for she had drunk very little alcohol herself that evening, she looked indulgently at the slightly dishevelled and *distrait* figure of Dr Crumpet, elegant in her flowery Laura Ashley dress, and at the neater, demurer, Sarah-Jane Moore, flushed about the face with wine, but still trim and shapely in her yellow blouse and tight grey skirt. Yes, it had been a successful evening. Tomorrow she and Dr Crumpet would take a trip to Hay-on-Wye. As it happened, all the next day's classes in the English department had been cancelled on Professor Bodgering's instructions—or so that idiot Napes maintained. He was apparently organising a departmental trip to buy Romanian novels. It sounded a pretty shambolic scheme. But she and Dr Crumpet would drive down in Mrs Quick's car—they would not be going on one of the coaches that Napes had booked. An hour and a half later, the sober Mrs Quick drove the drunken Dr Crumpet and the drunken Miss Sarah-Jane Moore back to their respective abodes, before driving carefully back to her cottage to get a good night's sleep, ready for the expedition to Hay-on-Wye the next day.

CHAPTER SEVEN

TALKING ABOUT CROCODILES

'A great scholar, in the highest sense of the term, is not one who depends simply on an infinite memory, but also on an infinite and electric power of combination; bringing together from the four winds what else were dust from dead men's bones, into the unity of breathing life.' (Thomas de Quincey, *Essay on Pope*)

'All the world has heard of a French treatise on the Miseries of Scholars, but none has appeared descriptive of their felicities....His toil is the only adequate reward which can satisfy the mind of a scholar.' (Peter Daniel Huet, *Huetiana*)

' . . . the books, the Academes,
From whence doth spring the true Promethean fire.'
(William Shakespeare, *Love's Labour's Lost*)

Amidst all the excitement that the Vice-Chancellor's letter had created, in the occasional odd corner the educative work of the University of Surleighwick was being carried on.

Ruth and Dr Hanwell were sitting in the latter's room at the end of their class, the Tuesday after their visit to Hay-on-Wye. They were drinking tea, and relaxing over buttered crumpets, those necessary antidotes to the cold, damp January afternoon. In their tutorial they had been discussing the writings of Liutgard of Tongern and Mechthild of Magdeburg, and then, as invariably happened, the conversation turned to lighter matters.

"Tell me about crocodiles in the seventeenth-century," said Ruth, spreading butter and strawberry jam lavishly on to her hot crumpet, freshly toasted in front of the three-bar electric fire, and then kicking off her shoes for the sake of comfort, and tucking her legs beneath her as she sat in Dr Hanwell's battered armchair.

"My dear Miss Henderson! What a question! 'The crocodile is shaped like itself, and it is as broad as it hath breadth. It is just so high as it is, and moves with its own organs. It lives by that which nourisheth it, and the elements once out of it it transmigrates.' The standard seventeenth-century treatise on crocodile lore is of course Hieronymus Allopedius' *De natura et historia crocodilorum*, a fascinating work printed at Padua in 1627 which is now, I believe, becoming rather rare. If I remember aright, Allopedius has a whole section on the incantantory songs and prayers with which endangered swimmers can invoke the god of the crocodiles, and thereby escape the danger of being eaten. He records several such instances from his own observations of the Nile, during his well-known trip down that river in 1594, when he helped to lay the foundations of the modern study of Egyptology. He also made some important observations on crocodile eggs, and the mating habits of the crocodile. Wait! I believe I have a copy on my shelves. Ah yes!" Dr Hanwell pulled a stout leather quarto from where it lay on its side on the bottom shelf of his bookcase. "Yes, here we are—this is rather amusing." Dr Hanwell proceeded to give an extempore translation from the Latin of some of the more bizarre and entertaining of Allopedius' anecdotes. He told Ruth about the chorus of singing crocodiles in the Nile Delta, and of the use of their tails in love-making, of the passion for paper weights made from crocodile claws in China, and by a natural association of thought discoursed on the history and development of ladies' handbags.

From crocodiles in the seventeenth-century, the talk passed to alligators, from alligators to the 1959 film *The Alligator People*, one of the all-time great alligator movies, and thence to the 1979 film *Crocodile*, one of the worst films ever made, and the 1956 comedy *An Alligator named Daisy*. From Daisy to daisy- chains as magical talismans in Celtic folklore, from folklore to witchcraft, from witchcraft to broomsticks, from broomsticks to saplings, from saplings to botanic gardens, from botanic gardens to the botanic gardens at Alexandria, Cordova and Padua, and thence on to gardens of pleasure, from gardens of pleasure to ha-has and the landscape gardens of William Kent, from pleasure gardens to *maisons de plaisir*, from *maisons de plaisir* to Buñuel's *Belle de Jour*, from *Belle de Jour* to *Les Hauts de Hurlevant*, from *Les Hauts de Hurlevant* to the science of meteorology, from Aristotle's *Liber de caelo* to Bacon's *History of Winds*, from the *History of Winds* to the influence of Chaos theory on weather forecasting. From there on the one hand to modern meteorological studies, and on the other to the views on Chaos of Bernard Silvestris and the creation-theorists of the School of Chartres—which had been the starting point that afternoon of Ruth's class.

"I didn't quite understand what you said about the theory of spontaneous generation in the thirteenth century," said Ruth, clasping her hand round her third mug of tea, licking the butter and jam from her fingers, and tucking into her third crumpet.

The room was dim now save for the standard light and desk lamp on Dr Hanwell's desk. Above, the rain hurtled down on to the deep thick panes of glass set into the ceiling of his room. The room was now warm and cosy, an isolated refuge against the rigours of the world outside.

"Ah, spontaneous generation. Now there's an interesting question. I don't know very much about it myself. You'll find a good deal about it though in Omphalius' commentary on Aristotle's *De generatione et corruptione*, a seminal work which first appeared I think in 1535"—he rummaged through a dusty volume. "No, I'm wrong, it was 1536."

From Omphalius Dr Hanwell's irrepressible train of thought led him to Omphale's spinning wheel, from the spinning wheel to the *Sleeping Beauty* and the Spinning Jenny, from spinning to theories of motion and impetus, from theories of motion to planetary astronomy, from planetary astronomy to exobiology, from exobiology first to Ufology, and secondly to panbiogeography, from panbiogeography to geography, from geography to Pomponius Mela, from Pomponius Mela to Pietro Pomponazzi and his writings on the immortality of the soul, and thence to poems about the soul in Latin, French and Italian, from the soul to the afterlife, from the afterlife to ghosts, from the ghosts of Borley Rectory to Baron von Reichenbach's theory that ghosts in churchyards were the result of marsh gas, from marsh gas to Boyle's law, from Boyle's law to gaseous diffusion, from gaseous diffusion to entropy, from entropy to the second law of thermodynamics and to the modern physical controversies about whether the universe would ultimately collapse back in on itself. From modern cosmology the conversation turned by easy stages to Hildegard of Bingen's image of the cosmic egg. And once again they were back at the subject of the class.

The time raced by, as Ruth occasionally interposed a question, and Dr Hanwell digressed. When he next looked at his watch it was 8 pm.

"Good heavens. I'm afraid I've made you miss your dinner again. Come on, let's go to the Three Blind Mice. I'm on foot today, so this time I can match you with the wine glass for glass."

Ruth put on her donkey-jacket, and, well-wrapped up against the rain and cold, they walked in the dark past unfrequented campus buildings, and then across the playing fields to the Three Blind Mice pub and restaurant.

Soon Ruth and Dr Hanwell were warming up again in the club-like anteroom to the steak bar of the Three Blind Mice, the hostelry that had been the scene of Professor Toady's first oration on the death of Professor Houghton.

They ordered their steaks, and sat in the lounge, which was pleasantly uncrowded on this uninviting January evening, sipping their gin and tonics, waiting for their table to be called. Over the second gin and tonic, Dr Hanwell for the first time noticed that Ruth Henderson was a rather attractive young woman, as she sat there unaffectedly in her dark red frock, flicking her slightly disarranged hair back from her forehead, her face full of colour from the brisk walk in the rain, looking at him with her light-grey, quizzical eyes and an expression full of mischievous fun.

"Where's your home town, Ruth?" he asked, as they were called to their table, to sit under the horse brasses and pictures of mice and farming implements in the half-empty room.

"My parents live in Bath. That's where I went to school too," she answered.

"Ah yes—the home of Adelard of Bath, author of a book of *Quaestiones naturales* and a work on psychology too, who introduced algebra to England in the twelfth century, as I expect you know."

Ruth shook her head with a wry grin, and then asked:

"What about you? Where were you brought up?"

"Oh, I was brought up in Switzerland," he answered. "My father worked for UNESCO."

"So that's why you know so many languages. I thought that wasn't normal in universities. Now"—changing the subject—"tell me what you've been reading for pleasure."

"Well, if you want to know, I've been reading the Meibomius I bought last week, and some of the other books from Hay."

"And was it interesting?"

"Well, the Meibomius is full of curious bits of information of the type I like."

"Yes—I had rather gathered that you did," said Ruth with a grin. "What is it about?—you can tell me, I promise not to be shocked."

"Well, it's a kind of historical survey of the social context of flagellation—e.g. in the religious orders, in early Roman religion and so on, coupled with anecdotes of prostitution from Babylonian to Classical to Medieval times. And I've also been reading the Jerry Lewis book you kindly bought me, and some biographies, and Balbo and Douhet's studies of the theory of air power, and a few novels."

They ate their way through their steaks in a leisurely way, and washed them down with a bottle of full-bodied Australian Shiraz of the sort that had only very recently made its way on to the menu of the Three Blind Mice steak bar. Then for dessert Dr Hanwell contented himself with a selection from the cheeseboard, whilst Ruth, with her more youthful and vigorous appetite, made short work of a long tall glass filled with a lurid mixture of chocolate, strawberry and peppermint ice-cream, candied peel and cherries, and mountainous swirls of cream, the whole smothered in hot chocolate fudge sauce.

"Gosh, that was good."

"And what are you going to do next year, Ruth?" Dr Hanwell asked Ruth

"I don't know. I'll have to see what turns up. Maybe I'll stay on to do research—perhaps I could write a thesis on theological poems about the soul," she suggested. "Or I may just take a year off and go backpacking round the world with a couple of chums. The only thing that I'm certain of is that I don't want to be a schoolteacher. If I did an M.Phil. it would put off the decision for another couple of years. Or perhaps I could work in a bookshop. I wouldn't mind working somewhere like Hay-on-Wye."

The talk turned to the romance of bookselling, of how the early printers of the fifteenth and sixteenth centuries were also publishers of the works they printed, and often they were scholars too. Dr Hanwell discoursed on the learning of men like Manutius and Froben and Stephanus, of printing in China and Korea, of block books and incunables, of the introduction of Italic type, of the wonderful Aldines which Erasmus had seen for sale in London in 1506 at 3/4d., of Gryphius and Plantin, of the Elzevirs and their duodecimos, of the booksellers of St Paul's, of printers devices, of Basle and Milan and Venice, of the first book auctions in the seventeenth century, of early proof-readers, and the printing industry.

"How did you come across all that information?"

"Just from collecting books," replied Dr Hanwell. "And from reading about them. That's what university education is all about in the Arts, you know, isn't it really—books? In the modern university professors are really pretty redundant you know. Certainly they are at Surleighwick. After all, as Thomas Carlyle said in *The Hero as Man of Letters*, if I remember aright, 'all that a University can do for us is to teach us to *read*. Once invent printing, you metamorphosed all Universities, or superseded them. The true University of these days is a collection of Books.'"

Dr Hanwell talked of books, talked of bindings in calf and vellum and russia, of the history of bookplates and bookmarks, of signatures and gatherings and raised sewings.

They drank their coffee and ate the After Eight mints supplied with it, and then lingered over their table for a brandy (for Dr Hanwell) and a crème de menthe (for Ruth).

The restaurant was now almost deserted, so Dr Hanwell felt able to light his daily Don Diego, and savour the first rich puff of smoke.

"Mmm, I like the smell," remarked Ruth, "though I don't smoke myself. Where do they come from?"

"From the Dominican Republic," answered Dr Hanwell. "They're the best cigars you can get, apart from Havanas from Cuba."

He restrained himself with some difficulty from giving a lecture on the history of smoking, the use of pipes amongst the North American Indians, *Carmen*, James I's *Counterblast to Tobacco*, the smoking of herbs, cannabis and opium, the history of the theory of Tobacco-related disease, the symbolism of the pipe of peace, the hubble-bubble in Arabia, and kindred matters.

After another brandy and a crême-de-menthe, the last four inches of Dr Hanwell's cigar were still in his mouth when he and Ruth left the Three Blind Mice. They walked up the hill towards the Surleighwick campus. Perhaps only at night did the city of Surleighwick and its campus ever appear beautiful. In the day it was a dismal wasteland of harsh jarring concrete, ceaselessly traversed by motor cars and lorries, overcast either with clouds or with endless industrial smoke. But at night the traffic stilled; and darkness softened the harsh edges of the concrete; and the distant glimmer of lamps lent the city an air of melancholy beauty.

Tonight, as Dr Hanwell and Ruth walked home, the sky for once was clear, and the stars and moon shone brightly down upon them. Relaxed and mellowed by the wine, they linked arms, and Dr Hanwell, his attention drawn by the sight of the sky at night, talked of Copernicus and Rheticus and Osiander, of Aristarchus of Samos and the *Almagest*, of Nicholas of Cusa and Franciscus de Marchia, of Kepler's *Harmonices mundi* and his laws of planetary motion and the five regular solids, of Aldobrandinus de Tuscanella, of Buridan and Oresme, of Villehard de Honnecourt, of Galileo's *Sidereus nuncius* and of recent discussions of the anthropic principle in cosmology.

They arrived at the shouting and noise of the carpark of Second Hall.

"Come and see how the other half live," suggested Ruth. "I'll give you a nightcap."

Dr Hanwell followed Ruth up the bare concrete stairs, along long, noisy, angular corridors in sore need of a coat of paint, to Ruth's tiny room at the end of the third floor of Second Hall. Ruth switched on the light and drew the curtains, and Dr Hanwell found himself in a characteristic student's room, a tiny box ten feet by eight, with a wash-basin near the window, a narrow bed, a desk, and an armchair, with a thin strip of carpet on the tiled floor. The room was however humanised by Ruth's books and possessions strewn around it. There were two cactus plants near the window, and two china ornaments on the desk. The wall was adorned with posters of Tunisia, where Ruth had once spent a holiday, a 'Save the Whales' poster from Greenpeace, some holiday snaps of Ruth and her family, and a few postcard reproductions of impressionist paintings. Propped in between the sheets of the bed was a large striped cuddly tiger, its paws stretched out plaintively on the quilted counterpane. ("That's Timmy the Tiger," said Ruth unself-consciously.) One side of the room was occupied by a diminutive wardrobe, and about twelve feet of bookshelves, in a row four by three.

"Make yourself at home," invited Ruth. "I'll just fix the coffee." Whilst she busied herself with cups and saucers, and fiddled with the coffee percolator, and looked in a tiny cupboard under the washbasin for spoons, Dr Hanwell looked at the books on her shelves.

There were the books Ruth had bought at Hay-on-Wye the previous week, and a half dozen books on cookery. There was a book about Tarot cards. There was a copy of the Bible in the King James version. There were some dull-looking books on theology, the textbooks for her course. There was a copy of Disraeli's *Sybil*, of George Eliot's *Felix Holt the Radical*, of Gissing's *Demos: a story of English Socialism*. There was a paperback of the revised version of John Fowles' *The Magus*. There was a book on medieval theology. A paperback on *The Universities: Their Past and Future* was cheek by jowl with a copy of Lord Dunsany's *King of Elfland's Daughter* and other fantasy writings, including the *Lord of the Rings*. There were half-a-dozen thrillers. There were paperbacks of Arthur Koestler's *The Sleepwalkers* and of Jung's *Man and his Symbols*. All in all, it was a not unimpressive collection of books.

"You like Wild Turkey, I expect," said Ruth, pouring out a generous portion of Bourbon into a plastic airline glass.

"Good heavens, Ruth," Dr Hanwell replied, astonished. "I hadn't figured you for a Wild Turkey drinker."

"I'm not," she grinned. "But I had an idea you might be! It's a bottle someone gave my father. He hates the stuff, so he passed it on to me."

Dr Hanwell thought that Ruth's father must really be a very nice person.

In spite of her disclaimer, Ruth nevertheless poured herself a small portion, just sufficient to fill the bottom of her tumbler.

"You sit down there," she said, gesturing to the single armchair with its wooden arms. Ruth kicked off her shoes and sat in relaxed mood on the bed opposite him.

"Cheers," she said.

"Cheers. This is good stuff," answered Dr Hanwell appreciatively, as he sipped Ruth's Wild Turkey. "As a matter of fact I've just been writing a little paper on spirits and the history of distillation—a little interest of mine that developed from reading about poteen—it ties in with the Arabs of course. The word alcohol is Arabic in origin. And in alchemy and early chemistry, and to some extent in the history of medicine too spirits were at first called *aqua vitae*, which means the water of life—hence in France today brandy is still *eau de vie*, and this is also the original meaning of *usquebaugh*, from which the modern *whisky* derives. Brandy was used as a stimulant by the Saracens in early twelfth-century Spain, you know. And before the end of the thirteenth century, Arnold of Villanova wrote on its amazing properties, and believed that it was called *aqua vitae* because it prolonged human life. Arnold believed that it preserved the health, dispelled superfluous humours, revived the heart, and prevented decay of youthful vigour; that it cured dropsy, paralysis, quartain fevers—a fever that comes every fourth day—and that it helped to cure lepers. In the fourteenth century,

aqua vitae was a universal remedy, for inward and outer application. Though in 1387, Charles the Bad, King of Navarre, died when
his physicians ordered him to be bandaged in bandages soaked in
brandy. When a servant went to free him from the bandages,
lacking scissors to cut him free, he applied a candle to the ties—and
Charles the Bad got fried up."

"How *horrible*!" exclaimed Ruth.

"Yes, its not a pretty way to go, is it?" agreed Dr Hanwell.
"Anyway, the paper I'm writing is on the theory of distillation from
the fourteenth to the sixteenth century."

"From a little treatise in Low German you happened to
stumble on in Hay?" suggested Ruth.

"Something like that," he smiled.

There was a short pause, and then Ruth said:

"Well, I suppose you've read your Harvey now, and know all
about the circulation of the blood."

"I haven't actually," he replied. "I've been too busy reading
my other books. Also I had to check some proofs of a forthcoming
article for *Annals of Science*."

"What's that?"

"It's a history of science journal—I sent them a piece about
sixteenth-century zoology last year. It will be out in July next."

"So you haven't checked up to see how much that book is
worth?"

He laughed. "No, I haven't. When I first started collecting
books, I used to check them out very thoroughly, but now that I've
got quite a lot, I don't always bother."

"So where would you go to find out about the Harvey?" she
asked, leaning her head back against the wall of her room."

"Well, I think I told you about *Book Auction Records*. Then
there's *American Book Prices Current*, which is a guide to prices
in the U.S. market. Then there's an equivalent volume for the
Continent, but I'd have to go somewhere else to look that up. The

library here only has the first two. Then, of course, one can go through the catalogues of book dealers."

"Could it be worth a *lot* of money?" asked Ruth.

He laughed. "I just don't know. I hope, at any rate, that it's worth at least what I paid for it."

There was a sound of sudden shouting and cat-calls in the corridor, and the noise of rushing feet.

"Noises off," grinned Ruth. "This place can be very rowdy at times. But I don't normally go to bed till gone midnight, so it doesn't bother me too much."

The disturbance passed. Ruth topped up Dr Hanwell's Wild Turkey, and added a drop to her own glass.

"This *is* nice," he remarked appreciatively. "Sure I'm not keeping you up?"

"No, as I say, I don't ever try to go to bed till at least midnight in this place," she answered.

Dr Hanwell found Ruth very easy to talk too, and far more unconstrained than most students. In fact, he thought, she was really rather unusual for a student. She was pretty, she dressed in an attractive fashion, and she seemed to have reasonably wide intellectual interests. He had never known a young woman before who was quite so interested in seventeenth-century attitudes to crocodiles. But Ruth seemed to be. All in all, he found her *très sympathique*.

At length the conversation came to a halt, and Dr Hanwell looked at his watch, and said that he must go.

"Oh, that reminds me, Ruth, I shall be in the States next week. Do you mind missing our class next Tuesday, and say having two classes the week following to make up?"

"No, of course not—after all today's class has lasted just over eleven hours! What are you going to the States for?"

"Well, strangely enough, I'm going to Surleighwick, Arkansas," he replied. "There's an Institute for the History of Science there, and I've been invited over to read a paper."

"What about?"

"Well, it's on intension and remission of forms in Matilda the Hermit of Debrecen."

"Intension and remission of forms. What on earth is that?"

Dr Hanwell hesitated.

"It's rather a long story, I'm afraid. If you don't mind, I think I'd better keep it until I get back, otherwise I really will be keeping you up too late. This had been a wonderful evening Ruth. Thank you so much for inviting me in for a chat, and for the excellent Wild Turkey."

"I'll see you out."

They went out into the corridor, and passed a group of dripping wet figures padding bare-foot along the tiles, leaving little puddles of water behind them as they shook themselves dry.

"They've been at the *aqua vitae*," smiled Ruth as she escorted her guest out. "Though I daresay they've done their health more harm than good."

At the front door Ruth stood on tip-toe, and proferred her cheek to be kissed.

Dr Hanwell touched her cheek lightly with a friendly kiss.

"See you in a fortnight," he said. "I'll send you a card, though I daresay I'll be back before it reaches you. Goodbye—and thanks once again for the nightcap."

Thoughtfully Ruth returned to her room, removed Timmy the Tiger from her bed to the armchair where Dr Hanwell had been sitting, gave him a goodnight hug, and then fell into a slumber that even the nightly noises of the Second Hall corridors could not disturb.

CHAPTER EIGHT

THE WILD GOOSE CHASE

'Before the Romans came to Rye or out to Severn strode,
The rolling English drunkard made the rolling English road.'
(G. K. Chesterton)

'God helpe the man so wrapt in *Errours* endlesse traine'
(Spenser, *The Faerie Queene*)

The day immediately following Dr Hanwell and Ruth's discussion of crocodiles, various members of the University of Surleighwick were making their way to Hay-on-Wye, with dissimilar and discordant motives, aims, and levels of awareness.

First on the road was Sarah-Jane Moore. Mrs Quick had driven her the previous night the three miles to her flat in the western suburbs of Surleighwick, for Sarah-Jane was in no fit state to drive home after Mrs Quick's little party. On arrival back home, Sarah-Jane had drunk a large glass of milk, had tumbled into bed, and had slept very soundly indeed, for she was not used to liquor in Quick-like quantities. Awakening at 6.30 am in the gloom and chill of that late January morning, she had quickly made herself a pot of steaming fresh coffee, cooked herself two poached eggs on toast, had a bath, and by 8.30 am was as right as rain. Since she was not working that day, she dressed in tight fitting cherry coloured trousers that showed off her long legs to advantage, pulled on fur-lined half-boots, donned a cardigan and leather-jerkin over her blouse, put a pair of driving shoes in her shoulder-bag, wrapped a silk scarf round her dark curls, and after a fifteen-minute bus-ride, was on the Surleighwick campus at 8.45 am, there to collect her Renault 5 from the library car- park, and begin the drive to Hay, which she had never done before.

Sarah-Jane's motives were two-fold. She wanted to buy a handsome book, preferably in vellum, and preferably the copy of *De motu cordis* that had been sold to Odds and Ends. She was also glad to take the opportunity of a day trip into the countryside, as a relaxation from the tedium and monotony of the Surleighwick spring term. So she drove carefully south and westwards in her little car, following exactly the route that Dr Hanwell and Ruth had taken, and like them stopped at mid-morning for coffee at Tenbury Wells.

*****

'Je veux me plonger dans l'infamie
Comme dans un lit très doux.'
(Valery Larbaud, *Poésies de A. O. Barnabooth*)

Next on the road were Mrs Quick and Dr Crumpet. Mrs Quick's prime motivation was the hope of buying the book that she now knew from Sarah-Jane had been sold to Odds and Ends in Hay-on-Wye, and which, unlike Sarah-Jane, she knew to be worth at least the £100,000 that Vice-Chancellor Tinker had said he was willing to pay for it. Mrs Quick had still not taken Dr Crumpet into her confidence about this matter. "Best to keep my own counsel on this till I see if anything comes of it," she thought to herself. "Of course, if I come into £100,000, I shall buy Antonia a really nice necklace." Dr Crumpet was on the road to Hay-on-Wye principally because she always fell in with her mentor Mrs Quick's suggestions. Mrs Quick was so *understanding*, so sympathetic, so mature, so wise. It was pleasant to sit in the warmth of Mrs Quick's car, and be driven effortlessly through the bleak and muddy countryside on the road to Hay. Dr Crumpet had slept well enough the previous night, for she had become inured to Mrs Quick's generous bottle-a-head upwards provisions at parties. Dr Crumpet had felt a little fragile when she woke at 7 am, but coffee and toast and a shower had made her feel fit to face the world again. Now, suitably dressed for the occasion in a wide black velvet skirt, belted at the waist, in a green blouse, in a dark blazer fastened with bright large brass buttons, the perfect foil for her long auburn hair, and wearing black leather boots up to just below her knees, Dr Crumpet felt relaxed and at peace with the world. She closed her eyes in repose as Mrs Quick's Peugeot nosed its way through the outer suburbs of Surleighwick, heading for the open countryside. In any case, Dr Crumpet was interested in having a look round Hay, which she had often heard about. Maybe she would find some books about Emily Dickinson or Julia Ward Howe or Louisa M. Alcott or Harriet Beecher Stowe. Yes, there was no doubt about it, few writers in the world had written with such feminine sensitivity as the great nineteenth-century American women writers, who had been unjustifiably neglected by scholars....

As Mrs Quick's car headed deeper into Worcestershire, she put a recording of Ravel's *L'Enfant et les Sortilèges* on the cassette player. There seemed no doubt that her incantations were working! There had been encouraging gossip from Jolly to the effect that Psycho Bodgering had taken a turn for the worse, and had spent several quite sleepless nights lately. Surely he couldn't go on as head of department for very much longer!

Mrs Quick broke in on Dr Crumpet's reverie.

"Tony dear, you know that little song we sang so gaily the other night:

'Stick the pin in
See it go in,
Do it with a grin. etc'

Now, tell me frankly: what did you think of its literary qualities?"

"I thought it was really rather good," replied Dr Crumpet, after a moment's reflection. "Of course, the rhyme scheme was rather simple, and the lines were end-stopped, but all in all, it seemed to me that it had considerable emotional intensity. And the repetition of 'die die die' at the end was very dramatic and effective, especially when followed by that mysterious 'Jeteh hantz dure!'"

"I'm not sure that I'd go all the way with you on that, Tony," replied Mrs Quick pensively. "I've been mulling the matter over quite a lot, and it seems to me that the key thing is the doll, which serves so to speak as the focus for our loathing of these clapped out old professors. The 'Jeteh hantz dure!' is important too, I'm convinced of it. Those are the magic words of power. But I thought we'd have another go tonight when we get back from Hay, and this time I was toying with the idea of changing the words. How does:

'Double double toil and trouble
Fire burn and cauldron bubble
For a charm of powerful trouble
Like a hell-broth, boil and bubble'

sound to you?"

"Oh, that's terrible," replied Dr Crumpet. "That's just a naive jingle, not half as good as what we had before. Anyway, we haven't got a cauldron."

"No, but we could get one. Still, if you don't like the rhyme, Tony, we won't use it of course. It's just that I thought we might get something a bit more *subtle*. You're right of course that 'die die die' has a certain intensity. But how about this for a couple of lines to start things off with:

'Can curses pierce the clouds and enter heaven?
Why then give way, dull clouds, to my *quick* curses!'

How about that?"

"Oh Pauline, I like that much better. How clever of you! How ever did you come to hit upon that? I'm sure it wouldn't do any harm at all to start like that."

"Well, there's no reason why we shouldn't still keep 'die die

die' if you like," said Mrs Quick generously. "And I thought of saying:

'I will drain him dry as hay,
Sleep shall neither night nor day
Hang upon his pent-house lid
He shall live a man forbid.'"

Dr Crumpet looked doubtful.

"It can't do any harm," responded Mrs Quick. "'Psycho' doesn't sleep well at the best of times, and this might help to wear him out a bit more."

"All right, if you say so, Pauline. You are clever to think up all these rhymes."

"How about:

'Hie thee to Hell for shame and leave this world
Thou Cacodemon, there thy kingdom is.'"

"What's a Cayco-demon?" (for that is how Mrs Quick had pronounced it).

"It's a a rather old-fashioned word. You must have heard of the Turks and Caicos Islands? They're one of our few remaining colonies in the Caribbean nowadays, you know. They're so small and remote they haven't been made independent yet. So a Cayco-demon means a devil from the West Indies, hence a black devil, and hence evil, like in 'black-hearted'."

"But isn't that racist language?"

"Oh I don't think so my dear. It's all right to use it in an old-fashioned context, like a curse. It gives an aura of the antique, you know."

"You are clever, Pauline. I wish I knew as much as you."

Mrs Quick gave Dr Crumpet's knee a friendly squeeze.

"But you will when you are my age, Tony dear. Don't forget I'm eleven years older than you."

It was now well past mid-morning, and Mrs Quick and Dr

Crumpet pulled into the car park at Tenbury Wells for coffee, arriving just a minute after Sarah-Jane Moore had left.

*****

'Complacency is the enemy of study. We cannot really learn anything until we rid ourselves of complacency. Our attitude towards ourselves should be "to be insatiable in learning" and towards others "to be tireless in teaching". (Mao Tse-Tung, 'The Role of the Chinese Communist Party in the National War,' *Selected Works*, vol. II)

As Mrs Quick and Dr Crumpet were discussing curses on the road to Tenbury Wells, the official Surleighwick University English department expedition to Hay-on-Wye was just getting under way, rather late in the day, at 10 am. Professor Bodgering had been hoping to come along, but his illness had taken a turn for the worse in the last few days, so little Jack Napes had made all the arrangements at Professor Bodgering's behest, and with full powers of attorney. Truth to tell, little Jack Napes had made a thorough nuisance of himself, pestering his colleagues to take part, and some of them had refused to come. But nonetheless, lectures had been cancelled for the day, two fifty-seat Surleighwick University coaches and two Surleighwick University minibuses booked, and for various reasons on that Wednesday morning about a hundred students and a dozen members of staff were waiting to board the vehicles. The scheduled time of departure was 9.15 am, but, as always happens at Surleighwick on these occasions, the coaches had been late and in any case many people who had put their names down to go had not turned up on time.

Staff and students went along for a variety of reasons—few with any real interest in the trip's ostensible purpose of buying Romanian books. To many of the students a free trip to Hay came as a welcome relief from lectures. Some wanted to see Hay, others just wanted a ride into the country, still more saw the whole occasion as a great lark. The staff too went for varying motives—not one of them with the slightest intention of putting themselves out for little Jack Napes. Dr Blodgett, Dr Showman, and Dr Spark were glad of the chance to visit Hay to look for books in their own fields. Dr Amersham, a researcher at the Centre for Marlowe and Elizabethan Studies tagged along because he had nothing else to do. Doctors Sword, Beaver and Festering had agreed to go because they saw it as an opportunity for an agreeable variation in their drinking surroundings.

At last, into the coaches piled dozens of laughing excited students. Little Jack Napes had drawn £5,000 in twenty-pound notes from the English department's maintenance grant. Aided by the fussy and self-important Dr Chittering, an American draft-dodger who had fled to Europe in 1970, and had been skulking at Surleighwick since 1976 *faute de mieux*, since no American university would now employ him, Jack Napes started to distribute this money a note at a time to each of the students who had volunteered for the expedition. For, as little Jack had said to Professor Bodgering, if the students did come across Romanian books, they had to have funds to settle the purchase on the spot. The students were delighted at this largesse, though Jack Napes made them sign for it in a large exercise-book.

Then it was time for the 'off' and at a little after ten, Jack Napes leaned out of the window of the first mini-bus, and excitedly waved 'Avanti', for all the world like the leader of a western waggon train. The four vehicles moved off, and were soon separated by the Surleighwick traffic. Fortunately, most members of the department had arranged to travel in congenial company. Clutching a case of whisky between them, and dragging three or four dozen six-packs of Ruddles County Extra Strong Ale, Doctors Beaver, Festering and Sword merrily occupied the rear seats of the

first of the coaches, and spreading themselves out they settled
down to continue with their serious drinking. Two or three dozen
of the less intellectual of the department's male students had
elected to join them, in the not unreasonable expectation that some
of the vast quantities of liquor visible on the coach would come
their way. But most of these had in any event brought along their
own six-packs. Some fifteen of the more rowdy and hoydenish
female students also elected to join this party as camp followers,
seated for the most part in a little cluster near the door of the coach.

Doctors Blodgett, Spark and Showman sensibly made for the
first of the fifteen-seater mini-buses, and they were joined in the
main by the departmental blue-stockings, ready to take the opportunity of an informal chat with their teachers.

Dr Amersham, Mr Napes, and Dr Chittering elected for the
second of the mini-buses, and they attracted to themselves some
of the more dull-witted of the department's students. The grouchy
Ivan Hoe sat all by himself on the back seat of the second coach,
not talking to any of the mixed bag of students who were travelling
on it.

Little Jack Napes was thrilled at the large turnout, and at the
success of his idea. Professor Bodgering would be grateful, the
whole department indeed would be grateful to him when the
Romanian books were bought, and the department laid successful
claim to the money that was to support Romanian studies! He
looked at the little book where the students had signed for their £20
notes with a thrill of pride—it was so good of students such as Jack
Horner, Thomas Cobbleigh, Harry Guerney, Michael Mouse,
Clark Kent, Bruce Wayne, Snow White, Fanny Burney, and Alice
Wonderland to have come! Yes! There was no doubt that Surleighwick had a deservedly high reputation for the quality of its staff-
student relationships. What a happy department it was! Jack Napes
took out his copy of *Teach Yourself Romanian*, purchased from
the Surleighwick bookshop the week before.

"Remember," he exhorted the students on his mini-bus, "Look for the *u* at the end of a word. Professor Bodgering says that that's the sure sign of a work in Romanian. We're going to start courses in Romanian literature next year, and that's why we need these texts."

"But why are we looking for them in *Romanian*?" asked Samantha Smart, a sharp intelligent and suspicious young redhead. "I did the option on 'Women in French Literature' last year, and we did *Madame Bovary*, *Mademoiselle de Maupin*, and Madame de Stael and Simone de Beauvoir and Françoise Sagan—but it was all in English."

"Yes," added her friend Harriet, "and I did Italian, and we read Petrarch's *Sonnets* and *The Leopard*, but they were in English too."

"Well, it's a new course," answered Jack Napes vaguely. "The details haven't been worked out yet."

In the first coach, Dr Beaver had started to sing 'Ten Green Bottles'. As yet, however, only Dr Festering and Dr Sword were joining in. An hour later, though, when the whisky bottles had been hospitably handed up and down the coach, and when most of the men and some of the women had almost consumed their first six-pack of Ruddles County, the atmosphere started to warm up. Soon Dr Beaver was standing at the front of the coach, conducting the choruses from *Mademoiselle from Armentières* that were now being roared out by the whole coach, accompanied by Simon and Paddy (Mrs Quick's dull-witted students) on a mouth-organ. West of Bewdley, this Surleighwick University coach passed through a tranquil village in which an opinion pollster was at work.

The University of Surleighwick had commissioned its local opinion pollsters, Surleighwick Surveys, to investigate the impact of the dog-food commercial filmed in its grounds against the backdrop of the chemistry building. 28% of those questioned had answered 'Yes' to the question 'Don't you think the setting of the

Doggo Dog Food commercial looks nice?'. As Mr Fadge, of Surleighwick Surveys, stood by the side of the road, he was indignant to be hit on the shoulder by an empty can of Ruddles Extra, thrown from a coach all too clearly marked 'University of Surleighwick' and occupied by drunken lager louts! Quickly he altered the 28% to 8%.

On the outskirts of Tenbury Wells, Doctors Sword, Beaver and Festering stopped the coach. They were tired of being jolted around, and ensconced themselves with a number of the students in the bar of the Black Swan, steadying their nerves with a little whisky.

*****

'Knowledge is a matter of science, and no dishonesty or conceit whatsoever is permissible. What is required is honesty and modesty.' (Mao Tse-Tung, *Selected Works*, I)

Last to join the crocodile leaving Surleighwick for Hay that day was Professor Eustace Toady. He had intended to make an early start, but he had over-indulged at dinner last night. His heartburn was not getting any better. So he waddled in to the campus at 10.30 am, just to make sure there were no urgent matters requiring his decanal decision. There on the blackboard was his inscription of the previous day: 'Demotu Cordis. MDCXXVIII= 1885?'

Below it had been written:
?De motu cordis= On the motion of the Heart.
MDCXXVIII=1628
Professor Toady grunted. Who could have done such a thing! Some prankster?—a student, probably, who had crept into his room whilst he was having coffee. (In fact it was Milly, the West Indian cleaner, who had received an old-fashioned and traditional

education in the British Virgin Islands.) Irritatedly, Professor Toady rubbed the blackboard clear, and went for an early coffee at 10.40 am. At 11.15 am he too was on the road to Hay, looking for a Romanian novel about angels to give to the Vice-Chancellor. An hour and a half later, his fat stomach was calling out for sustenance, and he pulled in to a steak house on the edge of Tenbury Wells, there to assuage his appetite with a T-bone and a plate of chips, washed down with a couple of pints of the local ale. It was not until 2 pm that he was on the road to Hay again.

*****

Sarah-Jane Moore was the first of those who had set out from Surleighwick to arrive at Hay-on-Wye. She quickly located Odds and Ends, introduced herself to the proprietor Mr Cantelow, and asked if he still had the vellum volume which the University of Surleighwick had disposed of.

"Well, no," he answered in some surprise. "As I told Dr Pratt the other day, the volume has been sold on. I sold it to Antique World and they have now sold it, I don't know to whom, I am afraid."

Sarah-Jane went to Antique World and there she learnt what the shop had been unwilling to tell Mr Cantelow, namely that the book had been sold on again to Old Leather Bindings. At Old Leather Bindings Sarah-Jane again found that the book had been sold—but there she found several other vellum volumes that looked equally attractive as objects. After a little thought, she paid £80 for a handsome quarto copy in vellum of *Télèmaque*, and then, pleased with her purchase, collected half-a-dozen novels and other books that took her fancy in the other Hay bookshops.

Half an hour later, Mr Cantelow was surprised to be approached with yet a further enquiry for the *De motu cordis*. Mrs Quick and Dr Crumpet had now arrived. Mr Cantelow told his tale to Mrs Quick too; and her opportunistic hopes of sudden riches were dashed. A little disappointed, Mrs Quick started to tour the bookshops looking for interesting books about Charlotte Brontë and other volumes by and about women. Dr Crumpet also made her own tour, looking for books about Emily Dickinson and the other great American women writers, and the two agreed to meet in the self-same tea-shop in which Ruth and Dr Hanwell had had tea a fortnight earlier. It was not long before Mrs Quick came across the Universal bookshop, with its shelves of 'New Age' and occult material. And from there she returned laden with several interesting volumes on the history and practice of witchcraft, which she took straightaway to the boot of her car, before returning to the shops of Hay to make various other purchases in preparation for the meal which she was giving Dr Crumpet later that night. Soon her car was full of provisions and bulky packages.

Between a quarter to two and 2 pm, the first of the Surleigh-wick University coaches and the two minibuses arrived. (The second, drunken, coach, was just preparing to leave the pub on the far side of Tenbury Wells.) Little Jack Napes, with Dr Chittering fussing at his side, self-importantly divided the students into little groups of four or five, and assigned each group to visit a bookshop and buy books in Romanian. Laughing and shouting and ignoring his groupings, the students vanished into the centre of town—some to sightsee, some to explore the bookshops for their own purposes, many to play the pinball and fruit machines in the local fish and chip shop. A few even looked for books in Romanian.

Charlotte and Emma and Elizabeth, who had been at Mrs Quick's party the night before, had been assigned by little Jack Napes to the Limited bookshop. And conscientiously asking if there were any Romanian books in stock, they had been directed to a bay where some four dozen books, bound in red, and priced at £5 each, rested on the shelves. These were odd volumes of President Ceausescu's commentaries on the works of Lenin, ghostwritten for him by a team of party hacks. The Limited bookshop had only that week bought 1,000 of these odd volumes for 5p each from Cardiff docks, where they had been used as ballast for ships. They had been priced at £5 each simply as books that looked nice on the shelves, rather than in the hope that they would find a buyer interested in them for their own sake. Charlotte, Emma, and Elizabeth bought three apiece for £5 each, and thus nine copies on the shelves were cleared out of the Limited. Pleased with themselves, the three girls left the shop and walked back to the coach. To their fellow students whom they met on the way they called out the good news that they had bought Romanian books in the Limited. As the news spread, within the next half-hour the assistants in that bookshop were surprised to receive five more enquiries for the *oeuvre* of President Ceausescu. The assistants went into the stockroom to bring out further supplies, and brought out another three dozen odd volumes, and these too were soon sold. Puzzled, the assistants brought out twenty-four more odd volumes, and this time priced them at £10 each. And within half an hour they too had been sold, as students drifted in in ones and twos and acording to their fancy bought one or two volumes with their twenty-pound notes distributed by Mr Napes. News of the find reached little Jack Napes himself. Flushed with pride at the success of his scheme, he hurried to the Limited waving a wad of 150 twenty-pound notes. Jack Napes was delighted with the bright red covers of the Romanian books. Soon, after a little haggling with the assistants, the Surleighwick English department was the proud possessor of the 934 remaining multi-volume odd copies of President Ceausescu's works. Soon Dr Chittering, Mr Napes, and various willing students were transporting them up the hill from the Limited to the luggage compartment of the coach.

As they did so, the sound of a hunting horn and of boisterous singing was heard, and the final Surleighwick coach arrived. Its occupants, encouraged by Doctors Sword, Beaver and Festering, had continued to drink after the hour-long pause outside Tenbury. The six-packs were now well and truly broken into, and washed down with increasingly large whisky chasers. As the coach had sped through the countryside, a stream of empty cans and half-a-dozen pairs of trousers (for the men had now started to fight amongst themselves) had been thrown out of the window at passers by, and there had been instances of 'mooning'. So far, 153 parents had been led by the behaviour of its occupants to discourage their offspring from applying to Surleighwick. The coach pulled into the car park, and vomited forth its raucous, singing, lurching, puking occupants, who made a concerted rush for the public conveniences at the entrance to the car park. Then in threes and fours they dispersed to discredit the University of Surleighwick in the eyes of the residents of Hay, for the arrival of the Surleighwick coaches had not passed unnoticed in the eyes of so small a community.

Dr Crumpet, emerging from one of the bookshops in a quiet and normally deserted street near the car park, suddenly came face to face with a group of eight now thoroughly drunken third-year men, along with half-a-dozen skittish girls. They were just in the process of removing the trousers of Paddy and Simon, Mrs Quick's guests of the previous evening! With a cheer the drunks tossed the trousers into the air over Dr Crumpet's head, where they fell behind a high wall into a garden. Dr Crumpet paused uncertainly for a moment, in part shocked and in part excited at the sight of the unfortunate Paddy and Simon as they struggled to escape the swirling mob of aggressive males and giggling females. But then the drunks wolf-whistled at her offensively, and made certain lewd suggestions as to the removal of her own attire with which she certainly was not going to comply! And so she turned tail and hurried away down the street, to be overtaken first by the fleeing Paddy and Simon, and then by the inebriated mob in hot pursuit. The incident confirmed Dr Crumpet in her view that men were nasty brutish creatures. As for their drunken female companions, they had obviously been led into bad ways by the men. She was more than thankful to bump the very next moment into Sarah-Jane Moore, who had emerged unnoticed from an alley-way just in time to see what was going on. They kept each other company for mutual support as the straggling throng disappeared down the street. A few moments later they were safely settled in the quiet tea-shop where Dr Crumpet had arranged to meet Mrs Quick.

"We're having a departmental trip," explained Dr Crumpet to the surprised Sarah-Jane. "Well, not Pauline and me—but the students and some of the staff are. Looking for Romanian books, I believe. But I'm afraid some of them seem to have got drunk and aren't behaving themselves very well."

"So I see," laughed Sarah-Jane. "Weren't those two of Pauline's students that I met last night? Poor chaps, how embarrassing for them! It's quite a coincidence we should all have come down to Hay on the same day, isn't it?"

*****

Dean Eustace Toady was the last to arrive. At 3 pm, taking it easy after his long lunch he parked his car and trudged to the entrance of the car park. And there he found himself knocked to the ground by a gang of six young hooligans who barged into him and rushed into a blue coach marked: University of Surleighwick! Picking himself up, Professor Toady followed the miscreants to their coach.

"I say you fellows, what is the meaning of this monstrous behaviour? Do you know who I am? I am the Dean of the Arts faculty of the University of Surleighwick."

But the jeers with which this announcement was greeted, and the empty cans of beer that were aimed at his fat paunch, soon persuaded him of the unwisdom of pursuing his remonstrances any further. Withdrawing with such dignity as he could muster, Professor Toady repaired to a tea-shop to soothe his shattered nerves with tea and buttered scones. Then, as the light was vanishing, he made the rounds of five bookshops enquiring for a novel about an angel in Romanian, by Demotu Cordis. His enquiries were greeted with a speedy, "Sorry, no, I can't help you, it's not the kind of thing we deal in." And at 5 pm Professor Toady, decidedly out of temper, started his long slow drive back to Surleighwick (he hated driving in the dark), cursing that fool Napes for sending him on this wild goose chase.

Little Jack Napes meanwhile was in his element. The expedition had succeeded beyond his wildest dreams! All in all he had bought upwards of a thousand Romanian books, all in nice shiny covers! Surely the Surleighwick English department would get the UFC Romanian money now, with all these books in their departmental library! The only slight cloud on the horizon had been that Mr Michael Mouse, Miss Snow White, Mr Jack Horner, Mr Bruce Wayne, Mr Clarke Kent, Mr Thomas Cobbleigh, Miss Alice Wonderland and one or two others had not rendered an account of how they had spent their £20. Still, with over a thousand books in Romanian to show for the £5000 that had been expended from the department's funds, no one could say that that wasn't value for money. At 5 pm he assembled those who had travelled down on the relatively orderly coach and two minibuses, and proceeded with his treasures back to Surleighwick. The other coach did not leave till four hours later, when it left with a police escort, containing thirteen frightened, sick young women, Drs Sword, Beaver and Festering, and half a dozen male students unconscious in a deep stupor. The remaining two women and twenty-five men were being held in custody at Brecon by the Powys Constabulary, whose football riot squad had eventually been mobilised after many indignant telephone calls from angry citizens, to clear the town of Hay. Charged the next day with being drunk and disorderly, and with committing a public nuisance, the students were fined £100 each. The report of the proceedings in the *Powys Chronicler* was picked up by the national press and TV. Two days later the University of Surleighwick found itself on the front page of the *Sun*, *Mirror* and *Express*, whilst the following Sunday all three 'heavies' ran features on 'Lager Louts at University: the Dimensions of the Problem'. All in all, Jack Napes' little expedition was to cost the university over six thousand applications for the next session, and in due course £500,000 from ten people who cut it out of their wills.

Mrs Quick had meanwhile arrived at the tea-shop, and she and Dr Crumpet had tea and scones with Sarah-Jane, agreed that it was a delightful coincidence that they had chanced to meet that day at Hay, discussed each other's purchases with much mutual admiration, and then departed by their separate cars, Sarah Jane in her Renault, Mrs Quick and Dr Crumpet in the Peugeot. They agreed to meet again soon.

*****

'Whenever in history there is a period of radical intellectual rebellion against long-established conservatism, hierarchy, and the like, there is always an effort to regard Woman as the fully equal, which means the superior sex.' Charles Leland, *Aradia, or the Gospel of the Witches* (London, 1899)

Mrs Quick and Dr Crumpet drove out of Hay a little before the arrival of the riot squad, their headlights picking out some of the students brawling and vomiting in the gutters, among them the dishevelled Paddy and Simon.

"How utterly disgusting!" said Dr Crumpet. "Men! How they can do these things I just don't know."

"It's quite simple Tony, they're pigs, simply pigs."

Mrs Quick placed her Ravel recording on the cassette player, and drove carefully back through the dark countryside, towards her cottage to the west of Surleighwick. Although she had not found the book she wanted, she considered the day a profitable one, for she had made some interesting purchases.

Two and a quarter hours later, the two ladies had arrived back at Mrs Quick's cottage. Mrs Quick went upstairs to change into a flowing ankle-length dress and sandals, whilst Dr Crumpet lit the log fire in the lounge. Soon they were relaxing over stiff gin-and-tonics. Mrs Quick had placed a casserole in a slow oven before she left for Hay, and now its savours filtered throughout the cottage, sharpening their appetites. Dr Crumpet had bought some interesting books on her subject, and was now meditating an article on the feminist language of nineteenth-century American female poets.

At last it was time to eat. Mrs Quick and Dr Crumpet went into the dining room, and Mrs Quick brought in her steaming casserole, together with an excellent bottle of fruity and oaky Rioja, the perfect complement to the casserole, and a little basket of bread. Mrs Quick poured the Rioja into two squat tall-stemmed goblets, and raising her glass declaimed:

Scongiuro te, o farina!
Che sei il corpo nostro—senza di te
Non si potrebbe vivere,
Scongiuro il sale.

And Mrs Quick sprinkled a little salt on to the casserole, and drank deeply of the Rioja.

"What are you doing Pauline?" asked Dr Crumpet, puzzled.

"It's a little magical invocation on our meal, Tony dear," replied Mrs Quick with a little smile. "I've been reading one or two books recently about how to make our spells more effective, and I just thought I'd invoke this blessing on our food first."

"You are clever, Pauline," replied Dr Crumpet admiringly.

Mrs Quick was an excellent cook, and her casserole was mouth-watering. The first bottle of Rioja was soon despatched via the capacious goblets from which the pair were drinking, and the second bottle followed, which was slowly emptied over the cheese and fruit which followed. Then they repaired to the lounge, lit by the flickering flames of the glowing fire and subdued lighting from one of the walls. Dr Crumpet took off her blazer, and reposed herself comfortably on Mrs Quick's deep cushioned sofa, as the coffee simmered in its percolator at the side of the hearth. She felt at peace with the world. From the sideboard Mrs Quick took out a tall liqueur bottle in the shape of a cone, and poured two generous portions of its colourful contents into little brandy glasses.

"What's that?" asked Dr Crumpet, curiously.

"It's Strega, Tony dear. It's an Italian liqueur that I've just disovered. I'm sure you'll like it."

Dr Crumpet took a cautious sip.

"It's delicious!" she replied.

"Yes, I thought you'd like it," answered Mrs Quick casually.

The time sped by. It was now midnight, and they were ready to cast spells again.

Mrs Quick went into the kitchen and returned with the two models of Professor Bodgering and Professor Toady, which she placed in front of the fire. Then she kicked off her left sandal, and stood in front of the fire with her left foot bare.

"I've been reading up a little on how to make spells more effective," she explained to the curious Dr Crumpet. "It seems that these little charms are more effective if you say them with one foot bare. I expect you remember that wonderful bit in Dryden's translation of the *Aeneid* when Dido curses Aeneas for abandoning her, and calls down a curse on him and on Rome:

One tender foot was shod, the other bare

Girt was her gathered gown, and loose her hair.

And Dido's curse was *very* effective. So I think we'd both better do it with one bare foot tonight."

Mrs Quick watched appreciatively as Dr Crumpet stood up, pulled off her left leather boot, hitched up her black velvet skirt and unclipped her left stocking. Then Mrs Quick went to the far side of the room where she had deposited some of the packages she had bought earlier that day at Hay.

"Look what I bought this afternoon," she said with a smile, bearing in each hand a pointed hat with a wide brim. "I thought they'd help to get us in the mood. They're called 'Welsh Girl' hats. All the young women in Wales used to wear them in time gone by you know."

"They look like witches' hats," exclaimed Dr Crumpet doubt-fully.

"Yes my dear."

"Oh Pauline, we're not turning ourselves into witches are we? I'm not sure I like that," said Dr Crumpet.

"Why do you say that?" quizzed Mrs Quick.

"Well, from what I've read witches seem rather unpleasant people."

"Exactly, from what you've *read*. But who wrote those books?"

"Oh, I don't know, various people, like say Montague Sum-mers and Charles Williams."

"Exactly so my dear Tony. Those books weren't written by *people*, they were written by *men*. Believe me, my dear, I've been into all of this quite thoroughly. Only women can be witches, so naturally the men who write books about them are not inclined to be very sympathetic to them. And what they call witchcraft is really nothing more than women trying to use their natural and intuitive feminine and emotional powers, which are in harmony with the universe, against the power structures of male-dominated society. Don't you see, Tony, that what were called witches were simply poor oppressed women trying to make their way as best they could in a world where men held all the cards. The time is ripe for a re-evaluation of their received image along feminist lines, and you and I, Tony, are leading the way!"

Mrs Quick gave Dr Crumpet a little kiss of reassurance on the cheek.

"So we won't use that horrid word again, will we? Just trust Pauline." She handed Dr Crumpet the pointed hat.

"Of course Pauline! I see now that you're right. I feel so much better now that you've explained it to me."

Dr Crumpet put the pointed hat on her head, and stood there whilst Mrs Quick went behind her and spread out Dr Crumpet's long auburn tresses down the back of her blouse.

Then Mrs Quick donned her own pointed hat, and intoned:
"Can curses pierce the clouds and enter heaven?
Why then give way, dull clouds, to my quick curses."
Then she continued:
"Re dell'abisso affrettati
precipita per l'etra
senza librar la folgore
il tetto mio penetra!
Omai tre volte l'upupa
dall'alto sospirò:
la salamandra ignivora
tre volte sibilò
e delle tombe il gemito
tre volte a me parlò!"
(also from her book of magic spells, as she explained to Dr Crumpet). Then she uttered the well-tried incantation:
" Stick the pin in
See it go in
Do it with a grin
Stick it in his skin
Pin go in

And die die die!
Jeteh hantz dure!'
Die, Bodgering die!"
Then she followed it with:
"I will drain him dry as hay,
Sleep shall neither night nor day
Hang upon his pent-house lid
He shall live a man forbid."
    And with a grin she stuck the pin into 'Professor Bodgering'.
Dr Crumpet then melodiously crooned the incantations, which Mrs
Quick had written out on a card, and then she too took delight in
driving the pin with heartfelt feeling, into 'Professor Bodgering's'
chest. The procedure was repeated for 'Professor Toady'. Far away
in Ratford Professor Bodgering tossed painfully and sleeplessly on
his bed, kept awake by chest pains, whilst Professor Toady decided
that he ought perhaps to see the Surleighwick University doctor
about his heartburn problems and stomach pains. At last, when
they had drunk another glass of Strega, leaving the two transfixed
dolls in front of the fire, Mrs Quick and Dr Crumpet sat on the
floor, and snuggled up in front of the hissing fire, until once more
Dr Crumpet fell asleep in Mrs Quick's tender embrace.

CHAPTER NINE

INTERLUDE IN ARKANSAS

'Tis evening now; beneath the Western star
Soft sighs the lover through his sweet segar,
And fills the ears of some consenting she
With puffs and vows, with smoke and constancy.'
(Tom Moore, *Poems relating to America*)

Two days later Dr Hanwell was on the Delta flight from
Gatwick to Surleighwick, Arkansas, via Atlanta. He whiled away
the long hours looking over the paper that he was to deliver at the
Surleighwick, Arkansas conference, and by drinking first the double gin, then the half bottle of wine, then the double brandy that
was served with the meal. Then he fell into a light slumber,
disturbed only by the dull roar of the jet engines. Nine hours later
the airplane arrived at Atlanta, and three hours after that, the
Atlanta to Surleighwick, Arkansas jet was touching down in the
spring-like sunshine of a clear February day.

As he came into the arrival hall at the airport, Dr Hanwell was
greeted by his old friend Professor Philip Rowlands, a historian of
science from the University of Chicago, a tanned and genial figure
in summer trousers and a checked shirt, who shook his hand, and
seized his suitcase from the carousel, and led the way to his
Cadillac, parked in the airport carpark.

"Have a good flight? It's great to see you again, Charles.
We're all waiting for your book to come out. And how is jolly old
England? Now, I'll tell you what we're going to do. I've booked
us in to a *real* nice place in downtown Surleigh-wick, and we're
going to take you there, let you have a shower, have a few beers in
the bar, and then I've fixed for us to have dinner with two *real* nice

girls who're coming to the conference and who are just dying to meet someone from the oh-riginal Surleigh-wick."

Soon Dr Hanwell was sitting in Professor Rowlands' Cadillac, listening to the gentle music of Beethoven's fourth symphony on the stereo, as Professor Rowlands drove expertly down the Arkansan freeway, with the cruise control set to a safe and steady 80mph, and the fuzz-buster checking out the way ahead.

Dr Hanwell always enjoyed his visits to the United States. It was pleasant to leave behind the gloom and depression of Surleighwick, England and arrive in the more relaxed ambience of Surleighwick, Arkansas, where waitresses greeted you with a smile, and remembered your order, and served it promptly. It was good too to see his old friend Professor Rowlands again, a kindred spirit with similar interests and a similar sense of humour, whom he had first met years ago at a history of science conference in Europe. Professor Rowlands had written a much acclaimed book on the reception and influence of Arab science in thirteenth-century Europe. And inevitably, as the Cadillac proceeded smoothly down the freeway, the talk turned to the ticklish question of the influence of the Arabs on Matilda the Hermit of Debrecen. Professor Rowlands believed that this influence had been direct; whereas Dr Hanwell believed that Bridget of Brnö had been an intermediary between them. Professor Rowlands conceded that the thought of Matilda the Hermit and that of Bridget of Brnö was very similar; but he denied that the one was an influence on the other. Dr Hanwell believed, however, that in certain contexts the language of the two was so similar that direct influence must be postulated. Professor Rowlands however believed that any similarity of language was coincidental, caused by the necessarily limited vocabulary in which scientific concepts were discussed in the thirteenth century. And as they were possibly the only two people in the world who were fully familiar with the writings of both Matilda the Hermit and Bridget of Brnö and with Arab science (in the original Arabic in the case of Professor Rowlands, via Latin and Greek translations in the case of Dr Hanwell), they argued the matter with all the friendly banter and enthusiasm that is possible only when two experts in the field, long deprived of intellectual companionship, come together.

Soon Dr Hanwell was checking in to the Old Plantation, a smart, cool, hotel in downtown Surleighwick. It did not take long to unpack, shower, note with approval that the hotel had a satellite TV system that carried the famous Monster Movie channel, and change into some cool cotton trousers and a casual shirt, before going downstairs to the bar.

There, in the half-empty room, sitting on comfortable, green, padded, leather seats, at a secluded booth, he found Professor Rowlands in the company of two extremely attractive young ladies.

"Hi there Charles," he called. "I want to introduce you to some *real* nice girls. Laura, Libby, this is Dr Charles Hanwell, from the oh-riginal Surleigh-wick, England. Charles knows more about Latin botanical poems than anyone in the world. Charles, let me present the charming Professor Laura Harington, from the History of Science department at CalTech, and Professor Libby Cyoote, from the Science History Institute at Florida State. Hey, let's all have some more beers to keep you company, Charles."

Soon Dr Hanwell was draining a cool glass of Heineken, whilst the lovely Assistant Professor Laura Harington, in a cool, flowery dress, and a melodious Southern drawl, was snuggling up close to him and asking all about the oh-riginal Surleigh-wick, and if it really was a cute old place? Professor Harington was an attractive young woman of about 28 years old, in her first year at CalTech, and Dr Hanwell found her very easy to talk to. After the beers, Professor Rowlands ordered first one and then another round of Margaritas, served in huge wide glasses, frosted at the rim, and the conversation became convivial as Professor Harington leaned her head against Dr Hanwell's shoulder, and put a hand on his knee, and told him that although she liked to let her hair down a little at conferences, she was really very happily married to her husband, who worked in New York and whom she visited faithfully at least twice a year.

Meanwhile Professor Cyoote and Professor Rowlands were chatting in an animated, but perfectly proper fashion.

At length Professor Rowlands looked at his watch.

"OK you guys, it's time to eat."

He led the way into a pleasant and spacious dining room, cooled by giant fans which whirled from the panelled ceiling. They were soon ensconced at an excellent and secluded table, sipping their iced water, and ordering aperitifs (another round of Margaritas for the two young Professors, a Fuzzy Navel for Professor Rowlands, and a gin and tonic for Dr Hanwell). They all ordered a fillet steak, and Professor Rowlands chose a couple of bottles of really excellent burgundy to accompany it. Few people in academic life on either side of the Atlantic drank less than Dr Hanwell; whilst until recently Professor Rowlands had been an almost total abstainer. But then his eighteen-year-old daughter Elizabeth, who loved her father very dearly, had read a book called *Drink your way to Health!*, which had recently swept its way on to the best-seller charts in the States. And, concerned that her father was not drinking enough, she had encouraged him to drink a moderate three or four bottles of wine a week; and just to please his daughter Professor Rowlands had started to do so. So Professor Rowlands and Dr Hanwell contented themselves with two or three glasses of burgundy with their steaks. But Libby and Laura soon polished off the second bottle of burgundy between them, and Laura waved the empty bottle at the waitress and signalled for another one. After the steak, the whole party drank coffee, and then whilst Dr Hanwell drank a Wild Turkey and Professor Rowlands an Irish Mist, Laura and Libby ordered a double Curaçao on the rocks apiece. Dr

Hanwell was now feeling pleasantly relaxed, as the even more relaxed Professor Harington sat on his knee and kissed him. Then, in the background, the resident pianist struck up the sentimental tune 'Smoke Gets in Your Eyes'.

"I just *love* this song," exclaimed Professor Laura Harington, kicking off her shoes and climbing on to the table, where she proceeded to dance and jive and kick her arms and legs about.

Professor Rowlands looked on wth tolerant amusement.

"Oh Laura, you are *awful*!" screamed Professor Cyoote, in her gentle Southern accent. "I do declare, your're *drunk*."

Faster and faster gyrated Professor Harington. Then she climbed down from the table, sat on Dr Hanwell's knee, and fainted.

"Well my boy," said Professor Rowlands, picking up Professor Harington's purse. "I guess this is your chance to be a *real* English gentleman and carry Laura back to her room. Her key's in the purse. What she needs is a good rest. Off you go my boy, mind you behave yourself, and we'll see you back here in ten minutes at the most."

Dr Hanwell left the restaurant with the senseless Professor Laura Harington draped across his arms. To curious glances, he walked across the foyer, climbed the stairs, opened the door of her room, and deposited her gently onto her bed. Then for comfort's sake he eased her gently out of her dress and hung it in the closet, placed a light coverlet over her prostrate form, turned off the light on the corner table, and rejoined the party in the restaurant downstairs. An hour and another Wild Turkey later, jet lag and tiredness caught up with him too, and he went to bed, ready for the first paper of the conference at 10 am the next morning.

*****

At 9 am the next morning, Professor Rowlands, fresh as a

daisy, was hosting the group over breakfast in the restaurant, himself cheerfully tucking in to a generous plate of fried bacon, grits, eggs, hush puppies, tomatoes and sausage biscuit, washed down with fresh orange juice and a revitalising pot of fragrant coffee. Dr Hanwell contented himself with juice, coffee, and a waffle, and chatted to the delightful Professor Cyoote. Professor Harington had not yet appeared for breakfast.

"I'm just longing to hear your talk on Matilda the Hermit," said Professor Cyoote, fluttering her eyelashes at Dr Hanwell. "She sounds to me like a real groovy lady. I've never read her works myself."

"What do you work on, Libby?" asked Dr Hanwell politely.

"I'm researching the image of the female scientist in the nineteenth century," was the reply. "I'm studying people like Madame Curie. That's why I'm so interested in Matilda the Hermit. Was she really a hermit?"

"Oh yes, she was a hermit all right," replied Dr Hanwell. "She lived all by herself for thirty years in a cave just outside Debrecen. That's where she did all her best writing."

Just then Professor Laura Harington entered the room, in a loose fitting yellow dress, looking rather pale about the gills.

She shunned Professor Rowlands' suggestion that what she needed was a cooked breakast, and poured herself a cup of neat black coffee.

"I feel terrible," she said, wiping her hand across her forehead. "What happened, did I drink too much? I don't remember getting to bed at all."

"You have Dr Hanwell there to thank for putting you to bed, my dear," said Professor Rowlands with a smile. "I guess you were suffering from the heat and the excitement, and you just passed out. You certainly weren't drunk so far as I'm aware. 'Course you did do a little dance on the table, but I guess that was just your exuberant high spirits."

"Oh no! Did I make a fool of myself?"

"Not at all my dear," answered Professor Rowlands with a smile. "We all enjoyed your dance very much. It was most decorous, and gave us a really great opportunity to admire your lovely knees."

"Oh no!" squealed Professor Laura Harington, putting her hand to her mouth. "I didn't really do that did I? He's kidding, isn't he Charles?"

"No, you did do a dance, but I assure you it was perfectly decorous."

"It's all your fault Phil, " exclaimed Professor Harington. "You gave me too much to drink. I guess I just lose control of myself completely when I've had too much to drink."

"Then you must certainly join us again for dinner tonight my dear," replied Professor Rowlands.

"Oh Phil! You are *awful*!" said Professor Harington, slapping him playfully on the arm.

Professor Rowlands looked at his watch.

"OK group, time we were off. I'll meet you in the lobby in five minutes time."

Soon afterwards the four of them were motoring in Professor Rowlands' Cadillac down the five miles of road that separated their hotel from the campus of the Baskerville Institute for the History of Science, a series of well designed, air-conditioned buldings set amidst thirty-five acres of grounds on the outskirts of Surleighwick. Some fifty invited participants were present at the conference. After the opening speech of welcome from the Director, Embury Jenkins, Professor Rowlands delivered his keynote speech on 'The *Metaphysics* of Al-Gazzali and its impact in Central Europe: the Case of Bridget of Brnö'. During the break for coffee which immediately followed, this talk was widely acclaimed by all participants as a masterly exposition of an abstruse and complicated topic. Professors Cyoote and Harington were quick to tell

Professor Rowlands how stimulating and enlightening they had found his talk.

"Well thank you," he replied genially. "Now Charles and I are really counting on you both to join us again for dinner tonight. We'll break out a bottle or too of the really excellent champagne that I noticed on the wine list."

"All right, Phil, as long as you see that I don't get drunk again," said Professor Harington with a flutter of her eyelashes.

"Of course not my dear. All you have to do is keep pace with Dr Hanwell there. He's a very moderate drinker, and never gets drunk. They don't in England, you know," he said, with a wink at Charles.

"Well, I do declare, that's *real* reassuring," said Professor Harington. "I'll certainly do just that."

Over lunch in the dining room of the Baskerville Institute, Dr Hanwell met many old friends from previous visits and from previous conferences.

"We're all looking forward to your big book on scientific poetry," remarked Embury Jenkins to Charles, as they were waiting to go into the afternoon session. "No-one here is into that kind of area. But maybe we ought to have someone," he went on thoughtfully. "Well, it's great to see you again, Charles. I'm looking forward to your paper on Matilda the Hermit. What a really weird, fascinating, brilliant writer she is!"

Dr Hanwell's paper on 'Intension and remission of forms in Matilda the Hermit of Debrecen: the theory of temperature in 13th century Hungary' was also well received. Everyone agreed over tea afterwards that the paper immediately following, delivered by a Professor from MIT on 'Giles of Rome, Averroes, and the Concept of Primary Matter' was positively lacklustre and dull by comparison.

So at 6 pm, back at their hotel, having bathed and showered and changed, the four were in a mood to relax and celebrate.

Professor Rowlands had ordered a magnum of champagne on ice to celebrate the two successful papers. Professor Harington took hers with a little giggle, and said, "Now I do declare that I am not going to drink too much at all this evening. What must you have all thought of me last night? Oh me oh my!"

"Well *I* thought you had *real* nice knees," said Professor Rowlands—at which Professor Harington slapped his wrist with a giggle, and snuggled up on the bench against Dr Hanwell. Three glasses of champagne later she was sitting on Dr Hanwell's lap again, and asking if he could not smuggle her back to England in his suitcase.

"I'm sure there's room for little old me in it," she maintained.

"And what would your husband have to say about that?" asked Dr Hanwell.

"Oh Charles"—she slapped his face playfully, and kissed him full on the lips, and looked at him with wide and lustrous eyes. "Don't let's talk about my husband. Let's talk about something *interesting*. Anyway, he goes his way and I go mine, so there!"

Then they moved out into the still-warm night air, to walk to a really excellent fish restaurant that Professor Rowlands had patronised before. And there they washed down their red snappers with a couple of bottles of chablis. Over the meal the talk turned to books.

"Well, Charles, have you bought any interesting old books lately?"

"Well, I did pick up an early edition of Harvey's *De motu cordis* at Hay-on-Wye recently."

"Hey, great, that must be worth a few Gs."

"It would be nice to think so. I paid £450 for it, which I guess is about the going rate."

Professor Rowlands and Dr Hanwell lingered over their coffee and drank their respective Irish Mist and Wild Turkey. They suggested that Professor Harington ought to stick to coffee, but she insisted on ordering a treble of 140 proof Polish vodka. Soon Professor Laura Harington was drunk and giggly again. They were however able to restrain her impulse to can-can on the table, and managed to get her safely back to the hotel in a state of semi-stupor.

Nonetheless, Professors Cyoote and Harington were both present at the breakfast table the following morning, dressed simply in bikinis, ready to swim in the heated glass-enclosed pool of the Old Plantation.

"Libby and I thought we'd skip today's session," explained Professor Harington. "We both feel we can live without talks on 'Henry of Harclay and Atomism', on 'John Dumbleton on Condensation and Rarefaction', on Ockham's *Summulae physicorum*, and on 'Walter Burley's concept of time in his commentary on the *De physica auscultatione*'. I ask you! Don't you think that sounds a mite tedious?"

"Hey, you're not serious?" exclaimed Professor Rowlands. "Why, I think today is the absolute highlight of the conference. I wouldn't miss those talks for the world."

"What about you Charles?" asked Professor Cyoote, leaning forward in her tight, black and exiguous bikini. "Wouldn't you rather stay and play in the pool with Laura and me? I've brought my floating rubber duck with me, and there's room for two on it."

"Well, no, I think Phil is right," replied Dr Hanwell. "I'd love a ride on your rubber duck, Libby, but today's talks are too important to miss."

Laura and Libby pulled faces of disappointment, but Professor Rowlands and Dr Hanwell were not to be dissuaded. As they left to drive to the Baskerville Institute, they waved goodbye to Libby, riding her huge rubber duck in the centre of the pool, and to the recumbent figure of Professor Laura Harington, who was reclining languidly on a floating sunbed, splashing the water lazily with her hands.

The afternoon session ended early, in order to give conference delegates a little while to explore the charms of downtown Surleighwick. Dr Hanwell went into the shopping malls to buy some postcards, including one showing all the attractions of Surleighwick which he despatched to Ruth. Then he went to the bookshops and bought half a dozen books on films and some of the latest volumes about the Kennedy assassination. Then, after buying a few ties and shirts, he returned to the hotel, poured himself a glass of Jack Daniels, switched on the 24-hour satellite Monster Movie channel, and settled down to watch a re-run of Roger Corman's *Attack of the Crab Monsters!* (1957), one of that director's most sensitive and exciting films.

*****

The conference proceeded on its usual course, and Dr Hanwell enjoyed the break from the dullness of Surleighwick, England. The company and the food were good, the sun shone down clearly, and the temperatures were just into the low seventies. He saw many good monster movies on the satellite TV late at night, and had many stimulating discussions with Professor Rowlands and the conference participants. In the evenings, there was the charming and attractive company of the two Professors Harington and Cyoote.

The last day of the conference came, and once again the bikini-clad figures of Laura and Libby tried to distract Professor Rowlands and Dr Hanwell from attending the afternoon session, before the final conference dinner.

"Surely you're not going to hear Professor Teedjus? He's sure to be *awfully boring*," said Professor Harington petulantly, standing by the pool with a huge beach-ball in her hand. "I can't even understand the title."

"Yes, and he's from Krakow, too. I don't think his English will be very good," put in Professor Cyoote.

But Professor Rowlands and Dr Hanwell were not to be deterred.

"Well, his talk sounds *real interesting* to me," replied Professor Rowlands. "It's on 'Modal Syllogistic in the works of Gaspar Lax and John of Glogovia'. I just don't know how you two girls can stand there and seriously say that that's not an interesting topic."

"But what does it mean?" asked Professor Cyoote, plaintively.

"John of Glogovia is one of the most important Polish Aristotelian philosophers of the fifteenth century," explained Dr Hanwell. "And Gaspar Lax has the reputation of being one of the most demanding of all the Latin logicians of the late middle ages. I guess Phil's right—it sounds like a really challenging paper."

"Oh well, you can tell me all about it in the bar before dinner tonight," said Professor Cyoote, taking Dr Hanwell's arm in her hands and stroking it.

So Dr Hanwell and Professor Rowlands set out for the final paper of the conference. Attendance at papers had been dropping off as the conference progressed, and maybe Professors Cyoote and Harington were not the only ones to whom its title sounded austere. And it was indeed true that Professor Osso Teedjus had given several papers at previous conferences that had been somewhat less than sparkling. Even the Chairman of his talk went down with a violent stomach upset minutes before the session started. And thus it was that Embury Jenkins had to chair the session at the last minute, and that Professor Osso Teedjus from Krakow delivered his *pensées* on modal syllogistic to an audience of precisely two: Professor Rowlands and Dr Hanwell. Professor Teedjus's delivery was a trifle hard to follow; and although the title of his talk was in English, at the last minute he chose to deliver it in heavily accented (and virtually incomprehensible) French. But Dr

Hanwell was able to follow the gist of the talk by reading the ten pages of extracts from Gaspar Lax and John of Glogovia that Professor Teedjus had provided. Professor Rowlands, in turn, strained to catch the drift of Professor Teedjus' meaning, and mentally recalled the salient features of the Arab logicians whom he had once read. So the two of them were able to initiate a lively discussion between themselves and Dr Jenkins at the end of the paper, probing the salient points of Professor Teedjus' paper, and exploring certain subtleties that he had omitted to draw out.

At the end of the session, Professor Teedjus hurried away, but Dr Jenkins invited Professor Rowlands and Dr Hanwell into his office for some iced tea.

"Poor old Teedjus," he sighed. "I fear that his reputation has gone before him. I'm grateful to you both for turning up, I really am. Otherwise I might have had to listen to him all by myself."

"A dull speaker, I readily agree," replied Professor Rowlands easily. "But a fascinating topic all the same."

The talk became general, as the three gossipped about the latest developments in the History of Science. But the subject of the *De motu cordis*, which Dr Jenkins wanted for his Institute, and which Dr Hanwell had a copy of, did not come up. When the two had gone, Dr Jenkins sat thoughtfully in his room. Dr Hanwell had seemed to him to be an amiable and well-read person. Maybe, when his book came out, they ought to think about offering him a research post at the Institute....

*****

After the conference dinner, Professor Rowlands drove Dr Hanwell and Professors Cyoote and Harington back to their hotel. As this was the last night of the conference, Professor Rowlands had agreed that there was no harm in them all settling down to unwind with a little serious drinking. So the four of them sat in the conservatory of the hotel, overlooking the heated and floodlit pool, drinking Pina Coladas (Libby), 140 proof Polish vodka (Laura), VSOP Remy Martin Cognac (Professor Rowlands), and Wild Turkey on the rocks (Dr Hanwell). It was pleasant to linger thus, drinking and chatting, beside the pool. And after three glasses of cognac, Professor Rowlands could see no reason at all why Professor Harington should not indulge her insatiable craving to dance on the table. Which she did. And so, at 2 am, after a memorable evening, the party broke up.

Next day, Professors Cyoote and Harington bade a fond farewell to Professor Rowlands and Dr Hanwell, exchanged addresses and telephone numbers, and agreed to meet up again at future conferences. Professor Rowlands and Dr Hanwell drove slowly north through Arkansas and Georgia, stopping off to inspect plantations, bars, restaurants, motels and historic sites on the way. Three days later Dr Hanwell was saying goodbye to his friend at Atlanta airport, and early the next morning, feeling much refreshed and invigorated by his brief break in the lands beyond the seas, he landed at Gatwick in the fog, snow, and ice of a February morning, and was soon struggling back to Surleighwick, England on a late running train where the heating had broken down.

CHAPTER TEN: IN MEMORY OF JIM

'Vale o magister! O Jamese, ave atque vale.'
(Walter Savage Landor, *Poemata et Inscriptiones* [London, 1847])

'. . . James to nature paid his debt
And here reposeth. As he lived, he died.
The saying strongly in him verified,
'Such life, such death.' Then a known truth to tell
He lived a godly life and died as well.'
(Epitaph attributed to Shakespeare)

The day of the memorial service for the late Professor James Houghton had arrived, and over eight hundred and fifty members of the University of Surleighwick had crowded into its Central Hall. Memorial services were popular events at Surleighwick. In the first place, for the teaching staff they were an excellent excuse for cancelling clases and not reading books. For the administrators, they provided a welcome break from the monotony of office routine, and hence all the ones with whom Professor Houghton had had dealings had turned out in force. The whole staff of the Envelope Section of the Stationery department were there; the university Carpets Officer, who had helped to acquire the wonderful carpet seized by Professor Toady, was there too, with his two secretaries. The Furnishings Officer was there. The Estates Officer was there. Forty-five administrators from the Registry were there in the front row (the Registry had been in charge of the seating plan). The Catering Office was out in force, for they had laid on the tea and cucumber sandwiches for afterwards. One hundred administrators from the Secretary's department were there. Dr Pratt and the Library Assistants were there. Every member of the

English department was there, to celebrate the loss of their leader. The Fellows of the Centre for Marlowe and Elizabethan Studies were there in force. A hundred lecturers from the Arts faculty were there. Then there was a reasonable turnout of students from the English department, together with five coach loads of academics, administrators and friends from the University of Doncaster, where Professor Houghton had taught before coming to Surleigh-wick.

For the Vice-Chancellor, the occasion represented above all a good photo opportunity, as he sat in his black suit, a grave look on his face, in the high central box to the side of the stage, where everyone could see him, and he could nod down to some favoured crony in the dense throng below. The Vice-Chancellor's presence at the Houghton Memorial Service would be the lead item in the next university *Factfile*, where two studio portraits of Mr Tinker and Professor Houghton would grace its first six pages, given over to recording the proceedings and celebrating Professor Houghton's life and works. For Professor Toady, the service was yet another chance to orate in a self-important manner and to rehearse his clichés. And of course, it provided another opportunity for all Professor Houghton's many friends and colleagues to remind themselves that he was dead, and they were still alive. The general rule at Surleighwick was that the less distinguished the death, the more elaborate the service. The death of a lecturer with no achieve-ments to his name save that of propping up the staff club bar and vinous bonhomie would usually pull in a thousand or so grieving colleagues, students, friends. Whereas Dr Hanwell would not have merited a service at all. Professor Houghton had not been utterly without achievement; but he had patronised the staff club bar, and he had been at the university for upwards of fifteen years. And so he merited most of the trappings which Surleighwick laid on on these occasions.

The Vice-Chancellor had entered his box a minute before the

service was due to begin, stood on his crutches for a moment or two, nodded curtly and gravely to the crowd below, and, resting on the arm of his Principal Personal Assistant, had posed for the first of his numerous photo-calls for the university Public Relations Office. Then Mr Tinker sat down heavily in his chair. The wailing music on the organ, jerky, cacophonous, excruciating, had been specially written by Professor Smelter, the professor of music, for the occasion. The music stopped, and Professor Toady rose to his feet, waddled self-importantly to the podium, bowed low first to the Vice-Chancellor and then to the Registrar, who was sitting in the middle of the front row. Professor Toady, coughed, cleared his throat, puffed out his chest, and began:

"We meet today to commemorate something of great joy" ('Yes, that Houghton's croaked' whispered Mrs Quick irreverently to Dr Crumpet), "that is, the life and works of Professor James Houghton, late Professor and Head of the Department of English in the University of Surleighwick, which were a blessing and an inspiration to all who knew him. Jim, dear old Jim,—and as one of his closest and dearest friends and colleagues, who feels his loss very deeply, I hope I may be allowed to call him that—is dead, but his memory is ever quick and green in our thoughts. Jim's keen wit, his sunny and amiable nature, his tact and consideration to all his staff, are matters on which I do not need to speak, for you all know them, you, all of you, who are his friends gathered here today. The very number of you that are here is testimony to how much Jim was *loved* in this university. Mr Vice-Chancellor, Sir: We, who were his colleagues in the Arts faculty, who had the high privilege of working with him, have lost a friend and colleague beyond compare. In the immortal words of Shakespeare, James Houghton was sweet and lovely in his life, and in his death, he is not divided from our hearts. We remember and honour him as a man; we honour him as one of the most brilliant teachers that this great University of Surleighwick and that this country has ever produced; we remember him for the depth of his scholarship and for his wide general reading. Jim bore his learning with great modesty. It was typical of him, for example, that although a great expert on the Romanian novel, he never embarrassed his colleagues by publicly flaunting his knowledge of the subject. No, Mr Vice-Chancellor, Sir, James Houghton was not one of those flashy scholars who believed that one had to publish all one knew. He was too much of a true, deep scholar, too much of *gentleman*, if I may be allowed to use a word that is now, alas, unfashionable, for that. In his latter years, he lamented the way in which modest, unassuming scholarship—scholarship in the best Surleighwick tradition—was crowded out by mere publication. No one deprecated more than he the tendency to judge a man merely by his publications—instead of by his true inner knowledge, by his taste, by his judgement, by his breadth of reading, by his discernment. Nevertheless, Jim did publish—and his publications were outstanding, and earned him an international reputation as a scholar, and deservedly made the name of the English department at Surleighwick one to reckon with throughout the world. It was sufficient for his students to say 'I did English at Surleighwick' —and those in the profession would know all that that implied. Later in this service, Mr Vice-Chancellor Sir, some of Jim's colleagues and students will be reading extracts from Jim's critical writings. Far be it from me, Mr Vice-Chancellor Sir, with my humble oratory, to attempt to do justice to the memory of such a man. One thing we do know—in the life to come, whatever it may be, Jim will be seated in an honoured place, far above the salt."

Professor Toady smirked first towards the Vice-Chancellor, and then to the Registrar, and twice bowed his head, and then thrusting his script into his trouser pocket, sat down with a self-satisfied smile on his face.

The organ now began to play again, and a music student stepped up to the podium in a long black dress, to sing a poem composed by Professor Bodgering, specially set to music by Professor Smelter. Professor Bodgering liked to consider himself an important poet, ever since he had won a second prize for nonsense poetry when he was a thirteen-year-old third-form schoolboy. From nonsense poetry he graduated to doggerel verse, and there his talents had remained. Occasionally, when there was little else to report, his doggerel verses appeared in the university *Factfile*. On the death of Jim Houghton, he had set his mind to work, tapping his *pensées* into the keyboard of his recently purchased Amstrad word-processor. And now the Surleighwick throng were to receive the fruits of his lucubrations.

First came the soloist:
"James Houghton's fled from this harsh earth
We hope he'll have a second birth.
We miss you Jim we really do
You dead, we don't know what to do."
Then came the refrain
"Poor old Jim
We miss him.
Yes he's gone
Dead and gone,
So, so long!"
which was sung now with passionate intensity by the English department staff-student glee club singers, to the stabbing, harsh cords of the organ.

Professor Bodgering swelled with creative pride as he heard his words now publicly performed. The tape recorders were whirring, the event was being recorded on closed-circuit TV. The service was being broadcast over the university's radio station, and would be preserved in the archives for posterity.
"Oh why was Jim thus sadly snatched
A plot the Fates so cruelly hatched.
Bless you Jim you're now in heaven
At least I think you've gone to heaven."

There were several more verses of similar sentiment, specially chosen as being the best and most emotionally moving of the eleven hundred that Professor Bodgering had printed out and pasted into his scrap-book, and provisionally entitled *The Jimmiad*.

Then little Jack Napes bounced up to the podium to read the first of eight readings from Professor Houghton's works—a book review from the *Kirke White Newsletter*. The review ended with the words: 'When all is said and done, this is not a bad book, but it would have been a better one if it had taken more account of recent scholarship—eg of a note by the present writer in *Notes and Queries* for 1955 (LXVII, N.S., p. 275).'

Then Dr Beaver lurched forward, drunk as usual, to read the whole of a 1,500 word essay on 'The Place of English in the Modern University' which Professor Houghton had once published in the university *Factfile*. This extolled the place of English as the supremely civilised subject, the great cultural yeast, the quickener of dead souls, the whetstone of the intellect of the modern university.

These sentiments caused a slight stirring in the audience, who could not help but be aware of the difference between the ideal as proclaimed by the late Professor Houghton, and the reality of his department.

Next, a weird dance in honour of Professor James Houghton was performed by the students in the department doing the drama option. After further readings from the Houghton *oeuvre* by Doctors Showman, Spark, Chittering and Blodgett and two students, the proceedings were drawn to a close by a further poem from the fertile Amstrad of Professor Bodgering, this time read out by Jolly.

"So here we meet.
It's only meet
To sing your praise.
Oh halcyon days.
You're truly missed,

We beat our fist
Upon our chest,
But we were blessed,
We loved you Jim,
So hence this hymn."

Then the whole congregation rose to their feet to sing *He who would valiant be*, and the proceedings closed with the singing of the Surleighwick University song, *O Surleighwick*, recently commissioned from an unknown poet at a cost of £10,000 by Vice-Chancellor Tinker, and now sung to the tune of *O Maryland*, as the organ thundered forth, and the choirs sang, and the dancers whirled around, and the Vice-Chancellor was helped to his feet, and the flashbulbs popped.

The members of the English department and the late Professor Houghton's closest enemies then returned to the Arts building for tea in the department.

"What a perfectly, ghastly, grisly occasion," exclaimed Mrs Quick as she left the Central Hall with Dr Antonia Crumpet.

Tea at any rate had been laid on in the English department, though the administration of the department was now generally in a complete mess. Professor Bodgering had not the energy to deal with correspondence, nor would he delegate it. Thus, the department had now lost, through omitting to book them, the three most popular times for the large lecture theatres of the faculty—Tuesdays, Wednesday and Thursdays at 11 am (the only times that did not interfere with weekends, morning coffee, or lunch). The department had now run out of stationery, and Professor Toady was blocking their requests for more. Its departmental maintenance grant had been cut, and thanks to Jack Napes' extravagance at Hay-on-Wye, its funds for the current session were drained almost dry. The department of English had omitted to order equipment. It had lost its secretarial help. Correspondence was in a mess. The admissions system was declining into chaos. The exams had not been set.

Two hundred favoured guests, together with the staff members of the English department, repaired to the Arts faculty coffee lounge for cucumber sandwiches, tea, and biscuits. The cost of these drained the last £300 pounds of the English department's depleted funds.

Little Jack Napes busied himself with handing out cucumber sandwiches and cups of tea to the numerous guests, who were jammed cheek by jowl into the crowded common room. At last he found himself on the edge of Professor Toady's circle, and he hovered on the edge of it until he could edge his way closer to the centre and pay his homage.

"May I congratulate you, Mr Dean, on your well-judged and indeed brilliant tribute to Jim?" Professor Stevenson, the Professor of French, was saying. "It was one of the most genuinely moving and timely tributes I have ever heard, Mr Dean, if I may make so bold as to say so."

Professor Toady smirked complacently.

"It's nice of you to say so, Cecil," he answered. "I don't mind telling you, Cecil old man, that I absolutely sweated blood over that one. I was anxious that our faculty's tribute to poor old Jim should be a worthy one. The faculty would have expected no less of me, I know. They look to their Dean to set the tone on these occasions, and to uphold the honour of the faculty before the other Faculties. But I don't mind telling you that having to fulfill these functions on the passing of a loved colleague is one of the hardest parts about being Dean."

He sipped his tea with self-satisfaction.

"You did splendidly, Mr Dean, if I may say so," remarked Professor Knatchbull, the short, cadaverous Professor of Art History. "I'm only sorry that I hadn't got round to commissioning his portrait to be hung in an honoured place in my department's Picture Gallery."

At last little Jack Napes wormed his way in to the centre of the Dean's circle.

"Mr Dean, if I may say so, Mr Dean, you did brilliantly this afternoon. Mr Dean, I've had a thought. The best way to keep Professor Houghton's memory green within the department would be to call our new Romanian option the 'Houghton' Romanian option. As you said in your brilliant speech, Mr Dean, Professor Houghton knew about Romanian novels. Mr Dean, we have many hundreds of books in Romanian in our departmental library. We will get some of the Romanian initiative money, won't we? We are the biggest literature department in the faculty you know, Mr Dean, and we did get a star for the international excellence of our research."

What on earth was that wretched Napes wittering on about now, thought the Dean to himself as he bit into the chocolate biscuits passed to him by the eager Napes. What Romanian initiative money? Then he remembered. Ah yes, that tedious little Napes had been hanging around eavesdropping when he had made up that cover story for old Cecil Stevenson, to cover his interest in Demotu Cordis. Professor Toady deliberated with himself for a moment. Should he string little Jack along any further on this one, so that he would keep on sucking up to him? But there was really no need. He had the English department over a barrel anyway, for stationery, secretaries, money, and the possible replacement for Professor Houghton. Resentment got the better of him, for he was still irritated by the long and tedious journey to Hay which he had undertaken at that foolish Napes' suggestion. Far more pleasurable to vent his anger a bit and crush the eager Jack's hopes! So he lied:

"Ah yes, the Romanian initiative. We won't be getting any money at Surleighwick for that. It's all going to Sussex, Kent, and Essex, as they're the three universities nearest to Romania."

Little Jack was flabbergasted, and could hardly believe his ears.

"But we've just spent £5,000 on buying Romanian books for the department," he exclaimed.

"Was there anything by Demotu Cordis among them?"

"No."

"More fools you then," Professor Toady retorted callously. "Clearly the English department has money to burn."

"But you said we were going to get the money!" wailed little Jack.

But he was speaking to the Dean's retreating shoulders. Still, the Dean was glad to hear of this further example of idiocy and incompetence in the English department. They'd be 'average' all right soon enough!

Professor Bodgering sat in his wheelchair, being fed tea and biscuits by Jolly.

Professor Toady approached him:

"May I say, Percy, how impressed I was by your moving tributes to poor old Jim. If I may say so, those were some of the most genuinely moving lines of obituary verse that it has ever been my privilege to listen to. And they fitted the music so well. I earnestly hope that we shall see them ere long in the *Factfile*?"

"Yes," gasped Professor Bodgering. "I've written eleven hundred lines so far, I'm calling it the *Jimmiad*. But they've said they haven't got room for it all, they only want ten lines."

"Percy old fellow! How monstrous. This must not be. I'll speak to the VC about it. Just leave it to me."

Professor Bodgering looked at Professor Toady with pathetic gratitude in his eyes. Maybe old Toady had his good points after all! And the publication of his verses was one of the few remaining pleasures in life for Professor Bodgering. He set so much store by them.

"You're coming to hear me lecture tomorrow, I hope?" he gasped.

"Of course, Percy old man. I wouldn't miss it for the world," lied the Dean. "I've been looking forward to it so much. Urgent faculty business permitting, of course." (It wouldn't.)

For tomorrow was one of the big days of Professor Bodgering's life, the day when he gave his bi-annual lecture. For the last three years, since his illness became acute, it had been Professor Bodgering's practice to advertise a big public lecture by himself in March and early November. Posters would be printed, and he would talk loudly about the importance of the event before it took place, and of its great success afterwards. This was Professor Bodgering's defence against any attempt by the Surleighwick administration to make him retire early on grounds of ill health.

So that afternoon the wizened figure sat in his wheelchair telling all his colleagues and anyone in earshot about his lecture on the following day.

"It's on *Tamburlaine*, you know," he said endlessly and self-importantly. "Marlowe's greatest play. I expect you've read my book on the subject. It's the book on the play, you know. Do come and hear what I have to say."

*****

The next day, Professor Bodgering waited eagerly for the moment of his public lecture in the faculty's largest lecture theatre. He had sent a special invitation to the Vice-Chancellor, which Mr Tinker had instantly thrown into the waste-paper basket.

Most of his colleagues never attended. However, there was usually a small student audience curious to hear 'the Sickko', most of whom had either never seen him, or had gaped in amazement at the strange, frail, mummified figure in the oxygen mask whom they had seen being pushed through the faculty corridors. Dr

Antonia Crumpet and Mrs Quick had decided to attend too, out of a certain grisly fascination to see how the man would perform.

At 2.15 pm, the desultory group of three or four staff and twenty-five students sat scattered amongst the four-hundred seats of the lecture theatre.

At 2.20 pm 'the Sickko' was wheeled in by Jolly and Bill the porter. Carelessly they bounced his chair down the stepped aisles, shaking him up considerably. Then Jolly and Bill physically lifted his wheelchair on to the large table at the front of the theatre, so that Professor Bodgering could see and be seen.

Professor Bodgering felt very proud as he sat there, very visible if a trifle precarious on his lofty perch. He felt that he was still a fine figure of a man, very attractive to all the girl students, at whom he leered with a sickly grin on his face. He was wearing the padded spiv's jacket which he had bought with the proceeds of selling nylons to the Hamburg tarts in the post-war black market of '47. His frail legs were covered by a tartan rug. For the first time in a week he had changed his shirt. He had trimmed the stubble that normally spread over his chin and neck. He had splashed deodorant over his face to cover the stink of his unwashed body. He had taken five-minutes pure oxygen, and a treble of vodka and lime immediately before entering the theatre.

Jolly placed the controls to the slide projectors in his hand— for this was to be a slide lecture, illustrated with scenes from the stage history of *Tamburlaine*. Professor Bodgering started on his lecture, and Jolly left the room, as she had heard the lecture more than once before.

In a voice just audible to the students in the first two rows, Professor Bodgering whispered.

"Marlowe is essentially a theatre man—by which I mean a man of the theatre." (Pause, cough, splutter.) "Only by seeing his plays on the stage can we understand the true greatness of his theatrical art. Here is a slide of that lovely and charming actress,

Miss Polly Pooper, as Zenocrate from the Old Vic production of 1956." (Here a slide was shown—but it was not of Zenocrate, but of a chimpanzee scratching its head in puzzlement.)

A stir went round the room.

"Isn't she beautiful?" said Professor Bodgering, misunderstanding. His back was of course to the screen, and he could not see what was being projected there.

"The next shot shows the slaves of Tamburlaine." A shot of a Mickey Mouse was projected.

The audience dissolved into desultory laughter and tittering.

Truth to tell, Dr Beaver, in a humorous moment, had crept into Bodgering's room and substituted all his slides.

"Yes, they do look funny, don't they?" said Professor Bodgering, pleased at the success of his talk. There was no doubt that he was one of the most brilliant and popular lecturers in the department. Perhaps he ought to make it three a year, not two?

Then, the projector bulb went.

"What's happening?" whimpered Professor Bodgering, in the total darkness.

Amidst cat-calls and laughter, his audience first threw books and pencils at each other, then slowly drifted from the room as the lights remained out and the screen stayed dark.

"Let me down!" cried a plaintive voice.

But everyone had vanished, and no-one could hear him. 'The Sickko' was left ludicrously elevated on the table in his wheelchair, in a totally dark room, cursing under his foul-smelling breath, until, at the expiration of the hour, Jolly and Bill came to free him from his ordeal.

CHAPTER ELEVEN

O WHAT A TANGLED WEB!

' . . . Do not let me hear
Of the wisdom of old men, but rather of their folly'
(T.S. Eliot, *East Coker*)

It was a normal day in the life of Surleighwick University. Vice-Chancellor Tinker lay dozing on his couch, propped up on a cushion, and sipping the cup of coffee which Miss Bimbaud had just brought him. Really, he thought, life was quite agreeable. He didn't actually have to do any *work*. The Registrar generally dealt with the administration, and told him what to say at meetings. His job, really, was just to be a presence, and have his photo taken for the university's publicity shots, and in general, to think about the future of the university. And, drowsing, Mr Henry Tinker MBE, B. Soc. Sc. Hon. MA (Surleighwick) had a sudden thought. If the Harvey book was worth up to a million dollars, maybe there were other books that were worth money too! And maybe Surleighwick had some of them! With a sudden spurt of energy, he called his second Personal Assistant's secretary to his side, and dictated some curt memos to all his Deans and to the Librarian, and to several arts professors, including Professor Bodgering. The terse, cryptic memos, delivered as usual in their distinctive envelopes, read:

'Are books worth anything? Report within the week.'
In his memo to Dr Pratt he added the PS:

'If a lot of money, shouldn't we sell some of them?'

Then, exhausted after the effort of the day, the Vice-Chancellor sipped the bowl of bread and warm milk which was all that his ulcer would allow him for lunch, drank a tumbler of whisky, and fell asleep.

As usual, the efficient Miss Sarah-Jane Moore had annotated the memo for Dr Pratt: Yes they are. We have several books worth more than £1,000. (She had checked with the rare-book librarian, and he had given her a list of twenty incunables worth over a thousand pounds apiece).

She attached the list of rare books to the memo, though she would be sorry herself to lose such treasures from the library.

*****

Professor Bodgering pondered the Vice-Chancellor's memo when he opened it three days later. Were books worth anything? He didn't know. His own book on *Tamburlaine* hadn't been worth much. The publishers had remaindered the edition after six months, and written their losses off to experience. Professor Bodgering had been invited to buy the 3,800 unsold copies of the edition of 4,000 at threepence each. (This was in the 'sixties, before decimalisation). So the Vice-Chancellor couldn't be referring to monetary value. He must mean what were books worth in non-material terms? A difficult question. Professor Bodgering thought, and then from the depths of his subconscious, through his feeble memory, a dim recollection of something he had once seen quoted somewhere crept into his fuddled brain. Speaking into the little portable dictaphone that he had recently bought to record his *pensées*, he declared, for Jolly to type up later:

```
Dear Vice-Chancellor,

As it says in the Bible, a good book is the precious
life-blood of a master spirit, a pearl of price, its
value is above rubies. As ever, my dear Vice-Chan-
cellor, I am

Yours sincerely
```

(Percy Bodgering
Director,
Centre for Marlowe and Elizabethan Studies
Professor of English
Acting Head of Dept. of English)

Another masterly epistle! Really, he ought to collect all his little essays, letters, poems and memos, and publish them as a little anthology of *Wit, Grace, and Style in the Twentieth Century! The Oeuvre of a Modern Master*!

*****

Since her return from the expedition to Hay-on-Wye, when she had failed to buy the *De motu cordis*, Mrs Quick had been wondering how best to use the information which she had extracted from Sarah-Jane Moore and Mrs Houghton, namely that the late Professor Houghton's copy of the valuable Harvey treatise on the circulation of the blood had been offered to the Surleighwick University library, and thrown away, with Professors Toady and Bodgering maintaining that it was of no interest; and that the librarian, Dr Pratt, had then disposed of the book to Odds and Ends of Hay-on-Wye as surplus to requirements. What, she wondered to herself as she sat in her room at the end of her day's teaching, was the best way to extract the maximum mischief from the information which she held?

Mrs Quick poured herself a generous half-tumbler of Manzanilla, and paced up and down her office, turning over the possibilities in her mind. She could of course go to see Dr Pratt, say that Mrs Houghton had told her she had given the Harvey book to the library, and ask to see it. But he would only fob her off, or say that it was being bound, or in Special reserve (for Mrs Quick had now looked up the computer catalogue on several occasions.) And then at last she thought she had it.

Switching on the new Macintosh wordprocessor which she had recently purchased, Mrs Quick wrote:

```
Dear Vice-Chancellor,
I know you want to get hold of a copy of Harvey's
De motu cordis because it's worth a lot of money.
(Walls have ears, even in the University of Sur-
leighwick.) Mrs Houghton, widow of the late Professor
Houghton, wanted to give one to the university. Just
ask her! But Professor Toady and Professor Bodgering
told her it wasn't worth anything. They thought it
was a Romanian novel! Dr Pratt took it away for the
library. ASK HIM WHERE IT IS NOW!
Yours,
AUNT JEMIMA
```

There, she thought with satisfaction, as she printed it out, confident in the knowledge that it could not be traced back to her, that would set the cat among the pigeons, and set the men fighting amongst themselves! In high good humour she placed it unobserved in the 'Internal Mail' tray of the porter's office as she left the English department building, and drove steadily home to settle down to a quiet evening reading up on witchcraft and spells from the books she had bought at Hay-on-Wye and elsewhere in the last two or three weeks.

*****

At 11.30 am the next morning, Mrs Quick's letter was at the top of the Vice-Chancellor's 'In-Tray', as he sipped his coffee and started to go through his correspondence with his Principal Personal Assistant. Miss Carstairs, knowing Vice-Chancellor Tinker's predilections very well, knew that such a letter would intrigue him. And indeed, to Vice-Chancellor Tinker, an anonymous letter carried far more weight than a signed one would have done. He felt a quiet glow of satisfaction run through his body. This was excellent! Anonymous denunciations were exactly the kind of thing he had been hoping to encourage at the University of Surleighwick. That would keep the staff up to the mark, and stop them getting complacent. Moreover, the writer of the letter seemed confident of the facts. Ask Mrs Houghton, it had said, and ASK DR PRATT. Well, both of these things could be done. For the next half-hour, Vice-Chancellor Tinker gave the matter his full attention.

Then he asked to be put through to Mrs Houghton.

"Mrs Houghton? It's Vice-Chancellor Tinker here. I'm just ringing to enquire how you're getting on now that the memorial service to your husband is over."

"How kind of you to ring, Vice-Chancellor," answered Mrs Houghton, surprised, for in all her years at Surleighwick she had never spoken to him before. "But I think I'm over the worst now."

"I was just wondering how the university could best commemorate your late husband's truly splendid services, Mrs Houghton? He was very dear to all of us at Surleighwick, you know, as was apparent from the large turnout at his memorial service."

"That's very kind, Vice-Chancellor. I'm sure he'd have appreciated your thought."

"I was thinking perhaps that we might set up a Houghton memorial room in the library, devoted to his books and writings. Is it possible that you would be willing to sell or donate some of his books to form the core of the collection?"

"Well," Mrs Houghton hesitated, and then unbent, warmed by Vice-Chancellor Tinker's consideration. "As a matter of fact, I did offer some of his books to Dr Pratt, but he didn't seem very interested. And I'm afraid that I've now sold most of them to a second-hand book dealer."

"Mrs Houghton! I'm shocked by what you say! Have I been

misinformed? I was informed that you had donated some valuable items to the library, including a seventeenth-century Latin book by William Harvey?"

Mrs Houghton hesitated.

"This is very difficult for me, Vice-Chancellor."

"Come, Mrs Houghton, you can be frank with me. This is strictly between ourselves. And we owe it to your late husband to see that his achievements are worthily commemorated."

"Well, Dr Pratt did take away a couple of books, and I thought one of them was a seventeenth-century Latin book. Dr Pratt said he'd put a label in saying they were from my husband's collection. Though Professor Toady told me it was a nineteenth-century Romanian novel, and I didn't like to argue."

"Ah, Professor *Toady*. Between ourselves, Mrs Houghton, I have my doubts about his capacities. I fear he's been overworking lately, and is not in full possession of his faculties. But I think I know the book you mean. Talk of your generosity has spread throughout the university. Would I be right in thinking the book you mean was the *Ex-erkitati-yo* (for this time the VC got the pronunciation right, picking up Fred the mail man's tip) *anatomica—De motu cordis* printed I believe in 1628?"

"Yes, that's the date I think," said Mrs Houghton, glad that she had been right all along.

"Well, thank you very much, Mrs Houghton. I'll get on to Dr Pratt, and we'll see if we can't make that book the centrepiece of the Houghton memorial collection. Just leave it to me. And—my condolences on your sad loss. Your husband is, I assure you, deeply missed by all of us at Surleighwick, and by no-one more than myself."

The Vice-Chancellor leaned back in his chair, with a satisfied smile on his face. This seemed a classic case for Creeps detective agency. He called in his Personal Assistant's secretary and dictated a memo to Arthur Singleton, the astute proprietor of the great

Surleighwick private investigation bureau. Vice-Chancellor Tinker first enclosed a copy of the anonymous letter from Aunt Jemima, and a covering note conveying the substance of his conversation with Mrs Houghton. Then he sent to the Personnel Office for the personal files of Professors Toady and Bodgering. Each of these contained a version of the university's already drafted obituary notice on the two professors, beginning with the standard Surleighwick formula:

Professor.....was one of the outstanding scholars of his generation/ famous in particular for/ his work on eighteenth-century spinning jennies/brilliant monograph on *Tamburlaine/* (fill in as appropriate); and sometimes (as in the case of Professor Houghton): his untimely demise has robbed the world of his great work on.....which would have been the worthy culmination of 5//10/15/20/25/30 years of devoted scholarship, and gained him an international reputation.

The Vice-Chancellor attached a copy of the Registrar's "Strictly Personal and Confidential. For Eyes of Vice-Chancellor only 'Frank Notes'" on the two Professors and the Librarian.

1) Professor Toady. Typical Arts faculty nonentity. Pliable and ineffective Dean, well under control of the Deputy Registrar. As Professor of Industrial Archaeology, undistinguished and with few publications. Pompous. Lazy. A time-server. Will always support Higher Authority. ?Consider for next Pro-Vice-Chancellorship?

2) Professor Bodgering. Low profile invalid, little seen in the faculty. Bumbling. Inefficient. Unproductive. Essentially a dead-beat. Lecherous. ?Consider as next Dean of Arts?

3) Dr Pratt. A technocrat. Not interested in books, but efficient so far as he goes. Malleable. No known weaknesses. Still rather young (thirty-nine) for Senior Surleighwick Position.

All this information was photocopied, and soon on its way in the Vice-Chancellorian Rolls to Mr Arthur Singleton, with a request in the Vice-Chancellor's own hand, delivered by his third Personal Assistant, for an urgent report.

Finally the Vice-Chancellor arranged for the following message to appear in the personal columns of the next *Factfile*:

AUNT JEMIMA. Your message received and much appreciated. Tell me more. Your grateful CUDDLES.

*****

Mr Arthur Singleton read the dockets and covering note, despatched a short note of acknowledgement, 'This will take a little time, but am now on the case', and then put his best men onto the job. He assigned three enquiry agents to shadow Professor Toady, Professor Bodgering, and Dr Pratt, and to report on their private lives. Then he himself changed into a smart, but not too smart, dark pin-striped suit, placed the bright, distinctive striped tie of St John's College, Cambridge round his neck, placed a pair of clear-lensed dark horn-rimmed spectacles onto his nose, picked up a file and a couple of eighteenth- century books, and boarded a taxi for the University of Surleighwick.

Professor Toady was sitting in his room congratulating himself on the excellence of his speech in memory of the late James Houghton, when his secretary excitedly put her head round his door.

"There's a gentlemen to see you," she whispered urgently.

"Oh, I'm far too busy," replied the Dean. "It's nearly my lunch-time anyway." And indeed it was now 11.40 am.

Excitedly the Dean's secretary pushed a white pasteboard card in front of the fat Dean's eyes.

With an air of languor Professor Toady glanced at the card and read:

Professor Sir Hugh Price, CH, FBA, D.Litt.,   Secretary,
Professor of Babylonian   Nominations Committee

**Trinity College,
Cambridge**

**The British Academy
20-21 Cornwall Terrace
London NW1**

Mr Singleton had found that this card unfailingly gained him instant access to the Professor Toadys of this world.

Professor Toady was all smiles when his distinguished visitor was ushered into the room, and he bowed low over the casually proferred hand. At last! It had come, the honour for which he had so long been waiting. At last the Academy had recognised the scholarly worth of his volume on spinning jennies, and surely Professor Sir Hugh had now come to inform him that he, Dean Eustace Toady, would soon be Professor Eustace Toady, FBA, the first FBA in the Surleighwick Arts faculty for almost twenty-five years. That would make all his fellow Arts professors sit up and take notice! There was no danger of any of them being an FBA, after all!

"Sir Hugh, such an honour! Please do sit down, Sir Hugh. Sherry, Sir Hugh? I have a very decent Amontillado here."

"Thank you—as long as you're sure it's from a decent Bodega."

"Oh Sir Hugh!"

Professor Toady poured two generous glasses. 'Sir Hugh' took a tiny sip, made a *moue* of distaste at Toady's supermarket sherry , and placed the glass down again. He didn't want to drink himself, but he thought it would be useful to loosen Toady's tongue.

Professor Toady sipped his sherry expectantly, waiting for Sir Hugh to welcome him to the Fellowship.

But 'Sir Hugh' crossed his legs elegantly, and leaned back in his chair.

Then he passed a photocopy of the title page of *De motu cordis* across to Professor Toady, the same one that had been sent to him from Vice-Chancellor Tinker when the Baskerville Institute had first enquired about the work.

"Have you ever seen this book?" he remarked.

Demotu Cordis again! Everyone seemed to be interested in that writer nowadays. First, the Vice-Chancellor, now the Academy. What was going on?

"I may have," he replied at length. "It does seem familiar. Of course a scholar such as myself sees so many books in the course of a week it's hard to remember them all."

"Think hard, Toady. Your election to the Fellowship may well depend on it."

What was this? A viva?

"Well, yes, as a matter of fact I believe I did see a copy the other week. A very dear colleague of mine, and a brilliant scholar, though alas death cut him off before his life's work was completed (no harm in praising poor old Jim now—he wasn't a rival for the Fellowship!), poor old Professor James Houghton, had one in his library. His widow consulted me about its disposal, and naturally I exerted myself to ensure that such a work should not be lost to the university. I think I can say that it was largely owing to my humble self that Mrs Houghton decided to donate the book to the university in memory of her late husband." He sighed. "Poor old Jim Houghton! Such a loss, we miss him terribly, you know."

Professor Toady sat back expectantly.

"Can you tell me a little about the book?"

"Ah," said Professor Toady, nervously. "What do you want to know?"

"Well, what's it about? Tell me the plot."

The Dean laughed nervously, and refilled his sherry glass.

"Well, to tell the truth, I didn't really read the book, just glanced at it you know, but I could tell it was an important work, and ought to be in the library here, so that's why I urged Mrs Houghton to donate it to us."

'Sir Hugh' smiled.

"I can understand that well enough, Toady. We can't all know every language, can we? And you're doing quite well to know even a little Romanian, on top of all the medieval vernaculars and of course Latin that you'll have to be familiar with as a professor of Archaeology."

"That's right," agreed Dean Toady eagerly.

"It's simply that the Academy would rather like a copy of this book, and we'd heard a rumour to the effect that there might be one at Surleighwick. Still, now that it's in the library, I suppose that's that."

"Well, normally, yes, but if it were for the *Academy*, I dare say the university might be willing to sell it or swap it. We don't actually do Romanian here you know."

'Sir Hugh' smiled pityingly.

"Well, I'll bear that in mind."

He was reasonably satisfied. Toady was a fool, but he was not a crook. He looked at his watch.

"Anywhere round here I can get a really decent lunch?" he enquired. "I've got a couple of hours or so to kill before my next appointment."

"Sir Hugh! Please be my guest."

And Mr Singleton let the gullible Toady take him to the Fox and Grapes restaurant on the Worcester Road, Surleighwick's luxurious business man's restaurant that was featured in the Good Food Guide. There the two enjoyed a very decent £80 a head lunch, washed down with a bottle of excellent burgundy, half a bottle of Chateau Yquem as a pudding wine, and two large brandies apiece. Mr Singleton let Professor Toady pick up the total bill, including drinks and service, of £350 (the burgundy and sauternes had been *very* good and *very* expensive, though Toady would of course reclaim this straightaway from the faculty hospitality fund), and then said with a wink as he took his leave.

"Oh by the way—about your election to the Academy. I'd keep a special eye on the post in the next week or so if I were you."
Professor Toady was over the moon.

*****

In the meantime, Dr Pratt had informed the Vice-Chancellor that the library did indeed have books that were worth a lot of money. The Vice-Chancellor therefore asked that an emergency meeting of the library committee be summoned, and exercised his right as Vice-Chancellor to attend it *ex officio*. The sole item on the agenda was to consider the sale of certain books of value from the university library (for Vice-Chancellor Tinker was still determined to get his helicopter).

Owing to the short notice at which the Committee meeting was called, only the Librarian, the Vice-Chancellor, Professor Toady, and Professor Zigmund of the department of Applied Economics were present.

Dr Pratt laid the list of twenty incunables before the meeting, and a note of their value, £20,000 at a conservative estimate. He pointed out that these books were in Latin, German and Italian, and had not been consulted for over twenty years, as the library records showed. They were in any case not available for borrowing. Their disposal would therefore make the library more efficient, and was in accordance with the library's accepted policy of disposing of unwanted and unused items.

Vice-Chancellor Tinker proposed a formal motion that the books be sold.

Professors Toady and Zigmund vied for the honour of formally seconding the motion. Professor Toady, as the senior of the two, won. The motion was carried *nem. con.*

"Now, as to where we sell them?" said Dr Pratt.

"Sotheby's or Christie's?" suggested Vice-Chancellor Tinker.

"I would recommend not, Vice-Chancellor. I take it we are not anxious to attract too much publicity—which we might get if we sold them in London. Representatives of the press go to those auctions, you know."   .

"Ah," said Vice-Chancellor Tinker thoughtfully. Certainly he could appreciate the force of that argument. The press were so apt to misinterpret perfectly sensible decisions taken by universities. Better not let meddlesome reporters get hold of this one.

"If I may suggest, Mr Vice-Chancellor, Sir?" put in Professor Toady. "Sell them to Hay-on-Wye. There's a lot of bookshops there. That way, the matter could be kept all very discreet."

"Right, Pratt, see to it, will you?" remarked the Vice-Chancellor. "I think that concludes the business. Thank you for your assistance, gentlemen."

"A pleasure to be of service, Vice-Chancellor, " answered Dr Pratt, Professor Toady and Professor Zigmund with one voice.

*****

It took a little longer for Mr Singleton to find an occasion when Professor Bodgering was at Surleighwick. But at last, he caught up with him during that brief window of opportunity between Professor Bodgering arriving for his weekly visit in Jolly's car in time for coffee at 11.15am, and departing after lunch at 2.15pm.

'Sir Hugh''s card was sent in, and Professor Bodgering felt the same surge of wild hope that Professor Toady had experienced. At last, after years of neglect, the outstanding merits of his short but superlatively brilliant monograph on *Tamburlaine* had been recognised, and he, Professor Bodgering, would be Bodgering of the Academy!

He signalled for Jolly to pour out two generous vodka and limes for himself and his distinguished visitor. After the usual pleasantries, 'Sir Hugh' got to the point.

"What do you know about the *Circulation of the Blood*?"

"Only what the medicos tell me," gasped Professor Bodgering. "That's the problem with my lungs, really. It doesn't circulate properly. But I'm in good shape you know! I'm not on the sick list. I'm up to the responsibilities of the Fellowship, no doubt about that."

"No, I fear you misunderstand," said Mr Singleton. "I meant the work by Harvey—it's your period, I believe."

Was it? Professor Bodgering thought hard. Dimly he remembered. Wasn't there a Harvey at Cambridge a few years ahead of Marlowe?

"Ah, you mean the writer?"

"Naturally."

"Well, we have his works at the Centre for Marlowe and Elizabethan Studies. Not a dramatist of course, but he wrote a famous Essex guide book, *Let's all go to Saffron Walden* I think it was called."

Mr Singleton began to feel that he was now getting out of his depth. Silently he passed over the photocopy of the *De motu cordis* book.

"This is the Harvey I mean," he said.

Professor Bodgering's eyes lit upon the nice engraving of the angel. Of course, that's where Harvey got his Christian name from, he had been named after an angel.

"Yes, that's the man, Gabriel Harvey, that's what his name is."

"I gather the late Professor Houghton had one of these. The Academy might be interested in buying it."

"Oh no, I don't think poor old Jim went in for Gabriel Harvey—not his period you know."

Professor Bodgering sat expectantly in his wheelchair, waiting for 'Sir Hugh' to tell him the glad tidings.

Mr Singleton decided he wasn't going to get very far with

Professor Bodgering. The man was either very very cunning, or a complete cretin. He would wait for the further reports from his agents before deciding which. Abruptly, he stood up to leave.

"About my election to the Academy?" wheezed Professor Bodgering, with hopeful expression.

"Ah yes—" 'Sir Hugh' tapped his nose. "Strictly between ourselves, of course—I think I can say that if you keep watching the post you may hear something to your advantage." Mr Singleton left, and Professor Bodgering eagerly riffled through the mountain of mail on his desk looking for one with the Academy's logo on it, but to no avail.

*****

Then Mr Singleton wandered over to the library and looked up William Harvey's *De motu cordis* on the computer. And on the screen the message programmed by Dr Pratt flashed up, 'Special Reserve Collection. In Binding. On Loan to Shanghai Exhibition. Readers wishing to consult this volume should type in their library card number.' Mr Singleton considered the matter thoughtfully, but did not type in any number. Then he returned to his office to consider the best way of approaching Dr Pratt.

Two days later, Dr Pratt was sitting at his desk when Sarah-Jane entered with an engraved pasteboard in her hand. Dr Pratt took it and read:

Dr Irving P. Hottlesham III	Vanderbuilt House
Librarian	Providence
Library of Congress	Rhode Island
Washington D.C.	

"Dr Hottlesham finds himself unexpectedly passing through Surleighwick. He apologises for the lack of notice, but he has read and admired your articles in the *Journal of Library Science*. He hopes that it will be possible for you to see him."

"Why, show him in, Sarah-Jane."

Mr Singleton was ushered into the room, with a pair of thin rolled-gold pince-nez spectacles on his nose. He carried a broad-brimmed hat in one hand, and a rolled up copy of the previous day's *Washington Post* and a silver-topped black cane in the other. In a cultivated East Coast accent, convincing enough to deceive anyone who was not a native American speaker, Mr Singleton began:

"Dr Pratt, it is a pleasure to meet you, Sir. I have long admired your brilliant writings in the library journals. I find myself quite unexpectedly passing through your lovely city of Surleighwick, and thought I would avail myself of the opportunity to pay my respects."

"Dr Hottlesham—what an unexpected honour. Please sit down. You'll take some tea, I hope. Sarah-Jane, will you bring us both some tea and biscuits?"

"I have taken the liberty of having a little look round your library here in the last half-hour or so. Dr Pratt, you have a real fine library here. Of course it's not as big as the LOC, but impressive all the same. And you certainly have gotten a lot of computer terminals in the place."

Dr Pratt was flattered and touched by this interest from the librarian of the largest library in the world.

"Yes, we're really very small here," he replied modestly.

"Even so, you have some mighty fine books. And I was rather surprised, I don't mind confessing, to see that you have a book for which the LOC has been searching for quite a while. I expect you know all about the wonderful mechanical collation of the eighty Shakespeare folios done twenty years ago by our sister library, the Folger? Well, the LOC has a project for applying this technique to other texts. Right now, we're doing it for William Harvey's famous work on the circulation of the blood, the *De motu cordis*. And checking through your catalogue, I see that you have one in your library. Dr Pratt, may I see the book? I don't supppose you'd be willing to sell such a treasure, but we'd pay handsomely for the loan of it for a month or two. Anyone who could help us towards this would certainly feel our generosity in full. How would you like to come over to Washington for a month with all expenses paid and an honorarium of say £10,000? Help me fix this loan of your copy, and we'd be eternally grateful."

The colour drained from Dr Pratt's face. Why on earth had he been so stupid as to put that fake entry in the catalogue?

Hesitantly he said:

"That's very generous, but we don't lend books from Surleighwick—not rare books, anyway."

"But Dr Pratt, your catalogue says 'On loan to Shanghai Exhibition'. If the Chinese commies can have it on loan, surely you wouldn't refuse it to the greatest library in the Western world?"

Dr Pratt did not know what to say.

"Well, I'll see what I can do," he lied. "I'll look into the matter, try and find out where the book is. It may be still in binding."

"When does the Shanghai exhibition start? I shall be in China next week. Maybe I can get a sight of the book there."

"Er, I'll look it up and let you know."

Dr Pratt stood up and held out his hand.

Mr Singleton ignored it.

"Goodbye, Dr Pratt," he said coldly as he left.

*****

Back in his office in the centre of Surleighwick, Mr Singleton consulted the reports of his agents. First, on Professor Toady:
'Professor Toady seems to live a regular, but boring life. Leaves house at 10 am. Into the Arts faculty at 10.30 am. Coffee from 11 am to 11.45 am. 11.45-12 noon, drinks whisky in his room. Noon

to 2.30 pm., lunches with cronies at the Three Blind Mice. Leaves
for home at 3.30 pm. Has dull wife and two daughters. Bon viveur
and extravagant, but not in debt apart from credit card debts of
£800.'

Then on Professor Bodgering:
'Most days can be seen staring vacantly out at the countryside from
his bedroom window at Ratford. Visits Surleighwick once a week.
Arrives Surleighwick c.11 am, leaves c. 2.30 pm. Lives alone. An
object of derision and scorn to his colleagues.

Finally on Dr Pratt:
'Private life appears blameless. Works library hours, arriving 9 am
and leaving often not until 7 pm or even 8 pm. Seems happily
married. No known financial problems.'

Then Mr Singleton wrote his report to the Vice-Chancellor.

```
Dear Henry,
    I have looked into 'Aunt Jemima's' allegations,
which seem to be true. Toady is a vain, idle, useless,
self-indulgent fellow. He apparently genuinely be-
lieves the De motu cordis is in Romanian. Gave bad
advice to Mrs Houghton, but not I think guilty of
deliberate fraud.
    Bodgering I find to have almost completely lost
touch with reality. He is clearly clueless about the
significance of the De motu cordis. Prone to
delusions. He seemed to think Harvey was the
Archangel Gabriel. He is probably mad. To be
perfectly frank, I am surprised that he is still in
full-time employment at Surleighwick. I know the
general standard of the Surleighwick professoriate
is mediocre, but even so! Bodgering is a virtually
total absentee, and only comes in for coffee and
lunch once a week. If I were you I'd sack him and
save his salary!
    The villain of the piece is certainly Pratt. He
knows about the book, and can't produce it. Is shifty
and evasive when confronted about the matter. He had
the book, and has undoubtedly disposed of it, though
whether his motive is criminal or not is unclear. I
```

suggest you bug your office and confront him with
the charge that he has disposed of the work. He will
not stand up well to interrogation. Why don't you
ask Chief Superintendant Mattingly at the next Lodge
meeting on Thursday if he'll give him a little
grilling? Looking forward to seeing you then, and
we can both have a word with him.
Kind regards,
Arthur Singleton.

Mr Singleton enclosed his bill for £12,000 plus £10,000
expenses, and sent off the letter.

*****

Vice-Chancellor Tinker was well pleased with the outcome
of this little investigation. It was well worth paying £22,000 from
university funds to have Bodgering, Pratt and Toady thus placed
in his power. He resolved to start first with Dr Pratt, and at the
lodge meeting Chief Superintendent Mattingly fell in with his and
Mr Singleton's suggestion that Dr Pratt should be questioned in
the Vice-Chancellor's office.

Three days later, Dr Pratt was startled to receive an abrupt
summons to present himself in the Vice-Chancellor's office. Such
a thing had never happened before. Nervously he reported to the
ante-room to the ante-room of the Vice-Chancellor's second Personal Assistant's secretary. There he was kept waiting for one hour
and a half, until he was at last ushered into the Principal Personal
Assistant's office. Then, after another hour's wait, by now demor-
alised, he was ushered into the Vice-Chancellor's office, where Mr
Tinker sat at his desk flanked by Miss Carstairs and Miss Bimbaud
to one side, and Chief Superintendant Mattingly, a stocky, run-to-
seed, florid, raddled individual in a crumpled, badly fitting suit, on
the other. Dr Pratt was not asked to sit down.

"Ah Pratt," said the Vice-Chancellor, sipping his tea. "This is

Chief Superintendant Mattingly of the CID. "He has some questions to ask you on a very grave matter. I should recommend complete honesty on your part."

Without a pause Chief Superintendant Mattingly began the interrogation.

"This is a very serious matter Dr Pratt. You are suspected of trafficking in stolen property, viz, a copy of the *De motu cordis* by William Harvey, worth at least £100,000. We know you had it in your hands. Now, you will either tell me the truth, in which case, in consultation with Vice-Chancellor Tinker, it may just be possible to treat you leniently, or you will tell me a lie, in which case I shall take you back to the station and have you beaten up. Which is it to be?"

Dr Pratt thought quickly. The game was up!

"All right," he said wearily. "If you want to know the truth, the book was sold by the library to Odds and Ends of Hay-on-Wye. My secretary can confirm that, as well as Odds and Ends too. I didn't know its value, but I tried to buy the book back when the VC first expressed an interest in it. Unfortunately it had been sold on. But I am not a criminal. I gained nothing personally from the sale. My only fault was not realising what it was worth. Professor Toady and Professor Bodgering told me it was a nineteenth-century Romanian novel, so I thought it was worthless. I believed them. It's all their fault. We have long had a policy of disposing of books in languages not studied at Surleighwick. It was approved by the library committee, and so, thinking the book was in Romanian, I was acting in accordance with that policy. But it's Toady and Bodgering's fault really, they're academics, and they said the book was worthless. Mrs Houghton will confirm that."

The story had the ring of truth. Chief Superintendant Mattingly nodded at the Vice-Chancellor. Dr Pratt was asked to wait outside, and then Chief Superintendent Mattingly started to speak:

"Well, er, as I see it, Henry, I'm inclined to believe that story.

Yes, I think I believe it. I mean, it's obvious, isn't it? I can of course check the details with Mrs Houghton. Yes, Mrs Houghton will soon say whether his story is true or false. Yes, Mrs Houghton will be able to confirm whether Bodgering and Toady said what they did say. I'm sure he's telling the truth. It can easily be checked. Why lie about something that can so easily be checked? Yes, I think it's clear that the story is true. I mean, why lie about something as easy to check as that? I think it's hard to see why he would lie on a matter that can so easily be checked. Yes, I think he's telling the truth."

"Thanks, Tom. I think you're right. You'll check with Mrs Houghton and Dr Pratt's secretary and Odds and Ends of course? And then I think we can call the matter closed. Many thanks."

Chief Superintendant Mattingly left the room, and Vice-Chancellor Tinker indicated to Miss Carstairs and Miss Bimbaud to show Dr Pratt back into the room, and to leave them for a private (though bugged) conversation, on which, whilst it was in progress, the two young ladies naturally eavesdropped through the hidden mikes.

Vice-Chancellor Tinker was irritated that Dr Pratt had disposed of a valuable book—but he was pleased to have such a hold over the man.

Dr Pratt, crestfallen, was ushered back into the room.

Vice-Chancellor Tinker offered him some tea.

"Well, Pratt," he said, "I'm glad to find that you are absolved of criminal intent. Apparently, you were just a fool, and misled by Toady and Bodgering. Now, I see no reason why this little matter cannot be satisfactorily hushed up. No one knows the whole story but you and I."

"But Professor Toady has been enquiring about the book," put in Dr Pratt, relieved.

"I don't think we need worry about him, do you?" said Vice-Chancellor Tinker. "Any trouble from him, and just refer him to me. As I was saying this matter can quite satisfactorily be hushed up. You made a mistake, true. Now, what I want you to do is this. The university urgently needs £600,000. There are plenty of rare books in the university library that no-one ever uses. So, and this is between ourselves, you just sell £600,000 of them on the quiet, and we'll say no more about this little peccadillo of yours."

"But they're all in the catalogue," protested Dr Pratt doubt-fully. "What if someone wants to read them?"

"My dear Pratt! Use your initiative. The catalogue's on computer, isn't it? Just delete them from the computer as you sell them. No-one will know. You said yourself that most of these books haven't been read for twenty years. After all, you wouldn't want the Library Association to know about your foolish mistake would you?"

"OK, I'll do it. It may take a little time, though."

"Oh, I think we can allow you, say, two months?"

"Thank you Vice-Chancellor. I'm truly sorry for the mistake. But it was Professor Toady and Professor Bodgering's fault really."

The Vice-Chancellor dismissed Dr Pratt, summoned Miss Bimbaud to mix a martini from his cocktail cabinet, and spent the rest of the afternoon savouring the roasting he was going to give to Professors Toady and Bodgering. Yes! He would give them a real fright with the information which he now had on them.

His determination in this respect was strengthened by another memo he had received from AUNT JEMIMA:

Dear CUDDLES,
Glad you liked my last. Why don't you ask to see Bodgering? He's senile and gaga—and a clapped out lecher to boot! His lecture last week was a shambles. Just ask anyone who was there. Why don't you sack him? Love,
AUNT JEMIMA

The Vice-Chancellor rubbed his hands in satisfaction.

CHAPTER TWELVE

SURLEIGHWICK MEDLEY: MARCH 1991

'La mort ne surprend point le sage:
Il est toujours prêt à partir,
S'étant su lui-même avertir
Du temps où l'on se doit résoudre à ce passage.'
(Jean de La Fontaine, *La Mort et le Mourant*)

Spring term had wearily unfolded at Surleighwick, and it was now the middle of March. The first crocuses and daffodils were trying to force their way through the frozen ground.

Amidst mounting disquiet at the way in which the English department was being run, members had assembled for the third staff meeting of the spring term. The meeting seemed likely to be a contentious one, since Mrs Quick had succeeded in having the question of the finances of the department placed on the agenda. She had been horrified to hear of the £5,000 which little Jack Napes had spent out of the department's funds, for she guessed that this was likely to affect the amount of money available for her and Dr Crumpet to travel to the next conference on Feminism in Nineteenth-Century Writing, to be held at the University of Skelmerdale in the coming July.

Moreover Mrs Quick, sternly moralistic, had seen the opportunity to make some anti-man capital out of the fact that twenty-five men, but only two women, had been charged with disorderly conduct during the English department trip to Hay-on-Wye. So she had come to the meeting prepared to do battle.

Professor Bodgering could dimly sense that there might be trouble brewing, and he was determined to meet it in his usual manner—by running away. He had arranged with Jolly that if he tapped the left arm of his wheelchair three times, she was to hustle him away to his car on grounds of ill-health.

As soon as apologies for absence had been taken, and the usual half-hour's editorial attention had been paid to the minutiae of the minutes, 'Chairperson's Communications' was reached. Before Professor Bodgering could say anything, little Jack Napes had shot up his hand and was unstoppably launched on to a speech.

"Mr Chairperson, may I be the first to congratulate you on two matters which really ought to be on Chairman's Communications, but which your own natural modesty prevents you from calling attention to on your own account? I refer of course to your impending election to the British Academy." (For Professor Bodgering had not been slow to spread the news of his imminent election to that body, which he confidently expected any day now after the visit of 'Sir Hugh'.) "Yes, Mr Chairperson, I consider this to be not only a worthy and much overdue tribute to your great scholarship, but also a tribute to the whole department, which got a star for the international excellence of its research under your leadership. May I formally propose a vote of congratulation to Professor Bodgering, FBA?"

Professor Bodgering bared his teeth in a parody of a smile as Dr Chittering hastened to say how thoroughly he agreed with every word that Jack Napes had said.

"There's many a slip 'twixt cup and lip," said Mrs Quick in a stage whisper to Dr Crumpet, to the approving nods of several members of the department in earshot. Really, if Bodgering of all people was to be an FBA, what was the Academy coming to? It was the old boy network again, thought Mrs Quick to herself bitterly. Women were notoriously under-represented on that body. But no-one had sufficient nerve to challenge the motion of congratulation, which was carried without the formality of a vote. Professor Bodgering grinned a feeble and sickly grin, savouring the first fruits of his soon-to-be-announced election. He had already sent off a statement about himself to the next *Factfile*, extolling the merits of his book on *Tamburlaine*.

Pleased at the success of his motion, Jack Napes also rashly proposed another motion of congratulation on the success of Professor Bodgering's latest lecture on *Tamburlaine*. Here, little Jack was a trifle ill-advised. He had not himself been present at the lecture, but had foolishly listened to Professor Bodgering's own account of its great success.

So Mrs Quick, who could stand little Jack's cant and humbug no longer, was moved to do something almost unprecedented at the University of Surleighwick, namely, to speak her mind truthfully.

"I find it surprising that such a motion can be brought to this Board—especially since the lecture in question was abandoned after two minutes owing to equipment failure."

"But the two minutes were really first rate," protested Professor Bodgering.

"May I seek to enlist the support of colleagues against the implied slur on our Chairman imputed by Mrs Quick?" said Dr Chittering angrily.

"May I say how much I agree with Dr Chittering's remarks?" added little Jack.

Doctors Showman and Spark looked up from their proofs and book catalogues. This was a bit more like it!

"I wasn't at the lecture myself," put in Dr Spark, "but I certainly see no reason why any colleague needs to be formally congratulated for doing what is after all her job, viz. lecturing. I move 'next business'."

The proposal was seconded by the grouchy Ivan Hoe. With a shocked expression on his face, Professor Bodgering, seething with rage inside, and wishing that he could murder Mrs Quick, proceeded to Chairperson's communications and the other items on the agenda.

"Let's have another session tonight," whispered Mrs Quick to Dr Crumpet. "'Psycho' is simply asking to be put down."

Dr Crumpet nodded vigorously.

Then came the discussion of the department's finances.

"Well," gasped Professor Bodgering, "it's difficult to know the present position. I haven't had a recent statement of account."

"My latest travel claim form was returned marked 'Insufficient funds: Return to Drawer'," observed Dr Spark cynically and helpfully.

"Ah," gasped Professor Bodgering.

"Mr Chairperson, is it not true that a large sum was recently expended on the purchase of Romanian books, and that this has effectively drained our funds?" asked Dr Blodgett.

"I don't know anything about that," gasped Professor Bodgering. "It's nothing to do with me. It was all Jack Napes' idea. But I'm sure there's lots of money left."

"No there isn't," put in Mrs Quick, who only yesterday had spoken to the Finance department in a gruff voice in the persona of Professor Bodgering, and had found that the department was now overdrawn, and that all further payments had been frozen, as a result of the expenditure at Hay-on-Wye of £5,000. "I know for a fact we're bankrupt this year."

There was wide concern at the news that no more travel claims or conference expenses would be claimable for the rest of the session.

"I believe, though, Mr Chairperson, that you authorised all payments from the fund?" continued Mrs Quick.

"It's nothing to do with me," said Professor Bodgering. "Ask Jack all about it. It was his idea. I have to go now."

He banged on his wheelchair, and Jolly hastily moved the smelly, wizened figure out of the room.

Mrs Quick opened the windows to clear the air, and then by general agreement took over the Chair.

"Well, perhaps Mr Napes would like to explain just what went on?" she said at length.

For once poor little Jack Napes was lost for words.

"It wasn't my idea," he lied hastily. "It was Professor Bodgering's fault. He told me to spend money on Romanian books. It wasn't my idea, no certainly not, I just did what I was told. I believe there was a hope we might get the minority languages money...." His voice tailed off, and he fell into an embarrassed silence, the focus of the hostile attention of his colleagues.

"Well," said Mrs Quick, relishing the chance to humiliate little Jack, "I think it's clear that Jack has behaved in a very foolish and improvident fashion, and that it's his fault we'll all get no conference grants for the rest of the year. And that brings me to another matter. The disgraceful behaviour of certain of the *male* students on the expedition to Hay-on-Wye, indubitably organised by Jack Napes there. As you know this got the department a very bad press indeed. I saw some of the vomiting myself, whilst poor Dr Crumpet there was dreadfully embarrassed by the loutish and quite unseemly behaviour of some of the third-year boys. I should like to propose a formal vote of censure on Mr Napes."

"Seconded," called Dr Crumpet, greatly daring.

The motion was put to the vote and carried.

Poor little Jack Napes, to Mrs Quick's immense delight, burst into tears and ran, extremely upset, from the room.

*****

The time had come when Professor Toady felt it advisable to seek advice from the university doctors about the stabbing pains in his chest and stomach which he had recently experienced. He stood there in his trousers and vest, as the newly qualified, but cool and competent Dr Janet French first took his blood pressure, and then moved her stethoscope over his pallid, flabbby skin. Then she unhooked the stethoscope from her ears, and made a few notes in a little notebook.

"Well, have you found it, why am I getting these pains?" Professor Toady asked anxiously.

Dr French did not answer directly.

"Tell me, Professor Toady, how much exercise do you take?"

"Oh, quite a lot. I never use the Arts faculty lift but always walk up the stairs."

"And what did you have for lunch today?"

"Oh, nothing very much, just soup, game pie and chips, a few pints of beer, a cup of coffee and two Kit-Kats."

"And would you describe yourself as a light, a moderate, or a heavy drinker?"

"Oh, a light drinker definitely. I rarely drink more than five pints at lunchtime, and not more than a bottle of wine with my dinner. And I don't often get through more than a bottle of brandy and a bottle of whisky a week."

"Well, I think I've found the cause of the trouble, Professor Toady," replied Dr French. She jabbed the index finger of her left hand first into his chest, then into his stomach.

"You're too fat, Professor Toady. You don't take enough exercise. You eat too much; and you certainly drink too much. I'm going to put you on a strict diet, and you'll have to cut out alcohol all together for the next year or so!"

"Nonsense my dear." Really, thought Professor Toady, it was too much to be prodded and treated in this childish way by a mere chit of a girl. Old Doctor Armstrong, who had just retired, had been so much more understanding of his ailments.

"You're newly qualified, aren't you? I think I'd like a second opinion from one of your colleagues, one of your more *experienced* colleagues," Dean Toady emphasised.

"All right. I'll ask Dr Chamberlain to come in."

That was more like it, thought Professor Toady. Dr Chamberlain sounded like a much more stable and reliable person. He was much put out when Dr Veronica Chamberlain, an attractive young woman of some thirty years, entered the room. She rapidly confirmed Dr French's diagnosis. Really, what was the university coming to, thought Professor Toady, as he put on his shirt. Why weren't there any older men doctors around at the Health Service nowadays? He was tactless enough to ask Drs French and Chamberlain precisely that question.

"Simple, Professor Toady," smiled Dr Chamberlain sweetly. "The University of Surleighwick employs very young doctors because we're cheaper. It's part of the economy drive you know. Dr Armstrong was paid much more than we are because he was older."

"Hmmppph" responded Professor Toady. "We'll see about that. I am the Dean of the faculty of Arts you know, and therefore a very important person in the administration of the University of Surleighwick. This policy of employing young women like yourself is clearly all wrong. I'll see what I can do to change it."

Professor Toady grumpily took his leave.

"Silly old sod," said Dr Chamberlain to Dr French, sticking out her tongue and pulling a face as the door closed behind Professor Toady's fat form. "I'm enjoying my social life here, and I'm damned if I'm going to let that pompous bugger interfere with it." And indeed both doctors enjoyed a good social life at Surleighwick, taking care only to date each other's patients for reasons of medical ethics. But they enjoyed the predominantly youthful nature of their practice, and Dr French, who had led a sheltered life, was now finding it an enjoyable and mind-broadening experience to accompany the Surleighwick rugby teams on their away fixtures, and join in their drinking sessions, and minister to their aches and pains.

"What did he say he was?" continued Dr Chamberlain. "Dean of the faculty of Arts, and an important member of the university?

Sounds like a case of paranoid delusions to me—he seems obsessed with his self-importance."

"Pity his wife, " giggled Dr French. "It must be like going to bed with a jellyfish. When I put my hand on his chest I really had to press hard to get to the bone."

The two sporting and robust young doctors broke off from their routine to make a pot of tea, and to gossip about their latest dates, determined that Professor Toady was not going to have any effect on them.

*****

Secretly and unobtrusively, late at night when everyone had gone home, Dr Pratt had started to abstract from the rare book room some of the items which he guessed might be valuable. Already two hundred items had been removed, and deleted from the computer. Above the Surleighwick University ownership mark, he had placed a stamp reading 'Surplus to the requirements of', and then he had inked out the whole. These he had then fed out to a certain number of book dealers at Hay-on-Wye and in a fifty mile radius of Surleighwick.

And thus it was that Dr Hanwell, paying another visit to Hay-on-Wye with Ruth a month after his return from the United States, was surprised to see a thirteenth-century manuscript of Clarbald of Arras for sale at Old Leather Bindings. This was priced at £600 (Dr Pratt had got £250 for it, neither he nor the shop having the remotest idea of how to price the work). Dr Hanwell was not sure of its value either, but he did not own any medieval manuscripts, and he reasoned to himself that for a work of self-evident rarity by an interesting author £600 was probably cheap, or at the very least a reasonable price. So he had charged it to his Barclaycard again. He was particularly intrigued to see the manuscript for sale at Hay-on-Wye, since he recognised it as one that he had consulted at the University of Surleighwick. Dr Hanwell had also bought, after even more hesitation, for £1,000, a copy of Aristotle's *De animalibus*, a handsome Venetian folio of 1476, which he happened to know was the first biological work ever to be printed, and which he had also had occasion to consult at Surleighwick. This also, like the Clarbald of Arras manuscript, had its library ownership stamp heavily blotted out by black ink, which had considerably reduced its value. Dr Pratt had been happy to get £500 for it. At first, Dr Hanwell suspected that these books had been stolen from Surleighwick University library. The proprietor of Old Leather Bindings had however assured him that the books had been sold by Dr Pratt personally.

So, with his credit card now strained to its limit, Dr Hanwell was proudly showing off his oldest book to Ruth as they sat in the tea shop at 4.30 pm, eating buttered toast and drinking steaming cups of reviving tea (for it was a rainy day at Hay, and the wind was driving down from the Black Mountains).

"Golly, 1476—that's over 500 years ago," said Ruth, her eyes like saucers.

"Yes, it's now my oldest book—and I'm unlikely to get one older than that."

Ruth too had bought some interesting books at a more modest level, including a beautifully illustrated *History of Stuffed Animal Toys*, which had a lovely illustration of a Timmy the Tiger looka-like, the *Collected Works* of Keble, and an attractive copy of Frederick Burnaby's *On Horseback through Asia Minor*, a cele-brated Victorian travel book. Finally, Ruth had come across a real find, *La scienza in cucina* (1891), by the merchant banker Pelle-grini Artusi, the Italian equivalent of Mrs Beeton.

"I've been after one of these for a long time," she explained. "It's a very famous book, and quite hard to get hold of now. Look, it has the most wonderfully original method for making farfalle in it."

And Ruth opened the book in the middle, and gave an extempore and fluent translation of the recipe.

"I didn't know you knew Italian so well," said Dr Hanwell in astonishment.

Ruth arched her eyebrows slightly, placed her elbows on the table, and rested her chin quizzically on the back of her hands.

A little smile played around her lips, as she said, in fluent Italian with a slight trace of a Genoese accent:

"My dear Dr Hanwell, you're not the only one who reads books and knows the odd language or two you know!" And, still in her excellent Italian Ruth gave Dr Hanwell a little lecture on the history of cookery books, from Athenaeus' *Deipnosophistae* and Apicius onwards. She told him about the medieval manuscripts of those authors, and about their sixteenth- and seventeenth-century printings. She discussed details of meals in Juvenal and Petronius. She digressed on alimentary metaphors in Pindar, in Quintilian and the Bible, and on the Indian philosophical text entitled 'The New-churned Butter of the Milk of Perfection'. She reminded Dr Hanwell that to St Augustine, God had been an 'interior cibus', and that Walafrid Strabo had called his prose life of St. Gall an 'agreste pulmentum' which he would flavour with salt. She observed that Gregory the Great had called St Augustine's writings 'wheaten flour' and designated his own as 'bran'; and that Eupolemius had ended the second book of his *Messiad* with the hope that his work might be milk for the tender and strong meat for the strong. From there, she was led to point out that Sigebert of Gembloux had written of ginger and pellitory root. She told him that St Francis de Sales had observed. 'Si la charité est un lait, la dévotion en est la cresme'. Finally, Ruth discoursed on the place of cooking in the hierarchies of knowledge propounded by the *Dialogo della rhetorica* (1542) of Sperone Speroni, and the *Il sogno* of Gabriele Zinano (1590). From cooking she was led, by a natural association of thought, to talk of Wyclif's arguments about transubstantiation, on the one hand, and, on the other, to a little excursus on perfumery throughout the ages, on nard and spikenard and basalm.

Dr Hanwell could tell that he was being teased, but he took it all in good part, and was impressed by Ruth's range of references and her quite clearly formidable knowledge of her hobby.

"Very well my dear Miss Henderson, you win! Come on, let's make a start, and you can tell me more about the history of condiments and spices over a good steak on the way back!"

They gathered up their books, and began the journey through the darkened lanes back to Surleighwick.

*****

Flushed by her victory over little Jack Napes, and greatly daring, Mrs Quick, who was on the faculty Board, had formally asked that 'English Department Finances' should be raised as an item of 'Members' Business'.

Dean Eustace Toady had joyfully included that item on the Agenda, and now, at the second faculty Board of the spring term, he was sitting in his padded chair at the centre of the table, waiting for Mrs Quick to introduce her points. Professor Bodgering was not present. The faculty Board always met on a Wednesday afternoon, and he only ever came to Surleighwick on a Thursday. Little Jack Napes was also on faculty—but he had taken fright, and sent in his apologies. Mrs Quick was not without friends on the Board—but Dean Toady knew that the English department had far more enemies than friends in the other departments, who had been irritated by the late Professor Houghton's superior manner, and the way in which he had always seemed to claim that the workings of the English department were ineffably superior to the goings on of all other departments in the faculty.

"For the record, Mr Dean, may I start by asking formally how much money is left in the English department's maintenance grant for the session?" enquired Mrs Quick.

The Dean had come prepared:

"The department has a debt of £176," he said gravely, and with a secret smile.

"I fear, then, Dean, that I have to request extra funds. Owing to an unfortunate misunderstanding, a certain sum of money was expended on books without proper consultation in the department, and now none of us can get conference grants."

A warm glow of pleasure suffused the Dean's body. He knew that all he had to do was sit there impassively and let Board members from other departments obstruct Mrs Quick's request.

Professor Stevenson, who had so often been himself criticised and ridiculed for dullness and stupidity at the Board, was quick to go on to the attack.

"If I may say so, Mr Dean Sir, I am surprised to find this item on the agenda. If the English department has run out of money already, that is unfortunate for them, but I do not see that it concerns this Board. Surely the administration of the fund is an internal matter, and should be so resolved?"

Fat Dean Toady nodded his head gravely.

"May I enquire Professor Bodgering's reaction?" asked the gloomy Professor Knatchbull, who knew that Bodgering was not present.

("Who's Professor Bodgering?" Professor Middleton asked his neighbour in genuine bewilderment, for he had only been Professor of Philosophy for four years, and genuinely did not know.)

"I fear that Professor Bodgering is not with us this afternoon," the Dean said happily.

"In that case, Mr Dean Sir, I move next business," put in Professor Stevenson." The matter cannot be of consequence if the head of department is not here to discuss the matter."

"Seconded!" called out Professor Knatchbull.

Dean Toady put the matter to a vote, and by a large majority the Board resolved to proceed to 'Next Business'.

'Next Business' was 'Any Other Business'. Professor Stevenson, pleased for once to have been on the winning side of a faculty Board argument, then raised his hand and said:

"Mr Dean Sir, if I may make so bold, may I say, Sir, how delighted we are, what a tribute to your wise leadership of the faculty it is, to hear the news of your imminent election to the Academy? May I propose a formal vote of congratulation? Your election will be a fitting honour for Surleighwick Arts, and a recognition of the high regard in which our faculty is held, not only in the University of Surleighwick, but also in other universities throughout the country and indeed the world. Well done, Sir!"

About half the assembled company banged their hands on the table. Dean Toady smirked, revelling in the respect, envy, and jealousy that he could detect in the eyes of most of his colleagues. The motion was carried by default, *nem. con.*

*****

Professor Bodgering was not in the least surprised to receive a summons to present himself in person at the Vice-Chancellor's office the following week. He had no doubt that the Vice-Chancellor had heard of his impending election to the British Academy, and wished to present his personal congratulations—and perhaps offer a *douceur* to keep him at Surleighwick, since no doubt other universities would soon be clamouring for him to accept a distinguished professorship elsewhere. Yes! Everyone would want him now! And then again, Vice-Chancellor Tinker would no doubt wish to congratulate him on the brilliance of his last lecture. A pity it had been curtailed by equipment failure, but one had to admit that the audience had loved it! So Professsor Bodgering sat in his

room leering at himself in a mirror, whilst Jolly brushed his
scurvy-ridden, thinning, wispy hair, sprayed deodorant all over his
person, arranged the tartan rug across his knees, and ministered a
ten-minute fix of oxygen and a treble lime and vodka. Then she
wrapped his yellow checked muffler around his neck, and pushed
him over to the administration building. There, to Professor Bodgering's surprise, instead of being ushered into the VC's office
straightaway, he was kept waiting in the Personal Assistant's
secretary's ante-room for a whole hour and a half. Ah well, no
doubt the VC was a very busy man. Finally, when Miss Bimbaud
had awoken the Vice-Chancellor from his afternoon nap, and
together with Miss Carstairs had assisted him to the seat behind
his desk, Professor Bodgering, now tired and exhausted, and badly
needing another treble vodka and lime, was ushered in to see the
Vice-Chancellor.

Vice-Chancellor Tinker was horrified when he saw the frail,
wizened wheelchair-bound figure. He could sympathise with a
disability, being himself in need of crutches. But Mr Singleton and
Aunt Jemima were right! Good heavens! Vice-Chancellor Tinker
looked with genuine amazement at the pathetic, shrivelled, diminutive figure before him, gasping for breath and wheezing
open-mouthed through stained yellow teeth. The man looked like
a living corpse. He was clearly unfit to fulfil even the minimal
demands which Surleighwick made on its professors. Why hadn't
that fat, lazy Dean Toady alerted him to this situation? Must he do
everything himself?

Professor Bodgering sat there expectantly, waiting for the
great man's congratulations.

"Ah, Bodgering, " said Mr Tinker disdainfully. "I wanted a
word about *The Circulation of the Blood.*"

"I'm all right, Vice-Chancellor," wheezed Professor Bodgering painfully. "Never felt better in my life. My lecture last week to
the whole of my department was a great success you know. Every

one liked it. I'm not ill, Vice-Chancellor, so I'm not going to retire on health grounds."

Aunt Jemima's observations were spot on, the man was clearly gaga! Vice-Chancellor Tinker went on:

"I understand you advised Mrs Houghton the work was not worth anything. That was a very foolish thing to do, Bodgering, and just showed up your ignorance of your own period. Fancy thinking that Harvey wrote in Romanian."

He passed over a photocopy of the title page of the *De motu cordis*.

Professor Bodgering dimly made out the figure of an angel, and was puzzled.

"It's a lie. I never did. *Let's all go to Saffron Walden* is in English," he gasped. "Anyway, how would I know? I never read anything but English, and only page three of the *Sun* at that."

Professor Bodgering stopped suddenly, realising he had been trapped into an indiscretion.

The Vice-Chancellor shook his head sadly. Aunt Jemima was right indeed. He should like to meet her! Bodgering was utterly and completely gaga.

"Yes, that brings me to another point. I'm holding you personally responsible, Bodgering, for the disgraceful, loutish, behaviour of members of your department on a recent expedition to Hay. I am informed that this was your idea. What have you got to say for yourself?"

"It wasn't my idea. It was all Napes' fault, a most irresponsible member of my department. He's to blame, not me. He organised it. I wasn't there, I was ill at home."

"Yes, you're ill, aren't you Bodgering? Don't you think you ought to retire sick?"

"Certainly not, I'm still an active lecturer," panted Professor Bodgering, groping for his oxygen mask. "Anyway, the Academy wants me, you know."

Vice-Chancellor Tinker saw no point in prolonging the interview. Bodgering was clearly a liar, a fool, and an idiot, and suffering from delusions to boot. Why on earth should the Academy, Surleighwick's well-known repertory theatre, want Professor Bodgering? Well, if they did, let them have him. He decided that in a day or two, when he had interviewed Professor Toady, he would have Professor Bodgering sacked for breach of contract. The man had published nothing for ten years—that would be sufficient cause, even without the absenteeism. It was typical of that useless Toady to be running such a hopeless faculty!

"Goodbye, Bodgering," he said coldly. "You'll be hearing from the Registrar within the week."

Professor Bodgering started to expostulate, but Mr Tinker signalled to Miss Bimbaud, who had been listening with boredom throughout the interview, to push Professor Bodgering's wheelchair out into the corridor. Without another word she did so, and Professor Bodgering found himself thrust straight outside the VC's door. It was not until two hours later, when the VC's staff went home, that Jolly, who had been waiting in the anteroom, emerged into the corridor herself to find the immobile and whimpering figure of Professor Bodgering, who was harbouring savage thoughts within his pain-racked chest.

*****

Dr Hanwell meanwhile had been doing a little research. With the aid of an ultraviolet lamp borrowed from his metallurgical friends, he had determined that his Hay-on-Wye purchases, the manuscript of Clarbald of Arras, and the edition of Aristotle's *De animalibus*, were the copies that had been in the Surleighwick University library. These items no longer appeared in the catalogue. The rare book librarian had recently taken early retirement, and Dr Pratt had refused to speak to him when he rang up to discuss the matter. So Dr Hanwell hacked into the library computer, quickly discovered the Librarian's personal password, ('Book'), and took a print-out of the minutes of the Special meeting of the Library Committee that had authorised the selling of the twenty Latin and Italian incunables. Then, back at his flat, he wrote a short article on the place of books in the modern university, suggested that the University of Surleighwick was behaving irresponsibly in selling off its incunables, asked what was happening to the money so received, and sent it off, signed 'Richard de Bury', to the *Times Higher Education Supplement*. Dr Hanwell enclosed a copy of the minutes of the special meeting of the Library Committee to cor-roborate his story. His piece was carried prominently in that newspaper a fortnight later, and was forthwith picked up sympa-thetically first by the *Times*, and then by the *Sunday Times*. Soon the University of Surleighwick once more found itself unfavour-ably in the news, to Mr Tinker's great fury. This was all that idiot Toady's fault! If only he hadn't given that silly advice about the Romanian novel, the Harvey could have been sold straight to the Baskerville Institute for a million dollars, and this whole sorry business would never have happened! It was characteristic of Surleighwick that no-one recognised 'Richard de Bury' as a *nom-de-plume*.

*****

SILVIO 'What may this be?
A woman or a Devil?
DUCHESS 'Tis a Witch sure.'
(Beaumont and Fletcher, *Women Pleas'd*)

Trusting and innocent and flushed with wine, the glamorous Dr Crumpet stood in the lounge of Mrs Quick's cottage, naked save for her Welsh Girl hat, drinking a glass of Strega from a tall-stemmed glass, and stretching out her hands towards the flickering flames of the fire. The scheming Mrs Quick had made great progress of late in her studies of witchcraft, and had drawn Dr Crumpet's attention to a passage in one of her witch books (or Female Emancipation Manuals, as she preferred to call them), which stated that the potency of a curse was tripled if uttered by a naked virgin in her twenties. Dr Crumpet had blushingly admitted that she fitted the bill (for she had shunned men since becoming a devotee of the women's movement at the age of sixteen).

"But do you think our spells are working?" asked Dr Crumpet, anxiously. "Things seem to be going well for Toady and the 'Psycho'. After all, they're both going to be FBAs."

"I'm not too sure about that," said Mrs Quick sceptically, as she leaned back on the sofa and admired Dr Crumpet's beauty, congratulating herself on the smooth-tongued way in which she had persuaded Dr Crumpet to take off all her clothes. "You haven't been at Surleighwick as long as I have, Tony my dear. When you have, you'll learn not to believe anything anyone tells you until you have hard, incontrovertible proof. I wouldn't put it past Bodgering to have simply made up the story, and Toady to have told a lie just to keep up with Bodgering. I won't believe it until I see the list in the *Times*. No, I think we're making progress. As a matter of fact, I happen to know that Toady went to the university doctors only last week seeking advice about his stomach pains. And Jolly says Bodgering is worse than usual lately. And indeed he's looking awfully ill. Haven't you noticed how pale and yellow his face has become? No, I reckon 'Psycho' is certainly on the way out."

"How do you know about Toady?" asked Dr Crumpet, curiously, strolling up and down in front of the fire (for she had gradually lost her first shyness in the presence of the sympathetic and understanding Mrs Quick). She felt delightfully decadent, and was starting to enjoy parading her loveliness for her older admirer.

"Dr Chamberlain told me, in confidence," replied Mrs Quick casually.

"But isn't that against medical ethics?"

"Yes—but we're old friends, and Veronica is sympathetic to the women's movement," replied Mrs Quick.

She poured herself and Dr Crumpet another glass of Strega, and then returned from the kitchen with a large baking bowl.

"I've a treat in store for you tonight, Tony. You're going to get the real liberating experience. This is a magic salve, which will make you feel wonderful."

"What is it?" asked Dr Crumpet nervously.

"It's from one of my manuals—it's a mixture of henbane, hemlock, mandrake, moonshade, tobacco, opium, saffron, poplar leaves, and one or two other very special ingredients."

Mrs Quick gently applied the sweetly smelling mixture to Dr Crumpet's bare shoulders, breasts, stomach, buttocks and thighs, and massaged it tenderly into her body.

Then, slowly and intensely, the two women chanted their customary charms, sang their spells, and hymned their hatred of the two old men.

Within twenty minutes, Dr Crumpet was in a kind of trance, in which she seemed to be flying through the air, stretching out her fingers, and directing streams of fiery darts from them towards the prostrate forms of Bodgering and Toady. And then she fell asleep as usual in Mrs Quick's embrace, in front of the dying embers of the fire, and gradually, over the next few hours, the hallucinogenic salve worked its way out of her system, and she awoke, late the following morning, feeling drained, shattered, and hag-ridden.

*****

Professor Toady had been racked by pains during the night,

and he hurried in to see the university doctors as soon as he arrived on campus the next morning.

"I'm in agony," he gasped, after they had kept him waiting for twenty minutes. "You've got to do something about it."

"You're sure you trust us, are you?" asked Dr Chamberlain. "I thought you thought we were too young and inexperienced."

"You were right in what you said," replied Professor Toady. "The university employs young doctors because they're cheaper. But I don't care about that now. I'm in pain. Just do something about it."

Dr Chamberlain and Dr French took off Professor Toady's shirt and sounded out his fat chest.

"What did you have for lunch yesterday, Professor Toady?"

"Oh, nothing very much, just a game pie washed down with a few pints."

"And for dinner?"

"Steak, chips, and a bottle of wine," he replied. "But I didn't have a dessert, just cheese and biscuits."

"Well, as my colleague Dr French told you when you first came to see us, the remedy is in your own hands. You're eating too much. You will simply have to cut out all that beer, wine, steak, chips and game pie."

"You've got to get me better again, Doctor. I'm needed at Surleighwick. I have to see the VC this afternoon you know. He relies on my advice. Arts is the second biggest faculty in the university. I'm an important man. You've got to give me some pills. It's no use just telling me to go on a diet. I haven't the will power."

Dr Chamberlain looked at the pathetic, quivering, wobbly figure before her, and then retired for a consultation with Dr French.

At length they returned, and gave Professor Toady a packet of pink placebos, solely to soothe his shattered nerves.

"What a fuss he makes about a spot of indigestion," remarked Dr Chamberlain after Professor Toady had left them. "What a pathetic, weak, lily-livered specimen. Do you think the VC really does rely on his advice? No wonder the university's in such a mess."

*****

That afternoon, at 2.30 pm, after Professor Toady had taken two pink pills, and confined himself to three pints of beer with his game pie, he presented himself at the Vice-Chancellor's office. No doubt the VC wanted to see him to congratulate him on his forthcoming FBA, which would be quite a feather in the cap for Surleighwick! He would be sure to get a good write up and his picture in the *Factfile* for that.

As a Dean, Professor Toady was kept waiting in the ante-room for a mere thirty-five minutes.

His face wreathed in smiles, the fat Dean entered Mr Tinker's office, and bowed obsequiously.

"Ah, Toady," said the VC, looking up from his desk at length, "I wanted a word with you."

"Is it about the Academy?" asked the fat Dean eagerly.

The VC was puzzled. Why should his Arts professors always wish to talk about the local theatre?

"No it is not. Toady, I am not at all pleased with you. I feel that you have been letting the side down. Under your Deanship, the faculty of Arts has been going down the hill. First there was that disgraceful episode with those louts from your faculty in Hay-on-Wye."

"Yes, it was disgraceful, Vice-Chancellor. I was there. They knocked me down, you know."

"What! Am I to understand that you were there yourself? This is even worse than I thought. You should be ashamed of yourself, Toady."

Professor Toady tried to explain, but the VC waved aside his protests impatiently.

"And there's another matter. I had occasion to speak to Professor Bodgering the other day, and I was *shocked* to see his condition. He is quite clearly an incompetent, and a chronic invalid into the bargain. Yet at the end of last term you recommended him to me as acting head of the English department. I'm amazed and dismayed to find you so lacking in powers of judgement, Toady."

Professor Toady began to feel unwell. It simply wasn't fair. He valued Vice-Chancellor Tinker's good opinion more than anything in the world, and now he was being blamed for things that weren't really his fault. After all, Bodgering was the next senior man, so he had to be acting head under the Surleighwick system!

"And there's another point, Toady," continued the Vice-Chancellor, "You signally failed to find me a copy of the *De motu cordis* that I asked you about a few weeks ago. I expect better than that from my Dean of Arts."

"But—." The Dean's face turned the colour of putty, and he felt a pounding in his chest.

"Furthermore, I'm told on good authority that you have been passing yourself off as an expert on Romanian, when you don't know any."

"Ah," Professor Toady gasped.

"I'm sorry, Vice-Chancellor, but none of this is my fault. It's all Bodgering's doing. He organised the trip to Hay, he told me he was in good health and could fulfil the duties of the headship. As for the Romanian, it's all a lie, a misunderstanding, I mean, why would I do that—of course Romanian is like Latin and French and I do read—"

Professor Toady cowered backwards as the Vice-Chancellor

lifted himself on to his crutches, and with a suprisingly swift sweep of his left arm swished his left crutch through the air just in front of Professor Toady's face. It was all that Toady's fault! He'd had the Harvey volume in his hands and told Mrs Houghton it wasn't worth anything! And now, just because the library had had to sell a few books to raise the money for a helicopter, the University of Surleighwick was being attacked in the Murdoch press for selling its books! And Toady had been at Hay-on-Wye too, when the university had been attacked by another Murdoch newspaper, the *Sun*. It was all Toady's fault—the useless, snivelling, pitiful sycophant. A fierce anger arose in Vice- Chancellor Tinker's heart.

"You idiot, you poltroon, you stupid incompetent! I'll see you sacked for this!"

In the office next door, Miss Carstairs and Miss Bimbaud were listening to every word with huge enjoyment via the hidden mikes.

Dean Toady backed away, as Vice-Chancellor Tinker lurched unevenly towards him, alternately swinging forward and trying to hit the Dean with his crutches. The Dean retreated into a corner of the panelled room. Dimly he could see the Vice-Chancellor's furious red face, contorted in vicious anger. There was no escape now! The Vice-Chancellor supported himself on his left crutch, seized his right crutch in the other hand by its base, and prepared to bring the thick, padded end like a club right down on the unfortunate Toady's head. Professor Toady cowered down and covered his head with his hands. Suddenly there was a strangulated 'Ah'. As William Harvey had described, the blood circulated faster and faster through the Vice-Chancellor's veins and arteries. The valves of his heart pumped more and more furiously, and the blood raced around his body. The beating of Vice-Chancellor Tinker's heart raced faster and faster. Suddenly it seemed to the Vice-Chancellor that his heart was seized in a vice and pierced by a chisel. There was a huge, blinding explosion in the centre of his body.

Vice-Chancellor Tinker's face contorted, the crutch fell from his hand, and he collapsed, dead of a heart attack brought on by extreme emotional stress, at Professor Toady's feet.

CHAPTER THIRTEEN

VICE-CHANCELLOR TOADY

'And some have greatness thrust upon them'
(William Shakespeare, *Twelfth Night*)
'As my career progressed and I worked my way up through
the party machinery to positions of power, nothing around me
changed. The corruption I faced simply became greater.'
(Boris Yeltsin, *Against the Grain*)

It took the fat Dean of Arts Toady a couple of days to recover
from the shock of being assaulted by Vice-Chancellor Tinker and
seeing him drop dead with coronary thrombosis. But then, with the
assistance of the odd bottle of brandy or two, his spirits began to
revive, and he began to enjoy the sense of importance that came
from having been the sole eyewitness to the Vice-Chancellor's
death.

"Such a tragic loss," he was saying, as he sat the following
Monday morning in the Arts common room, surrounded by a dense
crowd of professors and placemen eagerly hanging on his every
word. "I was there, you know, there when it happened. Henry had
called me over to ask my advice on some particularly tricky policy
matters—he relied on me so much you know—when, quite without
warning, he keeled over. I just don't know what the university will
do without him. He'd done so much for Surleighwick, he was one
of the finest Vice-Chancellors there was. You can imagine what a
shock it was to me personally, to be there when it happened. But I
like to think that it was some comfort to Henry, knowing that I was
with him to the last."

Professor Toady had never in his life called the Vice-Chancellor Henry, but such was the story that he was now relaying to

all and sundry. A murmur of sympathy went round the room. Poor old Eustace! What a shock it must have been for him! What shall we do without the VC? When will the funeral be? Will we get a day off? Who will take over?

"It was such a comfort to me that I could be with him to the last," Professor Toady told his fellow Deans that afternoon, at an emergency meeting of the Committee of Deans. "And I like to think that I was able to comfort him as he lay dying. 'Thanks, Eustace old man,' were the last words that he spoke. And you know, I may be an old sentimentalist, but I feel very humble that I was privileged to be with him in his last moments."

The fat Dean of Arts removed his spectacles, and brushed his eyelids with his hand, and smiled a brave smile as a murmur of sympathy and support went round the room from his fellow Deans.

"A truly tragic loss," said Professor Toady to the Registrar afterwards, "What we will do without him I don't know. He'd done so much for Surleighwick."

Two days later lectures were suspended at Surleighwick as a mark of respect, as the university buried its Vice-Chancellor. A long fleet of hearses left the Vice-Chancellor's house, bearing Mr Henry Tinker, MBE, B.Soc.Sc., Hon. MA (Surleighwick) on his last earthly journey. Dean Eustace Toady rode with the other Deans in two limousines in a place of honour near the front of the cortege, directly behind the limousine conveying Miss Bimbaud and Miss Carstairs. The six Deans, clad in frock coats and black top hats, walked gravely behind Vice-Chancellor Tinker's coffin, on which his two crutches had been placed as a mark of respect.

Dean Toady stood, with grave and solemn face, as Vice-Chancellor Tinker's coffin was lowered into the grave. With solemn demeanour he reached down and scattered a small handful of earth into the coffin! 'Ashes to ashes, dust to dust'. This was great! Tinker's death had certainly got the Dean out of a tight corner on this occasion! Serve that wretched Tinker right! He had been such a crude, insensitive bully, a real mediocrity and a pretty useless VC, when you came to think of it.

The ceremony over, Professor Toady and the other Deans met in an urgent afternoon meeting to consider the vital question: who should take over from the late Vice-Chancellor Tinker? All week the discussions continued behind closed doors—the Registrar was consulted, as was the university's Chancellor, the Earl of Brawdey, a remote, blind, aged member of the hereditary peerage, who lived in the Outer Hebrides. Senior lay members of the university's Council joined in the discussions with something like despair. It was only five years since they had been through the exhausting selection process which had resulted in the appointment of Vice-Chancellor Tinker, the 184th candidate whom they had approached. They knew perfectly well that no one of ability or intelligence would accept the job.

Dean Toady's grave demeanour had stood him in good stead. Even his fellow Deans had been touched by his moving account of how Vice-Chancellor Tinker had died virtually within his arms. Yes! When you stopped to think about it, Dean Toady was really a very sound man. Not too flashy of course, but then Surleighwick did not like flashiness. Toady was steady, he was *reliable*, and his counsel had been of inestimable use to the late Vice-Chancellor. He was *safe*. You knew where you were with him. The Registrar noised his name abroad. Toady, he knew, was amenable to advice. He was not a wild man. One could do worse. Even Professor Toady's fellow Deans could see some merit in his candidature. He was, they knew full well, basically weak, pompous, and vain—so he would carry on the Surleighwick traditions well enough, and would present no threat to their own fiefdoms. At any rate, the Dean of Science would rather have Toady than the Dean of Engineering or the Dean of Medicine. The Dean of Medicine felt the same. Better Toady than the Dean of Science or the Dean of Engineering. The Dean of Engineering agreed. Better Toady than the Dean of Science or Medicine. The lay members of council did not want an academic Vice-Chancellor. But, as the Registrar pointed out to them, Professor Toady hardly counted as an academic. At the end of the week all were agreed, and just ten days after Vice-Chancellor Tinker's death, Dean Eustace Toady was appointed in his place.

*****

Vice-Chancellor Toady found the first week of his new position extremely pleasant. Each morning the Vice-Chancellorian Rolls picked him up at home, and drove him into work at 11 am, where he was ministered to and soothed by Miss Carstairs and Miss Bimbaud. He spent an agreeable few days choosing new carpets and furniture for the official residence that would be his as soon as Mrs Tinker had moved out, and making, in consultation with his wife, numerous decisions about the interior decorations. He had many difficult decisions to make, too, about his new Rolls Royce. Would he prefer tiger skin or crocodile leather for the seats? It was a ticklish problem.

One had to admit that life in the Vice-Chancellor's office was really very agreeable. Miss Bimbaud ministered to every personal comfort, and no longer did he have to queue for morning coffee in the Arts faculty, or pour out his own whisky from the decanter. And Miss Carstairs managed his office routine and correspondence so well. Really, he was delightfully cocooned, and gazing from his office could see all the activity on the Surleighwick campus. And soon he would be really able to pay off some old scores against his faculty enemies....

Whilst he was thus musing at the end of the last afternoon of his first week in his new position, Miss Carstairs and Miss Bimbaud came into the office, and closed the door firmly behind them.

Vice-Chancellor Toady sat behind his desk, experiencing

some bewilderment as Miss Carstairs drew up two chairs, and as Miss Bimbaud poured three large whiskies from the decanter. The two young ladies placed their glasses on the desk, and leant forward in their chairs.

"Right, Vice-Chancellor," said Miss Carstairs briskly. "I think it's time we got one or two things straight. I hope you agree that Miss Bimbaud and I have done everything we can to make your first week an easy one?"

"Yes indeed," said Vice-Chancellor Toady, taking a nervous sip of whisky.

"Good. Miss Bimbaud and I have been thinking that we deserve a rise. What we had in mind was that our salaries should be doubled. Oh, and there's one more thing."

Miss Carstairs pushed a folder towards the Vice-Chancellor.

"You probably don't know that the Vice-Chancellor's office is bugged, and that all important conversations are recorded. This is a transcript of Vice-Chancellor Tinker's very last interview with yourself."

Vice-Chancellor Toady looked at the folder, and saw the torrent of abuse therein contained.

"We were wondering what you wanted us to do with this transcript?" continued Miss Carstairs. "Basically, there are two possibilities. We can either keep very quiet about it, or we can spread it abroad. Which would you like us to do?"

"Er—I think it would be best not to spread this around," answered Vice-Chancellor Toady. "And of course, I can see that two such hard-working and efficient girls as yourselves need a rise."

Miss Carstairs handed him the authorisation to sign, looked at Miss Bimbaud with a glance of triumph, for she had correctly assessed Toady's essentially cowardly and servile nature, and then lifted her glass.

"Well, cheers, Vice-Chancellor, I think you can rely on Cheryl

and me to be totally loyal and discreet." Miss Carstairs drained a
generous slug of whisky, and then continued. "Oh, just one more
thing, Vice-Chancellor. About Professor Bodgering. Do you want
to do anything about him? Tinker was going to sack him, you
know."

"Er, leave it with me—I'll think about it."

Sacking Bodgering would certainly be one in the eye for the
English department. But, on balance, it might be better to leave
him *en poste*. It had not yet dawned on Vice-Chancellor Toady that
he no longer needed to 'do down' the English department. So he
deferred a decision on the matter, and amused himself by reading
the transcript of Vice-Chancellor Tinker's last interview with
Professor Bodgering.

*****

Mrs Quick was ecstatic when she heard the news of Vice-
Chancellor Tinker's death.

"Don't you see, Tony, our spells are really working! It's
simply that our aim is too high, so to speak. We were aiming for
Toady, but we hit Tinker. Let's have another go again tonight."

*****

Dr Pratt had asked to see Vice-Chancellor Toady, and was
now closeted with him in the Vice-Chancellor's office.

"Congratulations on your recent appointment, Vice-Chancellor. I'm glad personally that a member of the library committee
has risen to such a post."

Vice-Chancellor Toady sighed.

"Thank you, Peter. Of course, it's a tragic way to succeed to
the office. Poor old Henry. Such a loss to Surleighwick. We were
very close, you know."

"I thought I should tell you, Vice-Chancellor, that I'm thinking of moving on. I've had a very attractive approach from the Australian National University in Canberra."

"Surely, not, Peter? I thought you were doing so well here."

"Well, frankly, Vice-Chancellor, I feel that I have not been a total success. I mean, look at all that publicity in the *Times* about selling off our early books. Though I have to say, Vice-Chancellor, that I do feel that it's not entirely my fault. It was you that said to sell them to Hay-on-Wye. I only had to sell them because the last VC wanted me to raise £600,000. And I gather I might have got that for that wretched treatise on the circulation of the blood. You remember? Mrs Houghton gave it to the library, and I didn't realise it was worth a fabulous sum of money. But you'd told me it was a Romanian novel, so naturally I didn't think it was worth anything. Anyway, I'm not here to indulge in recriminations. If you'll give me a really good reference for the Australian job, I see no reason why news of your part in all this should get out."

"Of course, Peter old man," said the Vice-Chancellor, with a sigh. There was always a price tag. "I wish you luck. Have a drink before you go."

He pressed a button, and Miss Bimbaud came in with a sweet smile, and poured two large whiskies for them both.

Dr Pratt returned from his interview well satisfied. Yes, it was time to shake the dust of Surleighwick off his feet. The ANU would be more his cup of tea. They wouldn't have all these old books there, and he happened to know that the 'Prattage' of their books was considerably higher than at Surleighwick. And it would be nice to live in a sunny country, away from the endless gloom and fog of Surleighwick.

He sat down at his desk, and looked at a small package that had arrived from 'Bibliophage Library Systems'. It contained a computer disc, and a covering letter saying that the disc was to demonstrate a new system of computer-controlled issues and returns. Interested, Dr Pratt loaded the disc into his computer. Half an hour later, a message flashed on to the screen of Dr Pratt's terminal.

'Ever been had? Well you have now. Your catalogue is now totally zapped. If you wish to retrieve it, send £50,000 to PO Box 35, Lima, Peru, and instructions will follow.'

Frantically Dr Pratt tried to check some items in the catalogue. It was blank. Very very furtively, he switched off his terminal, ejected the rogue disk and placed it deep in his briefcase, and hastily sent off his application to the ANU. As his telephone began to ring urgently and insistently, he left for home early, telling Sarah-Jane that he had a headache.

*****

. Sir John Dagger, KBE, CVO, FRS, FBA, MBA (Harvard), MA, Ph.D., D.Sc. (Cantab), Hon. LL.D. (Oxon), Hon. D.Sc. (Econ.) (LSE), the Chairman of the Committee of Vice-Chancellors and Principals, a man highly thought of in Whitehall, was lunching at the Carlton Club with a Very Senior Member of the government. Sir John, the Vice-Chancellor of the University of Skegness, was not a typical Vice-Chancellor. An FRS at the age of 32, he had gained his Nobel Prize for distinguished work in particle physics at the age of 36. His KBE had come as the result of his masterly chairmanship of the Royal Commission on the future of the Nuclear Power Industry, which had produced a lucid assessment of the comparative economic, environmental and technological advantages of the Advanced Gas Cooled Reactor as against the Pressurised Water Reactor. His brilliant history of atomic theory from *Epicurus to the H-Bomb* , a work of extreme scholarship which had also headed the best-seller lists for eighty successive weeks, had gained him a well-deserved entrée to the British Academy.

Appointed to the University of Skegness as the youngest Vice-Chancellor in the country, he had within the space of five-years speedily revitalised that somewhat moribund institution. Woe betide any professor at the University of Skegness who was not up to the mark! In his first year at Skegness, Sir John had forced the retirement or resignation of some fifty-five professors, by the simple expedient of threatening to list their publication and citation-index profiles, and circulating them publicly throughout the university. Eight unproductive but obstinate professors who had refused to resign found themselves simultaneously sued in the civil courts for breach of contract and for tens of thousands of pounds in damages. Sir John won all the cases, and eight professors who had published nothing for ten years found themselves forced to repay to the university one third of their annual salaries for each of the last ten years. In their place, Sir John appointed young, vigorous, active, outspoken scholars. Soon he was surrounded by a band of Young Turks who swept through their departments like a firestorm. Seven years after Sir John's first appointment, there was scarcely a member of the university who did not have at least twenty publications and thirty-five citations to his or her name. Research grants and external funding flooded in, and morale at Skegness rocketed as Sir John imported the best and brightest lecturers from all over the country to fill his new posts and chairs. (Surleighwick alone lost nine members of staff to Sir John.) At the time of the first review of research by the then University Grants Committee, fifty-two of Skegness's sixty departments had been awarded a star. The other eight were 'above average', and the luckless heads of these departments were publicly rebuked by Sir John at Senate in such savage, scathing, and sarcastic terms that one went home and shot herself, one took an overdose, and the other six handed in their resignations and fled the country.

And now Sir John was discussing the future of the British

university system, in the discreet and padded opulence of the Carlton Club dining room.

"You see, John, the PM's not really satisfied with the progress that has been made in cutting universities so far. True, there have been cuts. But he feels that he needs a visible achievement to go into the next election with. Universities are unpopular with the public you know, and the PM believes that to close one of them might be worth 150,000 votes. To be quite frank, he's furious—just like Margaret was—that no university has yet given him an honorary degree. To close one down would need an Act of Parliament, of course, but he's prepared for that. Now, which one do you think it ought to be?"

Over port, biscuits and coffee in a secluded corner of the library, the two men canvassed several suggestions. They started with the usual names that were inevitably mentioned whenever talk of closing a university came up—Keele, Essex, Stirling, Doncaster, Salford, Lincoln, Skelmerdale. Perhaps an hour was spent in reviewing these possibilities.

Then the Minister said:

"I wonder what you'd say to Surleighwick?"

Surleighwick! Of course, you only had to suggest the name to see that it would fit the bill.

"It seems to the PM that Surleighwick might be appropriate in several ways. First, none of the Cabinet went to Surleighwick, or has children there at the moment. Second, they've been getting some terrible publicity in the Murdoch press recently. You probably don't read the tabloids, but I have some photocopies here."

The Minister passed Sir John a folder containing details of the lurid headlines earned by the English department after its trip to Hay-on-Wye.

"For a start some of the Surleighwick louts pretty well smashed up the town of Hay-on-Wye. They had to call out the riot squad you know. Then there's been all this fuss in the press about them selling off their valuable books—and getting a pretty poor price too, so far as I can gather. And now it transpires that they let some fool penetrate their library computer, and wipe the catalogue clean. I ask you! But there's another point. We've had some secret surveys of universities done, and there's no doubt that in terms of what to do with the buildings after the university has gone, it would be hard to find one better than Surleighwick. Its student residences would make an ideal open prison, for example. Moreover, the whole campus is in a prime location. Do you know what the site's worth? We've had it valued at £600 million. And there's a further consideration—this is strictly between ourselves—the campus is plumb on top of an on-shore oil field. If we decided to let BP exploit it, we'd get nearer a billion. So the PM thinks that Surleighwick will have to be the one to go. Now, here's the point. He thinks that the whole business would go much more smoothly if the suggestion for closing Surleighwick came from the CVCP rather than from government. He's hoping very much that you will see it his way. What do you think? Do you think you could get your committee to say that the only way in which the next round of cuts could be implemented would be by the closure of a university? He'd be awfully pleased if you could. It would mean more money for all the survivors, and Skegness would be well placed to do well out of that."

The Minister winked.

"I'll put it this way. Get your committee to recommend Surleighwick for closure, and I think I can say that Viscount and Viscountess Dagger could pretty soon expect an invitation for a weekend at Chequers."

"Life or hereditary?"

"Oh, hereditary of course."

Sir John considered in silence for a few moments. Yes, he thought he would be able to carry most of his colleagues with him on this one.

"I don't see any particular difficulty here, Minister," he replied. "I think most of my colleagues will be quite amenable to closing any institution so long as it isn't their own. And I'll tell you one thing in our favour. The Surleighwick VC has never cut very much ice at meetings of my committee. Tinker, who has just died, never opened his mouth once in five years. And now I'm told that they have appointed someone called Toady whom no-one seems to have heard of."

The Minister laughed.

"Ah yes, I heard that Tinker had popped his clogs. Do you know the damned fool actually wrote to me more than once asking for an OBE? I ask you!"

Sir John lifted an eyebrow, and smiled with all the amused disdain of one who had got his 'K' at the age of thirty-eight.

"I have the impression that the whole university seems to be pretty mediocre," he replied. "The only person I know from Surleighwick is Charles Hanwell. He wrote some very decent articles on atomic theory that I quoted in my book, but apart from him I can't say I've ever heard of a scholar who was at the place. And Hanwell is a clever chap. I've been trying to find the funds to offer him a chair at Skegness. Just leave it to me."

Sir John returned home on the train from London to Skegness, reading the mass of adverse press cuttings about Surleighwick with shock and disbelief. When he arrived back at Skegness, Sir John called upon the department of Educational Sociology, and set that department to work to compile a complete list of the total publications of everyone who had held an academic post at Surleighwick for the last fifteen years, together with full details of how many times each of their publications had been cited in the various *Citation Indexes*. Then he started to phone around certain of his friends on the Committee who thought like he did. Such was the man with whom Vice-Chancellor Toady would have to do battle to save his institution at the next meeting of the CVCP.

*****

Doctors French and Chamberlain had decided to humour Professor Toady the next time he came to see them, which was ten days after being made Vice-Chancellor. Mrs Quick and Dr Crumpet had been practising their spells again, and Vice-Chancellor Toady had had another agonising night.

"Well well, it's *Vice-Chancellor* Toady now isn't it?" said Dr Chamberlain with heavy irony in her voice. "I can see now that you were right when you told us you were a *really important* man. Now, what seems to be the trouble. We can't have you dying, can we, Vice-Chancellor? I mean, it would look bad for the Health Service if you died. To lose one Vice-Chancellor is a misfortune, but to lose two would seem very like carelessness."

Dr French laughed, and then the two young women got out their stethoscopes and prodded Vice-Chancellor Toady's chest again, and took his blood pressure.

Dr Chamberlain frowned.

"Yes, Vice-Chancellor, your blood pressure is rather high I'm afraid."

"It's all my new and heavy responsibilities," the Vice- Chancellor added. "Of course, I had great responsibilities as Dean of Arts, you know. The last VC relied very heavily on my advice. But now I bear a much greater burden. It's a heavy responsibility running a great university like Surleighwick. It's not just academic departments I have to worry about. Even the Health Service comes under me now you know."

Gradually, Vice-Chancellor Toady had lost his distrust of the two young female doctors. Certainly the pills that Dr Chamberlain had given him last time had done him good. She seemed a competent young woman, and well, one had to be broad-minded these days, hadn't one?

"Tell us about it," suggested Dr Chamberlain, winking at Dr French behind the fat Vice-Chancellor's back.

"Well, one of my great responsibilities is to hire and fire staff," continued the fat Toady. "I have to decide whether to sack an old colleague of mine from the faculty of Arts, on the grounds of incapacity to carry out his duties. It's a grave decision, you know."

"Yes, I can see how that would keep you awake at night," put in Dr French, biting her lip.

"Exactly! And of course there is the financial responsibility. Do you know what the university's annual budget is? £90,000,000. That's a lot of money. I've already been involved in some very difficult decisions—like cutting back the library book grant so as to increase my hospitality fund. That wasn't easy, I can tell you. I didn't want the money for myself, of course, but it's so important nowadays, for the sake of the university, to give one's distinguished visitors the right impression."

"Well, you have been busy," remarked Dr Chamberlain. "By the way, we've been getting rather a bad press of late, haven't we, and I suppose it can't be very pleasant dealing with all those nasty journalists, can it?" she asked, massaging the fat roll of flesh in front of Toady's heart. "What are you going to do about it?"

"In the first place, we're going to get ourself a new logo, to enhance the university's visual identity," answered the Vice-Chancellor. " The corporate image of the institution is everything nowadays," he continued, delighted to give the young doctors some idea of his responsibilities. "It was me that took the final decision last week to spend £330,000 on our new logo of a tiger, rather than £300,000 on a logo of a lion. We had to pay extra for the stripes, you know. You'll see it when you get your next batch of notepaper."

"A tiger?" exclaimed Dr French in surprise. "Why a tiger?"

"It symbolises that the university is energetic and raring to go," explained the Vice-Chancellor. "Then again we're going to hire a good PR firm, It'll cost us a couple of million, but we hope to make people forget the bad publicity by stressing the good things about Surleighwick."

"What are they?" asked Dr French.

"Well, we've got a nice campus," answered the VC, importantly. "I bet you didn't know that more TV commercials have been shot at Surleighwick than any other university. That's a big selling point for us. Then again, we have great stability among the staff. Did you know that we have more people at Surleighwick who have never taught at any other university, than any other university in the country has? We commissioned a survey, you know. That proves people are happy here, and feel a loyalty to the place,"

"You're sure it doesn't mean that they're not good enough to be *able* to move?" asked Dr Chamberlain.

"Heavens no! What a suggestion."

"Then again, we've got a very good rugby team."

"Yes, I know. I have to deal with their injuries," answered Dr French.

"Well, it looks as if we'll have to put your stomach and heart pains down to your heavy responsibilities," said Dr Chamberlain, with a wink at Dr French.

"Yes, that's right. It's a responsible life, I can tell you. I've got to go to the Committee of Vice-Chancellors and Principals soon, you know, to represent the university, and discuss future government policy towards the whole university system."

"Well, all the same, cut down your drinking, and don't eat too much," said Dr Chamberlain. "And take some more of these." She handed him another bottle of the pink pills.

"You can count on me. Thank you, Dr Chamberlain," said the Vice-Chancellor, as he took his leave.

The two young doctors collapsed in hysterics when their patient had left.

"What a pompous fool! He really does take the biscuit," said Dr Chamberlain her eyes streaming with tears of laughter.

Dr French could not reply, for she was doubled up with hysterical giggling.

Vice-Chancellor Toady left for home, satisfied now with the treatment he was getting from the two doctors, who he could see took him seriously at last. He dined on roast lamb and roast potatoes, strawberry fool, cheese and biscuits, and confined himself by an exercise of will-power to a mere four glasses of wine and a double brandy, before retiring for an early night, ready for the onerous duties of the next day.

CHAPTER FOURTEEN

CURTAINS FOR SURLEIGHWICK

'Tombez ô perles dénouées,
Pâles étoiles dans la mer.
Fuyez, astres mélancholiques,
Ô Paradis lointains encor!'
(Leconte de Lisle, *La chute des étoiles*).

'Cut is the branch that might have grown full straight.'
(Marlowe, *Dr Faustus*)

The summer term had continued on its way at Surleighwick, and Vice-Chancellor Toady had now been in office for eight weeks, without anyone very much noticing.

On a fine sunny May day, Vice-Chancellor Toady strolled self-importantly through the crowds of students sunning themselves on the grass and trying to revise for the summer examinations. The library had been out of action for six weeks, to mounting protests, and eventually, in the first major decision of his Vice-Chancellorship, when all attempts at ridding the library computer of its virus had failed, Toady had decided to authorise the payment of the blackmail demanded. The virus designer had taken the money, and had replied: 'Thanks, but did I only say £50,000? I meant £100,000. Please send the extra £50,000.'

Now Professor Toady was on his way to his first meeting of the Committee of Vice-Chancellors and Principals. He drove down in his Rolls Royce, with only his chauffeur and Miss Carstairs for company. There was a wadge of papers for the meeting which he hadn't yet bothered to read. The Agenda consisted of just one item: 'The Future of the British University System'. Vice-Chancellor

Toady yawned. No doubt it would be a re-run of all the meetings he had attended on similar topics at Surleighwick over the years....Just a lot of talk, really, and nothing much happening afterwards. But it would be pleasant to meet his fellow Vice-Chancellors for the first time. There were quite a few knights among them! His FBA hadn't come through yet, but everyone knew that Vice-Chancellors had a pretty good chance of getting a knighthood after a few years, or at least a CBE. 'Sir Eustace Toady, FBA'— yes, it had a nice ring about it! No doubt, too, his fellow Vice-Chancellors would be very anxious to meet the new representative from Surleighwick.

*****

As the Vice-Chancellor was driving down to London, back at Surleighwick Dr Hanwell was despatching the newly arrived copies of his magnum opus on Scientific Poetry to various friends, including Embury Jenkins at the Baskerville Institute and Professor Rowlands in Chicago.

*****

Professor Toady had stopped for lunch at a hotel just off the M1. The lunch was excellent, but the service was slow. Hence Professor Toady was late in resuming his journey. Then his Rolls got stuck in a long traffic jam near St Albans. Later his driver lost his way in outer London. Consequently, Professor Toady was an hour and a half late in arriving for his first meeting of the CVCP. The Vice-Chancellors of most other universities had wisely travelled to London by train or plane, or had stayed overnight in a club or hotel, and had then taken the taxi or the tube to the CVCP headquarters. But then, the other Vice-Chancellors did not have a personal Rolls.

Hence Sir John Dagger had had an hour-and-a-half to outline his views on the future of the university system before the arrival of Vice-Chancellor Toady. Since Sir John had already primed his ten closest allies on the committee with his intentions, he had little difficulty in carrying the meeting with him when he said that in his opinion it would be better to go for 'major surgery'—viz the closure of one university, resulting in a small increase in funds for all the others, rather than to attempt to make the necessary savings by the 'death of a thousand cuts'.

The Vice-Chancellor of the University of Skelmerdale, fearful that his university would be chosen for closure, had expressed his strong reservations.

"I feel we should think long and hard before venturing on this unprecedented step."

"Oh, I'm sure that there would be no question of closing Skelmerdale," Sir John opined smoothly.

"As I was saying," continued the Skelmerdale Vice-Chancellor, "we should think long and hard before taking this unprecedented step. This does not however mean that we can shirk difficult and unpopular decisions. For myself I am of Sir John's view entirely—better to lop off one limb to ensure the health of the whole body than to endure the unending misery of cut after cut."

"I'm not sure that I'd go quite as far as that," put in the Vice-Chancellor of Coketown University.

"Of course, it's completely understood that no university in a depressed area such as Coketown would be affected," responded Sir John.

"As I was saying, Sir John," replied the Coketown VC, "In an ideal world, I'm not sure I'd go quite as far as that. But the fact is that we do not live in an ideal world. I agree, Sir John—difficult decisions have to be taken."

"I take it that the vital part that, say, the University of the

Cotswolds plays in the rural economy is fully understood?" que-
ried the Vice-Chancellor of the University of the Cotswolds.

"Absolutely," replied Sir John.

"Thank you for that assurance. I agree with you, Sir John, you
are proposing to us the lesser of two evils."

"I take it that for political reasons we would not expect to see
the closure of a Welsh university?" enquired the Vice-Chancellor
of the University of Powys.

"Certainly not—nor a Scottish or Irish one."

Slowly Sir John swung the whole committee behind him.

There was a sudden commotion, and flushed, dishevelled, and
very late, Vice-Chancellor Toady entered the room.

Sir John looked up with faint surprise.

"Yes?"

"I'm sorry I'm late, Mr Chairman, Sir—Sir Chairman Sir—
Sir John Sir I mean of course—" puffed the fat Toady. "An
unfortunate jam on the M1—not my fault."

"Ah, you must be the toady from Surleighwick we've been
waiting for. Come and join us." Sir John gestured towards an empty
chair at the far end of the table.

"Well, I think we're agreed so far, gentlemen. Now, I have
here some comparative performance figures for four universities
chosen at random. To protect their identity, and ensure an unbiased
discussion, they are called Universities A, B, C, and D. (A was the
University of Oxford, B the University of Cambridge, C Sir John's
own University of Skegness, D the University of Surleighwick.)

Sir John then launched his pre-emptive attempt to 'take out'
the University of Surleighwick.

His statisticians at the University of Skegness had done a
complete citation count for the work of every member of staff of
these four universities. These showed quite clearly that the worst
citation count was in University D.

"Let us observe these figures for a moment. University D

seems to be trailing the field here. Look at the dreadful figures for Achaeology or English for example. In University D, the Professor of Archaeology has only 2 citations in the last ten years, and two of the English professors only eight citations between them—a far worse showing than their equivalents in A, B and C."

"Disgraceful," nodded Vice-Chancellor Toady, who had never heard of the *Citation Index* and had not the remotest idea what Sir John was referring to.

Then Sir John looked at the A level scores of applicants for admission for the last ten years.

"Look, 3 D's seems to be the best that University D can do— but A, B and C come out at 2 A's and a B averaged over all subjects."

Professor Toady nodded sagely.

Sir John's figures showed that University D had the lowest number of FRS's (0) and FBAs (0). It had the fewest stars. It had the highest costs per student. It had the highest ratio of administrators to academics. In every area University D was the worst, even in the figures for audience response to campus commercials.

"I take it then that we are unanimous that University D is the one?" enquired Sir John.

Vice-Chancellor Toady, who was now sleepy, nodded his agreement with the rest.

"May we know which is University D?" asked the Vice-Chancellor of the University of Coketown.

"The Institution in question will be informed in due course by registered mail," said Sir John carefully.

He closed the meeting, and Vice-Chancellor Toady then had the opportunity to get to know some of his colleagues, who were not however over-impressed by the smell of alcohol that lingered on his breath.

******

Dr Hanwell's last class of the summer term was over, and he had taken Ruth to the Three Blind Mice for dinner to celebrate the publication of his book and to calm her nerves before her examinations the following week.

"I'm sure you've no need to worry, Ruth" he told her, as he walked her back to Second Hall in the still dusk of a summer evening. "Just remember to write your answers in English not Italian, and don't disagree too violently with Professor Bohring's views in your answers to the papers that he has set."

"Oh, by the way, I bought you a book that I thought you might like. I found it in a junk shop yesterday."

Dr Hanwell accompanied Ruth back to her room, and there she opened the window to the sultry heat of the summer evening, and told him to pour them both a couple of glasses of Wild Turkey. She busied herself with making coffee, and then said, "Here you are—a copy of *Book Auction Records* for the 1978/9 season. I paid all of 50p for it!"

"Ruth! How kind!"

Dr Hanwell stayed drinking Ruth's Wild Turkey, until at length she pushed the book into his arms, gave him a friendly kiss, and told him that she had to get an early night in preparation for her imminent exams.

Dr Hanwell left Ruth at Second Hall, and walked thoughtfully back to his flat. He would miss not having Ruth in his classes next year....

He arrived at his flat, poured himself a glass of whisky, and flicked through the pages of the volume of *Book Auction Records* that Ruth had given him. And there he was startled to see that the 1476 folio of Aristotle's *De animalibus* which he had bought on his recent visit to Hay-on-Wye was listed as having been sold for £20,000 at the Honeyman sale of Scientific Books and Manuscripts. He started upright with a sudden shock, and felt the hairs of his scalp tingle. He could hardly believe it. Then he turned to the H section, and there he found that a copy of Harvey's *De motu cordis* had fetched £92,000 exclusive of buyer's premium at the same sale. Good heavens! Had there been a mistake? He determined to check out the cumulative five year index in the morning at the university library, to see whether perchance an extra 0 had been added on by a printer's mistake. If these books really were worth all that money, then he would sell them. Well, he might keep the *De animalibus*, as that was in his area, but he would certainly sell the Harvey. One could get a lot of other books for £92,000, and do other things too. He would take Ruth out for a really super meal to celebrate....

*****

A week later a 'Personal and Confidential' registered letter, headed OHMS at the top, was handed to Vice-Chancellor Toady as he arrived for work at 11.30 am.

The Vice-Chancellor's heart leaped. He turned the imposing looking official envelope over between his podgy fingers. At last—this must be the first of the Honours traditionally associated with the high position he now held. What would it be? Surely a prospective member of the British Academy would not be offered anything less than an OBE at the very least? It was a bit early for the KBE, perhaps, which would not come till he had been in office for a year or so, but maybe the CBE was the most likely thing. With trembling hands he tore open the letter and read:

Department of Education and Science
Elizabeth House,
London,
23 May 1991
Dear Mr Toady,
Following the unanimous advice of the Committee of Vice-Chancellors and Principals, I am pleased to say that the government has made time in its legislative programme for a Bill to disband the University

of Surleighwick with effect from 1 October 1992. Arrangements have also been made for its Royal Charter to be revoked.

Members of staff still in employment at that date will of course qualify for the basic statutory redundancy payments. Arrangements are in hand for students still in mid-course on that date to be transferred to the Open University, where appropriate course credits for their Surleighwick experience will be given.

You will, I am sure, be pleased to hear that students without access to a television set may apply to the DES for an ex gratia payment not exceeding £15 for the purchase of a second-hand set.

On 1 October 1992, the site, buildings and property of the ex-University of Surleighwick will pass to the Property Services Agency, for disposal in accordance with the government's privatisation scheme. I am sure you will be pleased to know that in any share issues deriving from this, students and staff of the University of Surleighwick 'on the books' as at 30 September 1992 will be granted preferential treatment in applications for shares not exceeding fifty in number.

Commissioners have been appointed to assist in the winding-up of the affairs of the university at the earliest possible moment. They will arrive on campus on 10 June 1991, and I trust that they will be afforded every facility.

Finally, may I say that we at the DES much appreciate your own co-operation in supporting the CVCP in its decision, thereby making it a unanimous one. I have forwarded your name to the Prime Minister's Patronage Secretary with a recommendation that you should be awarded the BEM when closure is complete.

Yours sincerely,

W.A.T. Cheke,
Deputy Assistant Acting Under-Secretary,
Higher Education Division
Universities Section
(Grade 4 Institutions Sub-Section)

Vice-Chancellor Toady skimmed the letter hastily, and felt the colour drain from his face. The BEM! Much less of an honour than he had hoped for. Why, even Vice-Chancellor Tinker had had the MBE! Surely the BEM was a bit of a come-down? Then Miss Bimbaud poured him his customary glass of morning whisky.

"Make it a treble, please Cheryl," he said. He needed something to steady his nerves. Then, after the first three gulps of whisky, and a top-up, Vice-Chancellor Toady began to see matters in a more roseate light. Look at it how you would, the BEM was still undeniably an honour. It would give him a medal to wear at evening functions where decorations were *de rigeur*. And very few people at Surleighwick, apart from the occasional former member of the Armed Forces, had a medal to their name at all. The BEM was at least a start, and, who knows, might be upgraded to the MBE at least if he played his cards right.

Then, feeling that he would like to be alone, the Vice-Chancellor summoned his chauffeur and had himself driven out to the countryside to a really decent country-house hotel that he knew, where they did a first-rate lunch.

An hour and a half later, after Vice-Chancellor Toady had drunk two double gin and tonics, and a whole bottle of excellent Ducru Beaucaillou with his roast beef and Yorkshire pudding, and had a glass of Sauternes with his gateau and a double of Cognac Fine Champagne, he felt more able to come to terms with his fate. Yes, the BEM was undoubtedly better than nothing. It was a *medal*, and that was the important thing. And of course, it would give him some more letters after his name. Would it be E. Toady, Esq., BA, BEM, FBA, he wondered? Or did the BEM come last? It was important not to seem unaware of the etiquette on these matters. He must get Miss Carstairs to look up Debrett after lunch.

Thus comforted, the Vice-Chancellor was moved to take the letter out of his pocket and read it again. Hadn't there been something at the beginning about future plans for Surleighwick? What was that, closure? Surely not? Surely they couldn't be thinking of closing Surleighwick? "But the English department had got a star!" he thought to himself. And what was that about him supporting the CVCP decision? Vice-Chancellor Toady sat very still in his chair, and thought back. The CVCP! Of course, he had been there last week. He tried to remember what had been said at the meeting—of course, something about University D—he hadn't been paying much attention. Vice-Chancellor Toady felt a sinking feeling in his stomach. Everyone was sure to blame him for this—yet it was so unfair! He had never wanted to be Vice-Chancellor—he had in fact been almost forced into the job. And then he had an idea: perhaps he could organize a cover up, in the traditional way at Surleighwick. At any rate, it might be possible to keep it out of the press. But in his heart of hearts he knew that that would be difficult. Perhaps he could put a good gloss on the decision. What was that about shares? That was certainly something to sweeten the pill! Everyone liked to get something for nothing, and perhaps that was the way to play it. How had he got himself into this mess? The Vice-Chancellor thought back over his career at Surleighwick, where he had been since 1960, when had come as a young lecturer with some hopes of making a name for himself in Archaeology.

"I should never have let myself be elected to the faculty Board," he thought to himself. "That was my big mistake. Because I got in with all the drinkers, who used to assemble in the Staff Club bar after the meetings and buy me pints, and lead me into bad ways. And if I hadn't been on faculty Board, I would never have been elected to committees. And if I hadn't had experience of committees, I would never have become Dean. And if I hadn't been Dean of Arts, I could never have become Vice-Chancellor."

Suddenly, sitting in the hotel, the Vice-Chancellor felt lonely and sorry for himself. He was sleepy, so he asked his chauffeur to drive him straight home. There, in the warm May sunshine, he fell asleep until at 8 pm he was roused from his deep slumber. He was too frightened to tell even his wife of the contents of the letter which seemed to burn through his breast pocket. But two days later, he plucked up the courage to tell Mrs Toady that he was to have the BEM, and he had recovered sufficiently to drink a bottle of champagne to celebrate the honour.

For fully ten days, Vice-Chancellor Toady kept the contents of the letter firmly to himself, except for leaking the news that he was to be honoured in the immediate future. He made one half-hearted attempt to contact Sir John Dagger and Mr Cheke, but both men refused to take his calls. Miss Bimbaud and Miss Carstairs found him abstracted and nervous in his brief visits to the office, and they were unable to get any decisions from him, with the single exception that he declined to sign the letter that had now been drafted sacking Professor Bodgering. Even the full size mock-up of the snarling yellow tiger that was to form the new logo did not appear to interest him very much. But at last he plucked up courage to tell the Registrar. The Registrar's first concern was likewise to keep the news secret as long as possible, but he settled down to prepare an optimistic press release about the real value of the shares that everyone was to be offered, in an endeavour to look on the bright side. If the news had to break, as he supposed it must, let it break in the long vacation, preferably when the Registrar was on vacation in August in Bali....Thank goodness he was due to retire on 30 September 1992 anyway—so he would still get his shares. The Registrar breathed a sigh of relief. Yes, Surleighwick had lasted out his time, against all likely expectations.

*****

But as May turned to June, it was difficult to keep the news quiet. Ugly rumours began to surface in the world of higher education to the effect that Surleighwick was to close.

"But they can't do that," gasped little Jack Napes. "The English department got a star for the international excellence of its work! They couldn't close down a department that got a star!"

The university Information Officer, who had been kept in the dark by the Vice-Chancellor and Registrar, at once denied the rumours, in accordance with the Surleighwick convention that all discreditable stories were automatically denied, regardless of their truth or falsity. He quoted from Vice-Chancellor Tinker's last annual report:

'So we at Surleighwick, conscious of the traditions of this great university, are looking forward with confidence and hope to facing the exciting challenge of the next decade. The last ten years have seen great success. We are confident that Surleighwick is well placed to build on these successes. We know that our reputation stands high with employers, with our graduates, and with the general public, who have responded particularly well to the Doggo dog food commercials. We are very proud of the fact that no fewer than six of our ninety-four departments have got stars, which means that they are on a par with the best that the world can throw at us. We are also proud of our five "above average" and our ten "average" departments, which means that no fewer than twenty-one departments, or roughly a quarter of the whole, are average or above—a record we believe can stand comparison with other universities.'

This statement was issued to the Press even as the Leader of the House of Commons gave notice of the plan to take the Surleighwick University Disestablishment Bill through all its stages, via three-line whip and guillotine, in twenty-four hours.

Amidst uproar, he informed the House that Vice-Chancellor Toady supported these proposals.

When he saw the news on TV that night, Vice-Chancellor Toady judged it advisable not to come in for a few days. He took his phone off the hook, and for the next week spent the daylight hours being driven from country hotel to country hotel in his Rolls, leaving Miss Carstairs to fend off the numerous people who wanted to see him. On the Tuesday following the passage of the Bill, the Commissioners arrived at Surleighwick and set to work.

*****

A week later, Dr Hanwell was sitting in his office, wondering where to sell the *De motu cordis*, when a telex and two interesting letters were pushed under his door by Fred from the Post room.

The telex was from Embury Jenkins at the Baskerville Institute, Surleighwick Arkansas. In his admirably frank and direct way it read:

```
Dear Charles,
We all think your book is just great! The Trustees
have agreed that this area should be represented at
the Institute. Will you accept a research chair here
at 100 G's a year? Phone me soonest. We all hope
very much you'll accept.
Sincerely, Embury Jenkins.
```

Dr Hanwell poured himself a glass of whisky, to steady his nerves. Then he opened the other two letters.

The first was from the University of Surleighwick, England, and read, in the usual gracious tone adopted by that university in dealing with its staff:

```
Dear Sir or Madam,
As you will know from the Media, Surleighwick is
being closed down. We are therefore writing to give
you the earliest formal notice that you are offi-
cially sacked no later than 30 September 1992. A
leaflet setting out the details of the government's
statutory redundancy scheme is enclosed.
Yours faithfully
(signature illegible).
```

The third letter was also from the University of Surleighwick:

```
Commissioners Office
c/o U of Surleighwick
17 June 1991
Dear Dr Hanwell,
As Commissioners and Receivers in Bankruptcy for the
University of Surleighwick, we have pleasure in
enclosing a cheque for £3,156,234, representing the
balance of Foundation Funds due to you as Baskerville
Fellow, in full and final settlement of all claims
against the University of Surleighwick. Your ap-
```

```
pointment is accordingly terminated from 30 Septem-
ber 1991.
Yours sincerely,


p.p.
Mr A.D. Grumbel, MBE,
Commissioner and Receiver.
```

(This letter, though Dr Hanwell did not know it, was a mistake. Asked what to do about the Baskerville Foundation money from which Dr Hanwell's Baskerville Fellowship was funded, Mr Grumbel had said to his assistant: 'Send it to the Baskerville F.' (meaning the Foundation). Misunderstanding, she made out and despatched the cheque to the Baskerville Fellow. Owing to the speed and confusion with which the University of Surleighwick was dismantled, this mistake was never discovered.)

Dr Hanwell switched on his fluorescent light, and held the cheque suspiciously up to the light. But no, the cheque seemed good, the watermark was there, and it was drawn on the Bank of England. Hastily he called a taxi, and rushed into town to open a High Interest Cheque Account at the Head Office of the Midland Bank, the only one of the big four banks sensible enough not to have a branch on the Surleighwick campus. There, when the validity of the cheque had been confirmed by a telephone call to the Bank of England, he obtained a Banker's Draft for £2,500,000, leaving the balance on deposit. Then he took another taxi to Surleighwick Airport, and was soon on a plane to Basle, where he opened a deposit account in Swiss Francs at the Banque Suisse. Then, satisfied that the bulk of his funds were now beyond British jurisdiction, he bought some cigars, chocolates, shirts and a present for Ruth, and two days later was back in Surleighwick in the shabby basement office he would soon be relinquishing.

*****

'Tis but a case of mania, —subinduced by Epilepsy'
(Robert Browning, *An Epistle Containing the Strange Medical Experiences of Karshish the Arab Physician*)

At the university Health Service, Doctors Chamberlain and French, late one afternoon when their patients had departed, were gloomily discussing the impending end of their employment. It was not that they couldn't get a job elsewhere, but they were both aggrieved at having to move on, and were voicing a complaint common throughout the university, to which no satisfactory answer had been given.

"What I can't understand," said Dr French, "is why Toady went along with the CVCP recommendation. You'd have thought that at the very least he'd have voted against the scheme."

"I expect he was mad," answered Dr Chamberlain thoughtfully. "You know I always did say when he first came to see us that he was suffering from a paranoid delusion about his own self-importance. And look at that piece in the last *Factfile*." For, true to Surleighwick traditions, the *Factfile* had made no reference to the fact that the university was soon to be closed but had continued to report the Vice-Chancellor's little doings. 'VC to be honoured' the most recent leading article had said, hinting that Vice-Chancellor Toady was soon to receive an award for his public services. This piece was accompanied by a recent photograph of the VC with a sickly grin on his face.

As the two doctors were preparing to leave, the Vice-Chancellor's Rolls purred up to the Health Service. Mrs Quick and Dr Crumpet had been at their spells again, and Vice-Chancellor Toady was feeling distinctly unwell. So late that afternoon, he had dared to take the risk of coming on to campus for the first time for many days.

Hastily he staggered though the door, and was soon pouring out his troubles to the two doctors in their consulting room.

"You've got to do something about it," he gasped. "I feel terrible. I've got stabbing pains in my chest, I feel awful."

This time Vice-Chancellor Toady did not find the two doctors so sympathetic. They were annoyed at the thought of having to move away from their dates, their social life and their practice, and at all the upheaval that a change of abode would entail.

Coldly Dr Chamberlain prodded the Vice-Chancellor's chest.

"As I said before, you're eating and drinking too much."

"But it's worse than usual, Doctor, I fell really terrible. I've been under a terrible strain of late. Everyone is blaming me for the closure of the university, and it wasn't my fault. I did everything that I could, I tried hard," he lied. "I'm going to get a medal you know. It's not fair. No one else could have done better than me, and now they all say it's my fault."

Dr Chamberlain pursed her lips.

"But you agreed with the closure. It said so in the press and on TV."

"It's all a lie—misrepresentation. I never did. I didn't understand what I was doing. I was tricked! It was my first meeting. And now they're all out to get me. All the professors hate me now. I wish I'd never become Vice-Chancellor."

"And now Janet and I are going to loose our jobs."

"I can't help that," replied Vice-Chancellor Toady ungraciously.

Dr Chamberlain took Dr French away for a whispered consultation at the other side of the room. Dr French nodded vigorously.

Then Dr Chamberlain returned to the Vice-Chancellor.

"Will you stretch your arms out behind you please? As near horizontal as you can get them."

Vice-Chancellor Toady did so,

Dr Chamberlain slipped a white canvas strait-jacket over the

Vice-Chancellor's arms, and drew the tapes tight so that his arms were confined behind his back.

"What are you doing?" he asked.

"It's a new device to take blood pressure at your chest," she lied.

Then Dr Chamberlain placed another restricting canvas over that, and fastened it firmly around Vice-Chancellor Toady's chest, pulling in his stomach. Professor Toady felt tightly confined.

The two doctors checked the fastenings, and then moved over to the desk. Dr French took a form from the left hand drawer, and both doctors signed it.

"We're going to 'section' you under the Mental Health Act," explained Dr Chamberlain. (In the United Kingdom, any two doctors can commit a patient to the asylum under section 37 of the Mental Health Act, 1983). "We have just signed a form committing you to the Blackberry Hill Hospital." (The gloomy old Victorian building set in spacious grounds behind high walls on the edge of Surleighwick—the Blackberry Hill Insane and Lunatic Asylum as was, later the Blackberry Hill Hospital for the Mentally Ill.)

"But I'm not mad," protested the Vice-Chancellor.

"That's what lunatics always think," replied Dr Chamberlain unsympathetically, looking at the helpless Toady. "Dr French and I think you're mad anyway, and that's all that matters. You must be mad, mustn't you, to actually agree to the closure of your own university? It's also clear to me that you're suffering from paranoid delusions about your own importance. You're not important at all are you? Obviously you don't count for anything. And now you seem to be suffering from persecution mania as well."

"But I *am* being persecuted," protested Vice-Chancellor Toady, vainly struggling to free himself from the strait-jacket.

"That's what sufferers from persecution mania always say," retorted Dr Chamberlain. "Anyway, a forcible confinement of a few weeks at Blackberry Hill for a thorough examination won't do you any harm at all. I shall recommend a bread and water diet to get down your weight."

With a roar the Vice-Chancellor lowered his head, and charged at Dr Chamberlain, head-butting her to the floor.

Winded, she clambered to her feet.

"We'll have to knock him out," she gasped to Dr French, staggering to her feet and clutching her side.

Bellowing, Vice-Chancellor Toady lowered his head and charged at Dr French, his hands still pinioned helplessly behind his back. She neatly stepped out of the way, stretched out an elegantly-stockinged left leg, and tripped the Vice-Chancellor to the floor.

Dr Chamberlain quickly sat on the prone figure of the fat Toady.

"Quick—get the paraldehyde—10 cc, I should think. He's a crazy man."

Speedily Dr French filled a large hypodermic syringe.

"Where shall I jab him?" she asked breathlessly. "I can't get at his arm for the strait-jacket."

"Only one place for it," grinned Dr Chamberlain, gradually recovering her breath.

Vice-Chancellor Toady struggled violently as Dr French pulled off his trousers with a facility born from a year's experience of the Surleighwick Rugby club outings. Smilingly she jabbed the hypodermic into his bottom, and then, in a minute or two, the Vice-Chancellor's writhings ceased, and he was unconscious.

"What a horrible sight!" giggled Dr Chamberlain, as she carelessly tossed his trousers into a bag of medical waste, before phoning Blackberry Hill to arrange for the admission of Vice-Chancellor Toady. Then she rang his wife to say that he had been taken to hospital for observation for several weeks and must have no visitors, and then finally called for an ambulance to take Vice-Chancellor Toady away.

Doctors Chamberlain and French made themselves a cup of coffee to recover, and then, finally, a few moments before the ambulance arrived, draped a white medical gown around Vice-Chancellor Toady's recumbent form. Twenty minutes later, in shirt, strait-jacket and medical gown, Vice-Chancellor Toady, still unconscious, was on his way to Blackberry Hill. Dr Chamberlain accompanied the ambulance with her case notes to explain the situation.

*****

'Nutus est quidam praeambularius nuntius qui quodam inerrabili actu cordium secreta revelat.' (Boncompagno da Signa, *Rota veneris* (Strasburg, c. 1473).

The exam results were out, and Ruth had gained a brilliant First. She had done particularly well in Dr Hanwell's paper on Creation Theory, and he had given her a mark of 90%, which was upgraded by the external examiner to 94%.

"I'm so pleased for you, Ruth" he said, pouring her a glass of whisky when she came to tell him the news. "Come on—let's celebrate and have a last meal at the Three Blind Mice."

In spite of the champagne that Dr Hanwell had ordered to accompany the excellent steak, Ruth felt rather sad.

She would miss her little chats with Dr Hanwell, and the trips to Hay, and the good-humoured badinage she had enjoyed with him.

Flushed with champagne, they walked back up the hill in the tranquil summer twilight. Every sound seemed to carry in the still atmosphere. But Second Hall was quieter than usual, as many of the students had gone down.

Ruth settled down to make the coffee, and poured two generous portions of Wild Turkey into her airline glasses.

"Well, it looks as if I got out of Surleighwick just in time," she remarked, as she perched on the window ledge in her light green summer frock, which went well with her grey and intelligent eyes.

"Cheers! What are you going to do next year, Charles? I shall miss our classes, you know."

"So will I, Ruth," he said slowly, fingering in his left hand pocket the little gift from Basle he was minded to give her at any moment. "My, this Wild Turkey is good stuff. Actually, I shall be going to Surleighwick, Arkansas. They like my book, and they've offered me a research chair there. But what about you, Ruth, what are *you* going to do?"

"Oh, as a matter of fact, I'm going to Surleighwick, Arkansas too."

Dr Hanwell felt a wild surge through his heart.

"To Surleighwick, Arkansas!"

"But first, I'm going to Bath."

"To Bath?"

"Yes—I'm going to get married. Girls usually get married in their home town, you know."

Dr Hanwell felt crushed and depressed.

"To get married?"

Ruth looked at him sadly. Why were men so stupid?

"Yes. I'm going to marry a scholar. If he'll have me. I love him very much, and I think that he loves me."

"A scholar?" Numbness settled on his heart.

Her eyes misted over, as she continued.

"Yes. He's a historian of science." She gave a little sob. "I think he's very charming, and he knows more about seventeenth-century crocodiles than anyone I've ever met." A tear trickled down Ruth's face.

At last Dr Hanwell understood. He took Ruth's left hand in his right, and raised it to his lips, and kissed it gently.

Then reaching into the left-hand pocket of his lightweight summer jacket, he brought out a little jeweller's box, and from it took out the £30,000 engagement ring that he had bought for Ruth in Basle, and without a word placed it on the third finger of her left hand, and kissed her hand again. The ring, corruscating on Ruth's finger, was a perfect fit.

"It's beautiful," she whispered. "What lovely stones."

"Yes, it's sapphires, emeralds and diamonds set in gold. That's a very interesting combination of stones you know. Marbod of Rennes, in his treatise on jewels, says that...."

But the most eminently sensible Ruth cut off Dr Hanwell's explanation with the first of many moist, warm, long and lingering kisses.

EPILOGUE

'Redeamus ergo ad mentes humanas, de quibus iam pauca restant dicenda'
(Spinoza, *Cogitata Metaphysica*)

'Tempora mutantur, nos et mutamur in illis'
(John Owen, *Epigrammata*)

In September 1991, after a blissful honeymoon on the Isle of Skye, Dr and Mrs Hanwell were flying to Surleighwick Arkansas to take up their new lives there. As they sat in the First Class compartment of the Delta jet, nibbling at canapés and sipping champagne, their flight path took them over Ratford, Surleighwick, and the Welsh Marches.

*****

In Ratford, Professor Bodgering was as usual sitting dopily in his wheelchair, sipping vodka, popping pills, and gazing vacantly out of the window. Things had turned out quite well for him, really. The minor troubles of the English department, and the bankruptcy of its funds, had been forgotten in the major troubles of the university. He would have had to retire in a year or so anyway. He would get a pension. He could still afford to buy liquor. His health could be better, but then, he'd been ill for a long time now. He had, though, lost the services of Jolly. Jolly had departed in some bitterness. For over ten years now, first at Skelmerdale, then at Surleighwick, she had been his research assistant, amanuensis, and gopher. And what had it got her? Nothing. And now Surleighwick was to close and she had had a letter terminating her research assistantship from November 1st next. Over ten years of her life wasted, wasted at the beck and call of a specious, deceptive, lying invalid—for Professor Bodgering had often promised her a permanent job. She had been grossly exploited. It was time to make a clean break. And so she had said goodbye to Professor Bodgering before her contract expired, and departed for the Job Centre to look for a job.

Professor Bodgering was now being ministered to by Sukie, a blousy blonde nurse from a nursing agency. Sukie, who had read English at university, and knew by repute of Bodgering's proclivities, had suffered with unmoved indifference his feeble and usually unsuccessful attempts to pinch her bottom. Then one afternoon Professor Bodgering lapsed into a coma, and the best medical attention in the world could not save him. Two hours later, the breath of life slipped quietly away from that unloved, unlamented personality. No-one at Surleighwick noticed that he was dead, other than Mrs Quick and Dr Crumpet, who whooped for joy at this clear evidence of the efficacy of their spells.

"'Terrible hell make war upon his spotted soul!'" rejoiced Mrs Quick, opening a bottle of champagne to accompany a celebratory meal, and raising her glass in a toast to the naked Dr Crumpet, who was curled up in a langorous and relaxed fashion on the deep cushions of Mrs Quick's sofa.

"Right on!" responded Dr Crumpet with a mischievous and carefree smile, giving the thumbs up sign, and rising Venus-like from the cushions to be enfolded in Mrs Quick's loving and protective embrace.

*****

Soon afterwards, Mrs Quick and Dr Crumpet sold up at Surleighwick. Putting together the proceeds of the sale of their respective properties, Mrs Quick's alimony, and their redundancy money, they found themselves reasonably well off.

Mrs Quick now knew more about witches and the occult than she did about English literature. Together with Dr Crumpet, whom she had at last fully initiated into the delights of tribadism, Mrs Quick set up a Magic Women bookshop at Hay-on-Wye, special- ising in works on women and witches. Their business is now flourishing, and the two witches live happily together in a tiny cottage outside Hay, a hundred yards on the Welsh side of the border. There at night and sometimes in the grey dawn, they dance barefoot through the fen, darnel and butcher's broom, praying to the sun and moon with magic songs, invoking tree spirits, and caressing ancient stones with cheek and palm.

To their trusted female contacts in other universities they have circulated a card which reads:

SISTERHOOD SPELLS
Dr Antonia Crumpet Ph.D. Pauline Quick M.A. B.Litt.
Spells Sung   Charms Chanted
Dolls Devised Heads of Dept. Hexed
Is a man in your life bothering you? Why not consult Sisterhood Spells? Two liberated ladies (feminist, non-smokers) are ready to aid sisters in need. Proven record of success. (We have successfuly dealt with two heads of department and one Vice-Chancellor, and driven one Dean mad). Academics a speciality.
Consult Tony and Pauline on Hay-on-Wye 666.

Gradually, they are forming a little coven of like-minded feminists from other universities who come to visit them for spiritual advice.

Mrs Quick and Dr Crumpet soon adapted themselves to Welsh culture, and now regard themselves as genuine Celts. Shortly after arriving at Hay-on-Wye, they made contact with the Sons of Glendwyr, reproached them for sexism, and founded the very first Welsh chapter of the Daughters of Glendwyr. Two or three times in the coming year, at dead of night, dressed in combat fatigues, with blackened faces, they set out to burn down the Welsh second home of a male English professor. They made their debut with particular relish by gleefully hurling petrol-bombs through the windows of Vice-Chancellor Toady's holiday home on the Isle of Anglesey, before returning to their cottage for a bibulous meal and an evening of enchantments and tender nude embraces. Let us hope that these two engaging and enterprising witches are not one day shot through the nape of the neck by the SAS, who also operate in these parts.

*****

As Dr and Mrs Hanwell flew over Surleighwick, Vice-Chancellor Toady, wearing only his socks, strait-jacket, shirt and tie, was still head-butting the padded walls of his cell at Blackberry Hill, maddened and humiliated by the scornful smiles of the young nurses and sisters who fed him three times a day and kept him under constant observation as a demented pervert. His wife and daughters were well content to have him out of the way, as they opened at that very moment an elaborate package that had just been delivered, containing a polished heraldic wooden shield emblazoned with the new university logo of a striped tiger. And, as Dr Chamberlain had carelessly described her patient as V.C. Toady, enquirers after an E. Toady are invariably turned away. Vice-Chancellor Toady is not yet fully mad, but there is every possibility that he will be by the end of the year.

*****

One August night, Doctors Beaver, Sword and Festering, drowning their sorrows in the Staff Club bar, and then staggering down the middle of the campus road, were knocked down and severely injured by a drunken driver. The three drunk doctors remained in intensive care until some months after the final closure of the University of Surleighwick.

*****

Doctors Chamberlain and French wound up their practice, and moved to become the doctors at Hereford Polytechnic. From there, it is but a short drive to Hay-on-Wye, where the two doctors sometimes go to stay with Mrs Quick and Dr Crumpet. Many are the tales that are told of mad Toady, as the four women sit up late over port and brandy after one of Mrs Quick's excellent and alcoholic meals, and Doctors French and Chamberlain recount yet again their amusing narrative of Vice-Chancellor Toady's last visit to them, and how he was carried away without his trousers. In due course Dr Chamberlain lost her clothes and was inducted into Mrs Quick's coven, though Dr French has so far remained aloof, having doubts about her Hippocratic oath.

Sarah-Jane Moore is also often seen in the Hay-on-Wye area, and sometimes spends the weekend with Mrs Quick and Dr Crumpet. Sarah-Jane is now working for Dr Hanwell. Before he left Surleighwick, he advertised for a research assistant, to look up references for him in English libraries, and to scout around for interesting books. Sarah-Jane applied, and got the job. As the Surleighwick library was sold off cheaply by the receivers, Sarah-Jane was able to acquire many of the more interesting items in the history of science field for Dr Hanwell. She keeps an eye on the books at Hay-on-Wye on his behalf too. But so far, she has managed to avoid being seduced by Mrs Quick.

*****

Unbeknown to Dr Hanwell, another former member of the University of Surleighwick was on the same plane. Anxious to avoid a rise in the unemployment figures, the government had decided that non-EEC foreign nationals employed by the University of Surleighwick who could not get jobs elsewhere were to be deported. And now Dr Chittering was returning to the land of his birth, travelling in the back handcuffed to two immigration officers.

As Dr and Mrs Hanwell's jet crossed the English coast, and headed west for the States, a dishevelled, derelict figure, in patched and stained trousers, with unkempt hair, and unshaven stubbly chin, was swigging whisky from a bottle, and haranguing his fellow derelicts in one of the concrete underpasses in the centre of Surleighwick. Poor little Jack Napes had never recovered from the vote of censure that Mrs Quick had proposed at the English department staff meeting. And the news that Surleighwick was to close had virtually unhinged him. He could not believe it! He had taken to the bottle, and was now a stage or two beyond his alcoholic colleagues.

"We got a Grade 5 star you know," he mumbled to the tramps and drop-outs sprawled on the pavement. "We were one of the best departments in the country. It means 'international excellence' that's what a Grade 5 star means."

Dr and Mrs Hanwell arrived at Surleighwick, Arkansas, at 6 pm, and stepped out into the bright sunshine to be greeted by Embury Jenkins.

In Surleighwick, England, it was 11 pm. Drunk and dishevelled, little Jack Napes was still trying to explain the concept of a 'star' to his bored companions, when the Surleighwick Constabulary arrived for their regular round up of the city's down-and-outs.

"We got a 'star', you know," said little Jack Napes to the constable. And when he had been beaten up in the usual way and thrown out onto the pavement again, stars indeed were all that he could see.

THE END